To Richard
Ethan
Knew you'd love this!

EMINENT DOMAIN

DragonCon '97

by J. Cameron Thyme

Address all inquiries to the publisher:
Tales of Thyme, Inc.,
4805 Suite 116-304, Lawrenceville Highway, Lilburn, Ga. 30247.

Typeset and printed in the United States of America.

Library of Congress Catalog Card Number: 96-060729
ISBN: 1-889377-01-5

First Paperback Edition: June 1996.

DEDICATION

To my wife Carla, whose loving faith and patience indulged my endless hours of research, writing and ranting ...

To Stephanie, my daughter, whose energy seemed boundless (even in the wee hours of the morning!) ...

To my son, Winston, who is so new to this world, he doesn't know what I'm getting him into ...

To the other weavers of the dream:
Jon, Sheryl, Gary and Gordon,
whose extraordinary talent, expertise, and unwavering belief in this project, served as a yellow brick road to success ...

To all of my friends and relatives who lent their moral support to the inconceivable ...

Everlasting love and gratitude,
Cam

TABLE OF CONTENTS

PROLOGUE:	The Exodus Heresy	i
1	DANCE OF PASSION	1
2	EXPOSÉ	15
3	VISTA	26
4	A SEASON IN HELL	33
5	HOME SEARCH	40
6	BACK TRACK	47
7	FALSE HOPE	56
8	MODUS OPERANDI	67
9	NICHES	76
10	FLIGHT SCHOOL	82
11	BABBLE	89
12	ATTACKED	98
13	STAR WARS	102
14	SEIZURE	109
15	STEALTH TECHNOLOGY	115
16	"THEY WHO WAIT ..."	125
17	A RAT IN THE CAGE	129
18	SUPERHEROES	138
19	HACKER	147
20	ORACLE	157
21	THE HISTORY LESSON	162
22	MOURNING'S SOLACE	173
23	LA COSA NOSTRA	181
24	THE ART OF WAR	190
25	ESCAPE FROM ALCATRAZ	201
26	BATTLE LINES	215
27	ARMAGEDDON	228
28	SALVATION AND RUIN	238
29	PHOENIX	245
EPILOGUE		250
JING PEN TRANSLATOR		261

PROLOGUE: The Exodus Heresy

Hooves pounded the ground around the little rock. The rock seemed to be shrinking, sinking into a rising river of living fear. From atop the rock, young Nelky herdmaster, His Fa could see the direction of his boloks' stampede. The direction...and its cause!

The marauding predator was driving the herd forward, its appetite only whetted. Occasionally, it would peck at the few trampled animals at the floor of the gully, but they were motionless.

His Fa was not.

The sight of the amok Senori Pen rearing its head above the foliage was ghastly. It had the bloody, dismembered hind quarter of a Bolok dangling in its massive jaws. The herdmaster would be less than a mouthful to the pursuer.

The pachyderms he tended were a lucrative source of income for His Fa's family and many other Nelky ranches. They fetched a good price from the larger predatory peoples, Tralkyz in particular. Rich in high yield proteins, rapidly reproducing and docile when not immediately threatened, they could be moved under their own power for two or three dymes — halfway across the continent — at a time. Because Boloks were so large (four times the length of a tall Nelky and 10 times as heavy) and well protected, with three horns (one on the beak-like nose and a pair on the forehead) and a bony frill of armor framing their faces, their security was almost a non-issue. ...Almost!

The beast lumbered nearer.

Formidable armor and lethal weapons were no match for the destructive force of this killing machine. The Senori Pen were genetically engineered from the smaller wild Senori, who better respected the boundaries of civilized Efilu species, such as the Nelky. Perversions of their wild cousins, the Senori Pen were larger by a fourth or a fifth, and stood head above all but the tallest trees. The puny arms were useless and vestigial, but the shortcoming was offset by massive jaw muscles and dagger-like teeth. The thick muscular tail counterbalanced the large head and lean upper body. They were killing machines, pure and simple.

Destruction incarnate, each Senori footfall shook the rock, like rumbling of distant thunder.

Ostensibly developed to defend Sulenz towns from being trampled by herds of large grazing animals, the Senori Pen instead had become the scourge of the countryside. Never known to attack their Sulenz creators, they had nevertheless become harder to control and impossible to contain. Ironically, they were supposedly unable to digest wild game, and relied on their Sulenz masters for synthetic nourishment. This did not quell their voracious, predatory nature.

The carcass, now being flung from side to side by the beast, must have been the dominant Bolok male. It had turned to ward off what it thought was a lone Senori. The mistake cost just enough time for the slower Senori Pen to seize him. The herd was now without leadership and running wild.

His Fa's vision was momentarily blurred by a splash of blood in his eyes. A Bolok calf had not been able to keep up with his mother in the pandemonium. His Fa saw this as an omen. The young Herdmaster was trapped. He couldn't possibly traverse hundreds of stampeding Boloks to the relative safety of the rain forest.

The monster's moans of anticipation could be heard even now.

A member of the elite family of Super Hunter species, the Nelky were the smallest in size. They were less than one-sixth the size of the Senori Pen. His Fa's natural defenses — a whip-like tail, toe claws, agility and hyper-optical camouflage — were useless here. Although the Senori were more primitive members of the same Order, His Fa recognized no similarity between himself and his nemesis. Here, he was now prey instead of predator.

The distorted shadow loomed inexorably toward the rock in the mid-day sun.

His Fa had to continually shift his weight to maintain his balance on the tremulous rock. Now that the Senori Pen was within 100 head lengths of him, the herdmaster's movements betrayed him. The bulk of the herd had passed by now, and the beast had sighted its next target. Things didn't look good.

In spite of the ban on fission-powered arms, His Fa carried a forbidden energy weapon at his side. Its yield was only mid-range, but at least it afforded some reassurance. Herdmasters weren't supposed to come up against Threats to Life in the protected grazing reserves, so there was no legal excuse for carrying an energy weapon. He had gone with his instincts on this decision, for all the good that it had done. Even a lucky shot at point blank range would only wound the monster — he couldn't hope to kill it. There would be no time to squeeze off a second shot!

The Pen's scent was overpowering now.

His Fa gathered his strength and prepared a greeting to his ancestors. Visions carrying the collective memories of the world's first intelligent life forms filtered through the young Nelky's mind ... the collaboration between traditional enemies, herbivores and predators alike, to make the world they called Fitu a safer, more productive place ... the attempts to colonize the inner Stone Worlds of their solar system ... the exploration of the possibilities of settling even the planetary gas giants of the outer solar system ... all this would end for His Fa, but he could manage to record his unique experiences in his Animem.

ANImated MEMory/integration technique was an extension of astral projection, combined with gel/crystal integration technology developed by the Si Tyen scientist known as Dragon.

Dragon was less mystical than others of his breed, mostly dealing with the hard sciences. Still, he nonetheless was known as an eccentric. He accepted a few students from each race to teach the Animem art for general dissemination.

His Fa was one so privileged. He recalled that Dragon had once shared a premonition with him.: "I will be remembered not for what I have done or what I have said. Yet, sixty-five million years from now, the Si Tyen legacy will be known by my name only. Even then, we will be set apart from the other Efilu societies. We will Dance Life alone."

His Fa remembered the sorrow with which Dragon had spoken those words. He displayed no air of superiority to the other Efilu races; rather, he exhibited a sense of alienation. His Fa thought of those words as a prophecy he would always ponder.

The sensitive Nelky tongue tasted Senori breath now.

He unsheathed his little weapon, which now appeared more like a toy in his hand, when he saw them. Two Efilu dignitaries! Both must have been on their way to the parliament at the Great Hall and noticed the commotion. They were a large So Beni meg and a good-sized Alkz mer, who appeared unusually fit for her years. They had not seen His Fa yet, for their attention focused on the rampaging Senori Pen. Its raucous howl drowned out all cries for help.

They began to retreat, recoiling in disgust at the carnage, when the mer spied His Fa squirming on the rock. Fortune truly did smile, for if she had turned the other way to retreat, both meren would have missed him altogether.

They charged down the embankment in an attempt to distract the Senori Pen from the youth. The Senori Pen were bred not to be deterred once they locked on to a mark. It would of course dispatch any significant obstacle between itself and its target. Even this dull-witted beast recognized the So Beni meg and Alkz mer as significant obstacles.

The Senori Pen lashed out first at the larger of the two threats. While the So Beni was engaged, the Alkz seized the opportunity to pounce on the monster's back. Wrapping her tail around one of the freak's legs, she anchored herself by digging her sharp finger plumage deep into the soft flesh beneath its dwarf arm. She crossed his throat with a speared hand, first forward, then back. The action sliced through its armored neck, severing a major artery and several minor ones. The windpipe, however, remained unscathed.

The So Beni warrior then closed a huge fist and threw a well-cocked upper cut to the massive jaw. The Senori Pen was nearly twice the size of the So Beni, but having been weakened by the Alkz attack, its head was rocked slightly by the blow.

A set-up! The lethally spiked So Beni tail came around points-first into the lower rib cage. The spikes penetrated the armor and shed blood. The Alkz back-flipped to a safe distance. The Senori Pen were oblivious to pain, but not to anger.

The young Nelky felt his flesh crawl as the monster turned its full attention to the So Beni. It took a deep breath and drew its head back to strike. It was then that His Fa saw bubbles erupting from the Pen's flank wound and smiled. A bloody cough disrupted the Senori Pen's snap. Its eyes glazed for a moment, then it renewed its attack with vigor. The So Beni turned to retreat, losing a dorsal plate to the jaws of the monster.

As the crazed beast clutched the armored plate in its teeth, the Alkz had moved into position and stabbed a speared hand through the flank wound made by the So Beni, then twisted it.

The Senori Pen stumbled. Furious now, it glared at the Alkz and assumed a combat stance. It re-established a semblance of discipline, then poised to strike a death blow. The So Beni was too far away to intervene, since the creature had forced the Alkz mer in the opposite direction.

The meg felt helpless and frustrated, until he saw a peculiar mass of bubbling flesh on the back of the Senori Pen's head. The lethal attack on the Alkz missed its mark, and the marauder stumbled. As the beast struggled to regain its balance, the So Beni warrior spied the Nelky astride his companion's shoulders, the little weapon in his hand still glowing after discharge. The right eye of the Senori Pen freely bled bright red. The Alkz thought, *Good! An artery.* With the Nelky meg still on her back, she began to carry her little burden up the hillside.

The So Beni prepared to exploit the opportunity to strike a crippling blow to the beast when he smelled a paradoxically welcome scent. Natural Senori! At least five were in the pack, their scavenging instinct attracted by the scent of Bolok blood. They barely hesitated when they saw the injured Senori Pen. The hatred between the two species went beyond nature. To wild Senori, the Pen variant was an abomination.

The pack savagely tore at the Senori Pen. The slaughter was over in moments! Though wild Senori would not eat the tainted flesh, they obviously reveled in killing their genetically engineered kin.

The So Beni shared the sentiment from atop the hill. His companions, already inside a transport vehicle, urged him not to linger. He looked across the lush tropical rain forest with its rich flowers and dense ferns realizing these sweet days were indeed numbered. He resisted the urge toward melancholy, for remorse ill became the So Beni. This one, in particular, did not handle it well. Perhaps the Senori in the gully saw the nod of satisfied approval from the So Beni, as he turned to join his companions.

Just then, the warrior's foot slid a little on something slimy. A small, hairy tree mammal hadn't quite made it across the herd path and was trampled. The little creature had crawled up the hillside to die. *It Danced Life so poorly. Pathetic Jing. They never do seem to make it out of harm's way*, he thought, while scraping its remains off of his foot.

"Are you all right?" the Nelky asked. The big meg grunted. "I'd be better if I could have watched them finish off the damned thing."

Turning to the Nelky meg, he spoke again. "Your family lost a whole herd to that renegade. Are you willing to testify?" His Fa quickly answered, "Yes!"

"Then let's dispose of that weapon," said the So Beni. He crushed the weapon in one great hand and tossed the debris into the thick greenery.

* * * * *

"Let us dispense with the preliminaries!" The sounds and thoughts in the Great Hall began to die down at the silent command. Using Level One Intimate Communications as the universal telepathic language, the Alkz delegate repeated, "Let us dispense with the preliminaries! Please! "

"Now, as the second session of the Council will be called to order shortly, let's not waste time. We now have a quorum, so let's set an agenda." Shon Tai was undaunted by her ordeal earlier that afternoon. She sat at her designated place at the Round Table, center of power for the united Efilu races. Her voice projected clear and strong. Not a hint of the aching in her bones and muscles showed.

"First order of business: global status reports. Let's keep it brief and to the point. There'll be plenty of time for discussion later." She recorded the summarized data in a small crystal that rotated in a shallow basin of thick viscous fluid. The raw data would be archived for retrieval on demand.

"Second order of business: can the remaining meteors and radiation heading toward our world be diverted or destroyed, and can this defense be sustained over the next 30 to 35 years?"

Without pausing from her recitation, Shon Tai absently pounded a small rodent into oblivion as it scurried past her work station on the Round Table. "Third order of business: salvation of livestock and agricultural reserves. Both marine and land-based resources are at risk." She reminded her growing audience.

"Fourth: overcrowding in the newly protected Enclosed Areas. Many agoraphilic peoples find this setting most uncomfortable," she related, her thought projections edged with irritation. She spoke for her own now.

"Fifth—" Whomp! She swatted another Jing into the wooden table. The exasperated mer exclaimed, "Where are the damned Kas Pen? This hold is infested with fur mites!"

A young So Beni hoisted a lidded caldron from a refrigerated alcove and tipped it over. As the ophidians tumbled out, he scattered them across the floor. They hissed as the warmth of the chamber revived them. The vermin instinctively retreated for the false safety of the dimly lit corners.

Shon Tai, satisfied with pest control, continued. "Fifth: energy deficits. I would like summaries of sunlight measurements, damage control estimates including bionetic removal efforts in restricted areas," she paused here, for effect, and continued, "supplemental food produc—"

"You stop right there!" An unctuous voice interrupted, dripping with offense. Canad, the Sulenz delegate, went on. "This snide, never ending criticism of our efforts has got to stop!

"When the So Beni Union made a mess of the second planet in our solar system, it was called 'a miscalculation.' When the Nelky developed grazing Jing to clear the weeds from their Shath fields, it was called 'a clever use of genetic engineering.' So why are our accomplishments in that field — in all fields — viewed with such suspicion? Damn it, even your Kas Pen are artificial life forms." He snatched one of the scaled, slithering reptiles from the floor for emphasis and tossed it aside. "But you all make them out to be the Wilkyz's gift to Fitu! Why this very hall is made from a genetically altered hardwood!" He paused a moment for sympathy.

"We tried to develop an off world agricultural settlement and what happens: resistance from all quarters, threats from allies, interference from nearly everyone. It's no wonder we lost control of the power source. The only ones lost in the explosion of the fifth planet were us Sulenz anyway. The only remains left of that planet are a stream of Sulenz bodies and an asteroid ring! Yet, I haven't once heard anyone acknowledge the Sulenz contribution to the development of the Iridium Shield that now protects our home world from radiation and debris."

"Here on Fitu we tried to protect our meager arthropod farms from marauding animals and we get—"

"Away with murder!" The statement was accompanied by the slam of a massive fist on the Round Table. Shon Tai's recording device nearly disconnected from the crystal.

Merc dwarfed the Sulenz delegate as he loomed over his personal space, clearly on the verge of exploding. Canad was taken aback. The So Beni fist pounded again just short of the delicate, long Sulenz fingers as Canad retreated to his side of the table. Merc grinned sardonically as he taunted the emissary.

"This afternoon Shon Tai and I shared the pleasure of mauling one of your precious Senori Pen." The horror on Canad's face as he whipped his gaze between Shon Tai and Merc made the big So Beni grin all the wider. "It must have been badly wounded, head injured ..." he faltered. "The two of you alone could not possibly have—"

"You're right." Merc seemed almost charming for a moment. "It was wounded and its head injured ... after we finished with it!" There was no need to mention the Nelky's use of the energy weapon.

"We left it to a pack of Northern Senori. Gratifying to watch actually.

The pack rent your pet from limb to limb." Shon Tai's business-like facade slipped a little, broken by an involuntary smile.

"Order!" An audible roar accompanied an equally powerful thought projection, silencing everyone. The very walls seemed to tremble at the sound. The speaker continued, "Merc, your services are completed for the time being. You are dismissed."

Embarrassed, Merc approached his father submissively, and protested, "Forty of the Nelky bolok were slaughtered for no reas—"

Softly, the elder said, "Are you now Nelky, my son? The matter will be addressed ... elsewhen." A gentle gesture of Thair's head reiterated the command to go.

The powerful So Beni warrior was replaced by a more grand and awesome figure. Thair, supreme ruler of the So coalition, wielded much power — nearly half as much as all the other societies combined.

Canad had regained his composure, still in disbelief of tale just told. "We will tolerate this So Beni intimidation no longer! Your son threatened me. Right here in front of 70 witnesses. What do you intend to do about it Thair?"

The overlord stared for a moment, in silence. Canad whined, "I demand satisfaction Thair!"

When the So Beni ruler finally broke the silence of the chamber, it clearly bore no relationship to the Sulenz demand. "The Sulenz incident is simply another symptom of disturbances that have become more the rule than the exception. Let us address the matters at hand, shall we?" He strolled as he talked, passing Canad with not so much as a sidelong glance.

He reached around Shon Tai, who was no longer smiling, and reviewed the preliminary agenda. In a moment, he nodded approval, and gestured silently into the air. A recorded display appeared in the pools of charcoal gray fluid in each delegate's workstation. Returning to the head of the table, Thair crouched at the unique workstation reserved for himself. After a sweeping look around the room, he began. "Number one..."

It was a long night. Debates raged back and forth. Tempers were lost, but there was no violence. Even the nomadic Irfonde were civil in a vulgar sort of way. The Si Tyen contingent added little after their predictable opening argument for not evacuating Fitu.

Perhaps they had been counting on a widespread perception, especially among the lower orders, that Tyen were mystics to whom laws of nature did not fully apply. However, the more technically advanced races seated at The Round Table simply felt that the Tyen enjoyed a stark, austere lifestyle and were blinded by their own religious beliefs. Whatever the case, they were virtually alone in their position to stay. Only the Tralkyz also spoke in opposition to the evacuation.

"We have reviewed the data supplied by the So Beni and frankly, we are not convinced," challenged the Tralkyz delegate. "Perhaps you plan to establish a base from which to harass and subjugate the less technical species. Maybe you wish us to blindly follow you into your starships, only to be extorted into servitude in exchange for the promise of a return to Fitu someday!"

Thair was tired. "We have been over this," he said wearily. "The Pact establishes that the Lesser Societies of enlightened species shall form a greater society. That Greater Society will guarantee the rights of all of its members, regardless of size, environmental needs, dietary habits or body odor, and distribute resources appropriately to insure a uniform and comparable standard of living for everyone. Telepathic communication has been universally honed to at least a Level One conversational quality, so that the burden of either learning a flood of languages or vocalizing in one dominant language has become unnecessary. With a continued concerted effort, we can achieve anything as a united society."

"A tall order," said the Tralkyz, looking up at the giant So Beni, "no pun intended, but these are just intentions. When times get difficult, you, So Beni, will look after your own interests and forget the rest of us." His tone then became threatening. "All the same, you will NOT strand the Tralkyz here. If we are not convinced of the sincerity of these intentions, NO ONE will leave this world."

The silence in the room substantiated the truth of his statement. Such diversity of faces in the Council room was unprecedented. All eyes were on the presiding chair. Thair knew it was incumbent on him that the evacuation go smoothly and as agreed. He absently gripped the edge of the Table. As if for the first time, he noted how heavy it was. He felt as if he would be burdened with its weight from that moment on.

* * * * *

Jamom was just weak now. Hunger was a distant memory. He couldn't stand, so he crawled the long trail down the foothills of the abandoned Great Hall of the Round Table. He was not thinking clearly. Only his self discipline kept him on track. He looked up at his destination in the distance, obscured by the lavender, iridium smog that polluted the atmosphere now. The stench of the rotting land was stirred by a sudden gust of wind. Jamom's eyes tried to focus, as a dead tree toppled beside him. A spacecraft had descended.

The ship was large. A variety of peoples had already disembarked and begun anchoring machines around the base of the abandoned structure. A lone figure approached him through the dust. "You almost don't register on our sensors!" The Tralkyz commander exclaimed in disbelief.

Jamom was still dazed. "There are several Si Tyen corpses in the woods below us," he continued, crouching beside the emaciated wretch. "If my assistant hadn't noticed that your body was moving..." Now the Tralkyz's hands gestured expansively. "I am Pac Ard, the Commander directing this expedition."

Jamom reached up a feeble hand to grasp the strong Tralkyz's arm. "Then you're a restoration party?"

Pac Ard lowered his eyes in response. "No." Jamom's hand dropped to the ground. Pac Ard, seeing the Tyen's despair added "We're a salvage party. We've come to retrieve the Great Hall and any survivors we come across."

The Si Tyen, exhausted dropped his head back to the ground, rested a moment and said, "There are about ... eighty of us Tyen alive ... at last count."

"We can accommodate that," Pac Ard said thoughtfully.

"No, no. Not us. There are over 100,000 animals: avians, amphibians, small Jing—"

"We have no room for THEM. There are enough wildlife and vermin to suffice in the colonies.

He continued. "We have established three permanent colonies on the seventh, eighth and ninth planets of the solar system. The societies are flourishing, all of them. The Si Tyen that left with us are inspiring harmony and tranquillity. Some say there is a spiritual renaissance among the societies. The advances we have accomplished in the fifty years since the Exodus are amazing! Join us."

"What of Fitu?" Jamom insisted. "Without your help it will die. If you could just spare us a few shipments of grain we could—"

"Feed the rats? You're crazy!" Pac Ard shot back. "You're all crazy!

Look at you. You're dying. You can't even walk, let alone fly!"

It was true. The Tyen had no subcutaneous fat stores and his muscles were severely wasted by starvation. "Your precious Jing will devour your flesh before long. A final Dance of Life before nightfall...hardly a way to treat one's benefactors," chided the Tralkyz. He paused for a moment, as the Tyen drew a labored breath. "Face it. This world is dead, and you will die with it if you don't come to your senses."

Jamom closed his eyes, opened them slowly and focused on Pac Ard. "Fitu is our mother. We cannot all abandon her."

"It is only natural to outlive one's parent. Alum carries our fate to the stars. Why don't you Tyen listen to reason?" Pac Ard shouted in frustration.

Jamom placed a feeble hand against the Tralkyz's heart and said "Faith is a higher faculty than reasoning. We must keep the faith."

Someone called to Pac Ard. The Hall was secured, and the crew was preparing to leave. The derelict structure would be hoisted up by the main ship, which was in orbit.

"We're out of time," he said. "You keep the faith if you wish, but you won't live 'till nightfall ... if one could tell day from night on this forsaken hulk!" He turned and disappeared into the dust. The ship left soon afterwards.

Jamom lay there, his meager strength waning by the moment, and watched as the Great Hall rose into the purple haze. He steeled himself, spread his great wings and pulled aloft. Jamom ascended ever closer to the distant snow covered peaks with each beat.

EMINENT DOMAIN

Chapter 1
DANCE OF PASSION

"I'm not a philosopher. Oh, how I wish that I were! I'd be safe at home now, speculating on the 'psyche of our foe' or performing other such intellectual exercises. Then again, I might be theorizing precisely at what point during the Conflict it was that our fate had been sealed. Was the so-called Quatal Poisoning an act of desperation on the part of a vanquished enemy or a well calculated act of treachery.

"Well, as Saymon once said, 'Even the most humble of souls may be instantly venerated if the currents so favor.' I don't mean to sound pretentious. I wouldn't want to embarrass my clan by having the name Vit Na of Kemith become synonymous with conceit. I'm sorry, Vit Na Iku.

"I'm just an archeologist, and not accustomed to making decisions of such consequence. Actually my decision to use my Animem in this manner was a pragmatic response to a simple problem: how do I both debrief myself and brief you on so intricate a matter without being present? No, there is no mistake, I also said brief you. What we have discovered about the little furry vermin we left behind is of paramount importance to the Greater Society.

"I suppose that this narrative is my long-winded explanation for using my Animem to record this brief but intense chronography. As time was of the essence, the others telepathically assisted me in organizing my thoughts, hence the incongruous image perspective. The result is that this story is told from many points of view. Rest assured, High Commander Tur is not guilty of any coercion in this decision. The choice was mine alone. Please convey my regrets to my clan ... also, you may note that there is a coded segment herein. As is my right, access to this portion of the Animem shall be restricted to Tur for the duration of his lifespan. The content is of a purely personal nature, and of no significance to anyone else.

"Prepare to initiate sequence! Begin ..."

*   *   *   *   *

"It was wonderful! My entire brood was on our home grounds for an educational retreat. As Mater of our small house, I should have gone with them, to guide the lessons. Instead, I had to delegate the responsibility to one of my oldest sons.

"My excuse for freedom? A previous family commitment: to study (actually re-study) a set of hieroglyphs in the catacombs beneath the Round Table on Teist.

"The Round Table hieroglyphics, nearly 65 million years old, had been studied ad nauseam, but someone is always raising questions from the dead. You know how it is. Anyway, my job was that much easier — I had so little ground work to do, the task was no trouble at all. Everyone knew the condition of the Keepers at that time in Fitu's history. Most of them were so demented with malnutrition that they themselves didn't know what they were writing.

"As one of the few qualified archeologists in the quadrant, I was asked to render my interpretation. My family had already volunteered my services. I just couldn't refuse.

"A simple assignment for which I had been allotted a week took less than three days. How could any obligation be this easy? ... And timely! I was secretly grateful for a little break from the responsibilities of parenting.

"Teist, the seat of power of the modern-day Efilu Realm, is a magnificent world. A retextured gas giant, its surface area rivals that of a small star. Tectonic platforms floating at the outer limits of its dense atmosphere have fused at the standard G point to produce a pleasant gravity fraction that was only 1.031 of Fitu's natural. Fituforming is a feat of engineering so elegant, even a 'soft' scientist such as myself could appreciate it!

"The landscaping is artful even from orbit. Curvilinear patterns derived from various species of grasses and trees seem to form geometric patterns with unnaturally sharp edges, yet the design is subtle enough as not to appear like a contrived sand painting spread across the planet. That heavy-handed approach goes over satisfactorily on smaller worlds, but on Teist, it would just indicate "common taste" on a grand scale.

"The polar cap is impressively marked by the Forest of Feelings. The worldscape as a whole is a work of art, but the Forest is the crowning masterpiece. The formation appears as a circle bisected by a sine wave dividing a deep green semicircle above from an ash green mirror image below. For three hours out of every year, Teist eclipses the bright yellow star, coming between it and its distant red giant companion. As the reflection of the bright yellow star returns, it lights the rim of the northern pole, revealing the Tyelaj.

"The Tyelaj, is a most unique worldscape feature. Imagine an abstracted image of an adult Tyen in fetal position, with an over-sized wing gracefully spread to form the upper arc of a circle. Vapors curl out of a half-opened mouth, then under the body, to form the lower arc. The far wing is all but invisible through it.

"It is said that those graced by the sight of the Tyelaj are endowed with a touch the Tyen mystique for life. An accident of timing found me traveling during the annual eclipse. Was I so touched? Perhaps. Even so, that myth did not justify traveling during such intense radiation. I suspect that the legend is just an excuse for poor planning, developed by careless engineers.

"Central usually shut down traffic during this period. The pilot of my transport would probably be demoted, at least, for getting us caught in the solar storm. Still, what a spectacle it was to behold!

"As we neared our destination, we passed over a vast savanna, from the center of which rose an unnatural, broad-based plateau. Atop it, one could make out some details of the Round Table even at that distance, which grew greater by the moment. I had time to reminisce as the wind rider carried me northward. The Forest of Feelings was the perfect place to make up for lost time with my old friend Tur. We had known each other for over twenty years, but family and clan responsibilities had kept us apart. It seemed like ages since I had last seen him.

"The wind riders only stop at their home nests. This one only slowed enough where I indicated for me to safely leap off into a preselected clearing.

"Tur had arrived before me. He looked pensive. Well, I guess that's how I'd describe it. So Wari always look that way when they are in unfamiliar surroundings.

"Tur was as big as I remembered. Broad powerful shoulders supported arms as thick as tree trunks. His legs were like great pillars. The armored plates along his spine flapped absently as he basked patiently in the heat of the day. Wide and deep set orbs seemed to glow within the shadowed eye sockets. His long ears stretched out horizontally, changing orientation periodically to detect soft sounds that might be out of place or sudden shifts in the wind that might represent the silent movement of a foe.

"I realized it was an evolutionary trait to be wary of stalking predators. His short cropped pelt plumage was worn loosely in a neat conservative fashion, but that was a deception. The nearly impervious armor could be fused in an instant.

"Somehow, seeing Tur in that expectant pose struck me as funny. All at once I felt an explosion of joy and freedom. I felt like a cub again and cubs like to play. ...

"I sprung at his feet and hollered. The quality of his laughter told me he had missed me in kind. I assumed my most threatening warning posture, holding back laughter with all of my might. Tur must have caught the spirit of the moment because he turned and fled, still laughing. His usual military facade had dropped. My friend frolicked into the forest like a Shath fleeing its hunter ... me! A ridiculous sight it would have been, had there been anyone else to see it. A 500 lb. Melkyz mer chasing a 6 ton So Wari general! The game was so silly, yet neither of us could seem to stop.

"We must have roamed for miles into the Forest. Our little 'Dance' exercised instincts that had lain dormant within us for most of our adult lives. It was exhilarating! My heart was pounding in my ears, my nerves were on edge, my nose full of Tur's scent. His searching gaze was genuine, confirming the effectiveness of my cloak of invisibility. It felt good to 'Blend' into the surrounding glade, using my species' unique weapon. It felt ... basic!"

The self-conscious perspective of Vit Na's Animen was lost in the rush of the moment she recounted.

The huntress, becoming part of her environment, was invisible in every way to her quarry. Knowing the So Wari combat prowess and hypervigilance, clearly a stalker of her size was the one in danger. If she sprung on her friend unexpectedly, his reflexes could take over before his intellect could check them. She might go from a long absent friend to a pleasant memory in an instant. The element of danger only added to the chase.

Instead, she made a conscious effort to override her own instincts and stalk him from an upwind vantage. He would be much less likely to apply deadly force in a defensive maneuver if his nostrils were full of her familiar scent.

Just as Tur entered a clearing beneath a rocky bluff, Vit Na struck! She moved like lightning out-stretched foreclaw first caught his well-armored back, the downward stroke propelling her past him. Twirling her lean muscular body, she brought her feet to bear against an oakine tree, and rebounded toward her quarry. She struck him, midsection, with all the force she could muster.

Tur, still playing along, pretended that she actually knocked him off balance and rolled backwards a full 360 degrees on his tail. Breaking the action with his left foot, he came to a complete stop in a defensive posture, his massive arms raised in a mock threat as if to fend off a more formidable attack.

Vit Na braced momentarily, then bounded toward him with seemingly reckless abandon, suddenly spinning in midair just as her whip like tail came into range of his abdomen. In a blur of motion she delivered three powerful blows to solar plexus, spleen, and the muscular area of Tur's thick neck.

Pretending the attack was incapacitating, he feigned collapse but was unable to contain his laughter. Vit Na, mildly out of breath, stood triumphantly over her beloved prey, and Tur, not even winded, lay there on the soft humus, still laughing. They rested until Vit Na caught her breath, then they talked.

She began by telling Tur about changes in her family since he last visited her home grounds. Her clan had prospered since Yhm Vel had assumed the role of Mater Familias of the Melkyz. She now represented the entire Melkyz Lesser Society in Council.

Tur remembered Yhm Vel well: very vocal, innovative. They met years ago, when he had been called in as a consultant to assess the poor health of the Melkyz' Shath herds. The beasts had become anorexic and were wasting away. Forced feedings were only partially effective and had become very expensive. No known cause had been found, but Tur assumed a slow virus localized to the hypothalamus to be the probable culprit. Autopsies of affected animals revealed nothing.

One of Tur's specialties was body building for undersized So Wari sentries. He had developed a neurostimulation process for motor neurons of the lateral hypothalamus. Since the need for the treatment in So Wari warriors was rare, and the surgery expensive, this method seemed impractical for use on livestock. Then Yhm Vel had come up with the idea to deliver the stimulator via a parasite, which would be introduced into the herd. Brilliant! A young Vit Na had been assigned to help select the most specific, virulent host.

Although her specialty of choice was archeology, the fresh, new scientist distinguished herself by locating and cloning a variety of leech that was suitable for the task and had the added flourish of being both easily visible and removable. The Kemith Solution, as the process the trio developed had been named, was still in use.

Tur was remembering how taken he had been with her ingenuity. He came out of his reverie to discover that Vit Na's words had taken a darker turn. She was now projecting to him in hushed, focused, thought-tones, as if to avoid being overheard. To discuss the short-comings of one's mates was frowned upon, but to compare the scion of one mate with that of another was taboo. Yet, she explained, it had become glaringly obvious that her most recent brood was inferior.

It was not only intellect they lacked. They lacked judgment, instinct, enthusiasm, aggression, etc. They weren't slow enough to be classified as retarded, but they certainly were dull! For Vit Na, it was a relief to finally get these concerns out in the open. They had been a real source of frustration to her for some time now.

She half hoped for a sympathetic response from Tur, but instead he slipped back into his customary pensive mood, silent. For the first time, Vit Na noticed the real irony of their relationship. Usually, Melkyz such as herself were individuals of few words, solitary souls. The So Wari, by contrast, were social creatures, a bit more garrulous. It went all the way back to their respective roots, millions of years old, on a four billion-year-old rock named Fitu.

Tur stood, took several paces toward the trees, and stared into their shadows. He half turned back toward Vit Na and spoke more freely than he could speak to any of his own kind.

"There are weak ones in our broods," said Tur. "It's not just their size. It's their attitude. There are careless, even stupid, meren rising to positions of prominence. What really doesn't make sense is that they're born to reputable lineages, with pedigrees that have consistently produced great leaders for ages! What's more, they are breeding like vermin," he sneered.

"That's it!" Something had been nagging at Vit Na for months, but she couldn't quite put her finger on it. "The younger clan members have been spawning off season. It is bad enough for megs to rut out of season, but it is worse for mers to bare fruit of such unions. Come to think of it, the families of Wilkyz traders show similar patterns. ..."

She fell silent. These developments had been little more than a passing, if worrisome, observation to her, but Tur obviously had spent considerable time mulling them over.

"Vansar behavior has also been more than a little eccentric," He said, looking at Vit Na. "Doesn't it bother you that at least four different species that we've noticed between us have demonstrated significant flaws in their gene pools?"

"It's a known phenomenon, Tur. Every so often, most species, intelligent or not, develop groups of traits that are liabilities — usually the result of intentional selective breeding. The burden of tolerance reaches the critical level at intervals of 80,000 years or so, at which point the flawed genes must be purged, or else the species faces extinction. It's a healthy process, in the long run."

Tur leveled his gaze at his friend and spoke deliberately. "Yes, but have you ever heard of a time when more than two societies reached the nadir of competence simultaneously?" He paused as he watched her consider the question he knew was rhetorical.

"Have you discussed this with anyone yet?" she asked after a moment.

"No, of course not. I didn't realize until now that it extended beyond my people and the Vansar."

Vit Na thought gravely, to herself, *four that we know of ...*

She saw what had begun for her as a venting exercise about family problems quickly expand into the revelation of a social malady with no immediate solution. She also could see in Tur's eyes that he couldn't let it go. She needed to create a diversion.

Opportunity is where you find it, Vit Na mused. Her gaze wandered a short distance. She soon found herself peering into the mouth a large cave. Its outer lip was draped in a furry moss. The opening appeared to be large enough to accommodate even Tur's bulk. *Perhaps I can coax him into a little exploring,* she thought, as she dashed recklessly into its depths. She wasn't sure if her manipulation really had distracted Tur, or whether he too had seen the need for a lightening of the spirit. Either way, Tur's head soon emerged through the inner portal.

The cavern was much larger than its modest opening suggested. As Tur made his way up to Vit Na's level above the entry, he stopped and smiled. She was standing in ankle-deep water beneath a natural fountain. Water cascaded over her upturned head, and already, her thirst was nearly quenched. Tur's gaze followed the run-off away from the vestibule.

The lake broadened and extended into the distance under a huge, dimly lit vault. Bands of sun light streamed through the apertures in the ceiling, dappling the surface of the lake. As their eyes became accustomed to the dimness, the chamber took on an unexpected beauty. Several brilliant shards of light diffused luminescence throughout the cavern, as they reflected off of the walls and water surface. Brightly colored water flowers abounded in the most vibrant assortment of colors. Some floated in the pool, with tacit beauty.

Stalactites were enmeshed in a tangle of vines that bore succulent fruits almost as varied and fragrant as the flowers below them. The fragrance of the cavern bore a pleasant contrast to the damp dankness it had first impressed upon its visitors.

The twosome realized their hunger in unison. Tur's herbivorous lunch was easy. The large fruits were quick pickings and remarkably sweet for wild fare. The fish, on the other hand, were fast — a good challenge for Vit Na. She used her tail to herd them toward the shallows. However, the simple task of asphyxiating her game by plucking them from the water was confounded by a hasty miscalculation on her part.

The fish were also carnivorous, likely living on crustaceans and hatchling crocodilians. Their sharp little teeth sunk into Vit Na's feet and tail deep enough to irritate, but not enough to draw blood. Undeterred, she kept her focus, and soon discovered that a single claw pressed into the soft, fleshy protuberance just behind the gill caused instant paralysis and death.

Her appetite whetted, Vit Na cleaned the remainder of the little, clinging nibblers off of her lower extremities. She was too eager to prepare the fish in the customary Melkyz manner of spraying her prey with a fine mist of regurgitated stomach acid. She split one open and ate the flesh without preparing it properly, devouring it whole. She found the flavor unusual, but quite pleasing. This newly found delicacy, she decided, was best savored raw. Her hunger was sated after nearly 80 pounds of fish.

Tur had finished eating while Vit Na was engaged in catching her meal. He sat back and watched her with a touch of revulsion. Herbivores always experienced mixed emotions when watching predators feed. Yes, it was tolerable to witness the demise of dumb, defenseless animals, but never pleasant. Still, he found Vit Na's beautiful in the dim lighting of the cavern. Her coat was black, with a few silvery highlights. Her fluffy down, neatly clipped and shaped, glimmered with droplets of moisture collected from her fishing efforts.

During the quiet digestion of their meals, Vit Na detected a dry, cool breeze coming from the direction opposite to their entrance. She realized that the cavern was actually a tunnel. Pressing the playful mood that had prevailed for most of the short morning (the days on Teist were about a quarter less than Standard), she urged Tur on towards the hidden exit.

The cavern reopened onto a cliff. A natural path hinted at an ancient stream fed by the lake water, which had either dried up or changed course. The little mystery was solved by a glance over the edge. The water had eroded through the bedrock of the cave floor and was spilling out of the side of the cliff face. The dried river bed path beckoned the pair down the hill, but the thought of hiking the trail was at once swept from their minds by the sight they beheld above them.

A lone Tyen engaged in what could only be the legendary Dance of Fire was boldly framed against the calm azure sky. A large violet cloud of Abisund spores wisped and whirled about for its collective life. In hot pursuit, the lithe graceful figure of the Tyen expelled a crimson vapor intended to bind the spores and withdraw them into its hungry gullet for digestion. The last reported sighting of a Tyen Dance was over 18 years ago. There were just so few!

Legends are most deeply rooted where facts are scarce. It was said that:

The Tyen mated for life.

Each couple produced only one offspring.

They were immortal, living partly in the spiritual world and partly in the physical world.

They were endowed with omniscience and the ultimate wisdom of the Alum.

They fled their natural enemy, the Tralkyz, for sport only, and long ago had overcome their post-prandial vulnerability.

No other enlightened society was so enigmatic as the Tyen. No witnessed case of a Tralkyz/Tyen encounter had described a Tralkyz success in thousands of years. The Tralkyz would certainly never discuss the matter with outsiders in spite of their braggadocio ... or perhaps because of it.

In fact, the intent of the Tyelaj designers was to capture and endow Teist with Tyen-like invincibility, as well as to shroud Si Tyen leadership in divine mysticism. The attempt fell short, as far as most of the Lesser Societies were concerned. The truth be known, the Tyen as a whole were as flawed as any people. Certainly they were among the most intelligent of the lesser societies. Their fluid crystal systems formed the foundation of Animem and gel integration technology.

Their social structure, however, was limited and their numbers were clearly falling off, presumably due to some genetic flaw perpetuating infertility. Many an epidemiologist predicted Tyen extinction in the foreseeable future. If the Tyen truly were prescient, then they were oddly accepting of the end of their time in the sun. An eternal night approached for them all.

Tur's mind was a maelstrom of emotions as he watched the Dance. Time nearly stood still, his body frozen. *So beautiful, yet so disturbing!* he thought. Reminiscent of a hunt, the Dance obviously upset Tur. Intellectually, he knew the Abisund spores were flora — not fauna. Technically the Tyen were herbivores, hence Si Tyen, but the desperate struggle of the whirling spores lent the impression of fear, of helpless prey fleeing predator. *Very confusing.* Perhaps it was best for the So Wari psyche that the Tyen Dance of Fire was so seldom seen.

Vit Na, on the other hand, was enthralled by the spectacle. Her head bobbed and weaved in consonance with every swoop, soar and dive of the venerable meg. Tyen philosophy was highly revered among the Super Hunter societies of the Melkyz, Wilkyz, and Alkyz. Whatever the Tralkyz thought of Tyen teachings they kept discretely to themselves.

The Abisund quarry was a marvel: a semiconscious collection of spores that each generated just enough of an electromagnetic charge to accelerate to 2.1 of standard gravity. When coalesced into a cloud, they were essentially intangible to large grazing animals, even to avian feeders. Swarms of insects bent on savoring their nectar were discouraged by a stunning electrical discharge.

The parent flower, by contrast, was quite bitter in taste, low in nutritional value and very widely found in the most inconvenient of places to graze. It could best be thought of as a backward life cycle: with intelligence, high energy and maximum mobility characterizing the immature stage and reproduction taking place briefly at the end of an extended childhood.

The "behavior" of the Abisund suggested the presence of a rudimentary neurosystem, even a consciousness.

The Tyen solution to this unique defense was ingenious. Over the millennia since the Exodus, the Tyen had genetically engineered their salivary glands to ionize their digestive enzymes and organic acids. The mist they exhaled bound to the charged spores, immobilizing them. A low level tractor field was then generated in the Tyen gut, pulling the spore-enriched vapor back in through the mouth for complete digestion.

It was estimated that a Tyen would only have to feed this way three or four times a year. Still there was the question of a post-prandial heaviness that typically forced an immediate landing after the Dance was complete.

Unlike true avian wings, the Tyens' were overdeveloped dorsal plates. Although very muscular, they were evolved more for downward gliding than for true flying. Again, brilliant adaptive bioengineering intervened. To maintain flight, they built up a subdermal electron cloud that effectively decreased their corporeal density to less than the air around them — that is, until after they had fed. The digestion of the Abisund spores temporarily drained the field, forcing the individual to land and regenerate the charge.

This was the time of the Tralkyz. They were always attracted by the Dance and stalked a Tyen through the forest below for hundreds of body lengths. When it landed, there was always combat.

The Tralkyz were always at least thirty strong and formidable. Built much like the Alkyz, Tralkyz were smaller, and proportionately more muscular. Soot gray coats were accented by tufts of red orange plumage spreading from behind the ears. During a nocturnal hunt, quarry would find themselves surrounded by low-pitched moans that were ghostly in quality. The crimson tufts were incandescent and glowed like the eyes of much larger hunters. The effect made many victims panic — often the first of a series of final mistakes.

The Tyen always landed near water, or so the legend went. It was said that the battle took place half in the natural world, half in the supernatural world. The rest was shrouded in a mystery few Efilu eyes ever penetrated. If they did, they never lived to tell about it.

The Tralkyz were ravenous after such Dances, capable and cunning enough to devour any innocent bystander so foolish as to be in the wrong place at the wrong time. This unusual and violent ritual was respected by the Greater Society for ancient reasons that were largely forgotten. The Tralkyz rarely involved others or destroyed property in these affairs, so no other member society had a legitimate concern. The Tyen themselves never lodged a complaint.

The Tyen, although reclusive and often eccentric, were never reckless. This old one had selected a battle ground near the river, true to form. As he alighted on the clearing staked out by the Tralkyz pack, a grayish white fog seemed to issue from the forest floor itself. As the eerie haze wafted past the Tralkyz nostrils, their anxiety faded. The gas was innocuous and not completely opaque. They still would be able to attack.

The Tralkyz surrounded the lone Tyen and paired off for the assault. Vit Na was mesmerized by the combat unfolding before her eyes. Entranced, she began to move forward, gliding down the mountain path as surely as if she had done so a thousand times before. Tur was less sure-footed; but afraid for his friend, he followed close behind her as stealthily as his bulk would allow. As they approached the clearing, Tur took up position beside Vit Na, and forced the hypnotized mer into a less visible crouch. A thicket of brush provided them cover.

A solitary figure stood motionless in the center of the clearing, with the Tralkyz now nowhere to be seen. Only now were the voyeurs close enough to see the noble warrior's true splendor. The meg stood some thirty odd feet tall, but somehow seemed even taller. His visage was reminiscent of a lean, powerful So Wari general, the former distinguished by its deep set eyes and extended jaws accented by a tuft of downy fibers at the chin and cheek. Light filtered through the heavy forest ceiling, shining more like moon beams than sunlight. The luminosity of the fog gave a halo-like effect about the Tyen. The impression was like a still life image captured by a bolt of lightning.

The moment was heavy with tension. Only the mist seemed restless about the Great One's feet. Neither of the spectators saw the pack that surrounded the Tyen until the leader roared his challenge. Tralkyz chiefs were half again as large as their followers — a result of adolescent hormone surges, not genetics. Twenty-five feet of heavily muscled carnivore was flanked by two barely less menacing lieutenants, who were crouched in a threatening posture. Their stance was mirrored by the eighteen pair of Tralkyz maulers surrounding the Tyen. Tralkyz always attacked in pairs!

The lone warrior shifted his gaze to meet the gleaming orbs of the leader, as if the others didn't exist. Tyen mores held a leader culpable for the actions of those in his charge. The Tyen wings spread in warning, then retracted back for true combat — again, motionlessly inviting the packs advance. Two pairs attempted to blind-side their quarry, and the leader's lieutenants waited until the Tyen's attention was drawn to the movement before mounting a strike of their own.

The distraction was, at best, too brief. Action that could only be described as physical music flowed with the rhythm of the assault. Tyen defensive claws sliced the throats of the first pair, as another limb launched the second pair at the third pair with ballistic force. The sickening crack of impact heralded the departure of three souls from this plane. The fourth assailant was to rise again gratefully in several minutes with a dislocated shoulder and a few fractured ribs. The ease of the maneuver gave the remaining Tralkyz pause, but their leader was undaunted. This chief knew that tactic!

The Tyen strategy was to offer attackers the offensive until they recklessly lost their patience. The proverb went, "The patience of the Tralkyz is like a puddle; that of the Tyen, like a sea." The truth of it was evident here. The pack exploded into action from every direction. The rate of attacks accelerated so quickly that their strategy was lost on the inexperienced observer.

The Tyen's fighting style now mesmerized the warrior in Tur, as well as in Vit Na. The So Wari, like the extinct So Beni that they had supplanted eons ago, were widely regarded as the masters of the martial arts — but this! The Tyen fought not with six appendages, but with eight! His leg, arm and tail technique was the best Tur had ever seen, but the use of the head and neck was stunning! The Tyen would feint, then butt opponents off balance, only too strike a deadly blow with one of his seven natural weapons. The final weapon was the most surprising of all.

Vestigial Wings were always believed to be a hindrance in ground combat, and generally were recessed to the spine in the retracted position for protection. Today, this was not the case at all. This Tyen wielded his wings as swords, slicing or bludgeoning opponents left and right. He showed such efficiency! Nearly each blow either killed or maimed only one member of each pair. The psychological effect of that tactic soon took its toll on the Tralkyz. The leader signaled quarter, assessed his losses, then considered the Tyen carefully.

Again, the Tyen was motionless. There was a hint of a smirk on his lips, blood dripping from his claws, but otherwise not a scratch on him. He did not even appear winded! Thusly, the disciplined warrior hid his fatigue, as the Tralkyz chief looked around the clearing for a body count.

Fifteen casualties were incapable of combat. Most of them would not survive week's end, even with attention to their wounds. Those who remained standing bravely maintained combat stance. But they too had estimated the casualties, and felt the effects of the pummeling they themselves had taken.

The Tralkyz leader knew that to signal a second attack would cost him another seven or eight souls. It was too expensive. He acknowledged defeat to the Tyen, and ordered those troops still standing to bear the casualties back to their city for treatment or interment, never taking his eyes off of the victorious Tyen. He marked the grim smile on the Tyen's face, as his battered troops marched proudly back into the forest. Somehow, a sense of approval was conveyed in that smile. Perhaps it was a lesson well learned for them.

As the last trace of the Tralkyz faded into the forest, Vit Na snapped out of her trance, with her first conscious thought. *They're remarkably civilized in defeat.* She then noticed Tur staring at her with a concerned, puzzled expression.

A splash in the near by stream diverted his attention before he could project his concern. As they turned to investigate the sound, their attention was captured by a gaze of unnatural intensity.

The Tyen was still there in the clearing. His gaze locked with Vit Na's. The sense of danger was so overwhelming she dared not turn to confirm that it was shared by Tur, already tensed for combat.

So focused was she that the forest faded to nothingness in the shadow of the Tyen's presence. Mere moments seemed eternal as she struggled to remain still. Was it her imagination? Did the winged knight truly see her or did he merely peer into the darkness of the thicket?

Just when she thought she could stay still no longer, the Tyen vanished without a trace. No rustling of bushes, no flapping of wings. Simply gone! A second splash again distracted them as they realized that in spite of remaining absolutely motionless their orientation had shifted 50 degrees to face the stream. A serpentine head bobbed in the water, strengthening the popular connection between water serpents and the Tyen Dance of Fire.

Even after having witnessed such a spectacle, neither she nor Tur could confirm the myth of Tyen/serpent transmorphism. Bewildered, she turned to her friend only to see his head strangely cocked to one side, as if listening to something urgent. After a moment of listening herself, and hearing nothing, she spoke.

"Tur?"

His demeanor promptly changed. He was calm, cool and all business as he commanded Vit Na, "We must go."

Puzzled, she queried, "Where?" He answered absently, "To offer our services. There is a need."

Chapter 2
EXPOSÉ

"The evolution of language is interesting isn't it? I mean from an archeological stand point. Initially, the term 'Round Table' applied to the actual circular table that was in the Great Hall of the So Beni rulers." Vit Na paused for input. Tur seemed distant.

She went on. "At the time of the Pact, it was referred to as the Hall of the Round Table."

With her history lesson falling on deaf ears, Vit Na's monologue served more as a distraction to take her mind off of the matter at hand. "All records dating from the Return 50 years later show the term 'Round Table' to be inclusive of the table, the hall and the surrounding superstructure. Now of course it's taken for granted that 'Round Table' includes all of that and the plateau upon which it rests."

Tur seemed to have settled into a grim contemplation. Their transport had begun its deceleration. Vit Na was sure it had maxed out on velocity, and would arrive back at the Round Table long before sunset. It had taken her more than five times that long to get to the polar forest that morning. What could possibly merit such waste of fuel on this particular trip? In fact, the transport had met them right where they stood in the clearing of the Tyen encounter. The pilot had been sent especially for both Vit Na and Tur, and had even called them by name. All of these facts indicated business of the highest priority. *What are we caught up in?* she wondered.

She felt her heart beat quicken with a far more disturbing observation.

"There is a need," Tur had said. He had then mumbled something about the proceedings of a secured meeting at The Round Table — nearly 20 dymes away! That definitely was Level 3 intimate communications, beyond the reach of all but the most gifted and highly trained individuals among the So species. Even more amazing, though, was the appearance of the transport. If Tur had summoned it to their location — and who else could have, for she surely hadn't — then he was clearly capable of Level 4 communications. This was unheard of among the So Wari.

Tur, although very intelligent, had never displayed such talent. Vit Na looked at his solemn form and thought, *I wonder what is going on, and if Tur is as worried as I am?*

How would this proud So Wari deal with real fear?

*   *   *   *   *

Ralt reviewed the intelligence reports for the third time. He had been at it all night. It wasn't that he didn't understand them — he was a quick study — but he simply couldn't understand the "why" or "who" of it all. The security chief touched a control panel to reduce the dimensions of the gel-fabricated room and then sealed it, before expanding the holographic display. He was cautious even for a So Wari.

Even here in the security of the Round Table itself, modifications for added secrecy were in place. The So Wari had been the custodians of the Round Table since the extinction of the So Beni race. Even so, the formation of the Council officially precluded the maintenance of independent intelligence organizations. Most of the Lesser Societies adhered to this rule. The So Wari did not.

Ralt considered every conceivable facet of the raw data displayed before him. It was his extraordinary talent for radial thinking that had attracted the attention of the So Wari covert surveillance organization to him so many decades ago. Attention to detail and discretion accounted for his rapid promotion to the secret Inner Circle, whose members reported directly to Meeth. Ninety-seven years of loyal service and friendship kept him from saying no to Meeth when it needed to be said.

The Assistant Commander maintained a rank two full levels below his appropriate station to divert attention from his activities. Meren below the rank of commander seldom merit surveillance. Ralt often observed events without revealing his intent. It was Ralt's own keen vigilance which had detected a pattern in the data in the first place.

At least fifteen Lesser Societies showed signs of mental, psychic and emotional deterioration. Extinction or civil war was imminent in all but three of them. These factors were unprecedented, and certainly not accidental.

When he reported his preliminary findings, Ralt fully expected the investigation to be turned over to Council Intelligence, where it belonged. The expression on his leader's face told him otherwise.

He had known Meeth long enough to know when he was about to deviate from prescribed protocols. Sitting on information like this carried risks. Very high risks. After a furtive discussion, Meeth had convinced Ralt that there was far more to this Genetic Plague than natural selection bias. The data implied (or did Meeth just infer?) that there may be treachery involved.

That was the trouble with being insightfully paranoid: there comes a point at which you have to decide whether you're just being neurotic or you are actually seeing something that no one else sees. It was obvious where Meeth stood on this issue. Ralt, however, was undecided. He did not have enough information to make a decision, but the potential threat could not be ignored.

Could a faction of a Lesser Society truly be involved in polygenicide? It made no sense! The Council would surely eradicate the entire species if such a conspiracy was discovered. *No one would take such a risk,* thought Ralt. Members within a Lesser Society responsible for such a deed would struggle to crush such an effort once it was uncovered. *Therefore,* Ralt reasoned, *the culprit must be an outsider.*

In the 65 million years since the Exodus from Fitu, the Efilu had encountered only four intelligent alien species. Of those, they had been in direct conflict with only one: the Quatal.

The Quatal had near spherical body forms which were deformable into pseudopodia, giving them the advantage of shape shifting. They had had no need to develop tools until they encountered the Efilu. When they witnessed the Efilu fluid crystal space crafts, they became ... ambitious! They found that they could roughly duplicate the metamorphic Efilu technology with local resources. The essential raw materials were of course in short supply on their home world — ergo, expansion!

The Efilu/Quatal conflict had ended nearly 100 years ago. The Quatal, hopelessly overwhelmed by the awesome Efilu forces, had withdrawn from the disputed regions within six months. Hardly worth noting historically, were it not for the alien factor. The Quatal had been restricted to a single three-satellite star system. No further incursions had been attempted. Perhaps, until now.

Secretly, Ralt had sent four of his best agents into the field in search of Quatal traces. Those four, plus Moc, a young female warrior who came highly recommended, were the maximum number possible to investigate the anomalies in question without arousing suspicion.

Ralt had briefed each one individually, delicately, with his motives revealed strictly on a need to know basis. No two operatives were given the same limited scraps of information. They had been out for just over a day-and-a-half standard, when the siege began.

A silent alarm went off in the concealed room. Ralt immediately shut down the data display and prepared it for permanent erasure upon his signal. The erasure sequence would be entered into the security control cuff on his left arm. He exited the room quietly, collapsed it behind him, and walked briskly through the corridors to the public levels where he could already hear the ruckus.

The sound of security shields disintegrating impelled him to quicken his pace. Only his military discipline prevented panic when he saw ruptured security barriers at several outer portals. So Wari guards lay unconscious on the floor beside the outstretched wing of a dead Vansar. An Alkyz meg lay in a corner, motionless.

He hesitated just long enough to examine one of his own fallen sentries. There were no signs of trauma, respiration shallow, no detectable neurotoxins on the mucus membranes or in the air. *Neurodisruptors! But they are illegal except ... Oh, no ... NO!* He looked up and down the corridor. The trail of immobilized bodies led straight to the command center.

Ralt now found himself running through the ancient halls. He forced his way through several damaged containment doors to enter in the command chamber. Before him was the sight of his twelve remaining guards, the five So Wari on monitor duty and Moc, all in the custody of GS security officers.

"Who is the ranking officer here?" Weepf, the Council Intelligence chief asked tensely. Weepf was on guard. The Vansar mer was tall and slender with wings retracted. She stood eye level with Ralt, her wing plumes fanned out to give the impression of a broader back. Physically, her species was at a disadvantage in the relatively confined space of the Hall. "I am." He paused as her attention shifted then introduced himself. "Ralt, intercession commander of this installation."

She gazed at the newcomer with huge, gorgeous Vansar eyes. A luxurious mane the color of sunset, with golden highlights, dominated her crown. The soft fronds hung loosely about her hips, where they were neatly tied in a short binding braid. Still more plumage framed her face, sweeping down and forward. The gentle strands seemed to move with a life of their own, caressing her face and forehead. Yet the stunning beauty of that face deceived no one. This mer was a force to be reckoned with by any threat to the Council.

"I would like to hear more about this epidemiological study of Quatal landing sites," Weepf demanded.

Ralt winced inwardly. He hoped with all his heart that Moc hadn't tried to sell such a transparent lie. Quatal landing sites ... on Teist? That would have raised suspicion from anyone over 120 years old. Ralt looked at the Vansar security chief. The set of her wings told him that her intellect was offended by such a lame story. The Quatal had never come close to Teist, much less successfully landed there.

"This one claims to be completing a survey started eighty years ago by the So Wari xenobiology department," Weepf said skeptically. She displayed the holographic report summary for the assemblage, while the details simultaneously scrolled rapidly through a faded background.

The project had been deliberately left unfinished. They had detected no Quatal traces from a Level Three probe on and around Teist. Further investigation simply was not justified without some Quatal traced, even in the eyes of the most suspicious So Wari.

Such unfinished studies made for effective projects for young So Wari interested in learning the investigative process. It was not unusual for initiates, like Moc, to revisit such a survey as a training exercise.

Yes, Moc had done her homework, Ralt observed. Everything fit. So what gave her away?

He effected a bewildered expression as he looked from the captive to the captor. He was pleased that Moc's thoughts were inscrutable and just as confounded that Weepf displayed equal discipline. All the while, he hid the thought, *How much do they know? Were the others caught as well? The number one priority now: damage control!*

Ralt fiddled with his security control cuff as inconspicuously as possible. He had nearly completed the secret code to erase the data file when Meeth stormed into the chamber.

"What transpires here?" was more of a demand than a question.

Before the startled Avian security chief could respond, Car Hom, the Alkyz Delegate Emeritus, entered the chamber from the opposite portal.

"Yes, what is going on Meeth?" The question had an almost imperceptibly softer tone to it. Meeth's demeanor did not betray his relief to see his old friend among Moc's accusers. He and Car Hom went way back.

The society of the Alkyz represented the largest of the super hunter species. Sleek, agile upper bodies tapered into powerfully muscled lower bodies and tails. In Car Hom's case, long, thick arms extended from strong, broad shoulders that contrasted with the meg's advanced years. His sharp forearm plumage was slicked back. All claws were retracted, inconspicuous as lethal weaponry. His face, pleasant and calm, served to highlight Meeth's agitation.

"I come into MY hold only to be greeted by a multi-national invasion force? The entire plateau will be surrounded by So Wari defense forces in moments. Drop your weapons and start explaining this nonsense, now!" he thundered.

Meeth was half bluffing. It was true that the Round Table already had been surrounded by So Wari forces, but he knew only too well what the assault was about, and he believed it was about to cost him his life.

"Meeth, surely you recognize this 'multi-national force' as Greater Society Security and Council Intelligence," Weepf responded cooly. No more needed to be said. They all knew that council edicts superseded the authority of Lesser Society rulers, no matter how powerful they were.

Weepf spoke again."Your agent, Moc, was caught in a very lie."

"A BAD lie?" Meeth scoffed. "She was caught. In my opinion, that makes for a very 'bad' lie." *Brazen mer!* Still, Meeth had to admire Weepf's directness, even under these circumstances.

She continued. "Our interrogations reveal that you have a secret intelligence network. This is no surprise and by itself does not merit intervention. However, we have also discovered that you have been in possession of evidence that several Lesser Societies have been at immediate risk of extinction, for some time now — evidence which you did not choose to share with The Council."

"Concealing this kind of information represents a major transgression, Meeth." She paused, looked him squarely in the eye and said, "How do you explain this?" The question was moot. There was no explanation that would assuage the wrath of the Council now.

Car Hom saw the drama unfolding in the command center, recognized its requisite conclusion, and tried to divert it.

"I, for one, am in the dark." Car Hom said, trying to stall. "Exactly what is known, by whom, and for how long has that knowledge been available?" he demanded.

Annoyed at the distraction, Weepf reasserted her position. "Meeth knows, the Council knows, and I know. Although you are welcomed at these deliberations by virtue of your past service on the Council, you cannot interfere with these proceedings, Car Hom."

Car Hom replied slowly and softly. "As you have just indicated these are formal proceedings and not a criminal interrogation. Therefore the proper setting for this process is the Round Table chamber itself. The Council must be summoned and assembled before any action can be executed."

The clever old Alkyz had effected a stay of pronouncement against his old friend, if only for the moment.

It had been sixty years since Car Hom had yielded the Alkyz delegation to Yaw Doar, mostly because the young meg had shown such marvelous administrative talent and ambition. That, and good timing, had made it a perfect opportunity for a middle-aged meg to retire from active politics. Since then, Car Hom had been the Alkyz advisor, and over the years he had grown to trust Yaw implicitly. At least the Alkyz voice would speak fairly on this matter.

While these events were transpiring, Ralt had been searching his mind for answers to the questions around which everyone else was dancing. *Whoever or whatever is behind this "plague" has operatives on Teist. In high places no less. How did they overcome my security measures?*

It also was apparent that they had specifically targeted Meeth. Ralt took himself through the reasoning:

First, establish that there is a So Wari intelligence network.

Second, show that this network is in possession of vital information that has not been properly turned over to the Council.

Finally, concoct a So Wari plot of genocide against the other Lesser Societies, by deliberate action, or by deliberate inaction. Very neat, if they can verify all of the facts leading up to this "plot."

Again he considered the erasure sequence to his files on the lower level. The move could backfire, and there would be no turning back if it did. He saw no way out for his Sovereign, unless ...

The discussion had drawn attention away from himself and Moc. Ralt now made eye contact with her, but dared not project a thought.

His expression remained completely blank. If Moc were as good as she was reputed to be, she would read his intent without the aid of projected thoughts.

"This has gone too far!" she declared. Everyone in the room turned toward her. "I confess! The investigation was a family matter. I used my position at Hall Security to gain access to Council Intelligence files. I wanted information I believed would explain developmental deficits evident in certain members of my family. When I discovered that many So Wari were affected, and that we were not the only people, I began to look for a linking factor common to all.

"By single-handedly discovering a danger to the Greater Society, I would have advanced my standing within my clan much further than 70 years of work in the inter-society service could have done. Now I have jeopardized my entire family!"

Ambition. A nice flourish, Ralt thought to himself. He considered her lie as she feigned regret. The story was internally consistent and feasible. The motive for confession at this particular moment was perfectly timed and realistic. He silently held his breath as he awaited a reaction.

"This is very serious young one. If the facts bear out, you may be facing a penalty more severe than you know," replied Weepf. *She has taken the bait! Now to guide the follow through ....*

Ralt began, "As local commander I will take custody of the prisoner and—"

"This is now a GS Security matter. You have no authority here, Ralt," snapped Weepf. To her subordinate, she said, "Take them into custody." She pointed to both Meeth and Moc. *Still not off the claw yet!* Ralt thought grimly.

As they were led to the Table chamber, Ralt reminded himself of the fallen So Wari guards in the corridor. Unarmed and surprised, they had been able to mount an effective defense against superior forces. The dead security squad members attested to that. He was proud that he had chosen and trained them so well.

Ralt's reverie was interrupted as his liege's tail brushed his toes in passing. A subtle call for attention. They were in the chamber and Meeth had just been escorted to the head of the Round Table by respectful GSS officers. Ralt could not hide the shock as he gazed at the assemblage of delegates. All four hundred seats were filled.

The entirety of the Council was seated at the Table ... waiting. This obviously was planned by someone. Someone even more careful than he. Someone who was scared. *Whoever he is, he wants Meeth out of the way and badly,* Ralt thought. His mind raced as he strained to filter out extraneous matters. He needed to observe how closely each of the delegates was listening to the evidence being presented.

The individuals behind this conspiracy had already decided how this exhibition would end, he reasoned. They would be indifferent to argument, no matter how convincing. Meeth was still implicated.

Moc's testimony would be thrown out, of course. Her conviction would not serve a conspirator's interests. Council Intelligence may be just a pawn here, but if it was a willing party ... Ralt shuddered visibly.

Slijay, the Council Intelligence coordinator, intoned, "The overwhelming evidence indicates that there is indeed a So Wari secret intelligence network which has been collecting data for months that clearly show trends of physical and mental degeneration among several species of the Greater Society.

"These reports include documentation of intra-societal feuding. Acts of perversion, even homicide, are numerous. Criminal acts by those in power, committed for personal gain at the expense of regional ruin — with no remorse or sense of responsibility— clearly are evident. On a multi-stellar scale such weakness of body and spirit certainly would be disastrous.

"Although Moc was the first to be captured, she does not have the talent, experience or the resources to conduct a covert research project this extensive. Clearly, she is covering for her superior."

"Is that fact or conjecture?" Yaw Doar, leader and delegate of the Alkyz, questioned the Sulenz skeptically. "The case you present calls for a great deal of extrapolation beyond what Moc actually has discovered."

"Circumstantial evidence. Her story does not reel out. The study in question, although originally left unfinished for lack of interest, was finished some 47 years ago as a training exercise."

He couldn't know that! The outcomes of training exercises rarely were published, especially if the findings were negative. Only a So Wari Elder of that clan could have known the details of an obscure study like that. There would be no reason to dig it up. Not already knowing its content, there should have been no cause for suspicion. The only other way ... It came to him all at once. *Level 4 intimate communications!*

It was the only way they could have discerned the falsehood of Moc's statement. Only knowing that she was lying would have prompted anyone to investigate such pointless trivia. The culprit then had to implant in the minds of the investigative team the idea to look in enough places to reveal the security measures that Ralt had so carefully put in place.

Still, they did not seem to know everything. This was a credit to good defensive psychic training in Ralt's forces. Ralt found himself reanalyzing the available data in a new light. Who among the Efilu possessed Level 4 Intimate Communications Skills, he pondered?

The Si Tyen, perhaps; but they were so aloof, so above political aspirations. The Kini Tod were too timid.

Thea, the Ironde delegate spoke. "This council finds Moc not guilty of the crime she claims."

Ralt was not distracted by the machinations of this tribunal. The Notex? No. They were much more direct. They also lacked the patience to carry out this intricate a plot. Ejtok were limited to such communications within a single family unit, making them too easily traced.

"... Further, we find that the intelligence network is most likely responsible directly to Meeth."

Time was running out. That was the extent of species with natural Level 4 abilities. The only possibility left was ... *induced psychics!*

"Moc is free to go."

Someone with limited psychic ability is using technology to induce and coordinate limited psychic geniuses to an artificially advanced level, Ralt surmised. Only, there was no time to prove that theory to the Council.

With blunt Ironde candor, Thea concluded, "Meeth, you alone as delegate and leader of the So Wari, are hereby declared guilty of suppressing vital information. This violates the fundamental spirit of the Pact and disrupts the integrity of the Greater Society."

There was no time left. Ralt knew what he had to do.

"The punishment is immediate: death by—" Just then, Ralt bolted from his position beside Meeth and raced toward the portal on the far side of the chamber, knowing full well that he would be stopped before he could get there. He made an ostentatious gesture to trigger the erasure sequence on his security control cuff, while the three Vansar security sergeants seized him. As they struggled to restrain him, he tossed the big avian on his left arm across the Table.

At the same time, Ralt deftly unfastened the device from his arm so that it would appear to be accidentally thrown in the same direction. The Sulenz delegate shrieked a thought across the chamber. "Stop him!" Two Alkyz guards moved to restrain him.

Even now, Ralt was making mental deductions about Meeth's set-up. *Inducing Level 4 psychics would take at least Level 2 psychics to start with, but there are at least fifteen eligible species in the compliment of the Greater Society. The question then becomes, who is power hungry and arrogant enough to even attempt a selective purge of the Lesser Societies?*

Five security officers now held Ralt's struggling form firmly. *Now the final ploy!* He was still thinking, but simultaneous revealed a lightly cloaked thought,

" ... hidden files."

The Sulenz delegate projected to the council attendees. "On a lower level! Quickly, seize that control device." Several meren scrambled for the bait Ralt had thrown them.

Ralt, apparently apprehended in the act of treason, confessed to the Council freely. He cleverly filled his friend in on his ploy by pleading forgiveness for his crimes to Meeth.

"I knew that after you were executed, GS Security would seize all records. They would have eventually traced the cover up to me. The only way to protect myself and my family was to erase any connection between myself and this scandal. If there was nothing to be found after you were dead, they would stop looking and I would be safe. I just didn't want to be implicated. I don't want to die." Ralt begged at Meeth's feet.

Meeth was at once profoundly impressed by his friend's brilliance and touched by his loyalty. Meeth had but to play along and ... The Sulenz delegate, Slijay declared, "I want him thoroughly interrogated by Council Intelligence."

Ralt knew that he could not withstand the mind probing of the Ironde agents. He broke away from his captors, and ran straight at Car Hom. He knew Meeth's oldest friend would do the right thing when the time came. He knew he would carry out the execution of a traitor to Meeth, regardless of Council orders.

The So Wari fearlessly allowed Car Hom to grip his neck in the ensuing struggle. The two souls closest to Meeth exchanged a last glance, as Car Hom hoisted Ralt erect, still gripping the fugitive's neck tightly. A final thought came to Ralt simultaneously with the snap of his spine ... *The Ironde and the Sulenz!* The thought floated away from him, as the blood flow to his brain was interrupted. The urgency of that last thought was lost in the narcosis of carbon dioxide backwash from his paralyzed lungs. Ralt's world faded to a peaceful darkness.

Chapter 3
VISTA

Meeth stood before the oriel. The setting sun painted a vibrant collage of earth tones on a coat that normally was adorned in more subdued hues. Spinal plates of green and blue took on exaggerated form in the silhouette looming against the far wall. His face seemed even darker than the shadow. The deep creases of his brow and the corners of his mouth completed the grim portrait.

He did not see the great expanse of plains overlooked by his private offices. His mind still was fixed on the events of that afternoon. The whole sordid affair seemed to last forever, but in actuality the mid-afternoon siege was over well before the first hints of sundown.

The sun now brushed the horizon before him a soft orange hue. Meeth could not appreciate it. He could not erase from his mind the image of one of his two closest friends slaying the other. Even here, in the solitude of his office, he could not afford to show the smallest hint of grief for his fallen general. Still worse, if Ralt had learned anything significant, he carried those secrets to the mound with him.

A "traitor" could not be allowed to contribute his Animem to their Tarn — no matter what the circumstances. He knew some of Ralt's meren, but could not select one of them to replace him. Not yet. Some in Council Intelligence were not completely convinced that Meeth had no part in the incident. He had to assume that he would be watched carefully at all times.

For the first time in the 160 years of his reign, Meeth was without an independent intelligence network. Frustration boiled into anger as the thoughts Slijay had expressed came to mind again. "Justice has been served," the Sulenz had said. He had seemed a bit too satisfied with the outcome. *Satisfied? Perhaps relieved,* thought Meeth.

Memories continued to flow. He remembered Thea's vulgar Ironde habit of patting meren on the back while making a point. It grated on Meeth's nerves more than the point itself.

"Feels good to be alive, eh?" Thea had said, clapping him on the back. The Ironde delegate was shoulder height next to Meeth. Beautiful snow-white plumes stood erect on his body. The untrimmed down gave the appearance of a soft, puffy flower. The weathered dark gray skin of his face was nearly raw. Wrinkles fanned out from his eyes and the corners of his mouth — more a reflection of Ironde heritage than age.

Thea had looked down at Ralt's body and shrugged his broad, stocky shoulders. "What do you think, Meeth?" he had asked. Meeth resisted the urge to clench either his fists or his teeth and simply said "Justice."

"Cowardly scum. Your clan?" blurted an Ironde mer. Thea's was annoying, but his aide had social skills that approached barbarism. Thea himself recognized the insult and dismissed her. His apology reminded Meeth of the relative sensitivity that eighty years service on the council had fostered in Thea.

Just when Meeth's faith in Efiluan nature was on the mend, Weepf joined the growing ranks of those who could all but help saying exactly the wrong thing. "I assume you have some recording devices in place? Might it be possible to ..." She looked around abashedly, "... obtain a personal copy? For review, of course. I must make a full report and I don't want to miss any details."

The residual of the Blood Rush that all predator species experienced upon committing or witnessing a kill still had her on an obvious high. "A good kill. Bloodless though," she declared.

That didn't matter. Meeth knew the mixed feelings many predators had. Intellectually, they truly abhorred violence as much as any, but the blood lust ran deep. A recording of an earnest kill of a worthy adversary was quite valuable. Any recording provided to her certainly would be available on the Vansar black market by month's end. This weakness is what kept Weepf from the Vansar council seat. Neph, the Vansar delegate and Head of State, would have had more self-control.

The hiss of a Kas Pen brought Meeth out of his reverie, in time to see its coils embrace the struggling form of a herbivorous tree mammal. The unfortunate creature had ventured in through the open portal. The succulent fruit it sought to filch from a bowl on the conference table rolled silently from its hands, as it tried to loosen the death grip.

Meeth reach for the fallen fruit and replaced it in the bowl. He balanced the melon atop the pile overflowing the bowl, as he heard the little ribs crack. The gaping jaws of the ophidian dislocated to accommodate the limp animal.

Brought back to current events by the little drama, Meeth realized how long he had kept Tur waiting, but felt no guilt about the offense. He signaled his secretary to admit Tur to the outer office. *Now this!* he thought with exasperation. This virtually unknown meg had entered the picture. He was a governor of a quadrant of Porew, a major industrial center and military command base. On that scale this Tur was potent, but on Teist it was another story. Meeth's story.

The last thing Meeth needed now was another distraction. Weepf had already questioned Tur and claimed she had learned nothing that she did not already know. She had delivered promptly a succinct and detailed report to Meeth. They would be winding their necks for months to please him now. Many on the Council were embarrassed by the near blunder of executing a delegate and monarch of a High Society on so few facts. Many, but not all.

Meeth decided to use the prevailing situation to his full advantage. He reviewed her report. It was good, but he could not help thinking that Ralt could have turned it upside down and backwards to reveal something that she had missed. Still, it was an earnest effort. This almost bolstered Meeth's confidence in Weepf's trustworthiness; but what if she was trying to set him up again, he wondered?

Weepf, apparently impressed with Tur's deductions and assessment of the current crisis, wanted him included in the investigating team. Naturally, she had properly requested Meeth's consent before enlisting his aid.

Meeth himself was unimpressed with the dossier on Tur. Still, Weepf had pleaded with Meeth to grant him this audience in advance of the next impending session of the Council. Meeth had agreed, despite his misgivings. He found Tur's unsolicited involvement in the "Poison Scandal" aggravating, and nearly missed realizing the extraordinary nature of the feat itself. *It could be that Tur has excellent deductive skills, but what if ...* Meeth pondered for a moment. Tur's timing had been uncanny, pointing to knowledge that surely was impossible to obtain by research and deductive reasoning alone. The answer became obvious.

Such extraordinary psychic talent! He could be dangerous ... Too dangerous. Now he kept Tur standing outside of the closed door, just embarrassingly long enough to be seen waiting passers-by in the outer offices.

Finally, Meeth opened the heavy doors to his office using a gel console that currently was doubling as the conference table. They revealed a stoic Tur. Meeth looked the governor up and down, appraising him in an inappropriately casual fashion. Tur remained respectfully at attention.

"What are you doing here?" Meeth asked bluntly.

"I came to help," Tur replied, devoid of discernible emotion.

"Your help is not wanted," Meeth said dismissively.

"Its NECESSARY" Tur answered, in a matter-of-fact tone.

Meeth was on the verge of an eruption. "Who do you think you are?" He paused briefly, then blustered, "You're NO ONE!"

Without awaiting a response, he continued. "You can't begin to grasp the political nuances at play here. You come in here spouting off what you THINK you know about plagues, conspiracies and aliens, and you'll ruin our already tenuous standing among the other high societies!"

Tur strained to keep his composure. NO ONE spoke to him this way, not even the supreme monarch of the So Wari people! Tur was on the brink of getting physical with the older meg, but thought better of it. *That could be a fatal mistake,* he reminded himself. He tried to distract himself by allowing his eyes to roam across the ancient artifacts along the walls and ceiling. He noted that there were few objects on the floor.

"You have already focused undue attention on me," Meeth said. "There is some speculation that you seek to reestablish a secret espionage operation. If so, you can stop wasting my time with your delusions of grandeur. I have no use for you."

Tur leveled a gaze directly at Meeth, now furious. "Let's talk about embarrassment for a moment shall we?" he said. "Ralt had surmised that there was some kind of genetic tampering that involved several races of the Greater Society. Fine. But then he was too inept to report his findings to the proper authorities without bungling the effort, and got himself killed."

They were now facing each other, a mere head-length apart. Palms lay flat on the table, and arms vertically locked like the columns of two opposing ramparts about to launch toward one another.

Meeth moved suddenly. Tur felt the table begin to warp beneath his hands. Not one to panic, he instinctively responded to the potential threat below him by restabilizing his center of gravity.

The gel console, which had been serving as a table, had melted to a semi-solid "sol" state from underneath their hands, and was beginning to envelope them both from the floor up. Tur was momentarily intrigued by the liquid density of the until now inconspicuous device, as it filled the confines of the office in a gelatinous flood. As the console resettled into gel state, a comfortable fore-chair grew between Meeth's feet. A much less comfortable one shot abruptly upward from beneath Tur. As he tried to withdraw from its crude curvature, it clutched him firmly in place.

His pinnate plumes folding into a tight glistening mail, Tur braced to break the grip of the gelatinous extension when Meeth moved to defuse his anger. A gentle hand gesture indicated there would be no violence.

"The official report said that Ralt was conducting an independent investigation for his own purposes," Meeth said. He waited silently for a response.

Tur did not want to do "the expected" at this particular time. He remained silent. He thought to himself, *What has changed here?* The physical changes were obvious, but there was more to it. It was the strange mood change that was confusing.

He used his peripheral vision to examine the "new interior" of the room. Remarkable! The ancient office Tur had entered had displayed an austere charm that suited the So Wari ruler, but this!

Soft pulses of red, orange, and violet light focused towards the center of the parlor. The floor was now littered with several elegantly styled pedestals supporting replicas of large potted flowers and ferns. The gentle motion of the fronds somehow enhanced the illusion of life, interacting in a cause-and-effect fashion with the dioramas, as if they were open windows.

Real-time images shifting across the displays showed the worlds of the Realm at random. A fluid effect, like ink poured into water, mimicked wind-swept clouds so convincingly, Tur felt as if he could reach out and touch them, instead of the semi-solid walls of the cell. The sanctuary was a veritable island in the heavens.

Tur found the new, open feeling refreshing. The softly colored lights intersected to form a stern, white field that enveloped the two occupants of the salon. The harshness of that light hid nothing, reminding Tur that this heaven was ruled by Meeth. He was still under the leader's scrutiny. *He wants something,* Tur thought. *What?*

Tur filled the room with a deep rich chuckle that percolated up from the bottom of his heart. "How much of your mind do wish me to read?"

he asked Meeth. Tur was now staring him squarely in the eye, having a little fun at his Majesty's expense.

Not missing a beat, Meeth responded, "I have in mind more interesting things for you to read. I believe we have enemies in or around the Council."

WE, Tur thought, controlling his exuberance at being taken into the Great One's confidence. *He may be employing the "Imperial We" for all I know, he told himself.* Tur knew this really wasn't the case, but a little humility helped him maintain his composure. "Then you don't believe the Quatal are acting alone either!" he said.

Meeth drew his face closer to Tur's. "I'm not sure the Quatal are involved at all." Tur was taken aback by this consideration, but decided to hear Meeth out.

"The Quatal do have machines capable of transporting them to our Realm. That's true. But to do that without being detected by our surveillance posts? Impossible!"

Tur thought through this line of reasoning slowly before speaking. "How do you account for the Quatal traces found at multiple sites and verified by Ralt's own people, as well as Council Security?" he asked.

"How were they confirmed?" Meeth was patient, but intense now.

"The usual way," Tur said. He stood now, clasped his hands behind his back and paced slowly as he described the methodology. "Foreign protein scans, analysis of enzymes for known Quatal products. Sulfur, iodine, silicone ratios and concentrations in microsamples of secretions. These findings in the setting of the appropriate magnetic resonant disturbance are quite unique."

"Most environmental scientists would know just what to look for I would imagine," Meeth said.

"Of cour—" A look of consternation invaded Tur's face as he realized how long it had taken for him to see the obvious. Suddenly, the insults hurled at him moments ago seemed a little less trifling.

"If one knows what will be searched for, one also knows what to plant," Tur concluded grudgingly.

The signal from the outer office gave them both a start as the cell reverberated. "What now?" Meeth bellowed. It was his secretary, indicating that his next appointment had arrived. "Damn!" he cursed, under his breath. Meeth knew that he could keep the next appointment waiting, but it would look suspicious spending an inordinate amount of time with this Tur. He shifted the gel apparatus back to its original form and induced a holographic display of the outer chamber.

His secretary was chatting with Fath, who waited patiently for admittance. Meeth said nothing, but his eyes told Tur to remain at ease and silent. A brief gesture triggered the ancient doors.

Fath entered through the now opened portal. "I have fully interrogated Moc," he began. The newcomer paused to eye Tur inquisitively.

"And?" Meeth prompted, outwardly paying no more attention to Tur than to a familiar piece of furniture. Fath's momentary distraction by Tur's presence was terminated with a curt nod in the latter's direction.

"The 'family matter' story was a hoax, as we suspected. She now admits to protecting Ralt," Fath continued.

Not very well, though, Meeth thought to himself. "Did she admit this to council security?" he said aloud.

"No. She adheres to the story that Ralt had assisted her in her personal endeavor for reasons of his own."

Once again, Fath was distracted momentarily, this time by the bulge in the belly of the Kas Pen curled up in a corner of the room. He swallowed uncomfortably.

"There will be no disciplinary action against either Moc or her family," Meeth decreed. "As far as I am concerned, there has been no crime. I do, however, want a full gene probe performed on her before the sun rises. Dismissed."

The last command was addressed to both meren. Tur rose casually from his relaxed position, but Fath wasted no time in leaving.

As he reached the doors, Meeth called the security meg. "Fath?" He waited until the meg returned his full attention. "Don't go out of your way to make the probe ... comfortable. Understood?"

Fath acknowledged the order and resumed his exit. Tur manually closed the doors to the office after him, and watched the lights in the chamber dim.

Chapter 4
A SEASON IN HELL

"DEAD! "

"Ol, it makes sense to first find out if—"

"I said I want them DEAD!" The Tralkyz delegate was adamant to the exclusion of reason. "I don't want to discuss it with them in a civilized manner. I don't want to torture a confession out of them. I don't even want to listen to them squeal as they die agonizing deaths. I want them erased from existence! Not an egg, not a scent, not even funeral ashes will remain. I will personally wipe out every memory of them for all time."

Ol Ygar found himself standing alone at the Table. The rank-and-file of the council all stared at him in silence in the wake of his tirade. The sergeants-at-arms discreetly appeared at his side and gently urged him to take his seat. He looked down in embarrassment and saw his reflection on the surface of his work station. He noticed the bulging veins in his temple. His hands were shaking. He sat wearily, as Yaw Doar spoke.

"As I was saying, I think it prudent to extract as much information from the Quatal scientific community as possible. See how extensive this 'Poisoning' is. So far we know, it at least includes the tainted golden algae, which forms the basis of our food chain. Suppose it has also spread to grasses, common flowers—"

"Unlikely," Slijay the Sulenz Delegate stated. "The intent is now obvious. They wanted to minimize the risk of being discovered prematurely. The more levels they tainted, the greater the chance of discovery. Algae is the sole common link to the various food systems.

Destroy it and you have effectively destroyed the entire Efilu civilization and the supporting biospheres."

Thea objected. "That's an exaggeration isn't it? I mean, we certainly cannot allow a threat to any society, but truth be told, fewer than 5 percent of the Lesser Societies are at risk here."

"The Alom flows through all of us, as it flows through each of us," The Roog, Shem Ris, commented from his water-filled corpuscle. Skin now retracted from fins to reveal oversized hands and stubby arms.

"Yes, I appreciate the spiritual implications, but—" Thea began.

Neph interrupted the Ironde speaker. "We are not talking about spiritual jeopardy. Every animal life form derives an essential portion of its neuroendocrine function from the interaction with algae nucleic acid/protein domains. The system is so complex that our scientists don't fully understand it to this day." The Vansar ruler was obviously disturbed by the information he shared. Vansar neurobiologists were surpassed only by Roog and Sulenz in sophistication.

"There must be some way of synthesizing a substitute for the golden algae," Thea insisted. He looked around at his colleagues with growing alarm at the delay in a response. "Bioengineering is working on that as we speak, but ... the defect is so fundamental. We may not be able to synthesize it in large enough quantities."

Evem, the Tan Barr ruler, added to the Vansar pessimism. "It's not just a simple omission or substitution. This peculiar nucleotide sequence that characterizes 'the Poisoning' could permanently alter the neural synapses it contacts in victims. Eventually, an infected individual would end up with various parts of the brain and central nervous system unable to 'talk' to each other."

Sund Kai, the Denar delegate, queried with her typical practicality. "How will this toxicity manifest itself?" Evem looked to Slijay to respond.

"There would be difficulty in concentrating and logical thinking at first, with progressive dementia. Telepathy would begin to break down. In many cases, there would be paralytic attacks and seizures."

There was silence again. Thea spoke. "The Realm is so vast. I can't believe that all the algae is tainted."

"The actual field statistics are still pending, but sample data gathered thus far does not look promising." Neph answered, his head hung low.

"How 'not promising'?" Sund Kai pressed.

Evem answered. "DISMAL."

Meeth had been watching the exchange of information for patterns.

Nothing yet, he thought to himself. As he rose to speak, the assemblage fell silent. "The Kini Todd and Gen Rost have come up with an interesting approach that I initially thought too dangerous. This discussion has changed my mind."

All eyes were on the demonstration display projecting from Meeth's work station. "Their recommendation is for the use of another poison, of our own design." There was a telepathic undercurrent of dissenting thoughts.

Meeth went on. "The idea is to delay the degradation and excretion of nucleic acids, effectively stagnating the progress of 'the Poison's' symptoms. The interruption of the natural cycle of nucleotide clearance would keep them in contact with the synaptic micro-environment until they began to break down in several months. The stagnation will eventually cause malaise, anorexia and neuromuscular irritability, but there would be no permanent damage to the infected individual.

"As it stands now only 3% of the total sentient population has been directly exposed. We can now identify the affected algae, as well as any contaminated food products, and isolate them."

"A few months is not a long time, Meeth," said Sund Kai. "This proposed counter agent is fine, but we need a definitive solution to this predicament."

It was unsettling to Meeth that she could be so cool and rational under the circumstances.

"The Poison has a defined origin and dispersion rate," Meeth began. He had decided where he was going with the plan mere moments before sharing it with the congregation. "We have to search the most remote corners of the Realm. Even — no, especially failed world projects: planets that never got beyond the second stage of fituforming. With any luck, there will be some genetic remnants of the necessary organisms to replace the tainted golden algae."

"Unlikely," Evem said. "Those worlds were abandoned because there was some fundamental incompatibility with carbon-based life."

"Don't you mean Efiluan life?" Yaw Doar objected.

"No," insisted Evem. "I mean any carbon-based life. Remember, we utilized even hostile planets and worldlets to their fullest potential." Evem spoke momentarily with a hint of pride. "Those celestial failures were not near misses, they were outright disasters."

Meeth barely hid his disappointment. Before he could speak, the Ironde delegate preempted him. "We have nothing else to lose by searching at this point. Meeth, if you wish to proceed with the second phase of your plan, you have Ironde support." Murmured thought projections echoed Thea's sentiments.

Meeth struggled to obscure his second agenda. *How do I determine for sure what part the Quatal play in all of this, if they do at all?* He knew that something akin to the Blood Rush was boiling in herbivorous and predaceous peoples alike. In this atmosphere, there could be no move to spare the Quatal. Any attempt at that, and the Council would turn on him in an instant. He could not even be certain that his own So Wari society would back him. He had to take advantage of this mob mentality and the way it interfered with logical thinking, in order to flush out the real culprits.

A desperate idea came to him.

"The Quatal have made the fatal mistake," Meeth announced. "They have repeated the Threat to Life. This, in the wake of the generous mercy shown in the first Conflict, adds insult to the injury! There can be no question: they have chosen not to live in the same universe with the Efilu." He paused for effect.

"So be it then. They shall not live!"

A piercing demand from Slijay cut through the wave of zeal consuming the throng. "Specifics!"

Meeth was on a roll. "A ten-fold energy match for the entire Quatal system will be calculated. The Roogs will see to the details. The Melkyz will send their best strategist to lead a maximum grade assault against the Quatal. "

A delegate interjected, "A three fold match should be enough to ensure complete—"

"We will have their total annihilation! Any glimmer of Quatal existence must be extinguished," roared the So Wari.

Meeth stilled his mind momentarily to sense any suspicious underthoughts from the group. *Still nothing*. "The time is right, given the current solar storm on the Quatal home star. Our three surveillance posts will be maneuvered to the far side of the Quatal system. The trio will be sufficient to block any attempt at flight or distress summons." *Distress summons! To whom? They'll be all alone in this one,* he thought to himself.

For the first time, Meeth noticed the Tyen designate in the back of the crowd. Timon silently watched, as the Tyen were given to do of late, with a dolorous expression defining his face. *How will Chybon, the High Tyen, respond to Timon's report,* Meeth wondered to himself.

"Wait!" Slijay protested. "The Quatal don't yet know we're aware of their plot, but moving those listening stations is sure to raise their suspicions, perhaps even alarm."

Meeth turned deliberately to Slijay. "They have dealt a death blow to some of us right here on the capitol world. I'd venture to say WE don't know what THEY know or don't know."

Slijay said no more. It struck Meeth that the Sulenz ambassador had been unusually vocal during this Council session.

"The stations will shut down except for life support and grade zero propulsion. Timing is everything here." He drew them all in with a gesture. Projecting a real-time image of the Quatal system, Meeth indicated the turbulent solar activity.

"Our blockade will move into position under cover of the solar flares. They will be completely invisible to any telemetry sensors. The storm will reach it peak before this night is over. We must make our move now!"

If the Quatal are half as intelligent as I think they are, the solar activity will also afford them the perfect opportunity to slip past our spy network, Meeth mused. *Maybe they have been doing so all along. A few explorers, perhaps even a few colonies may have secretly gotten through the perimeter defenses to the Realm. The Quatal are remarkably adaptable. It will be a shame to see such a brilliant civilization extinguished over a matter that probably doesn't even concern them.*

A grim thought intruded into his line of speculation. *If we don't find a way out of this predicament, there may be no one left to write our epitaph. Mob mentality. I thought we had risen above it!* Meeth had to caution himself about careless thoughts. At least one other in the Council chamber was as cool and calculating as he was.

* * * * *

The nuclear fires burned brightly in their wide orbits around the Quatal star system in a short-lived tribute to the brave Quatal defense forces. The desperate tactics they had used were ingenious, even by Melkyz standards. They were, of course, hopelessly over-matched.

Nar Quy, the mission commander, was annoyed. It was nearly sunrise on Teist now. Although hastily deployed, he felt embarrassed that the strike force had encountered any resistance at all. He was amazed that the Quatal forces were so ... innovative!

It didn't matter to him that he had lost only twelve out of the twenty-five hundred ships he commanded. It also didn't matter to him that his forces had sent fifty billion Quatal souls to oblivion in the cold void of interstellar space. By the Roog estimates that represented more than half the entire population of Quatal civilization. What did matter to him was that he complete his task: erase everything Quatal from existence.

He pressed on, his ships dispassionately passing the miniature stars born of the power cores of the ruined enemy fleet. His advance squads already had ravaged the three worlds of the star system. Bombardment had already ruptured the tectonic plates of each world. The smoky atmospheres were now studded with flashes of volcanic eruptions, like twinkling jewels of death on charcoal gray blankets.

All defensive activity had ceased. The main body of the Efilu task force moved into position. Almost before he gave the order, the dissection of the charred planetary bodies commenced. Nar Quy felt somehow cheated that he could not hear or smell the carnage he inflicted. Like yolk welling up through cracks in an egg, the lava flows connected the volcanic fires.

Planetary rotation spun shards and huge fragments of the disintegrating planets into space. A wave of Efilu vessels had been assigned to atomize the newly formed meteors as they dispersed from their centers of gravity. The destruction wrought on the worlds of the Quatal continued to the end.

The station commanders all checked in with confirmation that the feeble evacuation effort had been obliterated. "Refugees consisted of mainly germinal centers, a few mentors and nutrient rations. There are no survivors. All debris has been pulverized," was the report of one commander. It was typical of the whole fleet.

Nar Quy ordered the outposts to withdraw to a safe distance. The withdrawing scavenger sorties vaporized scattered ice asteroids, knowing full well they could support no life at all. The sub-commanders were simply venting their pent up aggression at the Quatal skyscape. The solar flares died down as the native life in the star system was extinguished.

Upon reaching optimum range, weapons were focused on the star itself. The debris of the dead fleet winked out of existence as the last of the subatomic reactions consumed them. A line of Rid Sadox, the "Star Crushers," moved into position. The Sadox had not been deployed by the Efilu in hundreds of thousands of years.

Inexperienced meren directed the arcane operation that compressed antiprotons into a near planetary mass. Together, the powerful vessels rent a tear in the fabric of space-time through the center of the Quatal sun. Antimatter drew the core of the star into the singularity. The energy of the matter/anti-matter collision could not escape the growing gravimetric forces.

The dying star seemed to reach out to stroke her children with a last anguished caress before her implosion gathered them close to her celestial bosom. The star would shine dully for several months, perhaps even a year, before regressing to a dim glowing ember, its nuclear fuel exhausted.

"What a waste." Drik, one of the So Wari tactical officers thought aloud.

"Did I invite commentary?" Nar Quy snapped. "They were Poison incarnate. Malignancy like that has to be excised with wide margins." Then in a softer tone, he said, "Drik, sometimes there is greater value in sterilization than recycling."

The statement lingered in his own mind. *Sterilization. My resolution was absolute,* Nar Quay thought. *Why, then, do I feel more sullied now than when we left Teist?*

Chapter 5
HOME SEARCH

The shadow of the Round Table now began to loom over the sunny green patch of grass Meeth lounged upon. He hadn't been on a picnic in the open savanna like this in decades. The fresh citrus fruit tasted intoxicatingly sweet, the air was warm and exhilarating. The afternoon solitude was soothing. The hustle and bustle of life in the capitol seemed very distant.

Images of So Wari heavy equipment and construction activity came to his mind. His people had prospered with an intersocietal trade surplus in manufactured building shells. Their industry was not as aesthetically popular as Wilkyz styling, but much more sturdy, more durable.

Until now, he hadn't thought of how specialized nearly every member society had become in reputation: Melkyz interstellar security vessels, Vansar telemetric technology, Roog communication systems, Sulenz wildlife management systems. They all were interactive, but not interdependent. The fragility of that schema had been manifest at the end of the Golden Age on eons ago. The contemporary wisdom demanded that all societies maintain the means of independent existence.

When news of "the Poisoning" reached the general public, there would be social upheaval. Alkyz administrative skills certainly would be tested in the aftermath of that revelation. A new balance of influence would be established.

A disturbing truth became obvious. Energy storage and transfer enterprises would be of premium importance. The Ironde could be in position to dominate the entire economy of the Efilu Realm. What was worse, their lack of sophistication would likely alienate them from most of the dominant societies. The Greater Society could crumble.

Meeth's left ear twitched. He listened intently for a moment with long stiff So Wari ears, but heard nothing. Waiting for a threat to get within hearing range could prove fatal.

He focused on the grass around him. Insects. He actively sensed their collective life force, compared it qualitatively with what registered moments ago. *Less!* Something was driving them away. They should have been attracted by the scent of the fruit. Still he heard nothing and smelled nothing.

One hundred and fifty million years of adaptive evolution is not easily blunted. Meeth could almost taste the danger, but he knew that panic could play right into a trap. He leisurely reached for a fresh piece of fruit, scanning the horizon as he did. He felt a breeze on his back, caused by the flight of insects and mammals. It was faint, though. The threat was behind him. As he sat to enjoy his snack, he subtly braced to arm and snap to the occasion.

Meeth already had examined the landscape, and using his photographic memory, had formulated battle options ... when the lunge came. Razor sharp cowlicks of plumage raked impotently across his mailed neck. Meeth deftly evaded an Alkyz tail cast to ensnare his feet. His own tail launched the assailant into the grass in front of him.

Car Hom recovered and countered with another offensive, seemingly before touching the ground. Meeth was caught by this attack and suffered several shallow lacerations from the lightning-fast hands and clawed feet. He slipped the Alkyz Death Grip thrice, with no significant injury.

The adversaries circled one another warily. Stalemate. Meeth stopped and stood silently, watching his friend's determination in wonderment. Without dropping his guard, Car Hom asked, "Why did Ralt sacrifice himself in the Hall the other day?"

"Ralt was a coward and a traitor," said Meeth, his eyes narrowing "Are you with his cause?"

"Yes!" came the answer, with no hesitation. He dropped his guard as he spoke. "You can drop the charade Meeth. If I cannot eliminate a meg of your years, I should never have been able to best Ralt so easily."

"Your prowess is legen—"

"Stop! I fully expected to be defeated, maybe crippled in that scuffle. I wanted no more than to hold him at bay until reinforcements were available." Car Hom leaned forward and said, "but NO So Wari would leave himself open at such a critical moment as Ralt did. Not unless he was presenting a show for an audience."

So, legendary Alkyz arrogance yields to wisdom. ... and cunning to friendship, Meeth observed. "Does anyone else know?" he asked cautiously.

"Of course not. This was my first opportunity to speak with you alone. You weren't where you were supposed to be," Car Hom said, with a smile. "Very sloppy, I thought. I had to decide if you were beginning to weaken or if you were up to something."

Meeth also smiled and dropped his guard. "You honor and strengthen the So Wari people. Ralt was a great meg, but necessary loss. Something is going on, Car. Something I don't understand. We are at a distinct disadvantage here."

Car Hom sat on his haunches and caught his breath. "The Ironde have come up with a foolproof solution to 'the Poisoning' today." There was a hint of cynicism in his tone, Meeth noted.

"Oh?"

"They're taking samples of cerebral spinal fluid from uncontaminated individuals, now that we can identify them. They're running them through a modified polymerase chain reaction sequencer and plan to construct a series of retroviruses to re-write the altered sequences," Car Hom explained.

Meeth picked up on his line of reasoning. "Keep plugging them in until they get a functional algae strain again. Elegantly simple in its mechanics. Typically Ironde. Do you think it will work?" Meeth asked.

"No," came Car Hom's grim response. "But it's a whole-hearted attempt, just the same."

Meeth paced as he ruminated on the subject, then spoke softly. "Our only chance at flushing out the culprits is to feign complete ignorance."

"It is all well and good to avoid discovery, but what are we to do about crushing this ... alleged plot?" Car Hom asked. *Damn,* Meeth thought. Car Hom was with him, but not totally convinced. The liability of his hypervigilant reputation in this modern age of complacency surfaced again. And Meeth was out of the time he needed to convince his ally.

It came down to a leap of faith. "Here is what we will do ..."

* * * * *

Vit Na was uneasy. She didn't know what was going on, but she sensed the intensity of subterfuge around her. Tur had not contacted her in days. She had free access to everything in the southern sector of the Round Table BUT communications. The luxury of that section, with its lush garden district, park, museum, restaurants and entertainment, were obviously meant to placate its captives.

Her privileged standing in her society had in many ways blunted her sense of sensationalism. Now it simply sharpened her ability to see through a well-guilded veil of deception. Some, but not all, could correspond selectively with the outer world. Outgoing communications were being censored discreetly. Incoming tidings were being monitored. Vit Na was being held completely incommunicado, and she didn't like it.

Melkyz didn't believe in the concept of the "Inescapable Trap." There was always a way out. She quietly reviewed the boundaries of her confines as she bathed. Her tiered bathing pool seemed a bit extravagant, especially for a So construct. Still, she had to grudgingly admit to being quite pleased with the southern exposure the tri-level apartments provided her.

As she swam in the steamy upper waters, she pondered the motivation for her sequestration. The sun glared brightly through the large decorative transom above the portal to the sunken parlor. She realized she had lost much of the natural oils in her aniline colored coat and promptly spilled her body over the edge of the upper pool into the cooler environment of the lower tier.

The sunlight had just taken the chill out of the waters. She submerged in the cool basin to restore her body temperature and rinse the scented emollients through her downy pillage. Then, she emerged from the water and passed through the aquaphilic containment plane. As the water stripping effect chilled her body, she calculated how long it would be before she was able to Blend again. *Why did that thought cross my mind?* she thought with discomfiture.

Completely dry, Vita Na exited toward the bed chamber. She ran a comforting left hand down her right arm, then proceeded to her bed. She would dine in tonight.

* * * * *

"Why Tur?"

Car Hom's final question still echoed after he had listened to Meeth's stratagem in total. Meeth could have given his friend one of a dozen sound, legitimate reasons for placing Tur in command of the clandestine expedition to Fitu: he was intelligent, but could follow orders; he was creative, but would remain focused; he was born to lead, but was not overly ambitious ... The necessary experience was documented to justify Tur's appointment as team leader. Above all — and this was the very point his own skepticism could not overcome — he trusted Tur.

As far as Car Hom was concerned, it was all well and good for Meeth, safely on Teist, to trust Tur; but he was sending Car Hom off to parts unknown, subordinate to this brash young meg.

The matter was settled. With respect to the staff selection arrangements, Tur could select the personnel, subject to the Alkyz's approval. Effectively, each conscript candidate received either an immediate nod or rejection, with no room for debate between the two executives.

The official Search would prove futile, Meeth was sure of it. His own private expedition was an even riskier venture than Ralt's failed investigation. Meeth provided for a crew of two hundred and fifty, although he hoped they wouldn't take that many. How many good meren would he get killed this time, he wondered? He had to protect them as best he could.

Meeth had set the launch for dawn. The Repam would serve well. An old time survey ship, Meeth had seen to its reconstruction personally. A few surprises were added for the curious in case the ship were stopped in transit ... .and he had a good feeling about Tur and Car Hom. The Repam waited quietly under the inland sea for launch.

As Meeth looked out over the expanse of moonlit savanna from his office, he remembered his father's last meal with the family. Corp had been ill for many months. Wasted by starvation and emaciated by consumption, he lay dying.

The painful cancer had metastasized to most major organs in his body, but still he hung on. Pain had etched a permanent furrow in his brow, but he endured it. A lifetime of leadership and sacrifice had prepared him for nothing else. It was forbidden to bring more than water to the ill. Corp's strength worked to his disadvantage under a law designed to eliminate weakness.

In the privacy of his death chamber, Corp dropped the facade of courage and fortitude, issuing soft moans of agony. Meeth witnessed a moment of his father's despair. He remembered being demoralized by the patriarch's cowardice.

In the final days, the family could stand to watch his agony no more. Under the pretext of collecting the Animem, the whole family smuggled small bits of Corp's favorite foods to him one night.

Meeth was torn by guilt. He was watching his once powerful father waste away, all the while begging for death in the emptiness of his misery. His loyal family stood by, helplessly sharing his anguish. Yet to waste food on the dying. ...! How could Meeth ever honor any of his kin, knowing such shame?

The worn shell of a So Wari chief nibbled weakly on each offering from his family, the food falling from his mouth. Corp then spoke to his son after that last supper.

"Laws have held our peoples together in peace for eons," he whispered. "Sometimes though, there is no merit to blind obedience of the Law. We create laws to preserve our strengths and protect us from our weaknesses. It often takes a lifetime to realize that our strengths are our weaknesses, as much as our weaknesses give rise to our strengths. Fairness, patience, mercy, and generosity contribute to the strength of our civilization. When decisions are made, they are guided by the body of the Law, but executed in the spirit of Justice.

"That Justice is what is truly important. It preserves us no matter the adversity."

Meeth remembered thinking that his father had lied for the first time since he had known him. He had abandoned the province and his family and left them leaderless. He displayed such craven weakness, giving up like that! After all, pain and hunger were only feelings. What did they matter, when the mind and soul were strong? To make such lame excuses was an insult!

Corp ate next to nothing, but oh, how he savored those last meager morsels. Meeth's father hadn't seen the following dawn.

Now, Meeth was skirting the law, and he knew it. Was he just making excuses, as he once believed his father did, or was he doing what had to be done?

The Search, as it had come to be known at the last executive session, was fruitless. Meeth knew they would find nothing. Yet to admit that would be political suicide, and surely would precipitate societal chaos. He had to approach the dilemma from a desperate angle — one no sane individual would entertain.

Operation Back Track would not be recorded in any of the archives. It was an oversight during confusing times, if anyone asked.

I'm surrounded by enemies, Meeth told himself. *The only safe recourse is to feign ignorance, play along. With my most trusted ally away, no one will be here to save me if I make another mistake.*

He allowed himself a solitary moment of self-pity. *There will be no requiem for me.*

Chapter 6
BACK TRACK

"This is Tur, commander of the geological survey vessel Repam."

The transmitted image of the Melkyz officer eyed him long and carefully from the gel console display. On the Repam, Tur stood easily erect in his usual stoic manner. The So Wari knew that a geology ship lurking along the out skirts of the Realm would raise a few questions.

He surmised that this patrol ship sub-commander was the relief officer on duty. Likely this Desq Ja was trying to decide whether to awaken his senior officer over this minor irregularity. He appeared to deliberate for a long time before he spoke.

"If you don't mind me saying so, you're out a little far for such an old ship, commander. You haven't had any propulsion or navigation problems have you?"

"No. We are quite aware of our position and course," said Tur, without elaboration. Tur knew he was pushing this Melkyz officer.

"A craft like that is, well, obsolete," said Desq Ja. The survey class vessel he saw was shaped much like a spiral mollusk shell. The neutral configuration was ideal for burrowing when necessary. "We are the outer most Guardian ship in this sector," he continued. "Were you to suffer a malfunction, it would be unlikely that you'd get a timely response to a distress call."

Tur shrugged casually. He knew he was getting under the sub-commander's skin with his not-so-subtle contempt for the inquiry. Tur had always been good at reading people. He had this one down to a toe.

"Commander," said Desq Ja firmly, "your vessel's outer markings are dull, almost indistinguishable even at this distance. We almost passed you by. Our secondary telemetry systems are detecting mid-range EM emissions from your power core. Your propulsion efficiency can't be more than 47% of optimum."

With a touch of arrogance in his thought projection, Tur stated, "I have engineered certain modifications in the drive section to more than compensate for the losses, Sub-Commander ... Disc Jay, is it?"

A nearly exasperated correction came after the malformation of his name. "Desq Ja. Adding two additional Sekwoy generators to the stock drive is a dangerous 'modification,' Commander.

"It doesn't stop the power leakage. It just adds to the radiation spillage. The rate of loss will probably increa— "

"Are you authorized to probe ships on official business without notification or consent, Sub-Commander?" Tur asked, affecting indignation at Desq Ja's implication.

His patience wearing thin, Desq Ja explained, "Passive telemetry reveals much to a seasoned commander. There are few ways to get that kind of energy emission out of a ship of that design and age, short of completely gutting it and replacing the endoskeleton and viscera." The spiral/counter-spiral design was well known as the basic structure of geologic science vessels. "I know that it could not have been done because of the prohibitive waste involved."

Good! He knows So Wari mentality well. Tur guessed he also knew how some low-class So Wari held callous disregard for the feelings of physically smaller peoples.

"The blur in your communicated image and loss of background definition, in spite of efforts to enhance them, both betrays the EM field build-up." Desq Ja's ire climaxed in an attempt to humiliate the commander of the apparent scrap pile.

Still posturing defensively, Tur responded. "When you become a full commander, you'll probably understand that skill can make up for the inconvenient lack of technological luxuries." He casually looked back at his navigation crew members, who were conveniently out of the offended security officer's view field, as a final jibe.

This was enough! Desq Ja felt that he had wound his neck for too long trying to help this incompetent, arrogant So Wari and his foolish crew. *If he wants to risk losing their two hundred souls in the depths of interstellar space, let him,* the sub-commander decided.

Officially, everything was in order. There was no imminent danger, and assistance had been refused. He would bury the log entry in the mountain of insignificant passing observations made on his watch —

details not included. Desq Ja almost wished Tur would rot in space with that stupid grin frozen on his ungrateful face.

Tur waited until the security ship was well out of scanning range before resuming full dampened power. The EM field dissipated from the command center. The Repam's state of the art propulsion system returned to active status. A rift was formed in normal space and the Repam folded into the void.

No specific orders had been issued about divulging the grand-scale upgrades in the craft's viscera, but it was obvious by the deceptively modest exterior that this information was to be shared on a need-to-know basis.

No doubt, Meeth was covering his hindquarters in case the mission went sour. Tur wasn't sure he liked that. He had decided to protect his own tail by maintaining secrecy without actually "lying" about the true modifications himself. It would be tough to prove him guilty of anything during that last encounter, except vulgar behavior.

Tur rested on his haunches, ruminating. He looked up to see Car Hom with his arms folded in front of him, nodding approvingly. The Alkyz gave him a light pat on the back, as the High Commander rose and strode past. Tur ignored the silent accolade and continued on to his office. A curt gesture directed Car Hom to follow.

* * * * * *

Vit Na sat off to one side of the chamber, apart from the others, with her back against a wall. The other department heads and section chiefs were murmuring about the haphazard set up of the mission organization. The prevailing sentiment was that they all felt ill prepared.

The Tralkyz Bo Tep was at the same time animated and the most relaxed of the group. Vit Na felt uncomfortable around Tralkyz. The more relaxed they appeared, the more tense she became. *Head of Acquisitions!* she thought to herself. She shuddered at the thought of having him "acquire" anything from her.

Tralkyz were notorious for their unnecessary viciousness. Even worse, they had no fear or reservations about injury or personal loss. No enemy, no situation intimidated them. It was said that if a Tralkyz lost both legs in combat, he would chase his quarry on his hands and tail. Perhaps that chilling legend was exaggerated, but it was not so obvious in this very small chamber. This Bo Tep was reputedly tougher than most, but she found herself staring at him anyway. *Where do I know him from?* she asked herself.

The executive officer was due any time now and most of the department heads scrambled to organize their staff assignments. Car Hom would want reports immediately upon his arrival in the briefing room. The room went completely silent as the portal melted away to reveal Tur, flanked to the right by Car Hom.

The room remained open to the hall as Tur gruffly said, "Level Seven clearance and above." Car Hom made a short, silent gesture for all non-essential personnel to leave.

The remaining senior staff fidgeted restlessly. There would be no aides or support staff to help them through this meeting. The portal almost caught the tail of the last individual exiting as it closed.

* * * * *

"Outside of the Realm?"

Kellis looked around the room to see if everyone else was taking the news as incredulously as she. The Tan Barr mer had almost formed an objection when she realized the only other voice she heard was Bo Tep's snickering at her sudden discomfiture.

Tur and Car Hom stared at her impatiently. Her broad shoulder armor sagged slightly, in embarrassment. She found the courage to proceed more delicately. "I'm sorry for being a little thick-headed, Tur, but what is the purpose of going outside? If we are to look for uncontaminated golden algae specimens, we're not going to find any in unexplored space."

Car Hom waited for a nod from Tur before speaking. "We are not heading for unexplored sectors."

Bo Tep heckled, "But you just said outside the Realm. To me that means where no one has gone before. What are we doing, going in circles?" A stern look from Car Hom failed to check the Tralkyz's casual manner.

Tur spoke. "The Repam will retrace the path of the ancient Exodus as far as necessary to find algae remnants. Our thinking is that all the known worlds inexorably have been or will be contaminated."

"For security reasons this information goes no farther than this room for now. There will be a briefing for Level Three clearance and above upon our arrival at our final destination." He said no more on the subject, but stepped threateningly towards Bo Tep. It was clear that the next inappropriate thing he said would be his last.

Doh caught Tur off guard by breaking the silence. The short Kini Tod scientist was the only staff member who seemed truly thrilled to be there. "We are going all the way back to Fitu then?" he gushed. Vit Na's eyes rolled in the opposite direction with exasperation. The Kini Tod obsession with the mystery of the Keepers wore thin everyone's patience. The groans in the chamber echoed her sentiments.

Tur was uncharacteristically patient as he responded. "It won't be necessary to go that far. Our ancestors made numerous colonies between the current boundaries of the Realm and Fitu. We are certain to find appropriate specimens long before we reach Fitu, even in the ruins of those abandoned colonies."

"Unless someone has beaten us to it," Bo Tep interjected, his tone even and subdued. Tur and Car Hom shared an uncomfortable, silent acknowledgment of Bo Tep's insight. *This Tralkyz is a thinker,* Vit Na observed. *And suddenly, he's suspiciously quiet and attentive.*

Tur went on, trying to ignore for the moment the unexpected Tralkyz insight. "We have been inconspicuous so far. I believe we have escaped notice."

"Except that of the last patrol ship," Bo Tep said, somewhat more in character.

"That was handled adequately," Tur remarked. Nothing more came from Bo Tep, but he had made his point.

"I want every department up and running within the next three days. My apologies for the haphazard departure," Tur concluded. Before any questions could be asked, he had turned and moved to the exit, with Car Hom three head-lengths behind him. The remaining staff looked at each another with puzzled faces.

Ikara, in deference to the tasks at hand, spoke first with resignation. Long, beautiful Mit Kaim down mixed luxuriously with long feathers, covering the length of her muscular body and stiff tail. She looked incongruously vibrant, in contrast with her obviously tired posture.

"We all have a lot to do. I'll be in Xenobiology setting up my staff if anyone needs me." She hesitated for a moment to invite immediate curbside consultation, in the hopes of avoiding the inevitable interruptions later. She had no such luck. She hugged her tail once in frustration, then left. The others soon followed suit.

Vit Na felt a chill run up her tail as Bo Tep eased over to her side. "What would Tur have done if he hadn't been able to get that ship to leave?" he asked.

An interesting question, Vit Na had to admit. She thought about it, then answered. "Probably he would have impressed the ship into subordination. He has that authority as High Commander."

The Chief of Acquisitions was persistent. "What if the sub-commander had questioned Tur's authority? Under the circumstances, that wouldn't have been unreasonable, and he would have been within his rights."

Vit Na's apprehension continued to rise. "I don't know," she said unconvincingly.

"Yes, I think you do," Bo Tep replied. "I've heard you two have been very close ... synesprit, in fact." The earnest urgency in his face demanded an answer.

"If they didn't comply with the conscription order, he would have destroyed their ship and every hand with it," answered Vit Na. She found herself returning his resolute gaze. He answered the question forming in her mouth with more compassion than she had thought possible. "I had to know." Momentarily, Vit Na's anxieties vanished.

She found her anxiety returning as she realized that she would have to tell Tur about this conversation and that Bo Tep knew it. Then curiously, as she watched him stride away down the corridor, her tension again melted away and she felt reassured, as if she had just helped a close friend. The sudden change did not even disturb her.

* * * * *

"How did you come to select Bo Tep any way?" Tur asked.

"He is an accomplished leader and very well thought of in the Tralkyz community," Car Hom responded in a matter-of-fact manner.

"The traits that the Tralkyz find commendable, most of us find deplorable. For a moment, I thought I was going to have to kill him on the spot," Tur said.

"Yes, I noticed that," Car Home replied.

"And?"

Car Hom just shrugged in response. Tur, now irate, declared, "That should have been your responsibility, COMMANDER."

Experience and patience allowed Car Hom to recognized the disciplinary tactic for what it was and he took no personal offense. "I don't execute my senior personnel for their attitudes when making suitable observations." He deliberately omitted the honorific 'commander' in his response. He returned Tur's angry glare with no hostility or malice of his own.

Presently, Tur relaxed. "You are right of course. Still, he did seem out of character for a moment, did he not?"

Again, a shrug was Car Hom's sole response. Tur decided that this line of conjecture was going nowhere, and changed subjects. "Departmental organization and assignments seemed to be moving forward." He waited for Car Hom to chime in. He was given silent acknowledgment. "I've been especially impressed with Los, our Head of Astrophysics and Propulsion. He has retrieved ancient maps of the Exodus Corridor and is already coordinating with the liaison offices of the respective departments to be consulted."

Car Hom was not petty. He had shown Tur that he would not be bullied and the younger meg had learned his lesson. Taking his cue, Car Hom gave forthright personnel assessments. "I think the whole organization is solid and capable. We did a good job in the selection process if I do say so myself ... If I may make a comment, commander?"

Car Hom did not await permission. "This ship is not staffed solely with So Wari warriors, and no amount of discipline or intimidation will make them react as such. They simply cannot be as regimented."

"And? "

"I just think that this group's diversity can be used to considerable advantage, if the meren are given enough freedom to express themselves."

Tur nodded slowly, recognizing Car Hom's point without voicing agreement. "And should I have any misgivings about a staff member's performance?" he asked.

"I am at your disposal."

"I'll keep that in mind. When will you assemble them?"

"A Level Seven staff meeting is scheduled to begin in — well actually, right about now. If you will excuse me." Car Hom rose and exited the executive suite and crossed the Promenade garden to the chief of staff's office. The conference room where the meeting would be held was adjacent to it.

Tur allowed himself a reluctant smile. Meeth chose well. Not one for modesty, he mused that the same commentary could be extended to include himself. He busied himself reviewing the preliminary reports from the department.

* * * * *

Archeology was the fifth department to report. Vit Na was unsure of herself. Her department was one of the best organized, nonetheless. For the presentation, she even had constructed a holographic display of the surface of Fitu, the ruined cities at the time of the Return, and the most likely continental drift pattern over the ensuing 65 million years or so. Car Hom's appreciation of her talents deepened when he saw the surprise on Kellis' face.

Such accurate detail! And without help from Geotechnics. He almost chuckled aloud. He knew that Tur felt uncomfortable about Vit Na heading a department under his command, but as Car Hom had pointed out, she was easily the best suited to the task. She was the only crew member of noble birth on the Repam. There was bound to be some resentment towards her, but the others were professionals. They would get over it.

Faster than she will, Car Hom mused. The remainder of the staff meeting was gratifying. No one gave an unsatisfactory presentation. In fact, the vast majority of them were brilliant. Especially well prepared was Bo Tep's Acquisitions department.

The various contingency decision trees were well thought out. The choice of consultants well researched and integrated. The only presentations that were lackluster were the ones that should have been so. The nutrition and waste management departments, as well as medical section, were mere formalities. The mission was vitally important, but expected to be drearily routine. Supplies were more than adequate, and the passengers all young, healthy and free of the Poison. The only concerns pertaining to the medical department was dealing with the anticipated effects of the counter agent algae nutrient replacement, if the mission was prolonged.

The last thing they needed on such a crucial mission was the signature side effects: irritability and carelessness. Car Hom also knew in the back of his mind that there was no proof positive that the Poison had been screened out, with all the espionage back on the capital. The Medical department would act as a silent sentry for signs of infection.

The minor department presentations were quick, to the point, and over before anyone got bored. It was quite a feat of restraint. Car Hom thought of Brajay, the Sulenz Medical officer. The Sulenz, whether deservedly so or not, had the reputation for run-on thoughts.

The meeting adjourned on schedule. As he dismissed the group, Car Hom realized how hungry he was. He made his way over to Vit Na, intent on inviting her to dine with him. As he entered her personal space, she turned toward him to inquire what he needed of her. Suddenly, he thought better of his invitation. The request might engender bad feelings towards her from the other department heads. He decided to eat alone tonight.

Instead, he said simply, "Nice work." As he watched her depart to her quarters, he allowed himself a personal assessment of the young archeologist. *Most impressive.*

Chapter 7
FALSE HOPE

Car Hom was becoming full. He had finished the bulk of the well-seasoned Sindech and was about to stretch out to savor the last few morsels when the ripples in the portal barrier indicated that someone was there.

The door opened to reveal Tur. He had a queer, inquisitive look on his face that almost masked his disgust. "I've disturbed you," he said. "I'll just come back when you're done."

Car Hom replied, "No need. I've dined more than sufficiently."

Tur still looked hesitant. "Sorry to interrupt your meal," he said. The sentiment was genuine.

"It's all right. You saved me a lot of unneeded calories. I've got to watch it at my age." Tur pursued the apology no further.

Car Hom invited him to speak freely. "Now really, how can I be of help?" Tur appreciated his first officer's insight better each day.

As Car Hom rose from the table, the platter of scraps submerged into the gel table surface. Car Hom walked Tur to the door and lead him out, leaving the odor of dead flesh behind them. His growing concern that he had intimidated the young High Commander was short-lived, as Tur came promptly to the point.

"It has been four days since we entered the Exodus Corridor. Los has correctly located nine of the abandoned colonies. We have a seven phase telescien on each of them." That deployment dipped into their energy reserves a bit, but if it ended the mission early, it would be worth it.

The telescien were constructs driven by interactive programs with seven levels of artificial intelligence, which operated as the senses. Each unit maintained the pure energy equivalent of 100 pounds of unstable heavy metal. The telekinetic function worked as pseudopodia, which could excavate, manipulate, analyze, even synthesize simple inorganic objects on-site, from whatever native material was available. Guided from the safety of the Repam by a skilled Efiluan director, a telescien was a powerful tool for exploration. If there were any dangers, the unit could be withdrawn or sacrificed with minimal material loss.

"Reports have just come in from the last unit," he added.

"You don't sound very enthusiastic," Car Hom observed. "No algae? "

"No," Tur answered. Car Hom's shoulders sank.

"But there is something else. There are traces of alien organic matter that indicate recent contact."

Car Hom stared in disbelief. "Quatal?"

"No." Tur said impatiently. "Something completely different. We are tracking it now. That's why I need you in the command center. If this is a first encounter with an intelligent species, I'll need a Council member present as ambassadorial support."

* * * * *

Obb was pleased with his quarters. Everyone else was so busy setting up their divisions, they had little time to give personal space much thought. Most apartments were more than adequate anyway and no one wanted to draw Car Hom's attention unnecessarily by putting in unusual requests.

The Head of Paleobotany's selection went unchallenged. One reason Obb's choice drew no attention was that the occupants of Stratum Three were largely technicians and officers of Level 2 clearance and under. *Well, there's no accounting for taste,* he thought to himself. Most of the other senior officers were on the seventh stratum, centrally located and near the staff conference room.

Obb's parlor was situated below the tropical gardens on the third stratum. The chamber afforded open view to the glade at pond level.

Insects were kept out of the immediate environs by a neuro-disrupter field. Flying insects occasionally hit the water with a tiny splash as they were stunned in mid air by the field interface. Crawling insects simply avoided the growing discomfort as field intensity mounted. Lighting from the overhead ciel filtered dimly through the thick vegetation. These quarters were most suitable to Obb. The Gen Rost were amphibians capable of living under a variety of conditions.

The humidity almost reached saturation. The profusion of plants inside the apartments continued the jungle theme, with minimal interruption. Obb swung gently in a hammock as he cracked open a fresh seed fruit. Large hands extended from short arms to tip the treat over his beak-like mouth. The thick, creamy fluid trickled down his throat with a mild tingle. There was a paresthetic quality to the fruit that made it taste icy cold even at room temperature. Stubby legs terminating in big feet crossed in delight.

The reverberation of the gel portal signaled the arrival of Doh for his first consultation. Obb moved to trigger the open command with a gesture, but did not rise from the hammock. Gober Dil, his Wilkyz assistant, would escort the guest to the parlor.

Doh had a habit of miring himself in details, even those as trivial as the interior decor of Obb's apartments. Obb had had time to finish his fruit by the time Gober Dil completed the grand tour: the sunken den, the work area, sleeping system and data archives all had impressed the visitor. Dil had begun to show signs of impatience as he moved the chief paleozoologist through the dining area, hygiene pools and his own small adjacent suite.

Still, Doh was too preoccupied with the upcoming discussion with Obb to notice the apprentice's pique. There was audible relief in Gober Dil's voice as he announced the chief paleozoologist's arrival. Doh made himself comfortable as he set up the link to his own database for reference.

"So, do you really think there are still intelligent life forms on Fitu?" A bating opening line. Obb liked to start his debates off this way, regardless of whether he agreed or disagreed with the speaker.

"I do. I really do!" Oblivious to the form Obb had chosen for the discussion to follow, Doh jumped right in. "It has been over sixty-five million years since the Exodus — time enough for the heartiest of the surviving life to adapt, regenerate, repopulate and flourish.

"Now, I don't expect that they will have developed crystal technology or advanced thermochemical power, but I would expect that they will have formed complex social orders, maybe even groups of herds or tribes."

"That requires some degree of complex communication skills doesn't it? I mean, to join several communities together they would have to be able to share thoughts and ideas," Obb offered innocently.

"Yes, of course," Doh agreed eagerly.

Obb smiled inwardly at Doh's response. *This is going to be too easy.* "There are probably groups of interrelated codes in use. For example, both land and sea birds communicate with chirps and whistles. These tend to further organize into songs, which are then learned, and passed on to later generations who improvise upon them." Obb felt that he could do his opponent in right here and now, but he wanted to savor this session a bit more.

"Do you think that Fitu is currently inhabited by birds then?" he asked.

"Possibly, but—" Doh began.

"Possibly? Birds have small brains and high metabolisms. How do you propose that they build delicate devices and tools? The hind talons just can't be adapted that well, and their wings are useless for anything but flying and perhaps swimming." He paused as Doh floundered a while then struck again.

"Then there is the obvious question: where do they get their food? All vegetation was wiped off the face of the planet eons ago. None of the natural flora would have survived the iridium toxicity." Doh tried to raise an objection, but Obb rolled on. "Alright, forget the toxicity for a moment and answer me this: Autotrophic plants depend on photosynthesis for nourishment. What autotroph could withstand millennia of cold darkness?"

Obb paused there for effect, then stated, "With the basic food elements destroyed, Fitu's food chain had to crumble."

"Couldn't some autotrophs have survived on geological heat and enzymatically-released chemical energy?"

Obb became bold. He crossed into Doh's specialty for a moment. "And what about the effects of heavy metal poisoning on major organs? How could animals survive the inevitable renal failure, intestinal toxicity, not to mention central nervous system damage? Those ancient creatures needed every precious neuron to survive such a holocaust." He was openly laughing at the Kini Tod scientist now.

Doh was peeved, but managed to hold on to a little dignity. "Well I'll admit that the chances of surviving those dark times are slim, but some individuals are always sure to survive the demise of their species. Furthermore, they will pass those survival traits on to their progeny," he offered.

Still laughing Obb rejoined, "Oh that's the other thing: genital toxicity is the most common of all of the side effects of iridium poisoning. Every sexually reproducing organism on the planet was rendered sterile, including the Tyen Keepers.

As if suddenly realizing the cruelty he had just inflicted on his colleague, Obb's tone became more gentle. "No doubt the Tyen made some creative adaptations in those final years. We'll certainly see some unique settlements and dietary changes. Vit Na will be fascinated, no doubt."

From his place in an adjacent room, where he was ostensibly at study, Gober Dil discretely hid a snicker.

"I don't know what we'll see, I admit," Doh said. "I'm not smart enough for that, but I have seen enough surprises in my lifetime to expect the unexpected."

The remainder of the conference was much less lively. With Doh's feelings obviously hurt, Obb simply ran through a catalogue of raw data, and specific botanical trends and patterns.

* * * * *

"We are now 12 photodymes outside of the Exodus Corridor."

Tur acknowledged Los silently without turning around. He reminded himself, *so from here we might see images of the Corridor as it was a hundred and twenty years ago.* To study them would be a prudent first move. Who really knew what to expect?

The Repam entered the alien star system. "This complicates matters," Tur observed. "Searching for specimens in abandoned settlements is one thing, but here we are outside of our space. Military force cannot be authorized through official channels if resistance is offered by alien life forms." Not even by Meeth's convincing arguments. "And we don't have time for lengthy negotiations," he added aloud.

"There's no need for either," was Los' uninvited response. Tur breathed deeply, then exhaled, without turning around. Car Hom, taking the cue, said, "Just state your suggestion, please."

"We are no longer in the Corridor, it's true, but we're still in the Old

Dominion," Los spat out, his ego a little deflated.

"Then we still have jurisdiction," Tur concluded.

That could have been very difficult, Tur told himself. He considered Los without looking at him. *He knows his business, that's for sure. He has a flare for the dramatic though.*

The Notex scientist was more egotistical than most among his race, but he had their typical impatience. Notex had high metabolic rates for omnivores, accounting for their spare, lean physiques. More than restless, they were constantly in motion. Even when they weren't employing hyperspeed, they tended to mobilize their superjoints, presumably to prevent stiffness. The array of hooks and talons on their forearms made for great attention grabbers in an otherwise lackluster, mid-sized species.

"Display current parameters of the Old Dominion, Los," Tur commanded. A real-time image of the sector engulfed the command center. A yellow beacon marked the location of the Repam. A band of stars, which was bathed in a soft purple light, stretched from the beacon to a distant blue star cluster. No one could dispute the fact that this alien civilization had arisen in the shadows of Efilu space. The system contained fifty-three worlds of near standard gravity, with two-hundred-and-fifty less significant worldlets scattered about them in close orbits. The Fituine stone worlds were themselves in wide orbit around seven gas giants, the smallest of which was the size of Teist.

Kellis arrived in the command center at Car Hom's behest. The Head of Geotechnics enjoyed interesting planetary formations. The gas giants of the system were glowing with the intensity of dim, red stars, but in different colors: blue, indigo, red streaked orange, green with yellow and golden brown marbling.

"Unnaturally beautiful ..." was all she said when she came to a halt at Car Hom's side.

Tur half turned. "Unnaturally?" he asked.

"Of course. You don't think that those colors are normal, do you? Beside that, those giants aren't nearly massive enough to produce their own luminescence. "

"Are you certain?" Car Hom asked sternly, forcing her to shift her attention from the display to him. More formally, she answered, "I have identified this system from the survey records from fifty million years ago." She awaited the consenting nod before superimposing the archived image on the real-time display. She adjusted for the dissynchrony of the orbits before explaining.

"Here are the same gas giants, many eons ago. If that impossible glow we see in the present was a natural phenomenon, the ancient images would be even brighter. Yet as you can see, the gas giants simply reflected the radiation that fell upon them at the time of this old record."

"There could be an error in the recording. What about the possibility of a 'fade' effect on the visual? "

"The records aren't that bad. No. Those planets are artificially lit," Kellis concluded. The wonderment returned to her face.

Car Hom was more practical than scientific. "By what power?"

Los answered Car Hom's question. "About one hundred and fifty of the smaller solid bodies are mass drivers."

Tur lost his detached affect for a moment. "Are what?"

"Mass drivers." Los projected the thought in a deliberately patronizing tone — no doubt in response to the earlier disciplinary comments of the first officer. Tur noted this, but said nothing.

"Those small planetoids are equipped with magnetic feeds which take loose debris and gases from their own fields of gravity — atmospheres, if you will — and 'drive' them through an electromagnetic tunnel. The average tunnel is about a hundred times the length of this ship," Los explained, forming a tunnel with his hands as a demonstration display appeared showing the mechanism.

"The high velocity 'cloud' strikes a nuclear fusion field on the larger stone planets. This, in turn, causes a chain reaction to take place, forcing a small burst of high energy photons to explode into the upper atmosphere of the gas giants. The ionizing radiation is the source of the illumination as it disperses into the atmosphere."

"Mass to energy. Whoever created them at least has the first part of the unified field equation," Tur observed.

"I just haven't figured out how they utilize this energy," Los finished.

"We can't make that determination intelligently until we learn their root anatomy and physiology," Doh said, uncharacteristically somber after his encounter with Obb. "I recommend that telescien probes scan for life forms and communication patterns."

"Agreed," said Tur. He found Car Hom's waiting gaze and said simply, "See to it." He then left the chamber.

A day later Car Hom appeared in Tur's offices. At his command, Car Hom proceeded with the progress report.

"Well, as you know, our mysterious cloud dwellers have come to us for a closer look." He sat on a forechair, with his tail comfortably supported behind him.

"That should make our investigation of their biology and technology easy," commented Tur. He sipped a cool citrus concoction from a bowl, as he prepared for an upcoming briefing.

"I have Doh, Obb, and Ikara on the task force. Their preliminary conclusions can be summarized quite neatly," said Car Hom. "It would seem that our friends out their are actually carbon-based."

Tur didn't react. Car Hom continued. "Ikara has named them the Tomet. They are autotrophic organisms that feed directly off of the ionized clouds. Structurally, they have vascular membranes that roughly look like flower petals. In fact, the arrangement of these appendages attached to a single spiral trunk is very ... well, 'flowery'." He chuckled at his own description.

"Are you telling me that we're looking at a civilization of flowers?" Tur asked, also amused.

Sobering some, Car Hom finished. "No. They're actually closer to animal life. You may want to compare them to our native cephalopods. They spin their torsos when they want to move. Their appendages form a helix. As they rotate, the appendages cut through the dense atmosphere with a variable acceleration, pulling an individual with it. Direction is controlled by torsion of the body. The appendages even flap to provide sudden bursts of speed or drastic changes in direction."

"This is all very interesting, but what I need to know is: how do they manipulate the world around them?" Tur interrupted. "Specifically, how did they escape the atmosphere to create those orbiting power stations, for example?"

Car Hom rephrased the High Commander's question. "What you really want to know is 'what are they capable of militarily?'"

A wry smile preceded Tur's response. "No. What I really want to know is are we dealing with the most advanced society of its kind? Are they unified into a consolidated power?" Tur leaned forward on his haunches to get his first officer's response. He had learned to anticipate Car Hom's little games by now.

"Well, the life density seems to be concentrated near the 'gray world.' The mass supply appears to be the richest there, and all the ion trails of what Los calls 'transport clouds' lead to or from it." He folded his arms in satisfaction.

Tur too, seemed satisfied with the analysis. "So, we're dealing with a stellar empire," he observed.

"... and the Repam is poised at its hub." Car Hom said, ending the thought for him.

Tur turned in the direction of the foresection of the vessel and pointed with a nod of his head. "Now, to the present situation. "

"The Tomet's curiosity is giving way to frustration," said Car Hom. "Their probes are not penetrating the outer layers of our integument. They're still in the dark as to what we are and why we're here. I recommend that we let them churn for a while before we make our intentions known. At this rate, one of them is likely to lose its temper and take hostile action." The old Alkyz shrugged. "Then we have them."

Tur drummed his fingers a few times on the table as he thought silently. Then he spoke. "It seems to me that our interests could best be served by a direct inquiry."

Car Hom gave him a suspicious look. Tur reaffirmed his sincerity. "I'm very serious. Their political structure is sophisticated enough to make direct negotiation feasible."

Car Hom stood, and said, "I think you're right. This culture is fragile enough to crumble if thumped in just the right place."

"Let's hope that THEY know that."

* * * * *

Tur didn't understand the romanticism surrounding alien encounters. Obb and Doh were envious that Tur had decided to go alone. Ikara was downright angry. She felt that she had put too much effort into researching the Tomet to be left out at this point. Car Hom had been unwaveringly patient with his explanation as to why Tur wanted to proceed alone.

One: the energy drain of sending a telescien through that atmosphere was considerable. Sending more than one would be wasteful. Two: if a single, powerful alien being threatening the worlds of the Tomet, it would seem more like divine intervention. It was a shallow trick, but scale had a way of compensating for the lack of authenticity. Three: the High Commander was about to bring the Efilu to the brink of war with this unsuspecting race. No one must be responsible for this act, but Tur himself.

Naturally, he physically remained on the Repam. The data integration fields levitated his body into mid-air. They wove an intricate web of force fields around him, each transmitting and/or receiving different types of signals to or from a complimentary telescien generated out side of the ship. The basic form of the interlocking fields was spherical, but the telescien took on the self-image of the operator, which in this case, was Tur.

This telescien was potent. It had the power content of a small security ship — more than enough to do the job. If the Tomet challenged, or somehow destroyed the telescien, Tur's reappearance in a new telescien field would be psychologically demoralizing to them.

The decision not to be seen descending through the atmosphere, but to simply appear in the center of the Tomet empire was a risky one. The populace might panic and, in the ensuing pandemonium, destroy the ruins of the ancient settlements below. If that happened, the Efilu probably would never find any viable golden algae remnants.

Suddenly materializing, however, might be just the edge Tur needed to bluff his way through as a deity. He had decided to gamble.

The Tomet empire was ruled by a pentad, where one chosen individual spoke for a group of five equals. Tur's gambit paid well. When he materialized, there was no panic, only curiosity. *To look at the alien visitor!* Tur's image was inundated with questions.

They asked the expected "Who are you? Where do you come from? Why are you here?" All the while, they kept a respectable distance, unsure of whether they were dealing with some sort of hologram or a physical being. Tur was able to communicate with them in their own fashion, thanks to the work Jeen had done deciphering the signals that comprised their language. The Tal Genj communications expert lived up to her impeccable reputation.

Each of the common gases in the atmosphere could be forced to vibrate at a unique harmonic frequency specific to that individual gas. The code was complex, but consistent. All expressions followed 19 basic forms, with no exceptions. Tur had no particular flare for languages, but he managed.

He answered their questions patiently, but briefly. Explaining that this was once Efilu space and still technically under his jurisdiction was simple enough. The term jurisdiction obviously was understood, as were its ramifications. The Tomet Pentad didn't like it.

The speaker offered a hypothetical response to an unwelcomed expedition onto the worlds of Tomet. They awaited Tur's response, also hypothetical in nature — or so they hoped.

Tur saw their skepticism and decided on a remedy for it. They doubted whether or not he was real. As he communicated further, he began manipulating things with his hands and tail. He did it casually at first, in the course of conversation. When he answered the speaker's final question, he affected displeasure. With a wave of his hand, he seemingly caused an entire quadrant of the Tomet capital to shake and tremble.

Back on the Repam, Bo Tep realized that the harmonic effect could be scaled upward with seismic consequences. The telescien module was able to transmit the signal quite deftly, and to dramatic effect.

His point made, Tur apologized and explained that the problems facing his world represented a Threat to Life. The scenarios the Tomet had described were inconceivable. The fact that they could entertain such notions were deeply disturbing to him, he said. Any interference with the Efilu search could not be tolerated, and whatever steps necessary to corrected it would be undertaken, without hesitation. He then reiterated, "Whatever steps."

The desired effect had been achieved. The Pentad replaced the first offending speaker. It was not heard from for the duration of the visit. The Tomet made no objections to the neat excavation of one hundred sites.

Efiluan ruins had indeed sunken into the worldscapes of the Tomet Empire, but eons of ionizing radiation had wreaked havoc on the remnants of any recognizable DNA. The fossilized algae they found was useless.

The Repam telescien probes restored the disturbed strata and overhanging skyscape. The ruins were left as they had been found, as if the Efilu had never even been there.

The Tomet, however, would not ever forget this visit. Their history would be profoundly changed by their experience with the Efilu. The beginnings of a burgeoning interstellar civilization essentially had been brought to an end.

The scars of Efilu intimidation would prevent them from exploring any more of the neighboring star systems, for fear of trespassing on the space of Efilu or some other more advanced species. If what Tur had told them was accepted galactic law, the Tomet Empire had just reached its zenith.

The Repam resumed its previous course towards Fitu, oblivious to how dramatically it had changed the destiny of an innocent people.

Chapter 8
MODUS OPERANDI

A shadow crossed Vit Na's face as she slept. It reached the end of her sleeping nook before looming back to the center of the chamber. She did not stir. The silhouette of a hand stretched over her shoulder to darken her throat in the dim light of the room. Her eyes opened slowly at the gentle touch of that hand.

"What!" The thought was poorly formed, disorganized in projection. Her vision, focusing in the subtly waxing light, made out a familiar pair of eyes. "Vit Na?" Gober Dil asked. "I am sorry to disturb you, but you've been asleep for a standard day."

"A whole day? "

"Yes. I was worried and asked Brajay to look you over. The medical report went straight to Car Hom. You showed symptoms that might have represented degradation effects of the substitute nutrition."

"Substitute?"

"The counter agent for 'the Poison.' You know, the substitute they developed to ensure we had Poison-free food source on this voyage."

"Oh. Yes. Now I remember ... I think," Vit Na said, scratching her head.

"Tur heard about your collapse and waited for Brajay and Car Hom to make a decision."

"What do you mean decision?" Vit Na's head was clearing.

"Everyone was afraid that there was a gross foul up. Rumor was beginning to spread that some of the food might have been contaminated with the Poison. Los has been speculating that we may all be at risk if one mer was affected. No one would voice the obvious conclusion at which he hinted," Gober Dil said gently.

Vit Na nodded, and said, "That I would have to be eliminated as a source of contagion."

Gober Dil shook his head gravely. "No. That the mission would have to be terminated, and the ship itself destroyed with all hands aboard."

"Why would we not simply have to return and declared the mission a failure?" she asked, her thought projections becoming more coherent. "After all, 'the Poison' already is disseminated throughout the Realm. We are no more dangerous than anyone else."

Gober Dil smiled. "That scenario was not as exciting as heroic self destruction .... and Los was getting bored."

Vit Na returned his smile. "What other theories were there about my ... condition?"

"No one else advanced any. We just kept working," he answered. Then more seriously, he added, "Everyone else was worried about you."

Vit Na felt a little embarrassed. "I'm sure the High Commander may have been, but it was the Chief of Medicine's responsibility to deal with me. What did Brajay think?"

"His opinion was that you were exhausted and dangerously malnourished," Gober Dil said.

"And Car Hom?" she prompted.

"I think he felt guilty about pushing you so hard and ordered that you not be disturbed after you ate," the assistant paleobotanist said.

"After I ate? I don't remember eating!" Vit Na exclaimed. "For that matter I don't even remember retiring to my quarters."

"I brought you here. You were nearly unconscious. Car Hom reassigned me to your service for the duration of the mission."

Vit Na had been working for nine days since the departure from the Tomet system, without sleep and with precious little food. She vaguely remembered a meal ordered by a concerned Brajay. As the room's ambient light reached dusk intensity, she realized that her new assistant was not tall enough to reach her sleeping pallet on the upper tier of the chamber. She peered over the edge to see that the Wilkyz had grabbed hold of the ledge and pulled himself up to her level.

She also noted Kellis, waiting patiently below in the leisure area of the apartment. She was seated discretely, with her back to the recovering occupant. Gober Dil dropped softly to the floor after the offer to carry his exhausted superior down was declined. When Vit Na reached the lower level, she paused to groom herself for a moment, before addressing her assistant.

"Progress report," she ordered.

"We are now in the Fitu star system, tenth shell. Telescien modules are probing the ninth planet for storage receptacles."

"Any success so far?"

"None. The plan is to complete the reconnaissance per your descriptions of megaplex architecture of that era, in conjunction with the geographic data supplied by Kellis." He indicated that she was waiting, with a subtle gesture of his head.

"You don't seem very confident, Dil. What else?" Vit Na pressed.

"The Geotechnics of early retexturing technology were less stable than anticipated. Most of the artificial tectonic platforms have been swept away, with no chance of recovery. According to Kellis, this represents a basic design flaw, not a quirk. By extrapolation, the same results can be expected on the other two Gas Worlds that were colonized. The theory accounts for the deterioration of the settlement in the Tomet star system as well."

"The data will be of great use in planning and maintaining structural integrity of retextured Gas Worlds in the Realm proper," Kellis said, entering the private conversation while hiding her impatience. "Still, it casts the shadow of doubt over the likelihood of finding any of the city ruins intact. Examining the other giants will be an optimistic exercise in futility. I'd recommend against it if the goal was any less important."

Following the flow of circumstances, Vit Na summarized aloud. "So, Doh gets his dream fulfilled after all." Kellis and Gober Dil exchanged a weary look before affirming what had just become obvious.

"I suppose we had better start on plans to investigate the Fituine stone worlds then," Vit Na declared. "That's why I'm here." Kellis answered. "I'll start mapping sites of the old cities starting with regional capitals if you'll lend me some support staff," she offered.

Vit Na responded without a moment's hesitation. "Of course! Just let me conduct a short meeting on what your people will need. I suggest you appoint a liaison officer, if you haven't already."

Now the Chief of Geotechnics seemed more enthused. "We'll both be there at the appointed time," Kellis said, after which she turned and left Vit Na's apartments.

* * * * *

The general briefing session was off to a slow start. All department heads were present. The setting and format were formal. *So Wari formal, to be precise. This is a bad sign,* Vit Na thought. The meeting was called too urgently after Kellis and Vit Na had submitted their report that morning.

It wasn't that Vit Na couldn't handle Tur's strict style. It was just that the whole thing smacked of yet another edict, another major change of philosophy about the mission. *I'm sure he's going to pull another tooth from us before sending us out hunting again.* The old saying reminded her how much Tur hated predacious metaphors. She made a note to herself not to say it aloud.

Her staff was becoming disheartened. There had been so many disappointments already. Tur swept into the room with Car Hom right beside him, instead of the respectful two head-lengths behind him. *I knew it! Another tirade is brewing,* she thought. Vit Na took a deep breath and settled in with the others. *Let's just wait for the tail to swing.*

"I'm sure, by now, that many of you know that so far Operation Back Track has been a failure. The Gas Worlds are a lost cause. The stone worlds are, of course, our last hope," Tur said, remarkably calm and open, and somehow out of character. Car Hom looked as if his teeth were locked. *What has transpired between them?* Vit Na asked herself.

"As you may remember from your studies, the red fourth planet was never developed into a very fruitful colony. The thin atmosphere, lack of open water and scant energy resources made it a sink hole for any meaningful investment. Its limited use as a recreation center may have left some underground storage facilities intact." Tur was inscrutable now, his thought projections expressed in a deadpan fashion. *Where's he going with this?* Vit Na wondered.

"The second planet of course was wrecked by a poorly thought out fituforming venture." *Why is he dragging us through all of this?* "The first planet is not worth mentioning. Naturally, the best opportunity for recovering viable algae DNA is on the third planet...the planet of origin: Fitu.

"Now, I know that there is a certain amount of romanticism, even fanaticism, about the fate of Fitu in general and of the Keepers in particular. The purpose of this briefing is to set some basic rules. Number one: Car Hom and I will personally supervise this mission.

"Number two: There will be no digression into nature loving exploration. We are here to do a job. Nothing else.

"Number three: as we have seen in the Exodus Corridor, alien inhabitants may have visited or taken up residence on this husk of a world. There is a need for caution in any and all questionable encounters. Car Hom will outline the rules of engagement.

"Number four: There are bound to be some extraordinary findings. That fact is inescapable. Vit Na, Ikara, Obb, Doh, Jeen, and Egin will form a committee to customize a telescien module for recording incidental findings, as they present themselves.

"I want results by day's end. I know most of you are tired and I'm sorry. Finally: We are now over one month into the substitute food source. As Oot Su, the Head of Nutrition and Waste Management, will explain, there are certain toxic side effects that will become increasingly apparent." Tur looked briefly at Vit Na as he spoke. "It will be the responsibility of each of the surface scouts to monitor signs of toxicity in his or her comrades."

"Reports are to go jointly to Brajay, Oot Su and Car Hom. Car Hom will be responsible for actions to be taken in the event of impaired competency." *That's it!* Vit Na decided. That was the reason for the tension between the two. She thought about the conversation with Gober Dil. What would Tur do if effects of 'The Poison' were to manifest themselves? *Tur has charged Car Hom with the disposal of liable staff members, and he doesn't like it one bit! Poor meg. Car Hom the executioner!*

"Please turn your attention to Los' image of the Fitu binary system," Tur instructed. An image appeared before them displaying modern day Fitu and the white worldlet revolving around it.

"The geography looks nearly alien, but at the same time ... familiar," Tyot Da said aloud. The entire staff invoked genetic memories gleaned from their own families respective Tarns of Animems. This was Fitu, but continental drift had changed its surface since the Exodus. "Different from historical maps, but almost as we modeled it!" Kellis whispered to Vit Na triumphantly.

Slowly, as all eyes fixed on the shining blue world before them, officious masks of detachment melted away. Weepf raised a question that was several moments late in the asking. "Wait now. Did I hear you correctly Tur? Are we physically going down there?"

Car Hom spoke without waiting for Tur to respond. "We are going down in person because we need to. Telesciens are just not discriminating enough to separate the current life form remains from the fossil remains that we need. We have already tried using them on the outer worlds. Preliminary scans of Fitu show very subtle changes in microorganisms, since the Exodus. This project is going to require delicate, hands-on work."

"Current life forms?" Doh said, almost ecstatic.

"That's right. Preliminary studies show the planet is teaming with life," Car Hom answered.

Doh asked boldly, "Botanical or animal?" Car Hom ignored the question. "There are masses of organic activity stretching over large areas on the surface. They are intertwined in some areas, but most display indisputable signatures of advanced animal life. The oxygen content is consistent with a huge burden of plant life as well."

"What, exactly do you mean by 'advanced animal life'?" Doh prodded further. Tur intercepted his foray into zoology. "It doesn't matter what form of animal life is there as we will ALL be avoiding them." He then added, "Unless they get in our way."

Doh began another interrogative, only to be nipped by Tur's restriction. "If we do accidentally encounter any indigenous animal life, they will be dealt with in the most expedient manner possible." Tur then leaned over to speak directly to Doh. "You carry out your research on your own time, not mine!" Satisfied that he had been understood, he nodded to Car Hom to resume the briefing.

"The bulk of activity seems to take place during daylight hours. This leads us to believe that the dominant species is diurnal in nature. We'll send telesciens down at night so as to cause minimal disturbance."

Car Hom quickly looked to Tur for approval of the order. Vit Na read him well. *It's easier to be forgiven after the fact than to get permission for an unauthorized order.* Tur simply looked away.

Car Hom continued, unperturbed. "We will be within optimum range for telemetry survey before day's end. The probe module will be a Level One, launched on the dark side of Fitu. The search pattern will be modified by Kellis and Ikara, to optimize the yield. We'll know more when the probe data becomes available." He again turned to Tur, more deliberately this time. A nod from the High Commander signaled the end of the session. Car Hom announced, "Dismissed."

Vit Na had returned to her apartments to prepare for the surface mission. Her eyes were wide, her down erect, her tail writhing restlessly. The sound of the portal barrier signaling the arrival of a visitor gave her a start. She opened the door without thinking, only to see Tur enter furtively.

"The telesciens are back from the planet surfaces. They found nothing unexpected on the smaller stone worlds. Fitu, however, is going to be complicated," he said. The hustle and bustle had evidently infected even the High Commander. Vit Na looked up at him quizzically.

"It doesn't yet pose a threat. Just a lot of questions that beg answers." Tur's brow was furrowed deeply. "When it was just Doh asking them, I could ignore it — but now Los is becoming intrigued by a bunch of derelict mechanical satellites orbiting Fitu!"

Vit Na began to voice a response, but was cut off. "Car Hom is becoming paranoid about disturbing the masses of vermin that have infested the surface. Jeen is fascinated by the electronic echoes reverberating off those defunct contraptions floating in the sky. ...Now I hear that you want to investigate these floating artifacts for dating purposes?"

By now, Vit Na had ascended to the upper tier to reach eye level with Tur. She was hopping from the top of one wall ledge to the next, in cadence with his pacing.

"I cannot allow this team to get side tracked, but I also can't be everywhere at once. The expedition may have to be broken up into anywhere from five to seven teams," Tur vented. He came to a momentary standstill. "This world just presents too many distractions. I can't see how I can keep everyone in focus."

He unconsciously resumed his pacing. "This mission has already gone on too long! The entire crew could succumb to degenerate nucleotide toxicity. Here! Countless photodymes from home!"

"And that would be bad," Vit Na chimed in.

He turned to expound on her naïve reaction to his dilemma, only to find that she was no longer attending him. He whipped his head back and forth scanning the dim chamber. He found her sitting on the ledge of her sleeping nook, her feet dangling carelessly. "Are you listening to me, Vit Na?" Tur demanded.

"That's all I've been doing," she said with a humorous, yet chastising grin. "Obviously, if you wanted to talk to yourself, you could have done so in your own quarters. I assume you want some friendly and unofficial advice?" she asked rhetorically.

"You have a very disciplined and professional staff," Vit Na observed. "One that knows the importance of this mission as well as you do. Give them the freedom to use their own good judgment and stop insulting their intelligence."

This was the second time this mission that he had been told to ease up on his subordinates. He smiled, and said, "You said stop insulting 'their intelligence.' Why didn't you say 'our' intelligence?"

"Tur, you're not capable of insulting my intelligence," she said coyly. He playfully brushed her down from the ledge. Vit Na landed softly on her feet. "Tur, does Bo Tep seem oddly familiar to you?" she asked.

His brow furrowed deeper. "All Tralkyz seem familiar to me," he said deliberately. "Collective memories, I'm sure. Even superhunters fell pray to other superhunters in the dim times."

After a brief pause, he announced, quasi-officially: "Be ready to transport down shortly. You're with me." He left her quarters without a backward glance.

* * * * *

The surface team assembled before the crystal-gel launch spout, fifty strong. Tyot Da was giving last minute instructions. There was no hint of disappointment in his manner. The old meg addressed them formally. "My advanced years limit my usefulness on this trip. However, I have designed efficient, comfortable crystal gel-core headquarters for surface."

He noted Car Hom's skepticism, and added, "The size is deceiving. As you may have noted, telescien data has ascertained that the land has ample mineral content to supplement the substance of outer shell and inner support structures."

He looked around for questioning faces. He saw none. "May your search be fruitful," he intoned, and yielded to Tur.

"Everything that needs to be said has been said," Tur said tersely. He gestured for the encapsulation process to begin.

The gel oozed up from the floor of the compartment to envelop them all. Each team member effortlessly resisted the urge to hold his or her breath. The giant teardrop squeezed into a silvery thread, as it accelerated to prophoton speed through the tiny port in the vessel's hull. The thread arced across the night sky. It stretched for miles before disconnecting from the Repam. The Strand floated softly, slowly, inexorably, down through the thin atmosphere.

The Efilu visitors rained unnoticed as a single glistening drop onto the cold Egyptian desert. The near endless gel-stream pooled on the Egyptian/Sudanese border, making a shiny dome on the otherwise flat desert floor.

The first priority was to set up their headquarters as quickly as possible. The searchers toiled through the night, as the morphing gel construct absorbed the desert sands, fortifying an outer perimeter and expanding the walls of newly formed compartments.

Task team members activated producer sub-functions to raise necessary crystal and plasticine devices from the main gel core. These facilities were needed for the coordination of the expedition. Most importantly, the data systems and storage plants for managing reports and specimens, respectively, took shape.

The rising sun sleepily licked the sandy mound before grasping it with fiery midday teeth. Light from this star had not touched Efiluan flesh in millions of years. Few of Tur's meren were enthused by the primordial visitor. After an exhausting night's work, most slept through the brilliant welcome home.

The gel-base was more comfortable than Tyot Da had promised. Tur didn't notice, for he did not sleep. He stood atop the storage tower. The continual energy flow into the tower caused gentle vibrations throughout the whole structure. He surveyed first the little hamlet that would be home to his band of weary travelers for the immediate future. He was thinking, already, of how good it will be to get off of this rock.

Still, he decided that he was actually satisfied with his temporary headquarters. All chiefs had reported reaching optimal capacity, before retiring for the day. They weren't all So Wari, but perhaps they would do after all.

Tur turned his attention to the open desert. Heat waves were beginning to distort the horizon. He snapped to a combat stance as he peered into the distance. He had seen the apparition of a huge gel-wave crossing the desert directly toward them, at full speed, and with no warning. *Ambush! Some one has beaten us here!* he concluded hastily.

He had nearly completed the alarm activation gesture when the wave vanished without a trace. He recovered composure angrily, embarrassed at his reaction.

It was a good that no one had been there to see him panicked by a simple mirage.

Chapter 9
NICHES

The conference room would be full shortly and Tur had not rested all day. He had growing misgivings about this mission that he could not bring himself to discuss with anyone — not even Vit Na. He sensed an urgency that seemed to supersede even the obvious need to replenish the golden algae supply. He had been ruminating all day over the cause of his panic that morning, but found none. The thought that he himself had been the first to fall prey to the neuro-synaptic degeneration was repugnant.

Car Hom, as expected, was the first to arrive for the meeting. He took his place, silently, at Tur's right. The others filed in slowly, refreshed after their day-long repose. The oddly shaped auditorium accommodated each in individualized comfort. As the staff entered, Tur took note of how many department heads were included in the team. He counted nine. Doh was among them. His presence was another source of tension, but so far his discipline was exemplary.

Vit Na seemed to be doing alright, but still he worried about her. This was a hostile world. What if enemies of the Realm had made their way to Fitu? Meeting the Quatal would be bad enough, but an encounter with Efiluan traitors could be disastrous. He wanted her protected, but knew he could not conspicuously assign extra security meren to her.

The next best thing to assigning a So Wari guard, since there were only four or five others on the surface, was a Wilkyz. Not as big as an Alkyz or even a Tralkyz, the superhunter Wilkyz was more than a match for any animal that walked this planet! Gober Dil wasn't a security meg, but he was at Vit Na's disposal night and day ... and he had taken a liking to his new superior.

Gober Dil was a young but able specialist. Tur had checked his file. Dil was skilled in 'time-splitting,' a peculiar talent the Wilkyz had for briefly extrapolating themselves along different timelines at will. Depending on one's level of concentration, a Wilkyz could materialize as five to ten individuals of equal strength and intelligence for a few moments. It made for brilliant creative genius; but right now, Tur was thankful for the original purpose of the technique: defense.

He thought of the Repam in orbit above them. It was still within communications distance in case of the unforeseen, but there was no reason for unnecessary contact. Ga Win had been left in command. He was an able officer with typical Wilkyz discipline and patience. That unique Wilkyz 'time-splitting' ability made for excellent emergency response times as well. Tur thought about diversity for a moment. Car Hom had made a good selection in choosing that one as a sub-commander.

Los was a wild dart. Something about him and his preoccupation with those satellites made Tur uncomfortable. Los technically outranked everyone left on the ship, save Ga Win. Nothing could change that as long as he was Head of Astrophysics — and there was no justification for bringing him down to the surface. His forte clearly was keeping that ship running. The remaining support staff included assistant commanders Stihl and Dirm, both of whom were competent So Wari tacticians. Between the three officers, Los would be kept out of trouble, Tur decided.

Perhaps Car Hom and Vit Na were right, he speculated. He did worry too much. Still, switching Doh for Los would surely keep them both out of trouble.

After they had all assembled in the conference room, the ground team promptly began rounds of the facility. Tur and Car Hom were to see firsthand what resources were available for carrying out the mission.

The assortment of scanners would accomplish the first phase of analysis, of course. It would be possible to assemble telescien probes, but extremely impractical with the resources available.

Mini-waves were charged and ready for travel. They were more powerful than telesciens, but not quite as versatile. Composed of volumes of gelsol large enough to accommodate ten to twenty meren, the mini-wave could project force fields, deploy offensive weapons, and metamorphose into a limited variety of shapes, including the fluid state from which the name was derived.

The pest control devices were fabricated, but no real weapons had been synthesized for the time being. They were deemed unnecessary. The outer perimeter of the main structure was all but impregnable.

Nutrition, waste management, data storage and integration all were in order. The laboratories were operating at full capacity. Tur inspected these with extreme care and asked many questions of Doh and his staff. Doh certainly would be kept busy with his responsibilities for all paleobiology and active biology work. Ikara didn't at all resent being his subordinate for this part of the mission.

As he watched his people work, Tur reminded himself of the advice he had received aboard the Repam. The few department heads in the group did not always act as project managers here. Surrogate chiefs displaying the most capability naturally fell into leadership positions, without resentment from those with higher ranks. The limitations of echelons had their place in society, but here, it was do or die. Each in his or her own way knew this.

Efficiency — not formality — dominated here. Tur was learning the power of flexibility when strength is not enough.

A warm orange sun set in the West, as Sub-Specialist Kira Kesh presided over the first scan. The Denar mer was small for her kind, at barely half-a-head-length taller than the Ironde Weapons Master Devit. Her analysis accompanied the findings.

"This is a high density photomagnetic sweep of the grounds directly underneath us. As you can see, here and here, there are scattered remains of an Irfonde ..." she explained, pointing out various places in holographic display of the strata composition. Brown plumes swept back and forth along her crest, as she turned.

"Or, as we now say, 'Ironde' village. Obviously it was in shambles at the time of its burial," she said with typical Denar detachment. "Undigested bodies found everywhere suggest that there was no one left to perform last rites. The scattered plumes are more numerous than can be accounted for by the number of bodies found, further indicating a horrible battle."

"Which they lost," Devit added, masking his feelings for his fallen ancestors by affecting equal detachment.

"So it would seem," Kira Kesh commented. "Removal and subsequent enslavement of survivors would support the fossil record here."

"Is it worth excavating?" Devit asked, his ulterior motive obvious. Kira Kesh paused, but after looking for an excuse to comply, found none. "I don't think so. The storage buildings have been thoroughly demolished, and probably were raided beforehand." Devit said no more.

Kira Kesh swiftly moved along. "For our purposes, the remaining thousand mile radius is basically as barren as the desert above it. Scanning resolution at the microscopic level breaks down at about three hundred miles below the surface." It was a vexing limitation to her equipment. "Low resolution scan of the entire planetary surface did turn up one other peculiarity. Large circular burns appear across all of the land masses, as if from orbital bombardment. The odd thing is that they are only about thirty or forty million years old."

"Is there any relevance for our purposes?" The High Commander asked. "No sir," came the brief response.

"Well then." Tur began folding his arms across his great chest as he spoke. "We obviously can't scan the entire planet for these microbes. "

"Nothing's easy on this mission. What else is new?" Car Hom interjected. His manner seemed a bit short, Vit Na noted. Sensing the focus of attention shifting to her, she began speaking before her cue.

"We have identified the seven major mega-cities most likely to contain the material we seek." She triggered a two-dimensional representation of Fitu, which projected above them. She nodded to Gober Dil, who smoothly continued the presentation without missing a beat.

"There is a potential complication." The map shifted to a horizontal topographical display, as contours gave life to the face of the modern world. "Several of the these sites are now occupied by large populations of animals. Furthermore, there is evidence of towering mounds of metal-fortified stone villages, that are growing by the day."

Tur interrupted. "So, what's your point?"

"I would think that finding a way to work around them with minimal disturbance would be the most desirable option, sir. We could go for the minimally populated land site, as well as the marine site."

"Wrong!" Car Hom shouted. "We will not waste time limiting ourselves to two sites this late in the game." He paused to let Tur give the actual order.

The High Commander complied. "We split up, with five sub-parties of ten meren each. Assignments are forthcoming." He nodded to Car Hom to see to the details. Fatigue was beginning to tell on Tur, at least internally. He rose from his haunches to leave, hesitated, then turned to Doh.

Realizing he was about to unearth a nest of fur mites, he nearly turned to Ikara; but this was unquestionably Doh's department. He turned wearily to Doh and asked, "Just what do these new animals look like? I mean the main ones: 'they who construct?'"

"Oh, I can show you," Doh answered. He could not hide his delight at the opportunity.

"I mounted a magnetic scanner on a mini-wave fragment and sent it off that way," he explained, pointing south. "I haven't seen the recording myself yet."

The entire group gathered around, eager to see the successors of their forsaken home. Tur found himself no less intrigued than the others.

"The modified 'probe' was programmed to stop and record encounters with animal life of fifty pounds or more." Tur's weariness melted away as he stepped closer to the audio-enhanced holographic recording.

"I'm sorry there will be no tactile substance to the images. I didn't see the reason for the added detail, under the circumstances." Tur found himself embarrassed by the frustration of not being able to touch these marvelous sights. Doh had followed orders to the letter, *damn him!*

The small audience was astonished by not only the size of the beasts, but their shapes. "Doh, they look like animals with which our people coexisted a hundred and fifty million years ago!" Car Hom observed. "How do you explain this?"

Doh's chest pumped up proudly and he wished that Obb could be there to see this. He looked to Gober Dil, who was subordinate to him here on the planet, as the next best victim. "Dil, explain please."

Gober Dil, dumbfounded, could only shrug. Doh paused long enough for any speculation to surface. None did.

"This is a classic example of analogy. For instance, an insect's wings serve the same function as do a bird's wings. They are derived from completely different organs, but yet serve the same function.

"When we left the Jing and other animals behind during the Exodus, there were innumerable vacant niches to be filled. The eternal search for food presents problems that only can be solved in a finite number of ways."

The recording focused on giraffes feeding on acacia leaves. A rhinoceros raised its head to scan the savanna. "That looks just like a small bolok, but without the frill and forehead horns!" Bo Tep observed. Water buffalo and zebra were in the background, grazing. "The striped animals look a little like small streamlined versions of my own remote ancestors ... but minus back plates and tail spikes," Tur added. "Why don't they have tails?"

Doh answered quickly. "They do! The tails are small and vestigial, but they are there." He magnified several images and pointed out the appendages to the High Commander.

The scene shifted to hyenas being chased away from a freshly killed gnu by a pride of lions. "The more things change, the more they stay the same," Gren, the Roog botanist, commented from his water-filled corpuscle. Doh allowed the recording to go on to a wild dog pack bringing down an impala and a cheetah running down a thompson's gazelle, before terminating the show.

"Well, you get the gist of it." He knew they all wanted to see more, but wouldn't dare ask.

"What about the builders?" Tur asked a second time, with a little less patience.

"Oh them. I'm sure they're on here somewhere." Doh advanced the recording to a blur, and stopped it on the image of biped mammals living communally in a primitive village. The villagers were malnourished, but clearly resembled Efilu meren in their vertical proportions and basic facial features.

"They look like mutant variations of us!" a voice in the darkness said. Tur didn't even bother to identify Kellis as the author of that most revolting analogy.

The display showed a few emaciated livestock animals in a communal corral. Several huts made of sun-dried mud and grass were defended by the two-legged mammals. Largely hairless, their coats were limited to the crowns of their heads. They carried crude spears, and dressed in scraps of woven cloth.

"They do show basic signs of culture," Vit Na said, in an off-handed manner.

Tur cut his eyes at the sight. "Please!" he said in disgust. He rose and exited without another thought.

Chapter 10
FLIGHT SCHOOL

Tur awakened to the reverberation of his portal barrier. He rose slowly to his feet, winced briefly at the sunlight streaming through the window then gestured the 'open' command for the barrier. The door receded to reveal Weepf.

"You've rested for half a day," she said. The unsaid message was *and you've rested enough for my purposes.*

"You really must learn to be more direct, Weepf. It saves time," Tur said.

Ignoring his sarcasm, Weepf proceeded. "I've been thinking that we need more information about these sites. Those animals we saw last night certainly didn't build the towering structures we saw, but someone did. I think what we saw can be attributed to sampling error."

"What do you suggest?"

She almost began before he asked the question. "We need personal reconnaissance. Not probes. Not scans. Not telesciens. Someone has to go out there. Car Hom said it and you agreed: Technology is not sensitive enough to tell us what we need to know."

Tur found himself nodding thoughtfully. "Have you selected a party yet?"

"No, for this one I think a single mer will do."

"Anyone in this chamber?" Tur asked humorlessly.

"I am probably the ablest aviator in the group and my size will certainly intimidate anything in the skies of this world."

"Not to mention that you need to flap your wings a bit," Tur said pointedly.

"We don't have the extra personnel to spare on a mission like this. A single strange creature will be somewhat less threatening to Fituine life than a squad, and more likely to be forgotten or incorporated into vague legend, if these creatures have such concepts. Besides, there is no immediate need for security here. If there is a potential threat, which I doubt, it will be in those mound complexes. As Head of Security, I need to assess them firsthand. I can make efficient, on the spot decisions that can't be delegated to any subordinate I have here on the surface."

A good argument. She had probably spent much of the night preparing it. No doubt she had consulted with Ikara for the behavioral references to myths and legends. Tur had a good mind to call Ikara in and grill her for alternative scenarios to the one Weepf now presented. He might enjoy her discomfiture, but that would be useless.

Weepf was right. They did need good reconnaissance data and Weepf's flying proficiency was beyond question. Tur gave his permission and dismissed her.

* * * * *

Weepf had called Ju Kol onto a terrace overlooking the desert for a briefing session. The Alkyz security meg was the second highest ranking security officer in the unit. "I'm going to examine the animal herd over the nearest mega-city ruins." She indicated an easterly flight path. The sun was still rising in the sky. "I'll be back by mid to late afternoon. Prepare nothing special as far as security measures ... except ...

"On that recording last evening, didn't I see some large bird picking over carrion?"

"Yes. I believe so," Ju Kol answered.

"I'm probably developing some of Tur's suspicious nature, but I don't want any wild life wandering in uninvited, especially not if they come in flocks. I want the shield barriers for this base on stand by while I'm gone. I'll stay in communications with you by gel com link. You and I will review the data I collect this evening. That's all," she said, dismissing him.

Weepf fastened the gel apparatus to her torso. She arranged the transducers to maintain 360 degree recording during flight. She had eaten heartily that morning and felt eager to stretch her wings now. Discipline had allowed her to function in cramped close quarters for the weeks the Repam had been in transit, but upon seeing that deep familiar blue sky accented by fluffy white clouds she could stand being grounded no more.

She took wing and circled the base once, then took off eastward with steady, strong strokes. She waited until the base disappeared over the horizon before engaging in some aerial acrobatics. How had she tolerated so long a grounding, she wondered.

Accelerating along her prescribed flight path, Weepf felt the wind rushing by her. She felt the sound waves building up to maximal compression in front of her. The urge to press through it became overwhelming.

She waited until she was over a herd of hump-backed quadrupeds watering at an oasis before making her move, with anticipated results. The camels scattered, but there were those peculiar bipeds again. Apparently nearby, but unseen until the commotion started, the bipeds were frantically recapturing the other animals. *Interesting, but not worth recording,* she decided. She flew onward.

She enjoyed the cool sea air over the inlet separating the main continent from the eastern peninsula. The arid heat returned once she soared over land again. Weepf had maintained supersonic velocity for most of the morning, and was beginning to fatigue. She dropped to gliding speed and took advantage of the thermal updrafts to hold her aloft.

A glint of sunlight off in the desert caught her eye. The structure was too high to be a body of water. Ice? Perhaps, but an ice cap could not sustain solid form in this heat for more than a few weeks at best. Those peaks are so very high and narrow ... almost ...

Her wings beat now with a newfound fervor. She swooped down to collect for the recorder what her own eyes had seen from the greater altitude. It was a city! A full fledged city! More than that, it was occupied. This was more than a finding of interest, this was cause for alarm.

Who could have built this odd habitat? The style is not Si Tyen by any means, she speculated. *And it's brand new. Fifty years old maximum.* She broadcast an alert to headquarters, then zoomed into the towering spires without waiting for acknowledgment.

The avenues were narrow so she kept to the widest of them stopping to record gatherings of large numbers of bipeds and quadrupeds here and there. Mostly, she was intrigued by the network of electrical cable and the abundance of ozone in the air. Mechanical conveyances of assorted sizes and functions were traveling the broader trails. The air was heavy with oxidized hydrocarbons. A large stone building caught her eye, not for what she saw of its exterior, but for its content. She scanned it at length for review by Doh and Vit Na.

There seemed to be some kind of klaxon sounding throughout the city. The animals were scurrying for shelter. She scanned the horizon to the east, north and south. Nothing of particular interest there, just a small collection of broad, mid-sized vehicles with smooth cone shaped fronts resting on a field. The flat projections on either side suggested aerodynamic design, but why the three wheels? A few low buildings, bounded by a flimsy metal mesh, lay near the crafts as if serving as a storage facility for them.

She had collected enough. She beat her wings to regain altitude, then began to retrace her original route at subsonic speed.

Weepf had already begun to speculate on the origin of that city when she felt the transducers to the gel-com moving on her back. The Vansar Mer focused the view lenses on two of the three-wheeled metal vehicles approaching at supersonic speed. *Hello! What have we here?* she thought to herself. She maintained her present speed to allow them to get close enough for her to get a clear image recorded. She steadied, with recorders on multi-modalities, when the first projectile seared across her back.

One of the transducer cores was damaged. The whole apparatus nearly fell off her torso. It took several moments before she had even realized what had occurred. She regained her composure quickly, decided that she had better take the shortest route back to base. Weepf signaled her situation ahead to the Efilu headquarters. More missiles exploded around her, with deafening sound!

This is no game, she thought to herself. Weepf pumped up to supersonic velocity again, but found her pursuers matching her speed. Fear started to well up in her chest as she realized she was completely unarmed. She couldn't outrun these killing machines, but perhaps she could outfly them.

This arena is too much to their tactical advantage, she surmised. *I have to take them out by hand and talon. They have good speed, but they look somehow clumsy in the air.*

In a desperate move, she broke, 'pinning' on her wings, and made an immediate turnabout. The two jet-powered machines zipped right past her and kept going. They sped four miles before making the necessary bank to rejoin the chase. She performed three more deft aerial maneuvers, evading her pursuers without the slightest effort. Weepf almost laughed out loud before the site of another missile launched in her direction brought her humor to an end.

Those projectiles were not to be taken lightly. Her maneuverability could compensate for the hunter jet's excessive speed, but not for the missiles. She needed an equalizer and fast. She knew a mini-wave probably was on its way already with reinforcements, but she had to survive long enough to be rescued.

Her axillary plumes were singed evading that last missile. *Their aim is improving!* Weepf spied a mountain range off in the distance. It took her away from her home course, but it was her best chance. She moved toward the mountains.

She had been analyzing their flight technique for several hundred of her own rapid heart beats by now, and had come to certain conclusions. *They fly at speeds faster than those for which their guidance systems can compensate. I wonder how they'd handle a more restrictive flight path.*

The projectiles they launched were of two types. The small ones were most numerous and came in flurries. Following simple, parabolic trajectories, they resulted in nicks and lost plumage. The others were being deployed more sparingly, but with devastating results.

The concussion alone from the last projectile had bruised bone and sinew even without making direct contact. The noise from the attacks affected her equilibrium until she dampened her tympanic network. Only then did the gruesome din became tolerable.

Weepf had reached the mountain maze of cliffs. As she entered the chasm, her back showered by debris from a missile that impacted on the rock face behind her. *That's a good sign!* she thought. *They don't want me to go in there.*

She flew into the chasm for another mile or so at subsonic speed, all the while looking upward. As expected, the hunters prowled the skies above with no change in velocity. She noticed another tactical peculiarity: the jet flyers were maintaining a near constant distance and orientation with respect to one another. Perhaps they were automated and had limited programming. Or perhaps they were mentor and pupil on a hunting exercise. Both theories had merit, but somehow the thought of them having off spring so nearly identical in shape, size and coloration was unlikely. "Mechanical construct" was the best hypothesis at this point.

They disappeared again, only to be followed by a loud crash and a quake that shook loose rubble from the valley walls. *Trying to panic me into reckless flight,* she mused. She waited to test a new hunch.

Weepf picked a recess between two peaks and steadied her heartbeat forcibly. The pair skulked by at exactly matching velocities and that same fixed spacing. *A definite weakness!* They would have to bank to reconnoiter. She climbed by hand and claw to the underside of a precipice and waited. She quieted her thoughts again and listened to her own heartbeat. The blood pounded across her inner ears, then slowly, deliberately, the rumble of the jet machines returned.

She let the first pass unmolested. The second was her intended target! Her body launched from the crevice with ballistic might, hooking talons deep into steel wings. Clutched so tight to the mass of metal was she, that her legs went numb with the jerk. The torque threw the combatants apart like a sling suddenly released.

The Vansar recovered her altitude. The jet did not. The spin extinguished the combustion engines and the craft exploded against the chasm wall. The flash was unexpected, but nothing could have added to the stunning effect of that maneuver. Weepf was dazed.

Instinctively, she sniffed for the odor of death. Nothing. An imitation of life. She felt hollow in the absence of the blood rush which was so well earned. Weepf tried to hoist a rock into the air. It was a desperate challenge to the remaining fighter, but she found that her lower limbs were momentarily paralyzed.

The fighter came back to her, as she knew it must. Panic surged again in her throat as the terrible image of her vengeful foe grew against the blue sky. She imagined maternal rage, which could lead to the recklessness of one who had nothing to lose. The realization followed that this too, could be to Weepf's own advantage.

Weepf became emboldened, rising through the air in the glory of the afternoon sun. The light shone off of her tightly folded pile like a row of brilliant purple and golden flames. It was a blatant challenge to the lone marauder, signaling that she was eager for battle.

They have shown no hunting skills so far. Perhaps this one will be stupid enough to become careless, she surmised. The jet banked upward and over Weepf, preparing a rudimentary power dive. Slowly, it rose toward the sun, decelerating as its path approached vertical. Weepf found herself almost pitying the poor machine. ...Almost!

She darted up at its blind belly, as it naïvely strove to hide in the glare of the sun. The gun ports and missile bays were marked by her on approach. All were pointed skyward! Her talon strength now recovered, she began to slash structures that most obviously maintained the vital integrity of the aircraft.

The pull against gravity would soon bring the pair to a complete midair stop at the zenith. Weepf moved swiftly, disemboweling the craft with ease, first disabling its engines, then its weapons systems.

To gain leverage, Weepf had to climb over the edge of the left wing. With both hands grasping the lip of metal, she found her mid-section abutting the last explosive projectile the now flaming fighter carried. Later she would indulge a shudder, realizing how close to her ancestors she had come at this moment.

Weepf extended a talon to pry the lone remaining missile from the jet. It would detonate at a safe distance upon striking the desert floor beneath them.

As she worked her way around to topside she peered into the cockpit with amazement. She took it in all at once, in a matter of milliseconds. With her focus on the biped pilot, the electronic mechanisms were only subconsciously observed. She retracted her wing plumes to get her fingers under the edge of the shattered canopy.

Before the tug followed through, the clear canopy covering exploded upward. Weepf barely got her head out of the way in time to avoid the fragment. She looked down into the cockpit to see a tiny device in the animals hand. The last thing she thought of before the searing pain blinded her was how familiar the little instrument looked. Her right hand clutched an oozing eye in agony as her head and neck reeled backward.

Gravity was beginning to exert its grip in earnest. The masked pilot dropped its weapon in panic. Weepf recovered quickly, removing her hand from her right eye in order to grasp the occupant of the crippled jet.

The small form, now free of the restraints, was slippery with the exuded content of Weepf's eye. It was still alive, but subdued now. The little animal was not accustomed to dealing with so much activity in so short a space of time.

Weepf transferred it from her hand to her taloned feet and took flight. Guided by the blurry image of a receding sun, she glided homeward in near exhaustion. The ruined machine completed a nose dive into an unyielding sea of sand.

Chapter 11
BABBLE

"How are you feeling?"

"Nauseated! Otherwise no specific discomfort," was the response. Brajay had arrived from the Repam early that evening. He was regarding Weepf intently. She was trying to maintain some detachment from the events of the afternoon.

"Any disequilibrium? Any impairment in judgment? Any confusion?" he queried.

"No. No. And NO! I'm telling you, I was attacked by these killer flying machines. I barely escaped with my life. I can show you the exact site—"

"I don't dispute your account, Weepf," Brajay reassured her. "In fact, your injuries and the amount of shrapnel you've acquired cannot be explained in any other way."

He already had reviewed Weepf's log, primarily for an assessment of her injuries. The record was incomplete, the result of equipment damage from the battle. He began to deactivate his own probe device when Weepf stared down at his diminutive form and said with obvious irritation, "Well? What about this nausea?"

"Oh, that," he answered. "It's a manifestation of acutely decreased intraocular pressure. Are you experiencing double vision or is it just blurred in one eye?"

She closed her right eye for a moment before responding. The image of Brajay was as sharp as ever. "Just blurry on the right," she reported.

Brajay manipulated the probe to scan her right orbit. "You were a little slow in closing that one during the attack, huh?"

"No, I wasn't. The little slug threw something in my eye!" Weepf complained.

He probed at the next level of resolution. "Hmmm. This is inconsistent with the other pieces of shrapnel. It is constructed to be roughly aerodynamic. Still, that little creature could never have thrown it hard enough to penetrate your cornea. Are you sure it didn't use some sort of launching device?"

Weepf tried to isolate the image in her memory. "I can't be sure, but I think you're right."

"I'll remove it and restore the orb's integrity," Brajay said, raising a thin hand to silence the protest welling up in her throat. He then induced a force field tuned for deep, fine work and raised the power nearly to maximum. Weepf became nervous as the procedure commenced.

Where there had been silence before, a familiar chuckle now came from the shadows. Weepf struggled to ignore it. By the time she returned her attention to the procedure at hand, Brajay was done.

"I've placed a pseudo-cellular patch in the puncture wound. It will become permanent as it duplicates the genetic material from the surrounding natural cells, then proliferate normally after that. How are the optics?" he asked.

Weepf looked around the dark chamber. "Normal saccidic movement, a hint of a distortion at close range, but that's all." Although she dwarfed the concerned medical officer, she regarded him now with newfound respect. Back home, there was little use for medical intervention. The weak and injured either survived and recovered, or died.

"I still don't understand why there's no Blood Rush. Your endorphin levels are extraordinarily high," Brajay observed. His long, delicate fingers flickering through highlights of the battle record. "You were victorious against overwhelming odds, yet you're not the least bit intoxicated."

"Its a predaceous quirk, I suppose, but the Blood never rises fully when the conflict involves an inanimate opponent," she replied. Without thinking, she made a personal commentary. "It's very frustrating to work that hard and not get off."

Then suddenly embarrassed, she added, "If you know what I mean." She had remembered that they were not alone.

Bo Tep was beside Tur in the shadows of the room. They had listened quietly until this point. Waiting.

"Sounds like they pretty much dusted you off," said Bo Tep. The jeering comment was classically Tralkyz. "I thought you Vansar were supposed to be so good in the air." He laughed as he taunted her.

Tur placed a hand gently on Bo Tep's arm, ending the derision for the moment. The illumination in the room returned to normal revealing, the intensity of Tur's gaze.

"Where is Car Hom?" Weepf asked, realizing that her debriefing had been postponed pending medical clearance by Brajay.

"Car Hom is elsewhere," Tur replied, with typical So Wari economy of thought. His scrutiny was more intrusive than the metal fragments she still carried in her flesh.

The recordings of Weepf's sortie came to life around them. Tur leaned back on his tail, crossed his legs and commanded, "Fill in the blanks."

Weepf summarily recounted the missing segments and placed the recorded images into proper context. Both Tur and Bo Tep listened with stony expressions and without interruption. Brajay had remained, ostensibly to complete of her neuro-psychiatric evaluation. Weepf was as cool and efficient, as always.

"My impressions: The two machines communicated, I think, by some form of low frequency EM wave. Some of their navigation was automated I'm certain, but much of it was intelligent," she said.

"There was some form of electronic artificial intelligence at work, no doubt. It sounds like the machine was full of those devices," Tur speculated, while gazing into thin air. "The animal was probably a safeguard, in case of insect infestation," he added thoughtfully.

Weepf was surprised at his misinterpretation. "Oh, no. That little creature was piloting the machine," she insisted. Tur, Bo Tep and Brajay all snapped to peak attention in unison. Tur looked to Brajay. He shook his head. *No brain damage*. Weepf, recognizing the question on her interviewers' faces, clarified.

"The machines moved as I moved, adapting to my evasive maneuvers. They learned too much, too quickly to be managed by the machines I saw in the control center."

Tur initiated the intercommunication link. "What is the status of the creature, Doh?" he asked.

"It's really fascinating," Doh replied, sounding exuberant. "Did Weepf mention to you that this thing is wearing some form of woven garment?" Doh was off on a scientific tangent again.

Tur got him refocused in a hurry. "What are your immediate plans for it?"

Doh was right back on track. "Resonance scanning of brain and vital organs, tissue samples, uh, genetic sequencing, then I thought we could just release him into the wild." Tur was impressed. *Very goal-oriented.*

"Didn't you want to track it after release?" Tur asked, bating him.

"I would, but there would be no immediate gain. In my opinion, for this mission, it would be a waste of resources," Doh answered, with impressive discipline.

"Don't discard the creature just yet," Tur commanded. "I want an in-depth study of its intelligence and communications skills. If it can communicate, have it interrogated thoroughly. Report to me by first light. Understood?" After a brief pause which Tur could not quite interpret, Doh answered in a simple affirmative.

* * * * *

The mammal looked exhausted as it sat in the middle of the floor. The bright overhead light focused on a radius five of its head-lengths wide, with the pilot at its center. Doh approached from the darkness, brimming with excitement. He looked as if he would burst before his demonstration even got started.

He carefully and purposefully drew the animal's attention to his lips and spoke in plain English. The tones came out with a hollow, resonant quality.

"How much wood would a woodchuck chuck if a woodchuck could chuck wood?" he said.

The pilot looked perplexed. "What? What's this woodchuck crap?" it shot back.

Doh clapped his hands together in exhilaration. "You see? You see? I projected 'We come in peace,' in the most focused thought possible — right at it — and the only communication it comprehended was that nonsense verbal message. According to our research, that sentence has no substantive meaning, even to its own species."

"That doesn't prove they're solely verbal," Ikara protested from the darkness outside of the spotlight.

"No. Of course not," Doh agreed. "There is some component of body language that roughly corresponds to our own universal concepts. Perhaps some hint of vestigial telepathic ability, but nothing to speak of. No, no. Their communication is almost completely verbal."

"So, what's your point?" Tur said, trying to cut through Doh's scientific theatrics.

The Kini Tod continued. "There are about four or five billion of this particular animal living on or near the surface of Fitu. They have developed a rudimentary communications system made up of about five or six basic families of languages, each consisting of approximately 100,000 to 200,000 characters. It is this verbal language skill that allows unrelated tribes to coalesce into larger groups and accomplish amazing feats of technical and economic genius by cooperation. From what this creature displays I would say he was just above average in intelligence."

"Hardly 'genius,'" Tur said, his impatience penetrating the darkness. "So I repeat: What is your point?"

"The point is this: this individual and his kind constructed, maintained and piloted that machine and hundreds more like it. They communicate over long distances by way of transmitting verbal codes via low frequency EM waves, as Weepf suggested. Large quantities of data are managed through electronic integration networks, many of which are linked to monitor devices and automatons.

"It's all very sophisticated. They never could have developed this technology without help. I believe these Jing were genetically engineered to serve some purpose of the Keepers," Doh concluded. He was on the verge of giggling.

On a more serious note, he added, "Also commander, they do know something about us."

The chamber was filled with thoughtful amazement. Doh raised a stubby hand to quell the conjecture. "Not us on the mission team, specifically," he clarified. Then he performed a series of gestures.

A display of Weepf's excursion appeared. "This was recorded inside of one of their buildings." The holograph panned through a building named "The Arabian Museum of Natural History."

Assuming the display was a test of its knowledge, the mammal started to chatter in English. "Tyrannosaurus Rex, Triceratops, Stegosaurus, Pterodactyl, Brontosaur, I think."

Sensing impatience from the group, Doh moved to silence it. The pilot went limp.

"So they have a few mismatched collections of wildlife fossils. That has nothing to do with us," Tur said, standing now. He ran a finger along a dorsal plate of an enhanced image of the stegosaurus exhibit.

"There's nothing there to suggest that they know what we are here for. I see no threat for now."

Tur crossed his arms while he thought, now looking with disdain at the skeleton identified as "Tyrannosaurus." He shut the holograph off with a single gesture before returning his attention to the briefing session.

"Jeen?" he asked, calling on his communications expert.

The Tal Genj mer's antlers shook gently as she spoke. "I agree with Doh in at least one respect: they have very sophisticated data management. It's completely binary though, with data stored on magnetic strips and chips."

"That should be easy enough to access," Tur observed, while rubbing his chin. "We should be able to just—"

"I see where you're going with that thought, Commander, but believe me, it's a dead end," Jeen interjected. "The data is not coded in a uniformed pattern. A sensor sweep would alter the data almost simultaneously with the scan. What we get would be unreliable at best, but more likely, unintelligible.

Tur pressed onward. "It might be worthwhile at some time to access individual databases. That would be very cumbersome, but feasible. Our own gel/crystal technology can easily break in on any of these cables or fibrous conduits, and monitor, reroute, block or replace transmitted data. We would have to have a small number of selected terminals to experiment on first. We could download the raw data and translate it at our leisure."

Jeen exhaled with exasperation. Smooth short pile bristled slightly. "The spoken languages are even more difficult. Again, Doh is correct in stating that there are five or six basic groups, but there are a myriad of sub-groups further divided by dialect and mixed with elements of languages no longer in use. I selected this particular animals primary language of English. It's a poor language system with many syntactic contradictions, but it's the most widely, used all the same.

"It took me a while to master it. I spent most of the night teaching it to Doh, Vit Na and Bo Tep. Vit Na seems to be most adept at actually duplicating natural mammalian voices, because of the Melkyz phono-mimicking ability. At some point that may prove useful." With nothing further to add, Jeen relinquished the floor to Bo Tep.

"The bipeds are very security minded, in some respects obsessed, but their security measures are ridiculous. Visual surveillance, barriers of simple metal mesh ... Oh, and sentries. Whatever attacked Weepf probably was top-of-the-line technology. What's really interesting is that they have no defensive weapons at all." He paused to let the ramifications sink in.

"All of their weapons technology is offensive in design. I confirmed this with Devit. They have a deterrent/first strike/retaliation mentality. If we ever have to get past them, we will." Bo Tep made the final statement with the utmost confidence.

Vit Na presented her perspective in turn. "I have very little to add. Their 'civilization' is very young, but a complex of paradoxes. They have extraordinary wealth alongside abject poverty. Valuable skills are honed to an art, coveted, exploited — then relegated to those of lesser aptitude. All the while, the accumulated resources are squandered by the masters of each trade."

"The socioeconomic structure is not dominated by the gifted, but by the least inhibited, who are usually of average or below intellect. The next tier is composed of above average subordinates with special talents."

"And the commoners are at the bottom of the tree, scrambling for scraps. What's unusual about that?" Tur interrupted.

"Nothing!" Vit Na explained. "That arrangement would make sense, but it is not the case here. There are a disproportionate number of gifted individuals permanently incarcerated or surviving in the underworld. It's almost as if some of them are deliberately excluded from the mainstream."

"That doesn't make sense to me, but there must be some kind of survival value to the arrangement. Do you have anything else?" Tur asked her, preparing to adjourn for the time being.

"I can't explain why they keep a bunch of old bones around, if that's what you're asking. A cultural quirk, I guess."

Tur was about to end the session when Vit Na stood again. "Just one more thing, but it is a little out of my area." She paused for permission that she knew she would get. "Has anyone noticed a certain peculiarity about their anatomy?" She paused again.

"Yes. No tails!" A soft chuckle propagated through the audience at the anonymous quip. "Yes, that too, but there's something else even more fundamental." She paused once more, half for effect and half to decide for herself if her theory made sense.

"Their heads are too big," she finally stated. "Proportionately, their brains are larger than ours!"

The dying chuckle turned into a murmur of curiosity.

"Of course they are!" exclaimed Doh, apparently threatened by the proposal. "Their central nervous system is all in one place. We have relegated the lower level neural functions to the caudal center in the tail, and to peripheral neuromuscular plexi. We connect our diffuse central nervous system via a more sophisticated spinal/paraspinal cord network."

Doh obviously was insulted by the intrusion into his turf. Vit Na proceeded cautiously. "Yes, but taking all of that into account, they still should have far more intelligence than any of them display. They clearly have sacrificed strength, speed, endurance and other sensory advantages to the development of this relatively massive brain. What do they do with it?"

Doh was silent.

"They have no telepathic, prescient, or telekinetic ability," she continued. "It seems from Doh's observations that much of it is inhibitory. At some point during the last 65 million years, there must have been a survival advantage to this mutation: the tendency to suppress direct communication in favor of their ridiculous babble," she concluded. Her voice was beginning to falter.

Grudgingly, Doh concurred. "It may be that the Keepers pushed these Jing beyond their mental limits by narrowing their receptive abilities in an effort to override basic instincts and the barrage of superfluous psychic input around them." Aloud, it still sounded good to Vit Na. "They probably retained a number of neuro-psychiatric mutations long after the last of the Si Tyen died out," he concluded.

The staff's collective attention drifted back to the nervous subject sitting in the cone of light. Echoes of thought projections rippled through the theater.

Weepf spoke. "Well, this is all very interesting I'm sure, but we have a serious security problem on our hands. These Jing, or Jing Pen as Vit Na proposes, have gone beyond the level of 'pest'." The room was still dark. She brought up the lights and spoke again, without asking Car Hom's or even Tur's permission.

"If the essential research has been completed, get rid of that thing," she signaled to Ju Kol. "Remove its tongue, sedate it and release it back into the wild."

Predictably, Doh objected. "Why must we maim this animal? Can't we just—"

Weepf reasserted her position without missing a beat. "As I said, it's a matter of mission security — my department." That ended that discussion.

Tur and Car Hom remained silent as she continued. "These creatures tend to babble. You have clearly demonstrated that yourself. I can't have this one telling the whole world that we're here. Consider the silencing as an act of mercy. This creature will still be able to eat, excrete, reproduce and defend itself. What is lost?"

Sensing Doh's sympathetic sentiment, she added softly, but angrily, "By rights, I should put a talon in its scrawny neck here and now!" Regaining her composure she turned to Tur and Car Hom. "I also want a tactical officer with every survey team that leaves this base. With your permission, I'd like to requisition forty or fifty armed meren from my division on the Repam."

Tur looked to Car Hom with a look that was half galled and half amused at Weepf's brazen request, then simply, "Do it."

Chapter 12
ATTACKED

"I should have opened the little maggot's neck when I had the chance." Weepf muttered. It had been barely more than a day since they had released the jet pilot. She stood outside, looking over the heads of Doh and Devit. They were flanked by several of their subordinates. The light from the exploding missiles illuminated Doh's forehead and cheeks.

Sleek black machines suspended from whirling blades hung in the midday sky, slowly circling the Efilu Base. Shots struck harmlessly against the invisible barrier. A few painted bursts of colors against the exclusion field embracing the compound, but most just shattered dully. Shadows lumbered through the cloud of dust stirred by the swarm of crafts. Ground vehicles launched a continuous hail of incendiary cocktails of their own. It was a most spectacular pyrotechnic display.

Weepf was giving Ju Kol instructions on situation management when Tur arrived. By this time the show had drawn quite an audience. Tur stood with his hands akimbo, watching the muted sparks. "What's all this?"

"The price of mercy," Weepf answered sarcastically.

Tur restrained a satirical comment. "Just get rid of them," he said jovially.

With her nod, Ju Kol made a series of gestures. The mammalian assault force simply stopped moving. The darkly clad assailants fell silently where they had stood. The flying machines settled gently to the ground, blades whirling to a stop. Dust cleared as the futile attack came to an unceremonious end. Weepf took pleasure in neutralizing the armada. "This time, no loose ends" she projected and looked directly at Doh. He had no response.

The spectators lost interest as the commotion subsided. As they cleared the terrace, they filed haphazardly past a lone figure intently studying a mini-gelcom. Devit caught Tur's arm as he departed, not lifting his own eyes from the hand-held recorder.

"Fourteen bims," Devit stated, still not looking up as he spoke.

Tur looked down at his weapons expert quizzically. "No, you must have miscalculated. Fourteen bims would have ruptured the shield. You know that. Check again, you'll see it comes out to dae bims."

At that point, Devit initiated the display and triggered the repeat cycle. "No mistake, High Commander." He took a formal tone now, his facade grave as usual. "That pretty display generated fourteen bims of energy. It was low intensity — mostly wasted propelling metal projectiles — but a respectable discharge of power all the same." He watched Tur's brow furl as he confirmed the data's accuracy.

Tur activated the com link. "Car Hom ..." He waited for the response from his number one, then stated, "We're moving."

* * * * *

Tur drummed his fingers on his knee as he sat waiting. The amphitheater was nearly full. Only Ju Kol's party remained absent. Cleaning up the remnants of the shattered Jing Pen armature took longer than expected. They were so fragile!

Weepf was sitting quietly up front. Tur looked at her, and imagined a smug expression on her inscrutable face.

Damn her! he thought. *She was right from the beginning.* More than an inconvenience, this unexpected guerrilla fire power was developing into a full blown complication. The phrase "tactical retreat" would never be used to refer to the action he would take here today. Tur would see to that!

He commenced speaking as Ju Kol entered the room. The lights dimmed before any of the stragglers had a chance to find seats. Tur displayed an updated three-dimensional holographic globe of Fitu, now complete with the main urban centers.

"There is nothing of interest to us in this region," Tur said, indicating the base's current coordinates. "Today, we will split our forces into seven groups. They will be deployed here, here ..." He pointed as he spoke. "... and here on this hemisphere. Here, here, here and here on this one. The basic plan remains the same."

He paused a moment, for questions, then went on. "Car Hom will make team assignments. Weepf will assign security personnel. If there are no questions, you're dismissed." Doh poised to ask a question, but was cut off in mid-thought projection.

"If there are questions, direct them to Car Hom and Weepf." Doh was left with his mouth gaping as Tur left the hall.

* * * * *

It was nearly dawn in the western region of the very land mass to which Jeen had wished not to be assigned. Tal Genj had an odd habit of looking tranquil but dissatisfied all the time. Right now, Jeen was anything but tranquil ... and dissatisfied was an understatement.

The orders still echoed in her mind, "Be discrete!" *How do you remain discrete when there is no one to hide from?* she thought with exasperation. The desert was awfully big when crossed at ground level. ... And her mini-wave was too small for her party! So what she didn't have any of the really big meren with her? Why should she be cooped up with a Lau Rechin security officer whose feet constantly dragged on the ground, leaving tracks, she wondered?

"Uhn!" *Yet another groan from the "grunt."* Jeen had had it. "Enough of this!" she exclaimed. She reached down into the nerve center of the amorphous wave and shifted the control currents. The wave engulfed the whole compliment of her team and took on a giant arachnid configuration. "That's better!" she said aloud, looking back at the security meg with defiance. Her look said, *Report me. Go ahead.*

The going was a little slower, but a lot smoother with the well-adapted pseudopodia carrying her party easily over the undulating sandy terrain. Overall, it was much more "discrete." Even the Lau Rechin security meg couldn't argue that point.

The gel pod allowed visual perception that was apparently keener than that of the mammals they had been ordered to avoid. Twice now, troops of bipeds had come close enough to smell the traces of gel solution evaporating from the pod without spotting the immobile figure in the sands.

Jeen began to consider Weepf's security measures more as a burdensome exercise. She looked back at the security meg with contempt and returned her attention to the changing landscape. They were approaching the site of the ruined city of Meput. There was now more vegetation ... and more "Jing Pen" to contend with.

The name Vit Na with which labeled these bipeds had stuck. From the ancient word for tree mammal, Jing, the term Jing Pen implied Si Tyen genetic engineering. As she considered the possibilities, the Party leader suddenly felt her resentment for the Lau Rechin security meg turn to welcome. Jeen wondered how the other search parties were doing.

Chapter 13
STAR WARS

The Repam somehow seemed empty without its strongest personalities exerting their presence. Sub-Commander Ga Win had just walked the ship and was satisfied with its status. He was tired.

Car Hom had worked his staff to the quick. Super Hunters always expected more from their own class. Now it was time to rest. Ga Win lay down on his pallet and left Stihl in command.

He had no way of knowing the Department Head of Astrophysics would exercise the honorary Acting Commander rank provision to his own ends.

Los reveled in command, even if it was only "acting." There were more meren in the control center than necessary for the quiet third shift. Los crouched in the control groove. *Comfortable. No. Powerful!*

Stihl stood obediently at his left side. The assistant commander merely observed, silently making mental notes to himself.

Not accustomed to command, Stihl thought, eyeing the Acting Commander. *And preoccupied.* Los was still contemplating the shiny derelict satellites in orbit below the Repam. They appeared harmless enough. No reason for Stihl to step in ... yet.

"They may be mapping devices left by the Keepers you know," Los said. He was trying to engage the big So Wari for some reason unclear to Stihl. "We may be able to hasten this mission after all, if I'm right."

Stihl did not like games. "What are you asking?"

Los raised a slick, brown eyebrow. Stihl very patiently added. "... Commander."

"I'm asking for your tactical assessment, Stihl. Could any of those metallic constructs represent a threat to the Repam or our landing parties?"

In typical So Wari style, Stihl thought fast, but spoke slowly and deliberately. "They have neither scanned nor probed us since we arrived six days ago." Before continuing, he brought up the data on Pre-Exodus Si Tyen technology and compared it with the energy scans on the derelicts accumulated so far. There was no correlation.

"They appear to be machines of various designs. Their structures suggest specialized manufactures and very little adaptability. Some are clearly specialized for some form of celestial reconnaissance, but have not focused on us as yet. In fact, they don't even appear to have the capability to probe objects this close to their sensors.

"Most of them are designed for aerial and terrestrial survey. There is definite evidence of subatomic decay of heavy elements in some of them — no doubt they run on a primitive form of long-term power source, probably serving more vital functions. By contrast, some of the others are equipped with solar collectors. The technology is definitely of common origin to that encountered by the surface party."

"I concur with your analysis," Los drawled. "We are going to acquire one of those nuclear powered machines. My calculations show they are most likely to store data for long periods of time, data that may prove invaluable to our mission."

Stihl protested. "Wait now! Those machines are sloppily made. Although the radiation they leak represents no hazard to us or to the surface dwellers from this distance, bringing one on board is an unacceptable risk that I cannot allow."

The Notex's response was accompanied by the usual amount of hand waving. "I am Head of Astrophysics and Propulsion, as well as Acting Commander of this vessel. In my opinion, we can easily contain the radiation leaking from ten of those machines. We stand to gain far more than we risk losing. In fact, we are at less risk than our intrepid colleges on Fitu." He looked at Stihl triumphantly, knowing that he had won a reluctant ally should his judgment be questioned by Tur or Car Hom.

Stihl hesitated. The argument was a sound one. It just ... felt wrong some how. He wished that Ga Win was not in hibernation. Waking him now would be useless because he'd be mentally incompetent for at least a day.

"I acknowledge that you are in command, however, I have the responsibility of maintaining ship's safety. That comes directly from High Commander Tur," Stihl said, emphasizing the rank. "I will not allow this mission or this ship to be placed in jeopardy. The moment these activities even look like they are endangering this ship, I will terminate them and assume command pending the return of Tur or Car Hom."

Los started to respond, but was cut off. "—and I will restrain you if necessary." Stihl said. He then went back to his usual stolid vigil without further comment.

Los didn't have to say any more. He knew he had won, but he would have loved to have had the last word.

* * * * *

"ATTENTION COMMANDER OF CHALLENGER II. Switch to laser pulse frequency Epsilon."

Chip Rollins closed the door to his cabin and waited a moment after following the initial instructions. He knew what was about to happen and he felt a shiver run down his spine. This communiqué was Security Level 1.

The commander floated in the zero gravity as he waited for the President to appear on the view screen. The first encounter with extraterrestrials mandated presidential attention. Every astronaut dreamed about it, himself included, but the reality of the event hit him like a ton of bricks. He had not spoken to this president yet. He was nervous. This new Republican president had earned a reputation as a "hard-ass."

The Head of the Joint Chiefs of Staff appeared instead. The face of Air Force General Michael Chey was alert and intense. "Major Rollins, you are ordered to proceed with extreme caution. We have been expecting this call from you all week. Washington has reason to believe these aliens are hostile and dangerous. Attempt communication, but at the first sign of trouble, you will mount Operation Bethlehem ... and mind you, there will be no command discretion here. You will commence the procedure at the first sign of aggressive intent. This is not to be discussed with the rest of the crew. Chey out."

Rollins was left staring at the blank screen, absorbing the unsaid ramifications of the communication. Operation Bethlehem was the new code phrase for deployment of the Strategic Defense Initiative. *The President's maintaining his distance on this one. Why?* Rollins wondered. *And Chey. No encouraging "Good luck, Chip"?* Rollins found himself remembering the fate of the last shuttle named Challenger.

*   *   *   *   *

Disgust was becoming a part of Tur's normal disposition since the landing. He had stopped trying to mask his feelings since Geotechnics recommended straining the decayed liquid waste these Jing Pens were dredging up from the bowels of Fitu. All the same, it saved him the energy of having to excavate it himself. There was no arguing over economy for a So Wari.

They had found no golden algae yet, but a good number of microorganisms from that ancient time were being found intact. It was quite promising!

Since it was apparently common practice to harvest ancient Efilu refuse, the other sub-parties were ordered to duplicate the process wherever possible. An old So Wari axiom said, "Share the pain."

It was nearing time for check-in. The daily ritual was supplemented by security updates every quarter day by Weepf, who relayed them to the snowy northwestern peninsula of the land mass now called North America by the Jing Pen, for Tur's review. He was really beginning to like Weepf. *She'll make a good So Wari yet,* he chuckled to himself.

Tur looked up from the filtration unit for relief from the sickening process, only to notice Devit standing across from him. It bothered the High Commander a little that this one was consistently able to approach him undetected. *Ironde stealth technique seems even better than I've heard,* he noted. *We'll have to look into this some time.* The thought was lost as he noticed the little device in his Weapons Master's hand. Devit offered it to his commander. "Do you recognize this?"

Tur looked at it before taking it from his companion. "Of course. It's one of the weapons used by that biped pack that attacked our base." He tried to hand it back to Devit, but was refused. "No, no. Do you recognize the technology?"

Tur still looked puzzled. Devit tipped the weapon on its side in the commander's hand. Tur's eyes shone with a glimmer of recognition.

"Its a hand Lesad," said Devit, supplying the answer. "Named after the Sulenz inventor."

Tur shook his head slowly in disbelief. "That was invented over a hundred million years ago. How would they have access to such technology now?"

"A hundred and five million years ago," Devit corrected. "One might conclude that they had help, Commander," the Ironde offered.

"The Tyen Keepers were non-violent. Why would they provide these vicious little creatures with even primitive weapons technology?" Tur asked.

"I don't know Commander, but there are personnel available who are a lot more well-versed in Tyen psychology than I am." Both meren looked uneasy with this new problem. Just then, the Denar technician Kira Kesh, entered the small building.

"You two look as if you could use a lifting of the spirit," she said. There was a twinkle in her eye that piqued their curiosity. Following her lead, they stepped out into the night air and found themselves bathed in a familiar light.

Kira Kesh followed a bit behind them as she watched the effect of an old friend on weary travelers. "The Northern Lights," Tur recalled from Animem recollection. "Beautiful as ever." It was only then that he realized that he had come to regarding Fitu as an alien world. Just for a brief moment, he felt as if he had come home.

His warm moment was interrupted all at once by burst of something cold and wet on his back. He took a deep breath before turning to face the clumsy subordinate responsible for flinging snow in his direction. Vit Na crouched as she assembled another snow ball to hurl at her friend. In this environment, her coat was a milky white — an adaptation achieved without true Blending. Realizing that she was caught, she tossed the snow ball up and down, catching it each time in her bare hand as she addressed her commander.

"Isn't this great! I haven't played in the snow like this since I was a cub," Vit Na was grinning broadly.

"Weren't you assigned to Bo Tep's sub-party?" Tur growled. He was happy to see her, but enjoyed playing this game of feigning irritation.

"I think I was beginning to get on his nerves. He sent me to deliver the soil specimens we recovered this afternoon." It was half truth. She was delivering soil samples, but she had to coerce Bo Tep a little to let her do it in person.

Tur wouldn't probe too deeply of course. He was happy to see her. Who better to share the light show with?

* * * * *

Los had ordered the Repam to reduce its orbital distance from Fitu. They were now closer than the moon. The new orbit was on a deliberate collision course with the slow-moving shuttle. Los was obviously trying to bump into it.

Stihl was becoming more uncomfortable by the moment. He knew he should find a reason to notify Tur, but there was still no danger to the ship. The Repam's protection screen would deflect the shuttle with no effort at all.

Los slowed the ship once entering the shuttle's orbital path. Data on the small craft was collected even as it rebounded, shaken yet unharmed, off of the force field. The true object of intended study was just ahead.

As the Repam opened a port to receive the nuclear satellite, Stihl found his voice. "Abort. Abort! Close that lateral portal now!"

Los threw his hands up in the air in disbelief. "Have you lost your mind? What do you think you're doing countermanding, my orders? Don't you know who is in command here?"

His eyes blinked as the blinding flash caught him by surprise.

* * * * *

Ju Kol reviewed the data on the ruins below them. It was very warm. Jeen had supplied each of them with a working knowledge of the local wild life and the most popular languages in use. This place was called Venezuela by the resident Jing Pen. They were very close to the equator here, and the wide river posed significant survey challenges.

The heat in this region of the planet was different from that of the original landing site. More humid. The soil below him was rich in decaying organic material. The probe readings were less reliable than elsewhere. Of course, Weepf would not be interested in his excuses. He decided not to accept any from his own subordinates either.

Ju Kol was still berating his aide when Weepf stepped up to investigate the commotion. Almost whining he began, "We need accurate information on this site or we will really be in trouble. We'll nee ..." Just then he realized that she was not listening to him anymore. She was staring off into the midday sky at a glint barely perceptible to his eyes through the glare of the sun.

"Contact Tur and the other parties, Ju Kol," she said.

"We're in deep trouble."

Chapter 14
SEIZURE

Tur paced the floor of the conference room with heavy foot falls. The grinding of his teeth was audible even over the hum of the faulty transmission from the Repam. Car Hom listened calmly as Stihl recounted the series of events leading to the satellite explosion. Los was visible in the background, also pacing, obviously eager to give his side of the tale.

As the briefing came to a close, Tur locked gazes with Car Hom. He had stopped his pacing and settled on his haunches, motionless. Los took advantage of the momentary silence to interject his explanation. It ended abruptly with a slam of Tur's fist on the conference table. The communications link was broken.

"Car Hom, it would seem that a few soft meren have gotten into our little fold somehow," he said through clenched teeth. He looked away from his Chief of Staff. "Weakness appears to be rampant here. I was led to believe you could maintain our strength." In stating this, he invoked an ancient obligation that was never subject to criticism in civilized conversation. "See to it that the slack is taken in a bit up there, won't you?"

Car Hom stood without ceremony, and with no obvious sign of offense. He did not face Tur directly, but silently pointed to three technicians and gestured for them to follow him. "I'll have a damage report for your review before sundown. In the meantime, we'll stabilize the ship's orbit. I'd prepare to send all non-essential gel and crystal equipment up to the Repam if I were you." Without further comment, his party transferred to the damaged vessel.

With Car Hom gone, Tur drummed his fingers thrice on the table, and then stood. He was surrounded by his ground based department heads. He forgot the northern beauty he had grudgingly admired earlier that morning outside the temporary building. He could not even mourn the casualties resulting from the fiasco, right now.

"The danger from these Jing Penian tribes is unchecked at this point," he said. "Bo Tep, you will coordinate with Weepf, find out what else they're up to. I want a plan to neutralize this threat before sundown. Dismissed."

The staff left him alone in the conference room. Tur reached for the weapon Devit had brought to his attention, placing his smallest finger nail over the trigger mechanism and squeezing a harmless shot into his opposite palm. "If any of these miserable Keepers are still alive, I'll kill them!" he said aloud, tossing the weapon on the table. Then Tur subdued the lights, sat on his haunches, and folded his hands together on the table for the purpose of supporting his aching head.

* * * * *

The Repam crew was shaken by the blast. Twelve were dead, and twenty-seven seriously injured. Those with minor injuries continued at their posts.

The atmosphere was intense and Car Hom was in no mood to relieve any of that tension...especially not for Los. Car Hom had thought about destroying him for a moment, after surveying the damage, but he needed him. The mission needed him, but not on board the Repam. Los already had given his assessment of repair requirements. They were extensive of course, but could be implemented by maintenance personnel.

"Why do I have to go to the surface, my skills are best utilized here?" Los whined.

Car Hom looked around at the chaos and spread his hands at the pleading meg with a sarcastic shrug. After a moment, he added "We'll muddle through without you."

"Car Hom, what do I do about Tur?" Los asked, with uncertainty. "I mean, I would imagine he's ... a bit upset."

"Just stay out of his way, Los. You'll probably be all right."

Los fished for reassurance. "Probably?"

Car Hom could not resist the opportunity to torture him. "Well ... possibly," he replied.

"How angry is he?" Los asked.

Car Hom again looked around at the damages, then back at Los, and just shrugged. Los swallowed a little harder than usual, before shuffling slowly down the hall.

Somehow, Car Hom felt better than he had all afternoon.

*   *   *   *   *

Car Hom's report was in on time, as always. "The situation is salvageable. Please send ALL available gel and crystal tech for support," he transmitted in a manner reminiscent of So Wari brevity. Tur's culture was losing its monopoly on this stereotype more and more each day.

Tur saw that all key personnel were present for this latest meeting. It was time to begin. The meeting was lead by Bo Tep. The Chief of Acquisitions was well prepared.

"As we already knew, most of the Jing Pen assault forces are automated, at least the ones we're interested in right now." He and Kellis had come up with an elegant holographic system that utilized the dust and snow from the artificial cavern floor and was manipulated by personal field interactions. The gestures became mildly tedious for the holofield operator, but they communicated scale and spatial relationships rather well. *Leave it to Tralkyz ingenuity to employ talents that hadn't been necessary in eons,* Kellis thought with admiration.

"Jeen tells me that we can cripple their entire satellite system from either of two strategic centers in the region that I had been surveying before the ... accident." No one actually looked in Los' direction, but he certainly felt as if they did.

"They will try to locate us after the hit," Bo Tep warned. "At the same time, they may try desperately to re-establish control over their systems. We'll need a new base of operations from which to work — one that will afford us access to the same information flow the Jing Pen have. Under the circumstances, it needs to be some place close to our current location, but not too close."

He paused for a moment, then pointed. "Here!" The Tralkyz stabbed a finger at the large military base on one of the icy islands off the shore of the Alaskan peninsula they now were quartered on. Murmurs rose, only to be silenced by Tur.

"Intriguing. How?"

"I took the liberty of catching a few strays that were wandering around in motorized vehicles. Ikara feels she has a good enough handle on their psyche to emulate appropriate responses to any conceivable inquiry. Vit Na has assembled some of the best mimics in our group to match every Jing Pen voice in this nest. She can already match half of them herself.

"Brajay had been able dissect one specimen's brain. He's already gotten to the hippocampus and recreated fine details of memory. The crumb snatcher didn't survive the process, but we learned much of what we have to know ... and there are many more where it came from." He grinned at Tur. "With the help of Jeen's mastery of their digital communications web, we can follow their every move and they'll never even know anything is amiss."

Tur couldn't suppress a smile of satisfaction as he nodded approval. "Do it. Take any personnel you need."

* * * * *

Even Bo Tep was surprised at the ease with which the Jing Pen base fell. Most of the sentry animals were spared and taken for special retraining. Surgically. Fortunately the four-legged animals, were even easier to deal with than the two-legged ones.

All alarms were reset and routine was re-established, to emulate "situation normal." For the sake of comfort, the Efilu control center was set up in a series of connected hangars, after the disposal of excess aircraft.

The five top ranking Jing Pen were corralled in the control room for interrogation. There were no specifics on the "Repam Incident" recorded in their computer system, but Bo Tep knew instinctively that someone here had to know more than it let on.

"What are your plans for the alien ship that was attacked this morning?" Bo Tep questioned one of them, from a respectable distance. Its garment had been stripped away earlier, for examination. The little animal was pale and shaking uncontrollably in the open hangar. Bo Tep looked to Jeen to confirm he was speaking the correct language to the creature. She nodded, perplexed through her calm, confident exterior.

He repeated his question again more deliberately. This time, he stood a little closer.

The biped mammal, now cringing, still said nothing. The limits of Tralkyz patience being reached, Bo Tep snatched the wretched creature up in his left hand, drew it up to his own face and spoke a third time through clenched teeth. "Where and when is the next attack coming?"

"Ah, ah, ah ..."

"Don't give me that gibberish I know you—"

"Please don't eat me. PLEASE!"

"—understand what I'm ..." Just as the meaning of the general's plea sank in, Bo Tep realized that there was a copious flow of clear yellow fluid running from the man's legs onto his arm. Bo Tep dropped him almost involuntarily. He was unsuccessful in suppressing a dry heave.

"Eat it? How disgusting can you get? Eat it. Please!" He stomped at the fleeing animal to encourage its retreat, although that was wholly unnecessary.

All at once the hangar was filled with hearty laughter, as Tur slapped his leg in amusement. It was the first time Tur had really laughed since leaving Teist.

Bo Tep, now embarrassed, saw nothing funny in the situation. "Look, that urine could have been poisoned. It could have gotten into my eyes, my mouth ... you remember how vicious Weepf said they were. ..."

Now Weepf and several others had joined in on the laughter. The humor of Bo Tep's predicament now hit home, but he still suppressed his own chuckle.

Ikara approached the little band of confused humans and repeated each of Bo Tep's questions in a soft, calming voice. The humans were obviously less intimidated by her smaller form and harmless appearance. Still, they said nothing. Without cracking a smile she added, "If you don't answer me you'll have to answer him ..."

She pointed to Tur who had picked up on her line of thought and was no longer smiling. "... and we know when you are lying, too," she said. "The price exacted for each untruth will be a limb of your body, at his discretion of course."

The answers flowed freely and accurately from all five human officers until dawn.

Chapter 15
STEALTH TECHNOLOGY

What they learned from the interrogation confirmed the general Efilu pessimism. "The estimates from the computer database indicated dozens of platform-type satellites with scores of fission devices on each one," said Devit. Jeen and the Weapons Master had done well adapting basic crystal integration modules to read the simple binary data transmitted between the Jing Pen computer systems. Devit had taken over as Tur's assistant. His insights had proven most valuable.

He continued his report. "The good news is that none of them could match the maneuverability or speed of the shoddily constructed ship the Repam ran over before the 'Incident'." He indicated the space shuttle Challenger II, recovering its preprogrammed orbit about the planet. "It's simply a matter of how fast repairs can be made on the Repam."

Tur filled in the smaller meg on the state of affairs in orbit. "Car Hom has requisitioned virtually all high tech machinery to effect repairs. The hull was well preserved, but a third of the inner core has to be completely rebuilt. If not for Stihl's actions, the damage would have been much worse." He could feel his blood pressure rising already. He knew he had to get off of that subject, and fast.

"Progress reports indicate the repair process is consuming an exorbitant amount of energy. At this rate, we may not even have enough power to maintain orbit much less return home after the essential repair work is done. There is a minimal compliment of the original surface parties left here on Fitu." Tur thumped his tail on the floor to indicate ground level. His frustration was obvious. "Most of those personnel have been assigned to the restoration effort, and the remainder are engaged in keeping the Jing Pens occupied during this vulnerable period.

"Of the seven sub-parties on the planet surface, only Doh's group continues the algae search. Fortunately, there is minimal biped encroachment into the open oceans. Other mammals, so far, have proven much less troublesome."

Tur stopped walking as they came to the end of the hall and rubbed his chin. "Doh is on to something quite promising," he added. He then dismissed Devit and opened the folding door to begin his next meeting with his data integration chief.

"The interlocking computer network is proving more convenient than expected. Amazing how adaptable even primitive tools are when you're forced to use them," said Jeen, obviously quite pleased with herself. The soft antlers covering her protective head frill bounced gently as she looked from view plane to the High Commander, arms folded in pride. *She has every right to be proud,* Tur thought to himself.

"We've been able to not only follow the plans of our adversaries, but also to confound them. Fortunately, they are still looking for us in 'northern Africa,' as they call it. Weepf has seen to it that all traces of our presence were completely erased from the Siberia, Venezuela, American gulf coast, and Nigeria excavation sites."

"What?"

Jeen clarified. "I'm sorry Commander. These are the English designations for the locations we've occupied. It makes sense to refer to them with these Jing Pen designations, as the pre-Exodus geography is obsolete."

"Well, what about the old Senz city?" Tur asked.

"They can look all they want in the so called 'Arabian peninsula' region. Weepf had adequately probed it from the air.

"Our takeover of this Thompson Air Force Base has raised no suspicions here in the Aleutian Islands so far. In fact, in accordance with orders from their main military headquarters, a place called the Pentagon, we've launched several squadrons of Stealth bombers in search of the 'alien invaders.'" In anticipation of his next questions, she said, with a giggle, "Flying machines. And as Bo Tep said, 'top-of-the-line,' no less. Ikara plans to have the pilots report nothing back."

Tur was lost in a thought for a moment. A concerned look crept across his face. "No," he finally said. "Let them report nothing NEW. Keep track of reports from the other bases. If our Jing Pen report significantly less than the others, it may raise suspicions."

"Commander, I really think you're giving them too much credit."

"Maybe. All the same, have our pilots report only what they are expected to see no more, no less. Too much information may prompt a visit from one of their leading officers. Anything else from your perspective?" said Tur.

Jeen thought for a moment, then replied, "Not at this time, Commander."

He acknowledged her report's conclusion with the merest nod of his head.

"Bo Tep?" he said.

"We're ready to go with the invasion, Tur, but we can't hold another installation with the personnel we have available," Bo Tep answered. "If we were spread any thinner here, we'd start to make mistakes."

Tur nodded. He was really developing respect for this one.

The Tralkyz continued. "We need to get in, do some harm and get out before they know what hit them." He hesitated a moment. "I'm obviously too big to move efficiently through those halls. So are some of my seconds. There are only ten meren small enough to do the job. Of those, only three could do the job right. Los, Vit Na and Gober Dil."

Tur's distress was only momentary and was overcome by admiration for Bo Tep's surprising diplomatic skill. He had chosen the order of that roster carefully. First, Los, whose loss everyone could live with, had nearly supernatural speed; then Vit Na, followed up closely by the Wilkyz, Gober Dil. Intermediate in size between Tralkyz and Melkyz, Dil would have overwhelming strength relative to the Jing Penian bipeds. Also, the Wilkyz's special "time splitting" talents would cause enough confusion to draw attention from his friend. Naturally, he had the utmost confidence in Vit Na's own natural talents for survival.

"When will they go?" Tur asked.

"Very shortly," Bo Tep answered solemnly.

He nodded silently to affirm that there was enough time for Tur to say good by to Vit Na.

"We have just enough port thread left to get them inside undetected," Bo Tep said. Before he could finish, Tur demanded, "How do you plan to get them out?"

"Dirm and Stihl will launch an attack from the west of the base, using their personal fields to control a couple of prefabricated force fields I managed to salvage from a shipment of equipment that was returning to the Repam."

He waited a respectful moment for an admonishment he knew Tur would not voice, then continued. "The invasion team will then escape eastward in a similar force field, to a pre-arranged rendezvous in the marshes that Vit Na discovered while we were filtering the crude waste. We can pick them up later.

"The ones who will be in the most danger, actually, are Dirm and Stihl. The Jing Pen are going to throw everything they have at those two. However, between the force fields, some old style weapons we've fashioned, and their natural armor, they should be all right."

The plan was well thought out. The two So Wari could, of course, burrow to a safe depth under the dry, rocky soil and hide in a pre-arranged cavern until rescued.

"Wasn't Stihl reported as injured in the explosion?" Tur asked.

"Yes."

"Is he up to this?" The High Commander queried. Bo Tep answered with a noncommittal "Brajay thinks he is." Bo Tep shared the common tendency to overestimate So Wari recuperative powers, a myth that was self-perpetuated.

"Fine," Tur approved. "Send a summary of your proposal to Car Hom. Let's keep him in the loop."

* * * * *

"We're in," Vit Na announced. She got no acknowledgment from outside. *What next team leader?* she thought to herself. Neither Tur nor Bo Tep would fully trust Los with responsibility for a while yet, not to mention the doubts held by Vit Na or Dil. In all likelihood, had he been chosen, Los would have come up with some pride-saving excuse not to lead the assault himself.

They had split up to cover the key areas of the base depicted in the schematics scavenged from the Aleutian Island computer database.

"Los," Vit Na projected, her mind reaching through the man-made walls. "Report your location."

"Section two, level three." His thought projection was a little faint.

"Level three? Already? You really do move fast," she complimented.

"That's why I'm here. Uh, oh. Something's coming. Talk to you later," he projected. She felt the tension in his last thought. It made her a little nervous. Sooner or later she too would have to face one of these

Jing Pens.

It was time to check in with Gober Dil. "Dil? What's your situation?" she asked.

"I'm fine. Nothing has seen me yet. I think I'm safely out of sight for a while. I'll just wait for your signal to begin."

I guess it's all on me now, she thought. She took a cleansing breath before proceeding out of the air duct.

She reviewed the plan in her mind for the seventh time. *Step one: cut off all outside communications. I'll put the routine communication simulator Jeen designed in place first. It looks like a simple crystalline module. She says no one in here will know they've been cut off and no one out there will know the difference between our relay and their comrades' broadcasts for a while. I hope she knows what she's doing, I sure don't.*

Step two: we divert their attention from the weapons control center. That will be up to Dil, with some support from Los.

Step three: detonate that orbiting arsenal before it can do anymore harm to the Repam.

She didn't dare think about the fourth objective: get out of here alive.

Los sounded more than a little tense at this early stage in the operation. *It wouldn't surprise me if Tur had threatened his life if he allowed me to come to any harm*, she guessed. *I wish he'd quit doing that.* She took some comfort in the thought all the same.

Vit Na proceeded through the halls of the well-guarded installation, passing sentry after sentry. She "Blended" well in the dim lighting. She had closed all of her sebaceous glands to further minimize her already faint scent. It probably was a wasted effort on these limited creatures, but why take chances?

She entered the telecommunications center unseen. It was buzzing with activity. She saw her objective on the far side of the room, blocked by several alert-looking operators. *Why does the target always have to be on the other side of something?* she lamented. The tension level in the room was mounting rapidly. Vit Na didn't know why, but she had a feeling that something bad was about to happen.

Why can't I read their feelings? she wondered. Vit Na hadn't noticed before, but even in the newly occupied headquarters at Thompson Air Force Base, Efilu were subtly forced to supplement thought projections with physical communication.

The Inhibition Factor! it dawned on her. *It interferes with intimate communication.* She looked around the room again at the group of human beings. She remembered her theory on the reason for the big brain: inhibition of extraneous intrusive thoughts. Minds too primitive to cope with the myriad of intimate communications around them could be modified to block them out ... or suppress them within a given vicinity.

She tried to relay the information to Los and Gober Dil. "Los, report!" she projected. *Nothing.* "Dil, can you sense me?"

"Yes, but you're very vague. I'm getting little more than impression. Are you injured?" he said.

"No. The Jing Pens are having an unexpected effect on our communications. I think the interference is related to the number of active minds in the immediate area. I can't reach Los at all!" She had to try hard to keep panic out of that last projection.

"Adhere to the original plan for now," he answered. "If Los is still mobile, he'll do his part on physical cue. Just remember to try to reach both of us when we're clear of this facility." The feelings she picked up from Gober Dil were less reassuring than the content of his thought projection.

This really complicated matters, she thought. It was a small team to begin with. The first such operation she had ever led. *Now, this!* If anyone of them got into trouble, she or he would be unable to contact the others or even headquarters. *Why does Los have to be the one out of thought range?* He was unpredictable enough as it was. She didn't know him as well as she knew Gober Dil. She hoped the rumors about him were wrong.

Vit Na spotted an opening. The mulling Jing Pen were now settling down. She moved cautiously, but deliberately, towards a panel in the main computer complex. She placed a small piece of resin in her hand and manipulated it as Jeen had instructed. She worked fast. The resin hardened into the configuration Jeen had described. It fit inconspicuously into the empty parallel port in the central processing unit of the computer, with room to spare. She carefully eased out of the room weaving between the occasional ambling human that was still in motion. She retreated outside, to a corner of the dim hall, to await her cue.

It wasn't long before a klaxon went off. Armed men came running down the hall, right past her. *Right on time,* she thought nervously. She reassured herself that Dil would keep them occupied. They wouldn't know they were fighting only one being for hours, if at all. If Los was still on the loose, he would be cutting as many of the remaining outside cables as possible. She could check the volume of truly incoming messages to identify his work.

Good. The number was dropping off quickly. The integrating resin would act like a minicomputer, simulating appropriate responses to outgoing messages. At the same time, it would continue the usual routine updates in order to maintain the illusion of normalcy.

That's it. The last of the communication cables was out of operation. *Oh, no!*

One of the soldier bipeds had stopped and begun to inspect the corner where Vit Na was hiding. It was using a hand held light source to sweep the area. Vit Na could feel herself on the verge of panic. *Go away, go away, go away!* She projected the thought as hard as she could at the soldier, but here was no change in its behavior.

Vit Na could take it no longer. She reached out for the creatures throat and squeezed its larynx, remembering that they could project thoughts no better than they could receive them. The desperate squirming of the animal continued to heighten Vit Na's anxiety level. She instinctively gripped its neck firmly and tilted its head to one side with her thumb until she heard a little crack. The Jing Pen's body instantly went limp on the side opposite the injury. It struggled even more desperately for freedom as she tilted its head the opposite way with her index finger, to achieve total paralysis. Presently, she breathed a sigh of relief, as her victim succumbed to asphyxiation.

She tossed the carcass behind her, hiding it from sight. Then Vit Na resumed her vigil in the corridor, as if unperturbed by the encounter except for a tentative look back at the motionless form, followed by a shudder.

Soon, though, she decided to move. Her timing was a bit premature, but she could stand her proximity to the dead body no longer. She made her way down the hall toward what the schematic indicated was the "War Room." Dil was to have lured or scared the vermin to outer chambers.

Vit Na had indeed arrived too soon. One of the false images of the Wilkyz was still challenging the armed guards when she arrived. She carefully skirted around the activity and moved toward the detonation relays. She activated them in sequence.

One of the armed men in the room noticed the changing display on a Plexiglas screen in the middle of the room. It hesitated only a moment, then spun around to confront the intruder it expected to see at the control panel. Seeing nothing, it sprayed metal pellets in the general direction of the disturbance.

Vit Na made no sound as the stray bullets bit into her flesh. She spotted an air duct that she knew would lead her to safety and to the end of her portion of the mission.

It was her movement that gave her away. As she fled from the position where she had been injured, the blood that spilled from her wound became visible. The soldier saw it! He followed the trail to the opened air duct, and launched a grenade into it. It exploded.

As she lost consciousness, Vit Na became visible.

* * * * *

Stihl felt as if he had been beaten with a tree. He hadn't realized until now how badly the explosion on board the Repam had shaken him. As he crouched in the rocks, he felt the stiffness that had insidiously set in his body. Now his muscles rebelled against renewed movement.

The sun had set long ago on the military installation he was watching. The night remained quiet, lit sporadically by bright lamps that swept the area with their light. The sudden eruption of activity signaled the completion of Phase 2 of the Efilu strategy. Hopefully, Phases 3 and 4, were completed as well. The alarms were as easy to spot, as Bo Tep had predicted. It was pure pandemonium: their cue.

He signaled to Dirm, who was lurking some twelve head lengths across the pass from him. They moved out along divergent paths to initiate their assault. Stihl fired the first round of phosphorus grenades. The spread covered the entire compound with spectacular explosives. As the various animals ran out to their respective stations, Stihl cut them down with rapid fire bursts of force which he released from the storage field that enveloped him. *Amazing!* It worked perfectly.

Apparently, these creatures didn't even have a defense from a rudimentary force stream assault. Several biped groups seemed to triangulate on the source of the salvo and sought shelter behind a piece of heavy mecha. It only took a few pulses for Stihl to realize that he couldn't effectively penetrate the heavy metal with simple force blasts.

Damn, he thought. He needed to keep Dirm out of the fray for a little longer, as reserve fire power. Then it came to him. The Jing Pen had made the assumption that they were evading bullets that followed parabolic trajectories. It was then a simple matter of directing the stream of force around and under the vehicle shielding them. They were totally committed to their current position at this point, and were therefore, easy pickings.

Stihl launched another round of phosphorus grenades. It was surprising what one could create from handy natural material. The noise and glare of his assault were effective in maintaining a state of confusion, but Stihl knew it would also attract attention from other settlements. Heavily-armored vehicles would be more resistant to the relatively weak phosphorus weapons, and an attack force sent in from a fully operational base would be less confused by the distraction tactics.

Stihl was too far away from the sheltering hills to hide for cover when the human assault force came in. He had not expected them to be as well prepared as they were.

Armored hovering craft that suspended on whirling metal blades fired explosive missiles, just as Weepf had said they would. Larger aerial crafts clumsily, but quickly, unloaded land-based machines that immediately began tracking the source of the attack against their den. The direct impact of the missiles missed their mark, but the resulting concussion actually shook the ground beneath Stihl. His personal shield held firm.

He counted fifteen turtle like machines to the right, and twelve to the left. The aerial machines dropped back to continue the attack from what they must have determined to be an optimal distance. Stihl scanned the area. Most of the machines were within his personal sphere of influence. He had an idea.

Removing the remaining fifty phosphorus grenades from the folds of his integument, he then tossed them into the field bank that he had used as the source of his force pulses. Then marking individual objectives, he preset each pulse to target one machine. He planned to wipe out every war machine in sight in a single sweep. Of course, that would leave him totally without retaliatory capability against heavy weapons. Dirm would have to take over to give him an escape route. He was sure the Efiluan invasion team had done its work by now.

Stihl projected the plan to Dirm, who was still waiting quietly in the foot hills. Just then, a bright flash lit the night sky. Stihl did not have Weepf's acute Vansar vision, but he knew it to be a nuclear explosion in the upper atmosphere. Vit Na had done it!

The momentary distraction was his undoing. Three turtle-like machines charged over the horizon, firing missiles at close range. They caused his little "surprise" to detonate around him. Stihl's personal shield collapsed, overwhelmed by the blast. The other war machines intensified their assault as if they could somehow sense weakening in their unseen opponent. Stihl reeled back with the agony of the firestorm, fending off the continuing hail of projectiles with hand and tail.

He had mustered enough concentration to signal Dirm to begin his attack when he realized that the bulk of the attacking force was addressing another offensive. Dirm had picked up on Stihl's plan and launched a shower of grenades that were each perfectly on target. One of the little metal "turtles" continued its approach. Before taking a hit from Dirm, it fired an explosive missile at point blank range into Stihl's unprotected chest.

The impact sent his heart into spasms. Stihl crumbled to the ground, barely able to move. His peripheral circulatory system had weathered the assault well enough to supply some skin and muscle tone, as well as nourish his brain. His thick So Wari down remained fused into the strongest natural armor ever developed on Fitu or anywhere else in the known universe. These defenses would not be enough.

He sensed Dirm rushing to his aid through the embattled hillside, and stopped him with a faint thought projection. "You can't burrow and carry me at the same time, Dirm. Rescue was not included in this mission." After a pause that could only equate to a mental gasp, he said, "Tur cannot afford to lose us both. Objective achieved. Follow the plan!"

The logic was inescapable, of course. The fissionable material in those satellites threatening the Repam had been detonated. Dirm turned without hesitation. Brajay would never tell him how little first aid it would have taken to save his comrade's life.

Stihl watched his comrade disappear into the hillside as the heavy weapons swung back to fire on his now defenseless form. The bullets ripped through seared flesh even as Stihl crawled defiantly in their direction. He thought of that nuclear explosion and hoped the Repam had escaped destruction.

His final thought was, *We just can't lose to these vermin!*

Chapter 16
"... THEY WHO WAIT"

Car Hom waited as everyone else must have been waiting. He had faith in Vit Na. Oddly enough, he even had faith in Los. Nobody could botch an assignment twice. No, something else was bothering him. It had nagged at him even before he had left the surface, but what was it?

He looked out at the menacing satellites from the vantage point of the Repam's deteriorating orbit. It was losing its battle with gravity, in spite of repairs. There was just enough power to overcome the increasing atmospheric drag. Kellis had identified the ancient fuel reserves on the fourth planet, but it did them no good. He could not get a landing party there to retrieve it.

Suddenly, Car Hom almost laughed out loud. He didn't know why it had not occurred to him sooner. There was little enough time to prepare the command center personnel for what had to be done, let alone notifying Tur. He would not have had a choice anyway. Car Hom would tell himself later. He then pointed out an image on the tactical display, turned to his assistant and said, "Bring that one in closer."

*　*　*　*　*

Doh felt proud. *What a triumph!* Not only had he been right all along about the cycle of life on Fitu, but in the seas he had found a confederation of mammals, consisting of unrelated species. What a relief to find out that human kind was not the only intelligent life form left on the planet! He was slightly disappointed that even this civilization's collective memory did not reach back far enough to reveal what had become of the Keepers. However, the history of "Skeewii," as they called themselves, was nearly as interesting.

They all had, at one time, lived on the land. Those times were dim in the memories of the Collective. Somehow, they had migrated back to the sea. A guiding force they all called Wholu helped shape them to survive the new environment. Over time, they became aware of one another.— first locally, then worldwide.

Getting along was difficult at first. Many of the new neighbors in the community were convenient food sources. Eventually certain rules were made to govern behavior in intra- and inter-species encounters.

There has been heated debate over the status of their terrestrial cousins. Something important had happened among them millions of years ago, but no one in the Collective remembered exactly. Now the dominant ones were called human.

They did not have very good communication skills, those humans. They could apparently speak to one another sometimes, but were not always clearly understood. They had no concept of inter-species communication.

Still, there were those among the Skeewii who felt that humans had a right to at least establish some trade relationship with them. Who knew what riches lay on the land? It was potentially a reservoir of valuable resources. The objects that humans lost or discarded at sea were becoming more interesting by the day.

The humans seemed to rule the land. All other land creatures seemed to fear them. Human civilization had always been unstable, however, rising and falling over the centuries in the wake of great wars. In general, the Skeewii policy was to avoid contact with terrestrial animals, with the exception of feeding on the few that stumbled into the aquatic domain.

The fish-like creatures the humans had called dolphins were their greatest proponents. They often aided humans who were lost or in trouble at sea. Rarely did humans reciprocate with food or other valuable services. Instead, they hunted them.

The hunting of Skeewii and protected species took its toll. Some species retreated to cities and farms that had been developed in the network of undersea caverns tucked away beneath the continental shelves. There, basic needs, as well as exchange of ideas, were provided for more than adequately.

Only a few nomadic tribes and well-trained scientific expeditions went out into open seas these days, and then, mostly at night. Many races were seen so seldom in open seas that mankind had presumed that they were extinct.

All of this history was very interesting, but Doh knew that he had a mission to accomplish. He had described the yellow algae that the Efilu sought to a host of dolphin scientists. After conferring with a number of manatee colleagues, a group of them had taken off, presumably to confirm that they had indeed encountered such material.

Doh had transmitted his report to Tur and waited. The Collective had been entertaining Doh's search party with the history lesson ever since. What could be easier than to let someone else do your work for you?

Doh reflected on the Skeewii situation a moment, then became curious. "You have build this magnificent culture here, yet you have cut off all contact with the surface dwellers. They could obviously benefit from a lasting relationship."

The Sea Lion that Doh addressed curled his nose a bit and said, "We are waiting."

"What are you waiting for?" Doh asked.

"The final disaster that mankind will visit on itself," was the answer. He shifted on his fins uncomfortably, looking around at the otters, walruses, whales and porpoises that all interacted in harmony.

"As it stands, they have no real interest in actively destroying the ocean-going races, but if they thought we had more important resources to exploit ..." The Sea Lion's meaning was obvious. "These subterranean caverns will protect us from much of mankind's mass destruction when their final conflict begins. Many of the nomadic marine tribes, I fear, will be wiped out; but in the end, we will survive 'man.' Then we will reclaim the open seas and the land."

His determination was unsettling. It was a mission exactly opposite to that of the Keepers.

An otter splashed up on the ledge eagerly carrying a seashell full of golden brown silt. She offered it graciously to Doh. The Kini Tod scientist smiled and expressed the gratitude of the Efilu in the Skeewii language.

This was what they had come for: living yellow algae so close to Efiluan golden algae that little genetic manipulation would be needed.

The search was over. It was now a matter of waiting (and hoping) for the repair of the Repam.

Chapter 17
A RAT IN THE CAGE

Vit Na awoke in a reinforced concrete cell. There was a metal mesh stretched across the only opening. Steel bars, three fingers-breadth in diameter, supported the mesh from ceiling to floor at eight finger intervals. The mesh looked remarkably fragile until her eyes focused on a faint reflective surface just in front of it. The entirety of the barrier was encased in six inch thick Plexiglas.

Beyond the barrier she could make out six figures. Two were moving, the others were stationary. As one of the blurry silhouettes moved across her field of vision, she identified a portal framed in the same steel as the bars, hinged on the outside. *Hmm. There's no obvious opening mechanism on this side of the portal.* She had observed all she could without moving her head.

Her head was propped up on something soft with an unpleasant odor. There was a dim light source behind her and some type of electronic mechanism whirring at her side. She was laying on a table, with a white sheet draped across the length of her body. *The texture suggests a blend of various plant fibers,* she observed. She estimated its weight at 10 ounces, based on the average pressure she felt exerted on her chest.

Vit Na turned her attention inward. She assessed her volume status and metabolic reserves. *Odd. Metabolic reserves are disproportionately low in comparison to circulating volume. Which is correct?* She had no idea how much she had bled. Her loss of consciousness may have been due to vascular reflex syncope. She had no way of being sure. She had never been injured before.

Vit Na hesitated in her analysis. *Well, I had better go through this methodically,* she decided, even as she realized she was afraid to learn the extent of her injuries. *What if I'm permanently crippled?* That line of thought had to be terminated immediately. She went on to her neurological review. The results were inconclusive. She decided she would have to learn more about her new surroundings first.

Then, without moving a muscle, she swept her attention up and down her body. Both motor and sensory functions were intact. All visceral organs were functioning adequately. Her chest wound had some sort of complex dressing on it. A contraption of metal wires sheathed in a plastic material that wreaked of decay, and thin tubes made of a similar material, carried fluids and gases in and out of her body. For all its associated paraphernalia, the apparatus provided no anesthesia, but did seem to supplement her fluid deficit and provide a few nutritional calories. That explained the discrepancies in her diagnostics.

The wound itself was deep. A piece of her left lung was missing, along with part of the ninth rib. Necrotic tissue had been carefully cut away, and bleeding minimized with some kind of electric cauterization. She could still smell the ozone trace. Breathing hurt a little, but she would manage.

Vit Na avoided extending her sphere of influence to scan the "guest room," for fear of revealing her return to consciousness. *Better use passive senses,* she thought.

The Melkyz listened. The sound of fluid rushing through the tiny tube leading into her side could be traced to a source three head lengths away from her. She shifted her half shut eyes ever so slightly to her left to see a pole supporting a mechanical pump.

Suddenly, another sound caught her attention. It was to her right, and nearly out of sight. She almost reacted instinctively by turning her head, but checked the urge. Her peripheral vision detected a vague, furtive movement towards her bed. Long moments of silence followed. She waited.

She heard a scurrying sound to her right. This time, the movement was more distinct ... and there was more than one source! She inhaled through her nose. *Jing scent. My captors, no doubt,* Vit Na thought to herself.

She remained still as something tugged at her sheet, then let go. Presently, she felt tiny hands grip her tail, which was hanging over the edge of the table, but resisted the urge to shake them off. One of the mechanisms attached to the ceiling moved as if tracking movement on the floor wherever she heard sounds. *Surveillance! I knew it.*

The scurrying activity in the room increased. *What next? I can't play dead forever. They'll poke and prod me until I have to react,* she guessed. *Better to respond to them with the most non-threatening posture possible. I may even learn what happened to the rest of my team ... and the Repam.*

Vit Na now drew a deep breath. Pain lanced through her side, but fortunately, no air leaked from the wound. She sat up. They had not placed any restraints on her.

She looked around for her hosts. What she saw were small, hairy four-legged mammals with tapered snouts, whiskers and hairless tails. These were like the mammals she remembered on her world. She waited for one to approach, but they kept their distance.

She swung her legs off of the table. The apparatus attached to her side was designed to be mobile. *This thing won't encumber my walking ... for all the good that will do,* she thought. *From the looks of this chamber I'll be staying for a while.*

A gray animal approached first. The largest of the bunch, it bared its teeth aggressively. Its hair was a bit more coarse than that of the others, its skin and ears scarred. Most of the others appeared more kempt, almost delicate, and had soft, white hair. These creatures kept to the shadowy corners and huddled together.

A few other unkempt grays were lurking under the table. With the leadership of the big one, they advanced.

Sharp, little teeth sank into Vit Na's flesh. *Is this some kind of greeting ritual or are they trying to do me harm?* she wondered. When the leader drew blood, Vit Na decided she was not going to participate in this custom, no matter what its purpose. She shook them off of her as gently as she could. Then she tried to make contact with the big one. *Maybe some of these smaller creatures retain the ability for direct communication*, she reasoned.

The large rat had become bold, perhaps sensing helplessness. It climbed onto the table, then into her lap. Vit Na could see it well now. It was male and malnourished, with a broken tale. The scars of narrowly won battles were visible in its sparse hair. Its breath was concentrated squalor.

She brushed it aside, a bit more vigorously this time. The group of them scrambled and cowered in a dim corner. The broken-tailed rat still peered at her with that hungry look.

Great! she thought to herself.

Vit Na realized that her movements had attracted the attention of the larger animals patrolling outside of the cell ... and perhaps more importantly, those contraptions on the ceiling.

She lifted the tubing and with her eyes, again traced it to the machine on the pole. The fluid levels in the containers were low. *Whatever they're pumping into me is almost done,* she realized. She concentrated on the differences in the content of the blood returning from the damaged area of her body.

Hmm. Lipids, carbohydrates, electrolytes and water. There was something else that she could not quite identify flowing with the nutrients. She made a specific effort to metabolize it at the source. She would take no unnecessary chances.

Vit Na knew she would be in need of real food soon enough. She drew her knees close to her chest and rested her face between them.

*   *   *   *   *

Tur reviewed Doh's data on the algae specimens. "Perfect! You say that these Skeewii were cooperative with you?"

"Yes. We've collected enough algae to replenish our supplies by using cultivation methods alone, with some help from accelerated maturation technology, of course."

"All the same, I want the genetic code recorded and duplicated for each team leader," Tur said.

"As you wish," Doh said. He excused himself to made preparations.

"One more thing, Doh." The Kini Todd scientist stopped at the door to the conference room, at the So Wari's request. "I want your gel network. We are basically defenseless here and I've heard nothing from Car Hom since the explosion. Until we know for sure what happened to the Repam, we're on our own. We're going to improvise a bit."

Doh understood the gravity of the situation and went off to comply with his commander's wishes.

*   *   *   *   *

"Are you sure about her anatomy?" Javier Mendez asked, as he pressed fast forward to scan through the video tape.

Bruce Stahl responded with confidence. "Absolutely, her metabolic rate, eye structure and position, teeth and general physique all point to a hunting meat eater. She's a predator all right. I'd stake my reputation on it."

"Add that to the fact that she mauled a few dozen armed men at Graham AFB last week and I'd say that pretty much clinches it," Hollingsworth interjected. Max Hollingsworth was the animal trainer/behavioral specialist assigned to Project X. He and Stahl had worked together before and as far as he was concerned, when it came to analytic anatomy, Stahl could walk on water.

The lab was a state-of-the-art affair: arranged in such a fashion that each work cubicle contained equipment tailored to each team member's needs. Swivel chair on castors allowed each individual to role easily out of his or her cubicle for spontaneous discussions. If all the chairs were 180 degrees from their respective work stations, they formed a circle for convenient, impromptu conferences with minimal interruption of work time.

"We've watched and waited now for three days," Mendez said. "It hasn't killed a single rat. The IV fluids ran out thirty-six hours ago. We're going to watch the first alien in captivity starve before our very eyes if we don't come up with something soon." He scratched his head. "Maybe there are proteins or amino acids that we missed in the screening process that it perceives as toxic."

Stahl answered with bewilderment, "We were pretty thorough. The rats have everything it needs for survival."

"What about trying to broaden its diet a little? Some predators are taught to eat only certain prey, aren't they?" Clyde Olsen said.

Mendez, Stahl and Hollingsworth exchanged an embarrassing glance between them. No one wanted to admit that the computer geek had a good point less than did Mendez.

Without meeting the younger man's questioning gaze, he gave a nod of agreement and said, "We'll take that under advisement. For now though, we follow our current plan of letting her demonstrate some of its hunting techniques under carefully controlled conditions."

"Chuh!" Robyn Washington blurted over her shoulder as she reviewed visual analogs of the sounds recorded in the holding cell the previous night. She looked over in Olsen's direction and smiled.

"Excuse me, Robyn, is that some language that I don't know? Chuh?'" Mendez asked.

"Well, I don't know Dr. Mendez, do you understand the words 'thank you'? It's English, I believe. Used when someone has helped you out, you know? It seems to me that Mr. Olsen came up with an idea that was somehow overlooked by the mountains of gray matter shared between the three of you guys."

She left him and the other two to figure out what "chuh" meant. "Pompous asses," she whispered under her breath, and went back to her work with a grin.

Soon, though, the grin faded as frustration crowded the good mood out of her mind. "I just wish she'd made some noise!" Washington exclaimed.

"You know, I thought only guys made that wish the morning after, Robbins. Now I guess we have something in common." Bruce Stahl sneered. He knew the linguist didn't appreciate lewd innuendo, so he enjoyed his joke all the more.

Robyn "Baskin Robbins" Washington wouldn't let him get under her skin. She would banter in a friendly manner with her colleagues, but she would never participate in any ribald jokes. She was unique in many ways, and all jokes aside, the whole team appreciated her importance to the project.

Washington had an uncanny flare for languages. Not only was she "fluent in 31 different flavors" as she was fond of saying, but she could quickly pick up languages unrelated to any she had ever heard and even duplicate the accents perfectly and she hated the Baskin Robbins joke!

Everyone of them knew the story of how this African American woman had shocked the Chinese delegation to North Korea a few years ago when she was working for the Clinton Administration. The Chinese translator had taken ill prior to a state dinner. The two camps had struggled to communicate as best they could when Washington stepped in and translated for both the Chinese and the Koreans, with perfect accents in both languages. If any human being could communicate with the alien, it would be her.

One final member of the Project X team was arguably the most important at the moment. Dr. Hoyt Matthews spoke as he analyzed tissue samples for the umpteenth time. "Well hell! I don't know why it won't eat. I guess it's sore from that injury. Intense pain can sometimes cause anorexia. Ah betcha that side of hers is just as sore as a risin'."

The veterinarian scratched his neck as he turned towards Olsen. "... Or she's just a very finicky eater," he added. His warm smile accented the laugh lines around his eyes. With that comment Mendez had no way of putting it off any further. He had to arrange to "feed" her something else.

* * * * *

I wish it would stop looking at me that way, Vit Na thought as she watched the broken-tailed gray rat watch her. The big one somehow had taken on the collective presence of the whole pack. They had exchanged places, she and the rat. It stood on its hind legs on top of HER table. She sat on her haunches against a wall of the cell. Vit Na felt cornered by the rat. She also felt as hungry as the rat looked.

She was light-headed. Her eyes glazed. *Properly prepared, I might be able to hide the gamy taste of that little vermin,* she thought. Revulsion snapped her out of her reverie. She looked around the cell again in order to remind herself of her circumstances. The large gray was looking back at her with a puzzled expression. *I'll never get that hungry,* she resolved.

Deep in her heart, Vit Na knew she would ... eventually. Her glycogen stores were already depleted and auto-digestion of muscle protein was a conscious choice and hard to accomplish at that. A hundred million years of plenty had reduced her species fat reserves to a minimum. She needed food, and soon.

A sudden stirring among the guard animals outside of the cage interrupted her fantasies of food. *Or were they hallucinations?* She wasn't sure. A large biped approached the door. *Jing Pen. Human.* She reminded herself. It was dressed differently from the others: all in white, except for leg and foot coverings. The newcomer was a bit older than the others and over fed. Not very intimidating at all. It carried something with a white cloth draped over it.

Well, the interrogation at last! Maybe I can communicate with them if I can just hear some more of that babble and watch their reactions. If I'm lucky, they'll speak English like the other Jing Pen we've studied. She moved a body's length away from the door to indicate she meant no harm, and awaited the greeting. To her surprise, the Jing Pen slid his burden just past the door, whipping the drape off as he did. He quickly retreated through the open door, which closed immediately behind him.

Vit Na was puzzled until she recognized the raw meat on the tray. Something she only later recognized as hunger overpowered her. She seized the gift from its place on the floor before her "roommates" could get at it. Not only had her desire to parley vanished, so too had her unspoken treaty with the rats. She brushed them off the table with her arm sending them tumbling across the room.

Vit Na then grabbed the cotton sheet that had covered her body several days before and spread it over the table. She promptly sat on her haunches and surveyed the setting. She placed the tray on the table and set to work preparing her meal.

The meat was lean and thick — not the way she liked it, but she really didn't care. She raked her claws across the steak at an angle then again at an angle 90 degrees to the first. She turned it over and repeated the procedure on the other side. She sat back and for a moment looked as if she were going to vomit as she regurgitated stomach juices into her mouth, then evenly sprayed them onto her meal. She sat patiently as the digestive enzymes cooked her food right there on the tray. Again, she did the same for the reverse side of the steak.

Satisfied with her culinary effort, Vit Na carefully bisected the now crispy meat four consecutive times until the pieces were bite sized. For all of her hunger, the consumption of the meal was leisurely, almost dainty.

The observers in the outer room and in the control center watched with fascination. There was something very familiar about the process, like watching an aristocrat dine through a cracked kitchen door or an outside window.

When she had finished, she drew a deep breath and exhaled slowly with satisfaction. Vit Na rose from the table carrying the now empty tray. She reached down and retrieved the small cloth drape the human had left behind. She covered the tray and replaced it exactly where the man had left it. Then she stood back and waited.

Shortly, the same overfed biped returned and opened the cell door. As he reached down to fetch the tray he was frozen by a familiar, but impossible sound. "Thank you very much. The meal was delicious!"

The man's complexion went white. He dropped the tray and fled, shutting the door with all of his might. Then he nearly collapsed and had to be physically assisted from the anteroom.

Vit Na, upon seeing this reaction, immediately retreated to the far corner of the room to indicate neutrality. There was obvious confusion outside. *In here too,* she thought to herself, as she replayed the exchange in her mind.

She hadn't done something that she was expected to do ... or she had done something that she was not expected to do ... *I hope I didn't get that response all wrong,* she worried.

Chapter 18
SUPERHEROES

Now that he was back on the main floor, Hollingsworth felt like getting on the wagon. Then he remembered that he hadn't had a drink in months. The MPs had brought him into the observation center, where Washington had forced him down into his seat and raised his feet. She then left the room to get him a cool glass of water. Hoyt Matthews, who was the only person with medical training, came to his side and took his pulse.

"Look at him! He's sweatin' like a pig an' pantin' like a puppy," exclaimed Matthews.

"Y'all want me to go fetch a cool glass o' lemonade from Aint Bee?" Stahl said mockingly.

"No, but you can go get me that paper bag on your desk. This ol' boy's gonna pass out if he keeps hyperventilating," Matthews answered. Just to show that he too had a sense of humor, he added, "Oh, you might stop to empty it out first son. Wouldn't want him to aspirate that 'London' fried chicken you've got in there."

Rebreathing the carbon dioxide from the bag slowed Hollingsworth's respiration to normal. Olsen, however, was still excited. "We heard it too, Max," he gushed.

Stahl shook Hollingsworth's sweat-soaked shoulder in congratulatory fashion. "She sounded just like Katie Couric on 'Good Morning America,' guy."

Olsen corrected, "Katie's not on 'Good Morning America,' she's on 'The Today Show,' Bruce."

"Shut up Clyde!" Mendez snapped, as he tried to re-establish order in the room.

"Think carefully Max," he continued when the babble had died down. "Did she say or do anything else that we might have missed? Anything hostile?"

Hollingsworth tried to clear his head. "Not that I can think of, Javier. Of course, we'll need to review the tapes to—"

"Been there, done that!" Olsen blurted out. "Her back was to the camera. We couldn't see her face when she spoke."

"Well then, we'll just have to ask her to speak to us some more now won't we?" said Washington, who was now back with the water. She handed it gently to Hollingsworth.

"Seems to me that someone is out of a job, hon.'" Stahl teased. "How so?" Washington responded.

"If she already speaks American, we don't really need a translator do we?"

"Fine. We'll send you in next. Then IF you come back, you can tell us about her language skills ... and table manners." She enjoyed his discomfiture with that last suggestion.

"We've got to inform the President." Hollingsworth said all at once.

"Fuck the president!" Mendez exclaimed. "He'll have his bully boys from Department D down here pumping her full of the truth serum du jour before night fall. Then we'll have nothing but a corpse from outer space." Mendez raised his hands for everyone's attention. "This is the discovery of the millennium, folks. No, this base is on radio silence as of now. I may be on inactive commission, but I still outrank the major who commands this base. No information gets in or out without my say so."

He looked around for any challenge to his edict. Seeing none, he went on. "I'm going in there next. You all have an hour to prepare. I want a minimum of twenty intelligent questions from each of you for me to ask her. Try to stick to your own disciplines, please."

"Some ego! He'll probably claim the credit for inventing '20 Questions' too," Washington said under her breath to Hoyt. He chuckled and added aloud, "Can the first question be 'is it bigger than a bread box?' Javier?" Everyone, including Mendez, had to laugh at that one.

"And now the disciples of Professor X prepare themselves for the mission of their young lives. Into the Danger Room go the X-Men, ready to save the world!" Olsen intoned dramatically.

"Will you quit it, Clyde?" Mendez asked, his patience sorely tested.

"What ever you say, professor."

"Don't push me, son, I'm not in the mood." Everyone suppressed a laugh. Only Olsen could really get under Mendez's skin, and without really even trying. That was the beauty of it.

*　*　*　*　*

Six hours later, Javier Mendez was in the guard room outside of the holding cell. Vit Na watched him interact with the others. *Ah. This one's different,* she noted. *He has the same body covering style, but obviously carries more authority.*

A submissive posture should be most effective, she decided. She backed slowly toward the table and sat on her tail and haunches. She affected the facial expression with which they all seemed to greet superiors. *A smile,* she reminded herself to call it.

Two guards entered with "the Chief"; a four-legged animal leading a two-legged one by some kind of tether.

Mendez had walked through the door boldly, but seemed more wary now that he, too, was confined by the cage. He pulled up a chair that had been brought in specifically for his comfort, and sat. Vit Na noted that the four-legged guard also sat, while the two-legged guard remained standing. *A pecking order perhaps?* She watched the seated human produce a sheaf of papers bound at the top by some sort of resin. He looked down at it a few times before speaking.

The first question was predictable. "Where - do - you - come - from - ?" Mendez gestured in crude sign language after each syllable, as if to clarify his question. He spoke slowly and loudly. *English,* she confirmed.

Vit Na noted the flurry of activity the question stirred in the rat pack. They scrambled for the shadows. She waited for the big gray to give some verbal response to "the Chief," but there was none. Realizing that he may be addressing her, she cleared her throat and answered the human in clear, soft tones. "Are you speaking to me or to your friends?" She gestured toward the rats huddling in the shadows.

Mendez smiled. "Friends? These are only rats. We use them for scientific experiments and sometimes as live fodder for 'carnivorous guests.' Most of the time though, they're just pests. Basically harmless, though. We were very surprised that you failed to catch any of them."

Vit Na was not sure she had mastered the spoken language yet. She looked puzzled and asked, "Why would I care to 'catch' one of them?"

"It's obvious from your physiology that you are a predator by nature," he answered. "Study of your anatomy reveals to us that you were either created or evolved for hunting. Our specialists believe that your species is closest to a carnivorous kangaroo, except that you seem to lack some basic features, such as breasts.

"Your hair is also peculiar and light, almost feathery. It's certainly softer than anything we've ever felt. For such rudimentary biology, you're astonishingly complex. Your digestive system is much like ours, but simpler and shorter. This is a tribute to your ancestors' adaptation to a very harsh environment, no doubt. Tell me a little about you planet and life there."

Vit Na hesitated. *What can I teach him that he could understand without a year-long prerequisite course?* "Oh, it's much like this place, but warmer."

"Go on, please."

She shrugged her shoulders realizing this was a universal gesture of perplexity. "We ... work for food, for ourselves and our families. We try to maintain good health. There are no doctors, as you have here. Most of our medical efforts go into prevention and education. We have no social support for the handicapped or deprived."

"That's too bad," said Mendez sympathetically. "We try to live in peace and harmony with each other and with nature.

"Were there others like myself loose in your facility when I was captured?" Vit Na queried.

"Don't you know?" Mendez asked suspiciously.

"No, I don't. I just remember a great deal of commotion, then I was attacked."

Vit Na had never lied before. As all Efilu were telepathic, lying was very difficult to accomplish among them. Being caught in a lie was considered an insult to another's intelligence. Fortunately, this was not a concern here.

"What were you doing at Graham's Air Force Base?" Mendez asked. There was a moment of tension.

"I had orders," Vit Na replied.

"To do what?"

"I'm not sure."

"Did you accomplish your objective before being captured?"

Make him guess a little. "My objective?"

"The explosion."

"There was an explosion?"

"Yes. Were you trying to set off those warheads?"

"Warheads?"

"You mean you didn't know the potential of the devices that you detonated?"

Vit Na thought for a moment. *Let's see how far I can take this act.* "I'm sorry, but I don't understand enough of your technology to work any of the equipment I saw."

Javier Mendez thought about her response for a moment. Vit Na interpreted his expression as doubt. He stroked his chin. *That's a strangely familiar gesture,* she thought to herself with amusement.

He spoke again. "We have much to teach each other. We would like to learn what space travel between the stars is like. It's a pity that the starship was destroyed in the blast. What was its relationship to you? Was it chasing your people? Are you a slave or worker, or something?"

The Repam destroyed. Vit Na was stunned by the prospect of never being rescued from this ancient wasteland. Mendez saw she could not answer his flurry of questions. He began again.

"How do you call yourself?" Mendez asked belatedly.

"I am Vit Na," she answered.

"You could end much speculation, Vit Na, about alien life forms. There has been much conjecture about alien physiology, but you are not very different from the earth life forms we know well."

Before she could speak again, the little "Chief" asked, "Just how is it that an alien is so well-suited for life on our world, Vit Na?" He stroked his chin again.

Irritated by his tone, she snapped, "Well, it's only natural as we evolved and developed here." Suddenly, she felt stupid. *How could I have reacted to such a dangerous question without thinking?* she chastised herself. *There must have been a thousand ways of exploiting that opening. I'll have to avoid telling them anything that they can exploit or don't already know. I'll satisfy enough of their curiosity to remain valuable, but keep them from figuring out too much more.*

"This was once our home, long ago," she began. Before he could ask, she went on. "Millions of years ago, we were forced to leave this place. This world became ... inhospitable to us."

Mendez forgot the questions on the page in front of him. "How many millions of years ago?"

She answered his question directly. "Sixty-five."

The guard almost dropped his weapon.

"Then you mean whatever it was that drove your people out was what killed off the dinosaurs?" Mendez asked intensely.

Vit Na had heard this word before, but did not understand its meaning. "What is a dinosaur?" she asked.

Mendez groped the air in desperation. “Big lizards ... reptiles ... like snakes and alligators.”

Vit Na floundered for a moment. “I still don’t underst—”

Mendez flipped the page and began to draw; first a snake, then a crude version of an alligator.

Vit Na said, “But what have these to do with—”

Then he furiously drew a picture of a stereotypical dinosaur, with large hind legs, semi-erect posture, short arms and sharp teeth. He turned the tablet to her.

Vit Na stared at it for a moment before taking the pad first, then the pencil. She drew over the same picture modifying the ears, eyes, mouth, and skin. When she was done she held the page to face him, offering it back to her host.

Mendez hands trembled as he took the tablet back and stared in disbelief. The drawing had been altered to resemble her. His mouth made several contortions before forming the words, “OH MY GOD!”

* * * * *

After a brief recess to collect his composure, Mendez returned to the cage. “We have tried to solve the puzzle of how the dinosaurs died out for two centuries. Now you’re telling me that they didn’t go extinct at all? They just ... left?”

Vit Na suppressed a smile. “Something like that.”

Mendez was still skeptical. “If this is your natural home, then the wild life here is your natural prey. Right?”

“It was,” Vit Na agreed.

“Then why didn’t you eat the rats when you were hungry? You’re certainly capable of catching and killing them. You could have prepared them and eaten them the same way as the other meat.”

Shocked, Vit Na glanced at the rats and heaved from the abdomen involuntarily. “What would make you think that I would eat vermin?” she scoffed.

“We had little information to go on, so we extrapolated from our knowledge of modern predators on Earth. They’d eat anything that moved, if hungry. Especially snakes.”

"The long limbless animals?"

"Exactly!"

Vit Na sought a simple way to clarify the relationship between Efilu and reptile, when she froze. "What kind of meat was that I ate earlier?"

Mendez said congenially, "That, my friend, was a twenty-ounce center cut steak you had."

Vit Na was almost afraid to inquire further, but found that she had to. "... And what kind of animal does that come from?"

"The cow. A large grazing animal that lives in herds and is used as a food source." Vit Na felt relieved. At least it wasn't pressed rat meat.

Mendez added, "The cow is a mammal, just as your people are reptiles." He had no way of knowing that just as he lumped all reptiles and saurian species together, so too did she fail to distinguish between various species of mammals. *I can't believe I ate giant fur mite meat!* she thought. *That accounts for that rancid odor.*

"So, how do you like beef? It's quite a delicacy for us." Mendez asked misinterpreting, her reaction. "How does it compare with the meat you eat at home?"

Vit Na leaned her back against the wall. She pressed against it in an effort to relieve her nausea. Her facial pallor was invisible behind the soft black pelt of her face, but nearly all the blood had drained out of it.

"Can we take a short recess? Perhaps an hour or so? I don't feel very well," Vit Na announced. She saw hesitation.

Desperately, she said in a weak voice, "I need time to more thoroughly assimilate your culture and vernacular language, in order to answer your questions better."

Mendez reluctantly nodded his consent and left the cell with his entourage. Vit Na closed her eyes and choked back the explosion of gastric content threatening to erupt at any moment.

She opened her eyes after regaining control of her stomach. There was "The Rat" with two of its friends, within an arm's length of her again. They appeared to be sneering at her. Her reaction was like lightning.

Vit Na lashed out with her tail, sweeping all three rodents off balance, then almost simultaneously crushed them all with a second blow of her tail. She hadn't even looked at her tormentors as she struck.

She brushed the carcasses under the table out of sight, half turned away from them, folded her arms across her chest and muttered to herself, "VERMIN!"

* * * * *

"What happened in there? Why did you break off the interview, Javier?" asked Bruce Stahl, who was waiting for him at the door to the 'Lab' as they were all beginning to call the observation center. "I can't believe the things that were coming out in that session."

"Why did you stop Javier? She didn't look like she was in that much pain," Max Hollingsworth said, echoing Stahl's question.

"She became 'ill,' I think when we began to talk about food." Hoyt said, joining in with a laugh. "Clyde guessed it, she is a finicky eater."

Ignoring everyone in the room, Mendez went directly to his work station, spouting orders along the way.

"Stahl, I want everything you know or need to know about dinosaurs laid out neatly. Hoyt, help him.

"Clyde, listen because I'm only going to say this once. Tap into the Library of Congress and the Smithsonian's archives. Download everything on the evolution of life on Earth from the Triassic period to the present.

"Also, I want A&P on amphibians, reptiles, birds and early mammals—"

"What's A&P?" Washington asked Stahl.

"Anatomy and Physiology," was the condescending response.

Mendez continued his orders to Clyde without interruption.

"Pull the files on molecular bio and biochem from my computer in Manhattan. They'll be on CD. That should be a good start. Hoyt and Bruce will update you as to any additional requests."

"Robyn, you still have a job," he continued. "Our friend, Vit Na, speaks English fine, but there seems to be some conceptual and maybe some cultural hurdles we'll have to help her over. I think she could be slightly retarded for her kind. She seems to have a lot of trouble answering very simple questions.

"Robyn, get to know her. By her voice, I assume she's female, but we don't know for sure. Teach her. Teach her about us, anything she wants to know, but try to keep it simple ..."

"I know, she's a little slow," Washington said, her voice heavy with sarcasm. "But how do you suggest we all interact with her without falling over one another?"

Mendez put on that silly look of his that said "I don't know."

"We could each go into her cell in shifts," Washington offered.

Mendez had not given any thought to that problem yet. If the team was to do its job efficiently, each member would need access to Vit Na. That feat was impossible in such a small cell! He would have to meet with Major Dixon about adapting the gymnasium to accommodate their visitor.

Fortunately, he had access to all the Plexiglas one could imagine There in Carlsbad, NM. They made the stuff there. The military had been storing the government surplus here at Hennessy Barracks. The small army base was not even on the map. It served well as cover for Project X. The small, but state-of-the-art research facility was secretly under the authority of retired Colonel Javier Mendez, Ph.D.

An official commander was named to put on the public books, but in actuality, he was directly subordinate to Mendez. Major Dixon had wangled this command by proposing and demonstrating that waste Plexiglas could be economically recycled. It was quite an accomplishment for an officer with less than a colonel's ranking. It looked great on his resume.

The warehouses were full of Plexiglas scraps. Now their task was just a matter of escape proofing the gym. Major Dixon's entire battalion would be working all night to finish it. Mendez didn't care. The men could gripe all they wanted, they still reported to the Major ... and the Major reported to Mendez.

Dixon turned out to be a rather eager fellow, and very cooperative. *He'll make Colonel before forty yet,* Mendez thought.

He had told Mendez, "These boys can tell their kids and grandkids someday, 'I helped guard the first alien ever captured in history.'"

Mendez had added, "Or the first dinosaur."

Chapter 19
HACKER

Vit Na had put in a request with Dr. Matthews for fish, chicken or domesticated alligator ONLY for meals. The look she got after requesting that last menu item told her she wouldn't be tasting any crocodilian meat for a while. At least he guaranteed she would be served no more Jing meat.

Her cell was modified to annex the anteroom where the guards had been stationed. This gave her a bit more room. The bars and Plexiglas had been removed and the table had been replaced by a bed of soft feathers covered by a cotton afghan. It rested on a king-sized water mattress.

The soldiers working on Vit Na's new quarters had begun to complain bitterly about the rodents that were getting underfoot and into their lunches. The humans were unbearably clumsy about catching the creatures. The men managed to kill only one of the twelve pests she had counted — and they had made a mess of it, at that.

Vit Na, seeing an opportunity to rid her chambers of the annoyance, asked, "May I be of assistance?" The sergeant heading the work detail answered, "Yeah, build a better mouse trap."

The man held a spring-powered wooden trap in his hand, with a look of frustration on his face. Quietly accepting the invitation, Vit Na had eleven rats neatly executed and piled in a corner for removal before late morning. She thought it was the least she could do.

Her hosts had proposed to modify a larger room to accommodate her needs. The Chief was being very hospitable. Had they better technology, Vit Na would have professed these creatures were acknowledging her proper station. She knew better than that though. This Mendez bore careful scrutiny.

The intensity of their questions was picking up. It seemed as if these people, as she had to remind herself to call them, wanted to know every detail of the past 65 million years, TODAY! At the same time, they wanted to know everything about space travel and whether or not there were truly alien civilizations out there. This seemed to be a "hot issue," as Washington liked to say. There was some bizarre belief in alien visitations and abductions.

Vit Na had honestly answered that she had never personally visited Earth prior to two weeks ago, and she didn't know anyone else who did. The idea of "flying saucers" made her laugh. Her left side still hurt when she did.

Descriptions of strange lights whisking people away from remote areas seemed familiar. Stellar Fletts. *They really don't need to know about them,* she thought to herself. She decided to verify Jing Pen knowledge through the Internet when she felt confident enough to elude detection.

Olsen had used his computer to create a mock-up of the interior design ideas Vit Na described to him. She had to simplify the more elaborate architectural concepts according to the limits of her hosts' technology and resources.

Finally she came up with a livable, practicable arrangement for the gymnasium. An old oak tree was cut down and defoliated. Raw cotton fibers were woven into a mesh work that formed a large tent/hammock and stuffed with soft goose down.

The bleacher steps were covered with indoor carpeting, the kind that changes hue when brushed against the weave pattern. Footprints of the clumsy showed easily in the patterns. Vit Na may have been at Jing Penian mercy, but she could still know when they were coming and going.

As she watched Olsen's fingers dance across the key board, she memorized each command he entered. She had been testing all of them individually, to ascertain how sensitive they were to increasing variations in her personal field of influence. *Not very!* she decided.

This is my opening. These Jing Pen cannot process information they have never experienced before, so they ignore it. Plus, they blindly rely on these computers to interpret and organize data. Their machines are only designed to respond to a finite number of algorithms with limited heuristic capacity, and no internal monitoring systems!

Neither the Jing Pen nor their computers have been able to detect my personal field fluctuations yet. With a little time, I can build my own computer access field, complete with an override system to rewrite their programming, right under their noses. I'll be running this whole complex within a week. She maintained an inscrutable facial expression while plotting her coup.

Vit Na probed through the circuits and along the nuances of the underused microchips with impunity. She sensed the stream of data in the so-called cyberspace just beyond the confines of the facility. *Jeen is sure to be monitoring the Internet,* she assumed. She stopped there, as she sensed the safeguards Mendez had put in place to prevent unauthorized external communications from Hennessy Barracks.

Patience, Vit Na, she thought. *Just wait. Their next mistake will come, all in good time.*

* * * * *

Washington returned later that afternoon with a bundle of newspapers. "Now Vit Na, I'd like you to go through these very carefully. Tell me if any of the pictures or symbols are familiar to you."

Vit Na saw that the photos showed pictures of dolls or mannequins in strange clothing, and people in costumes. The captions under the pictures generally said "alien abduction this" or "close encounter that kind."

"No. I've never seen any of these characters before," she said. She turned to one of the pages casually, to hide her recognition of a familiar image. It was distorted for sure, but the pattern was still unquestionable. *The Tyelaj!* It had been reduced to its simplest form: a circle bisected by a sine wave, leaving one light half and one dark half.

This was hard evidence that the Keepers were at least partially responsible for the perversion that was now Earth. She unfolded the page further and could no longer conceal her shock.

There, unmistakably, was an etching of a full grown Si Tyen!

Washington made a mental note of her reaction, then questioned, "What's wrong, Vit Na? You look as if you'd seen a ghos—" She turned the page that lay limp in Vit Na's hand. "A Dragon? That's a dragon. What do you know about dragons, Vit Na?"

Vit Na regained her composure. "I might ask you the same question. How do you come by this name, Dragon? Are these creatures real or are they figments of your collective imagination?"

Washington knew she was on to something and secretly signaled to Olsen to record this session in high resolution video and enhanced sound. "Both, it would appear," she answered.

Vit Na realized she had underestimated Washington. *Another mistake.* They were getting to be a habit for her.

When Vit Na didn't respond, Washington expounded: "Well, dragons are known to nearly every civilization on Earth in one form or another. European mythology describes monsters terrorizing the countryside in ancient times. They were kin to devils and gods — usually the former. The legends peaked and faded in the Middle Ages with the advent of scientific thought and reason.

"In contrast, many eastern civilizations regard the dragon as a mystical figure, bestowed with great wisdom and strength. Whole philosophies have been based on dragon lore ... or is it dragon history?"

Vit Na realized that Mendez, Matthews, Stahl and two guards had moved into the immediate area to listen to her tale of dragons. *I didn't give them enough credit. Their communication skills are better than I thought. Maybe there is some latent telepathic ability. Yet ... this Inhibition Factor seems to behave a great deal like the Poison.*

Did the Keepers ... This last thought frightened her more than she could admit at the moment.

"They were — are called Si Tyen. They are of my people," Vit Na said solemnly.

"Then they do exist!" Mendez exclaimed frantically.

"They did exist here. They must have died out millions of years ago on Earth. Before their extinction, they must have made quite an impression on your ancestors."

"But you don't understand," he persisted. "The legends of men fighting dragons is within the span of our recorded history. They must have lived longer than you think. Maybe they still live here." Mendez was now standing in front of Vit Na as he spoke, unintentionally pushing Washington into the background.

"That seems unlikely. They could never have survived the Holocaust that drove us all out."

"Tell us more about this 'Holocaust,' Vit Na."

"Tell me more about this 'fighting of dragons' first," she countered.

Mendez looked at Matthews for a second, then shrugged. "In times of old, men would slay an evil dragon to save a village or a damsel in distress. It was a feat of great strength and courage."

Images of the Tralkyz confrontation with the Si Tyen she and Tur had seen in the Forest came to mind. "What kinds of weapons were used?" Vit Na asked.

"Traditionally ... broad sword, lance, cross bow, armor and shield."

Vit Na mentally accessed images of the weapons Washington described. *There's no way of killing a Tyen with those weapons. There must be more to it than that.*

"No cannons, no bullets or bombs?" Vit Na asked suspiciously.

"Not back then. Those weapons were not generally available ... and not manageable by a few men when they were," Washington explained.

"Are there any artifacts left of these slayings?"

"No real ones. Sometimes precious gems or ivory are referred to as 'dragon's eyes' or 'teeth.' Dragons were often purported to guard vast treasures." Robyn Washington seemed to be remarkably knowledgeable about dragon lore, Vit Na observed.

"Usually red crystals and gold?" the Melkyz offered.

"Why yes. Now what do you know about such things?" Mendez demanded.

"The Si Tyen often recorded data within crystalline devices. Your ancestors probably stumbled onto those data modules, which were guarded by Animoid sentries. Is the word 'Iku' familiar to any of you?"

Mendez answered question with question. "Should it be?"

"I don't know. I'm just trying to help you. These artificial guardians might have been disrupted by the weapons you described, especially if they were very old and degenerate."

"Vit Na, you said the Tyen were 'of your people.' Are you a baby? Will you mature into a dragon?" Hoyt Matthews asked.

"Or were they the masters you fled?" Bruce Stahl chimed in.

Vit Na couldn't help laughing. "Definitely not! And no. We are a union of nations with no geographic boundaries. Each is comprised of a sea of individuals who act together for the advancement of a common good. Our philosophy is 'May the all live as one.' The Si Tyen are but a single race among equals." She paused. "They have largely withdrawn from social participation in the last several eons."

Then Vit Na sighed. "In many ways, they were the best of us."

The subsequent moments of silence seemed like an eternity. *It's as if they have some sort of latent reverence for the Keepers,* she observed. *Yet they don't seem to consciously acknowledge the Animem Iku state. Maybe I can use that.*

"Your people are the survivors of an awful accident, an accident of our making. We saved some of your ancestors, as many as could be carried in the time left before the end ... or what we thought was the end. Your progenitors grew in the darkness of a crippled planet — A planet that has miraculously healed itself with the help of the Keepers."

"You mentioned the Keepers before. Just who were these Keepers?" Mendez asked.

"A cruel joke. The Keepers of the Faith, were the Tyen — I mean dragons — who stayed behind to heal this world and its wild life from our folly. Your remote ancestors were a part of that wild life.

"The word 'dragon' is strikingly like that of the name of a historical figure of Si Tyen race. The Keepers could not tolerate the toxins and famine that followed, so they died out. Your kind could not understand the knowledge left in the modules, but I can.

"I can light the darkness of your past, Javier Mendez," Vit Na lied. It was becoming easier for her.

"We'll need to assemble a group of specialists. We don't have the expertise to take advantage of this opportunity. Give me twelve hours. ... By the way, Vit Na, do you think you could operate one of these computer terminals if Clyde helped you out?"

Mendez turned, as Vit Na answered with a simple nod and a smile.

* * * * *

"Okay, these are the rules. One: No one knows what we have here before they actually arrive at the base. Two: They tell no one where they're going or who called them. Three: They are to bring any essential equipment or paraphernalia with them. There's no going back until their part of the project is over," Mendez instructed the group.

"What if they ask questions? They are very intelligent people you know, Javier. They're bound to ask questions," Max Hollingsworth interjected.

"Tell them to plan on ten days if they can. Other than that, tell them anything you have to in order to get them here."

After the approval of a short list of experts, each was contacted by a familiar face from Project X. Mendez was surprised and a little uncomfortable at Clyde Olsen's popularity with so many of these intellectuals. As it turned out, Olsen was the computer expert for many a scientist on his off-time. It was yet another credit to his abilities.

The names read like a "Who's Who" of the scientific community. Sometimes the most highly esteemed individual in a particular field was deliberately omitted if the area of interest was "high profile." Their absence would likely attract media attention.

Mendez was good at this. Too good, Hoyt Matthews and Robyn Washington had decided. He was too sensitive to the needs of security not to have had some covert operations in his background, but they could not figure out how a molecular geneticist could be involved in such operations.

The guests of Project X began arriving within hours, brought in by army mail planes. They were mostly dressed in jeans and flannel shirts and carried back packs.

Among the first arrivals were the likes of Claude Morgan, the noted Princeton astronomer; Julian Hardacker, physicist extraordinaire; Will Parker, the flamboyant dinosaur fossil hunter; and Saul Pothel, the famous theoretical mathematician.

Allister Brumbellow, and Neil Cassidy came in the next morning from the UK. Between the two of them, they brought a practical sociological perspective to the table.

All the guests were very inconspicuous, except for the one wheel chair user. That evening a one-way video link would introduce each specialist to Vit Na's voice, while allowing her to both see and here them.

Each scientist suspected they were being prepared for a drill to test their readiness for the eventuality of alien contact. Each was very cooperative and obeyed the rules set forth by Mendez. Vit Na noted that none mentioned the encounters with Efilu so far.

Curious. They seem to take this all in stride. I wonder how much they really know? How does Hoyt say it: I'll "play it close to the vest" for now. I'll let each of them ease into this relationship with me, she decided. *I'll just answer questions.*

"So, Vit Na, where are you from?" Morgan began, speaking in a patronizing tone. Vit Na explained the location of the Efilu Realm and displayed the region on a star map displayed in the computer.

"Oh, I see. And how did you get here?"

"By spaceship of course," she answered. She was amused by his tone. *He's rather casual, as if he receives dignitaries from the Realm everyday ... either that, or he doesn't believe the situation. Is he in for a surprise!*

"Where is this spaceship now?" Morgan asked politely, anticipating a nebulous answer.

"Either destroyed or damaged beyond repair in an expanded orbit. Didn't you see the explosion?"

"What explosion?" Morgan asked with genuine interest.

"The big one two weeks ago."

"You mean the one from the collision between the meteor and that satellite. Yes, that was amazing, but there was no space ship involved in that. I personally saw the recording taken from Hubble. Try again, now." *There's that smug tone again,* she noticed.

"What about the second explosion? It was larger than the first. How do you explain that?" Vit Na probed.

"It was in all the papers and on CNN. The end of the Cold War a few years ago, and the new trade relations with China, prompted the elimination of orbiting nuclear weapons. It was long overdue."

How interesting. A cover up. I wonder if I can safely deviate from the official story? Maybe a strategic slip of the tongue might work. "What about the invasion and destruction of Graham Air Force Ba—" audio transmission was interrupted

She was cut off mid sentence by a voice only she heard. "Vit Na, we need to maintain a few secrets. At least for today. Try to sidestep those questions if possible. We'll help you whenever necessary," Mendez said from monitor screen in front of her. *So I'm being censored. Okay for now.*

"I'm sorry, I'm not a physicist myself. I'm just an archeologist and I don't have a very strong background in the hard sciences," Vit Na admitted truthfully.

"Of course not," The human said condescendingly. *Arrogant little garbage crawler, isn't he,* she thought to herself. She looked forward to meeting this Claude Morgan face-to-face in the morning.

Her interview with Julian Hardacker was most interesting. A victim of rheumatoid arthritis, Hardacker was limited by deformed hands and wrists. He was wheelchair bound most of the time.

Vit Na had never before seen an adult as crippled as he. *How has he survived puberty, much less adulthood,* she wondered? *If he was injured as an adult, who would even try to save him?*

Hardacker was considered one the most brilliant scientists on the planet, however. He certainly was less pompous than the others. Vit Na somehow wanted to like him, but felt uncomfortable around such physical limitations.

At home, should she encounter such an individual of her race or one with which her people had diplomatic relations, she would have been required to kill him to strengthen the race. She knew she had no such obligation here, but didn't someone, she wondered?

She typed out a mathematical equation in answer to his question as to how she arrived here. He made a sound that she could not interpret. He said nothing more that day.

* * * * *

Vit Na made herself as comfortable as possible in her new quarters. She bathed in the warm water of the gymnasium pool out of necessity. The practice, normally enjoyed in leisurely fashion, had to be cut short. The irritation caused by the chlorine made the process of bathing more a chore than a pleasure.

Fortunately, there was no detergent in the water that would wash the precious oils from her downy coat. Her ability to blend was her the most reliable weapon left to her, even if not currently in use. It would do little good now, anyway. They watched her every breath. A sudden unexplained disappearance would set off alarms every where. She needed more than mere invisibility. Vit Na needed a plan.

Vit Na had begun requesting to have certain musical selections with particular rhythms piped into her quarters. The humans had no concept of personal fields, spheres of influence or force fields at all. Occasional references to personal auras only scratched the surface of what humans called parapsychology. She wove power siphoned from the surrounding structure into a force field she constructed from her sphere of influence.

This is a dangerous gamble, she surmised. The power dynamics would have been easily detectable to any Efiluan, even by simpler peoples. *The Inhibition Factor not only prevents intimate communication, apparently it also prevents the sensing of auras and personal fields,* she observed.

Vit Na wove her secret power source right before her captors' eyes. When guards asked what she was doing, she frequently answered, "dancing." *Soon, I'll be prepared to attempt an escape.*

* * * * *

The afternoon went quickly for Vit Na. Now that she had regained her strength, she felt penned in. Even if she just knew she could go out of doors, she would have been more comfortable. Since she could not, she took every opportunity to peruse Animem experiences pertaining to Tyen customs, technology and culture. Most of these took place under open skies.

She found it funny that this was one of the many lessons of her youth for which she had thought she would never have any practical use. Now her knowledge of Tyen Animems presented a chance to manipulate these beasts called "men."

For right now, this knowledge was her sanctuary from this madness, and her only way into a peaceful slumber.

Chapter 20
ORACLE

The warm sunlight streamed across Vit Na's sleeping pallet through the wide Plexiglas windows. It was her only consolation for the limitations of her surroundings. She awoke rested, but wary.

The next round of meetings with 'the experts' were scheduled for that morning. The humans were eager. They would be looking into both the future and the past, through her mind. Vit Na would be doing the same, in effect, through their history and myths. As she did, she would be exploring the age-old question: how does an advanced culture make the transition from savageness to sentience?

This meeting will be a two-way window through time, she thought to herself. Finally the veil of speculation would lift and the secrets of the Keepers would come to light. *Well, this is the day. Mendez's day,* she reminded herself.

Her first meeting would be over breakfast. Washington thought it would be a nice "ice breaker." The victuals were better than usual. Eggs, an unexpected delight that she had forgotten to mention to Dr. Matthews, were plentiful. There was salmon, trout, and catfish — which she developed a genuine fondness for — and fried geese. Big ones at that, just dripping with grease.

To drink, she had plenty of ice water and several gallons of heavy maple syrup at room temperature. She would have to make a note to further investigate this obsession with brown colored beverages. *All these people seem to drink is coffee, cola, tea, both hot and cold, night and day,* she had observed. *Then there's that beer.* The latter was more distasteful than the rest. *Fermented swill.*

Vit Na greeted each of her guests graciously before starting to eat. As expected, they were all dumfounded. Julian Hardacker was the first to find his voice.

"May I be the first from this assemblage to wish you a good morning, Ms. Vit Na." He extended a gnarled hand, which she shook gently with no hesitation. Will Parker just stared for long moments, nodding, apparently sizing her up.

Vit Na smiled triumphantly. *He's thinking, "Now how did they accomplish this hoax,"* she told herself. *He must have seen all of the same newspaper clippings that I did.*

"I'm sure you ladies and gentlemen must have as many questions for me as I have for you," Vit Na began graciously. "If my eating does not offend you, let us begin."

It was a very casual and civil meal. Will Parker and Claude, as Professor Morgan insisted that she call him, dominated the conversation with Vit Na.

"So you're both a dinosaur and an extraterrestrial. How long has it been?" asked Parker.

"Approximately 65 million years, Will. Give or take a few millennia."

"But the fur? When did you develop the fur?"

"We always had it. Most species did anyway, in one texture or another. Most of the larger peoples developed dense pelts for protection."

"Why haven't we found any fossils of creatures like you?" Parker asked.

"People like me? From everything I've seen, you've found less than one percent of the fossil remains of animals from 'our day.' When you have, you lumped together primitive mammals with more advanced animals.

"It's unlikely that you would have found remains of any civilized peoples. The vast majority were disposed of decently, according to our customs. The occasional individual that died while traveling through the wilderness would have been completely devoured by wild animals."

"What about you? Are you a predator or omnivore?" Will Parker asked. He had no way of knowing what an insult that question represented. The "Super Hunters" were elitists and did not appreciate comparison to lesser meat eaters — especially not to scavengers!

Vit Na answered with no obvious offense. "We don't hunt for food anymore, so I guess we wouldn't be called predators, but we are strictly eaters of meat ... and eggs." She punctuated that last item by hoisting an opened, soft-boiled emu egg to her lips. They had been brought in by Hollingsworth, just for the occasion.

"Why don't you need to hunt anymore?" Morgan asked.

Vit Na swallowed before answering, impressed with the logical line of questioning. "Well, we raise livestock now. We only hunt for sport nowadays," she clarified.

"How many different species are there in the Efilu society?" Parker asked. "Oh, about four hundred or so. That includes avian, terrestrial and aquatic peoples. There are several hundreds of thousand of complex wild species, not to mention millions of species of insects, arachnids, crustaceans and other simpler animals." *No need to emphasize that we include Jing in the category of vermin,* she reminded herself.

"Can any of you tell me how this verbal language developed and diversified?" Vit Na looked to Washington for an answer first.

Allister Brumbellow answered instead. "No one is certain how the various languages came about. The origins of individual words are based in antiquity, probably relating to sounds made by various animals or natural phenomena. The possibilities of reproducing these sounds would naturally be limited by the phonetic constraints of the human voice. This would tend to explain why there have been similarities in languages spoken by cultures that never encountered one another."

Vit Na was again impressed. "Something of a natural onomatopoeia, in other words?" Vit Na offered in summary.

"Why yes. I've never heard it put that way, but that's quite correct." Brumbellow said.

"You have incorporated into your language a few terms that are very familiar to me. Words for which you people should have no frame of reference. You describe not only dragons, but also fire birds you call the Phoenix. You also have written about in detail, and even etched, serpents with which you should never have had direct contact. How do you explain this knowledge?"

Answers were so close that Vit Na could almost taste them coming.

"Vit Na, I think you're taking these coincidences a bit too far," Neil Cassidy interjected. "I must admit that I have exaggerated connection between events for theatrical purposes, but what you propose is incredible. These mythological creatures can have no basis in reality. The powers attributed to them defy all the laws of science as we know them." He paused as he considered the source of the implications she made, then urged her to continue.

Vit Na went on, somewhat frustrated by their lack of ancestral memory. "Your legends tell of magical creatures that are like men, yet have the extremities of horses and goats. You describe small, slender men with pointed ears, called elves, and large powerful creatures called ogres. What about them?"

They all looked at one another in wonderment. "Did these creatures really exist?" Harold Goldschmidt asked. Even in retirement, his knack for asking pointed interview questions set him above the average television journalist.

"That's what I want you to tell me!" Vit Na exclaimed in frustration. *How could they be so stupid?*

"Alright," she continued. "What about references to giants four, often ten times the size of men? Your West African cultures describe a race of giants who became so powerful they were banished from the Earth by your gods. They call these giants by name 'Soa,' in some dialects, even as 'So.' Certainly, this is no accident!"

"We don't understand that reference, Vit Na. What is a So?" Hoyt Matthews asked.

"Who! Who are the So? The So Wari, the So Beni, the So Rikhi ... Does none of this strike a note of familiarity with any of you?" Vit Na was beginning to lose her temper. *Such stupidity!*

She forced relaxation to return, before elaborating on her discoveries. "Among the Efilu, there is a race of exceptionally large, powerful people called the So Wari. In the final days of the Efilu on Earth, they were a fledgling race who rose to power in the shadows of their kin, the So Beni.

"In studying your civilization, I perused your most ancient history and art work. West African lore has it that the people who inherited the lands vacated by the So now call themselves the Chi Wari. They are robust, powerful warriors compared to their neighbors. The similarity is too close to be mere chance. You people have a habit of naming yourselves after those you either admire or fear." She watched for responses. All she got was more dumb looks.

Better drop this subject, she cautioned herself. *You'll only give them all headaches, not to mention yourself.*

"Vit Na, what did the dinosaurs look like? I mean the ones we do know about?" Will Parker asked with child-like curiosity.

"Well, as you guessed, the Bolok —which you have descriptively renamed Triceratops — looked much like mammalian pachyderms similar to rhinoceros, elephants or hippopotami.

"You're a ways off on many of the other ancient species, though.

The Stegosaurus, for example, looked more like a robust horse than the monster you portray. Brontosaurs had colorful, feathery manes that helped them blend into their surroundings." *Careful with that term "Blending,"* she told herself.

The questions went on and Vit Na began to notice a peculiar habit among her hosts. *Why do they keep taking liberties with my coat?* she wondered. Morgan casually stroked her neck and shoulder as he passed behind her. *Nearly every one of them has either rubbed me or attempted to all morning. I'll have to put a polite stop to this right now.*

"That is a very offensive practice, rubbing another's integument. It is reserved for family members only. From anyone else, it is usually taken as a hostile act."

A hush fell over the room and Vit Na began to ask herself if she had gone too far with that warning, when she realized they weren't looking at her anymore.

Another man had entered the room. He was dressed in military garb and was flanked on both sides by several armed men with weapons drawn.

"Well, Javier, it would seem you have actually proven the rumors going around Washington these days. We really do have our very own alien."

The man stepped up to Vit Na and stroked her chin. "Hello. I'm Colonel Kenneth Doyle. From now on, I will be your host." He turned to the persons seated at the table and added, "In fact, I will be host to you all for the next several months. Please finish your meal everyone. We'll talk later."

His smile seemed to make even Mendez uneasy. "Javier, you and I have a lot to talk about right now," he said.

"You've been a bad boy."

Chapter 21
THE HISTORY LESSON

"Goddamn Hoyt Matthews!" Colonel Doyle had taken his feet from their comfortable position on the desk he now called his own. "How the hell did he get a former president here so easily? Do he and old Jimmy go fishing together or did Matthews just save the Carter cat?" He threw his hand up in frustration. "Good ol' boys!"

Major Ernie Dixon stood patiently at attention as the Colonel digested the bad news. Former president Carter had been called in as a "humanitarian representative" of the USA. Doyle was really perturbed. "We can't keep a former president holed up here against his will!"

"I didn't hear that sir." The major jutted his chin forward as he spoke, to emphasize the mistake.

Doyle became silent and focused on the young major. "And I didn't say that either," he stated. He waited for another comment from Dixon, but got none.

"Shit, you are ambitious. Okay. Damage control now takes a priority. Carter has only honorary status nowadays, and with this new Republican administration in office, he won't throw that around too much. When does the good President arrive?"

"He did arrive. About an hour ago," Dixon said.

"Dixon, if you're going to work for me, you're going to have to handle yourself better than this. Why am I just hearing about Carter now?"

"You're hearing about it exactly four minutes after I first heard about it, sir. Matthews must have had help overriding the communications lock-out."

"Olsen! The little schmuck," Doyle cursed.

"My guess too, sir," said Dixon.

"Well, what are you doing about it Major?"

"Whatever they did to get President Carter here, they couldn't have given him many details. We'll have to keep it that way. We can completely shut Olsen down, permanently."

"Don't kill him, Major, just break his fingers for me," Doyle said, chuckling at his new protégé's enthusiasm.

"I had nothing so dramatic in mind, sir," Dixon replied, without humor. We can place Olsen and Matthews in the brig. There will be no more hacking for him this go round.

"The secret service will keep to themselves as long as the President is safe and content," he continued. "They never think, they just follow orders. We'll have to keep him in the dark as long as we can and away from our 'guest.' I observed the other guests when they first spoke to the alien over the computer phone link. They thought it was some kind of drill. Perhaps we can help Mr. Carter to the same conclusion."

"Without actually lying to him," Doyle reminded him. "Now, transferring you from your branch of the service to mine will be tricky, but I think we can do it with my connections. Major Dixon, I'd dare say you have a very promising future in my organization."

"Yes, sir."

* * * * *

There appears to be a new chief in the village, Vit Na mused. *It's certainly got most of the natives riled up. I wonder if they'll dispose of the deposed chief by execution, imprisonment or exile? They don't appear civilized enough to simply demote their rivals.*

She looked at the pool and thought about how relaxing a swim would be now, if not for the chlorine. Things were very tense around Hennessy Barracks, but quiet. There were no more questions, no visits from 'the experts' or Mendez's people.

Perhaps this change of leadership will work in my best interests, she thought. *Where there is change, there is confusion. Little things slip. With what I've accomplished so far, chaos can only serve me.*

She continued to fold energy into her personal field for later use.

Now and then, her manipulations drew quizzical looks. When human music was playing, she moved to the rhythms with perfect timing. Her dances were endless entertainment to the men. When no music was playing, she simply smiled and said, "I just can't get this tune out of my head, you know?" and continued her work.

She had been waiting for Hoyt Matthews to visit all day so that they could update her menu. She had some new ideas on food preparation that she thought human technology could handle.

As she waited, she noticed that her guards' uniforms had changed subtly. Their color had changed from green to tan. The little insignias were altered. *How significant is this change?* Vit Na wondered.

One of the new guards came into the gymnasium uninvited. "How are you feeling today? Ya feeling all right?" he asked.

She looked at the name tag over his breast pocket from across the room. "I'm just fine Sergeant McCray," she answered.

He continued to approach her. She noticed the other guards of lesser rank were standing at the open door with weapons drawn. "Can I help you sergeant?" she queried. He was close now.

"How's your side, Vit?"

"Vit Na. You can say it as a single word if that's easier for you."

"Whatever. You don't recognize me, do you? I'm the guy who shot you at Graham AFB. Sloppy aim, but not bad against an invisible target, huh? How did you do that anyway?"

This is too clumsy for an assassination attempt, she thought. *This is more like some kind of provocation. Maybe they're trying to learn more about the blending process. She shivered inwardly.*

"They say that you never forget the face of death. The face of someone who almost killed you. Do you remember this face?" he taunted. Vit Na remained silent.

"No, obviously not. Will you remember it in future?" He shrugged, then extended his index finger in her direction, cocked his thumb up and jerked his hand as if it were a gun. "Sure you will. I'll be watching you, Vit."

Vit Na watched the sergeant exit her gymnasium. *Great! Just what I need, a new ripple in the stream of my life. At least he didn't follow up on that question about invisibility.* Yet she knew that if this one was going to be in charge of security, the subject was going to come up again. *I had better have answers for him next time,* she decided.

Fortunately he seemed even duller than average ... and filled with pure hate. She felt this emotion spilling through the inhibition field. There was something else nearly submerged in the hatred. *Fear!*

Vit Na decided to ignore the chlorine irritation, and paddled around in the pool for a while. She surfaced after a few moments, to see Robyn Washington squatting at the edge of the pool. "Good afternoon Vit Na. You must be confused about all the sudden changes going on around here," Washington said.

"Change is a part of life, Robyn. When you can't direct the stream, you just have to go with the flow." They both smiled at the witticism. Vit Na climbed out of the pool and shook most of the water out of her down.

"I admire your serenity Vit Na. You're very accepting of the situation. You're very interesting in many ways, I'd say."

Vit Na was curious now. "Oh? How is that Robyn?" She moved closer to Washington and lounged comfortably on the indoor/outdoor carpeting.

"Well, for one thing, that coat of yours reminds me most of a leopard or a mink. Yet you seem to enjoy the water so much." *She's stalling,* Vit Na thought. *Both leopards and minks like water. Either SHE doesn't know it, she doesn't know that I know it, or she's making small talk.*

Just wait. She'll come to the point.

"Your people ... Did they go through the changes we're going through?" Washington asked.

"Specifically?" Vit Na prompted.

"Greed, prejudice, selfishness, short-sightedness. These are problems my people face today. We think we root them out and make laws to protect ourselves from them, and yet they keep coming back to haunt us."

Vit Na still sensed hesitation. "These are very general things that any species must go through on the path to civilization. There is something else more specific troubling you Robyn. What's wrong?"

"Do you understand the concept of genocide, Vit Na?" Washington asked.

Vit Na rolled off of her back and propped her head up on her hand to look directly at the linguist. *Now this is interesting. Does she know something about the Poison situation?* "I know the definition of the word, but like many words it is inadequate in and of itself. Context adds another dimension to give the word true meaning."

"We are in danger," Washington let out.

"We are?" Vit Na responded, not sure how the pronoun in question linked her with her inquisitor.

"No, not you. US! Not just this country, but probably the entire human race. We exploit anyone or anything that has what we want, without conscience. We're out of control! I don't know if this means anything to you, but this is not the first time we have encountered aliens."

Vit Na didn't move, but she gazed at Washington with greater intensity. "It's not?"

"No," Washington said gravely.

"You don't mean those ridiculous fakes in your news papers?" Washington shook her head before answering. "No, but they are close to the truth. An alien space craft did crash on Earth fifty years ago. The creatures on board were dead or dying when we found them." Washington looked around furtively. "This is highly classified information. The kind for which people disappear for divulging."

"Go on Robyn. Nothing could be more classified than me. And I doubt that there are any more secure settings than this base," Vit Na said reassuringly.

"Well, the military came in then, as it has now, and dissected the lot of them. Then they analyzed the technology retrieved from the ship."

Vit Na was intrigued. "So what did they learn from that encounter?"

"Nothing then, but the data was stored. I think some agency, I don't know which, has been making slow, but steady headway on those secrets for the past fifty years.

There must have been a breakthrough. Recently we've gained a considerable edge on our competitors in weapons and electronics technology. In fact, we've basically eliminated the competition over the past ten years."

Vit Na interrupted "... You mean the Soviet Union and the Chinese Republic?"

Washington nodded. "I think my government has been deploying some of that technology in covert operations and counter-espionage."

"And you think they may use some of it on me?"

"It wouldn't be the first time. They moved this site from Roswell to Carlsbad, but the intention is still the same."

Robyn Washington again looked nervous. Vit Na appreciated the risk she took, but also realized that Washington was at least as cautious as any human being she had met so far. "Robyn, you've done something to the surveillance systems, haven't you?"

The sharp look she returned was all the confession necessary.

"How long do we have?" Vit Na asked.

"Ten more minutes. Fifteen at the most," was the answer.

Vit Na hesitated for just a moment as she assessed Washington's veracity. Then she said, "The aliens that you describe are unknowns. They sound primitive, but of course I don't know the circumstances of their visit." She whispered the next few words. "I do have a theory about your mysterious abductions though."

Robyn was stunned. "But you said no Efilu has been to Earth since the extinc— the Migration."

Vit Na said, "Very true, but this world has regular LOCAL visitors."

Before Robyn Washington could organize a question, Vit Na decided to take a chance. She might never leave this world. If she were trapped here, she would need something with which to barter. *These people do value information even if they can't use it,* she surmised.

"They are known as Stellar Fletts. Normally they're docile, and avoid larger concentrations of biological life forms. They feed mostly at night, when the Earth's magnetic fountains peak.

"Some humans and their domesticated mammals must be oblivious to the proximity of a magnetic fountain. Apparently, some wander into them when a Flett is browsing. They just get sucked into the funnel. Their unprotected minds are disrupted by the field, and subject to major defects in memory, like confabulation. Extensive DNA damage would certainly lend credence to reports of abduction and experimentation."

After a brief moment of reflection, and a glance at her watch, Washington steered the conversation back to her original point. "The U.S. government, at least certain factions of it, are engaging in various forms of biological warfare."

"At first, their activities included modifying of natural diseases. Then, they began the development of artificial viruses."

Vit Na chimed in. "You mean HIV."

Vit Na was not in the least impressed with her own conclusion, but Washington was. "How did you come to that—"

"Robyn. A virus that is nearly one hundred percent lethal to a single species, that appears abruptly in a single community the larger society deems undesirable, can be nothing but an artificial weapon. That's painfully obvious."

"Are there any precedents from your time?"

"My time is now, Robyn."

"Sorry. I still tend to think of dinosaurs as creatures of the past."

"People, Robyn. Like you, we're just people." Vit Na took the opportunity to plant the seed of empathy in this fertile emotional soil.

Washington said apologetically, "I am sorry. I really meant no offense. I just mean examples from your history— and solutions."

I've got to think carefully about this, Vit Na deliberated. *If this is a set-up this conversation is bound to be monitored. I can't afford to align myself with a weak faction of this culture. Still, there may be a way, if Washington is bright enough to think this through ...*

"Do you know this symbol, Robyn?" Vit Na drew a circle bissected by a sine wave into two equal parts.

"Of course, the yin and yang," Washington answered.

Vit Na nodded approval at the knowledge. "The meaning of this symbol is universal and it governs the Dance of Life everywhere."

She saw confusion in Washington's face. She knew direct explanation of the statement could be considered subversive if overheard or recorded. That could weaken her negotiating position if she ever had to deal with the U.S. Intelligence community, she reasoned.

Vit Na formulated a way to encrypt the answer into fable that was seemingly innocuous.

"There is a tale that has long been told among my people. It has its origin deep in our antiquity, some one hundred and ten million years ago — before we were truly Efilu.

"Our cultural origins are complex and not pertinent to this discussion, but suffice it to say the times were wild and in many ways savage. Intelligence was our greatest weapon against the protomammals and reptiles."

"But I thought—"

Vit Na raised an opened hand to silence a tangential question. "At the time, there was yet no highly developed food source, and we lived on domesticated animals and harvested wild grains. There were only 250 or 300 enlightened species then. International law was young, rigid and naïve.

"There was a particular expanse of terrain right here ..." She pointed directly downward. "... if memory serves me, that was of interest to a race called the Kalkin. They were, for the sake of comparison, much like large ground squirrels. They were exiled from their people for developing different cultural practices and beliefs. They moved in what was then a northward direction, to this area.

"They were few in number, perhaps one hundred or one hundred and fifty thousand strong. There were not enough of them to develop this land into what they needed it to become. Their plight was not a unique one, they discovered, so they struck a bargain with a tribe of — well again, for the sake of reference — a species of powerful antelope the Kalkin had encountered on their travels. They were known as the Tal Lurd.

"A contingent within the Tal Lurd community was eager to explore new frontiers and were curious about the strange Kalkin. The Tal Lurd were adventurous and strong: natural explorers. When they heard tales of the new lands the Kalkin had located, they joined the strangers for the purposes of joint colonization. The leader of the Kalkin surveyed the new country alongside the Tal Lurd chief, and plans were agreed upon.

"The Tal Lurd, being herbivores, cleared the land of trees and unsavory brush the Kalkin could not manage. The Kalkin were omnivorous, eating mostly grubs, berries, mushrooms and a few varieties of shellfish. The clearing process opened flat highlands for burrowing new Kalkin towns. In return, the Kalkin supplied sterile mud which could be fashioned into bricks for Tal Lurd village construction.

"The arrangement worked out quite well for decades ... until the Tal Lurd became too comfortable. There were no predators for them to flee, so the young Tal Lurd spent much of their days engaged in mock battles for dominance and mating rights. It was mostly 'rough housing,' as you might say, but it did get a bit noisy sometimes.

"The Kalkin flourished and developed an aristocracy of sorts. Their industry was limited only by the availability of viable land on which to raise crops and livestock.

"The Tal Lurd ranged over large tracts of land in semi-nomadic fashion. Kalkin nobles began to covet the open territory grazed by their neighbors. They started disturbing rumors about what overwhelming strength the Tal Lurd had, and how unstable were their temperaments. It was said that if the Tal Lurd were to run amok during their wild games, they could wreck an entire Kalkin settlement. A Kalkin could lose an entire lifetime of work, without compensation. That rumor became widely accepted by the Kalkin working class, whose members lived marginally, on the allowances of their lords. They too came to resent and fear the Tal Lurd.

"The Kalkin merchant class devised a plan to exploit the Tal Lurds' competitive nature. In secretly approaching frustrated and rejected Tal Lurd youth, they found that the desire for respect and power ran deep. So, the Kalkin developed potions designed to enhance the Tal Lurd natural abilities. Young megs who found themselves excluded from mating after being legitimately vanquished in the mock battles now learned that they had an alternative.

"A new contingent of strong, aggressive, undisciplined Tal Lurd arose. They not only fought each other, but they pillaged, and killed brothers, elders — anyone who stood in their way. The problem was that as outcasts, they did not have enough training or focus to know 'their way.' They were culturally isolated from their kind.

"Frustrated by lack of identity and ignorant of their proper heritage, they formed rogue mobs. However, the groups seldom grew large enough to effectively challenge the main herd, and suffered from poor leadership.

"Enter the Kalkin merchants. They provided guidance and built a hierarchy for Tal Lurd thugs. Loyalty to the new system was cemented by drugging the young megs with a neurotoxin which made them susceptible to Kalkin telepathy. Within a few generation the Kalkin had honed these lost souls into sterile monsters, capable of nothing but destruction and terror.

"The Kalkin grew rich on the ruthlessness of the new Tal Pen. As slave labor, bodyguards, and suicidal warrior hordes, the Tal Pen wiped out any threat to their Kalkin masters. As gifts for their service they were given captured Tal Lurd mers, but of course, they were sterile. The virile Tal Lurd were slaughtered by Tal Pen rape gangs, to the extinction of the parent race.

"The Tal Pen were further depersonalized by the next development of Kalkin perversion, the Salt Pits. Tal Pen clones were grown inside eyes plucked from the giant serpents of the inland seas. The giant orbs served as incubators, where genetically enhanced Tal Pen were cultivated. The result was a race of biological robots, to use your terminology, who's only purpose in life was to serve the Masters."

"So the Kalkin won," Washington concluded.

"Not exactly. The Kalkin took advantage of Tal Lurd weakness because the Tal Lurd elders ignored a growing problem: an ever growing, disenfranchised population. The Kalkin did not create the depravity, they simply took advantage of an opportunity that was already there."

Washington scratched her neck uncomfortably. "Weren't there any laws to protect the innocent from such temptations as those to which the Tal Lurd youths were exposed?" she asked.

"You must understand, the Law applied to many species then. It had to be adhered to quite strictly. 'Each race shall have its freedom as long as it does no harm to another race.'

"A very naïve statement. You see, the Kalkin found ... how do you say it? ... a loop hole. The Tal Lurd youth took these potions of their own accord.

"In fact, they actually petitioned for their rights to take the drugs. Because the resulting damage and devastation was visited on their own kind, there was no violation of International Law. It was, by definition, an internal Tal Lurd affair — one the Elders would not admit existed until it was too late.

"The problem for the Kalkin was that they failed to recognize their own fatal flaw: they never learned how to stop growing. The Kalkin overused the resources available to them. They were always trying to squeeze more out of their working class than it could produce. When their own workers said 'enough,' the new aristocracy used fear of the Tal Pen to force production out of exhausted Kalkin workers."

"But you said the international community would step in if there was a violation of one race against another," Washington protested.

"So it would," Vit Na conceded. "However, the Kalkin had thought their actions through carefully. Since the Tal Pen were grown from cloned embryos, and not born of Tal Lurd mers, they could no longer be recognized as an independent species. They were property of the Kalkin. As always, the rich got richer.

"Neighboring peoples, however, did not tolerate unchecked Kalkin expansion. Indirectly, they cooperated to undermine Kalkin economy. Eventually, the Kalkin merchants began to squabble and feud over their dwindling resources. They used Tal Pen gangs to attack each another as the Kalkin Republic crumbled around them.

"Finally bankrupt, their food supply exhausted and the population unsustainable, Kalkin civilization fell. Many Kalkin starved. Stagnant water and rotting flesh caused many more to die of disease. There was violence and killing to rival that of the nearly forgotten Tal Lurd riots. The Tal Pen were completely destroyed in the violence, while protecting their Kalkin lords.

"The Kalkin aristocrats fled back to their parent nation and were reabsorbed. We suspect that their descendants rose again as the Sulenz people, but no one is certain."

"The four horsemen of the apocalypse rode even then," Washington murmured. *Biblical references,* Vit Na observed.

"So the moral of the story is that the Tal Lurd should have disciplined their young better and the Kalkin should not have coveted their neighbors' lands. That still does not give me any answers," Washington said.

Vit Na smiled, and thought, *Now for the useless information that she really wants.*

"To answer your interpretation, specifically: yes. Following the perversion of the Tal Lurd, a law was enacted to prevent the development of sentient weapons and slaves. However, in the ages to follow, some of the Efilu found yet another loophole in the law. That is how those monsters you know as Tyrannosaurus Rex came to exist. Of course, we collectively dealt with that problem, permanently."

Maybe someday when she repeats the story, it will dawn on her that the tale has more than one moral, Vit Na thought hopefully. *There will always be weak individuals in any group. If they are disgruntled and disillusioned, they become easy prey for corruption and can be turned into an irresistible force of destruction. On the other hand, exploiters are inherently parasitic and add little value to any system. Once fat, they will eventually feed upon each other in order to maintain their hedonistic existence.*

Vit Na contemplated. *There must always be a struggle, an ever shifting balance of force, a Dance of Life. It's not easy, but it does provide both stability and passion — a reason to exist that strengthens its participants.*

The fable had always been an interesting bedtime story for cubs, designed to amuse and teach. Under these circumstances, it didn't seem so amusing to Vit Na.

Washington began to leave the room when she turned with a curious look and said, "I can see why the fable has survived as long as it has. She eyed the camera on the ceiling. It was still disabled.

"We are in danger of perverting our own so-called undesirables into monsters, so that some bastard's unthinkable dirty work will get done. How does a society ensure the rights of the individuals?" Washington asked.

Vit Na's shoulders shrugged. "The people must move beyond intelligence, to enlightenment."

Humbly, the linguist asked, "How?"

Vit Na acknowledged her candor and said simply, "The usual way. First, learn the difference between what you want and what you need. The path becomes easy after that."

"Where to begin?" Washington said, seeming overwhelmed by it all.

"I don't know, Robyn. It really doesn't matter."

Vit Na smiled, then thought silently to herself, *It didn't matter then and it doesn't matter now.*

Chapter 22
MOURNING'S SOLACE

"Nothing yet from Car Hom?" Tur asked. The question had become almost rhetorical by now. Tur generally was pleased with the intelligence reports Bo Tep gave, but it had been over two weeks since the Repam was last seen. No communications of any kind were forthcoming.

He had long since stopped asking about word on Vit Na.

"We'll recheck the receptor field, it may need recalibrating," Bo Tep replied.

Everyone was now centralized in the northern sanctuary. Thompson AFB was still secure under Weepf's efforts. After its acquisition, Bo Tep had turned over the Aleutian base of operations to her.

It was time for the bi-daily update with the staff.

"At least our technical support is improving," Devit began. "In spite of the limitations, we've been able to arm and monitor this entire quadrant. Fortunately, the local tribe is routinely monitoring the activity on the rest of the globe and transmitting directly to us at regular intervals. We've been enhancing their signals via sensor fields."

"Any new arrivals from beyond the atmosphere, Los? Even crystal beacons?" Tur's thought projections were solemn.

"Not so far. We're using the most advanced of the orbiting equipment with modifications that Devit and I came up with, but no activity so far, Commander."

Tur looked down the table with concern. On top of this latest news, he was noticing that Ikara had been withdrawn for the past two sessions. She had provided no useful reports on the U.S. government activity, or broadcast news interpretations. Jeen and Kellis had voiced concerns about her coping mechanisms.

Doh broke the silence. "I wish Car Hom would at least signal us with an estimated time of return ..."

"He's not coming back you idiot!" Ikara screamed, with searing thought projections. "He's dead! The Repam's not coming back because it was destroyed. Who are we kidding? We all saw it go up in a ball of flames!" She walked over to Tur, and began circling him as she shouted hysterically.

"We're trapped here! Stuck on a mud hole crawling with hairy monsters!" Her shouting had turned to ranting.

Tur grabbed her by the shoulders, and shook her thrice. "Ikara, we number only twenty here now. You six department heads, and a few technicians. There are only ten or eleven of us that can function as security or combatants if it comes to that. You are large enough to help in a tough situation, but I need you to be in control of yourself.

"I can't afford to have one or two of my meren nurse you. WE can't afford that right now. As much as I need you, I'd be forced to take more PERMANENT action. Do you understand?" He shook her again to drive the point home.

Ikara was no longer raving. She projected her next thoughts with the utmost clarity. "That famous So Wari efficiency. Eliminate any internal hindrance to the operation. What does the So Wari code of battle say about allowing emotion to interfere with war campaigns?"

Tur's eyes narrowed and he tilted his head to one side in confusion. "Your losing it Ikara. We're not in battle."

"Turtle spit we're not! We've lost thirty meren on the Repam. We lost Stihl in direct battle with these animals. *Stihl,* a fully trained So Wari warrior!

"Now we are hiding from their patrols like grubs from a Sulenz pup, while you lament the loss of your friend, Vit Na." She beat her fists against his chest. "Now tell us all again how we are not at war!"

"They're just fur mi—" one of the staff members tried to interject, but Ikara never took her eyes off of Tur.

"NUK! These fur mites destroyed a Class Five interstellar Efilu warship! We destroyed the entire Quatal race for less than That! Is this any less a Threat to Life than 'The Poison' itself?"

Los added, "How DO we know that none of us have been affected by The Poison? We have no way of scanning for it without the Repam's equipment."

A group shudder seemed to move through the room. No one wanted to comment on that very real possibility ... or its ramifications under these circumstances. *Leave it to Los to stir an already volatile situation,* Tur grumbled to himself.

The High Commander looked around at his assembled meren. All were attending the exchange, but not even Bo Tep had anything else to say.

"They're beating us Tur!" Ikara continued. "These bugs are not only beating a So Wari high commander, but they're intimidating him as well." He silently turned, his expression inscrutable, and walked toward the door.

"TUR!" Ikara pleaded.

The warrior half turned to address the distraught mer. "Ikara. Your point has been made. I trust my point was equally as clear." Then to the group as a whole, he said, "We'll reconvene by dark. I want a complete analysis of the enemy's strengths and weaknesses, as well as our opportunities to exploit any natural threats to Jing Pen life.

"Dismissed."

*　　*　　*　　*　　*

"So, what have we got?" All twenty of the remaining Efilu had assembled in the big hangar next to the conference room. Tur was resting on his haunches as he spoke.

"Well, we have something special for you Commander," Devit announced, smiling for the first time since the landing. Tinkering with scarce materials was his forte, and the reason he had been selected for the mission. "How do you like this?"

Tur looked up at the gelatinous mass lurking in the shadows of the hanger.

"Is this what it looks like?" Tur asked in amazement. Devit grinned. His long plumage seemed to dance around his deep teal face.

"How did you make a mini-wave?" Tur asked in genuine astonishment.

"In the Roog corpuscle. It's the basis for the gel synthesizer, anyway. Dru Log let us use his while he swam around in the cove outside for a few hours."

"Devit, this means we now have PRODUCER equipment! We can make anything we need!" Tur exclaimed, openly exuberant.

"Hold on now commander. It's not that easy. This is a very limited mini-wave. We can't funnel enough energy through it to make anything fancy."

"We don't need anything fancy." Tur said firmly, more in character. "All I need is a few more gel consoles for basic equipment production and a telescien or two ..."

"That we can manage, Commander."

"Great. Bo Tep. Weepf. These are the things I'll need from you ..."

As the meeting progressed, Bo Tep and Weepf reviewed holographic plans and made the appropriate changes and additions.

"Ikara, I want you focused now," Tur instructed. He pointed to a tree diagram with various characters on its branches representing what was known of the U.S. Government.

"I want to know these individuals better than their own litter mates do. I'm going to pay their chief a little visit."

* * * * *

"Are you saying we got them all?" President Rhodes asked skeptically. The ad hoc committee on the Alien Invasion had attended the meeting well prepared. Jonathan Rhodes would accept nothing less.

"We are not prepared to make that assumption just yet, Mr. President, answered the Secretary of Defense, Henry Mason. "We haven't seen any sign of disturbance of the wilderness or caverns. Meanwhile, the army has been gassing, then bombing every cavern within five hundred miles of Graham AFB.

"We're now at Phase Two: searching for bodies. We have had nominal human casualties so far in this operation I'm told." The Secretary of Defense was an old hand at the word game. He seldom lost because he never chose the wrong word. "From what our reports show, they're too big to hide in anything more crowded than a small rural city." They'd be too conspicuous.

The President's secret task force included Wilfred Chatham, Secretary of State; Mason, the Secretary of Defense; General Michael

Chey, Head of the Joint Chiefs of Staff; and Major General Dale Schmidt, Head of Department D.

General Joseph Ashy, Dale Schmidt's superior and head of US Space Operations, was on Rhodes hit list to be replaced. His absence sent the message to those in attendance: unofficially "kicked upstairs."

"Mike, what do you make of all this?" The President asked.

"As the Secretary says, sir, we're taking it one step at a time. We haven't found any aliens yet, but we haven't stopped looking."

"That's the kind of answer I was looking for gentlemen. Any word from Major Rollins, Mike?"

"Yes, sir, but all reports are negative for new activity," answered Chey. "Challenger II has been in orbit for over two weeks now. We've been feeding the press all kinds of double talk, but sooner or later they're going to demand some answers."

"So we tell them that its a matter of national security and there's no further comment. What's so difficult?" said the President.

General Chey deferred to Secretary Chatham with a glance. "It's against the law, Mr. President," said the Secretary. Without waiting to be asked why, he said, "There is a little known law that's been on the books for several years. It's known as the Declaration of Principles of Conduct in the Event of Contact with Extraterrestrial Intelligence. This declaration requires sharing of any and all information that pertains to alien encounters of any kind."

Rhodes slammed his fist on the studded leather arm of his chair. "What JACK ASS signed that bill into law?" he demanded, alluding to the opposing party.

After some hesitation, Chatham volunteered, "It was signed eight years ago, sir." Feeling some mild embarrassment for his own party, the President laughed. "At least it was a kinder, and gentler jack ass!"

The other men joined in with soft laughter.

"Okay. So, who are the watchdogs we're dealing with nowadays? What's the name of that group ... SETI?"

"I believe General Schmidt is better prepared to answer that question than I am, Mr. President," Chatham said. After a nod from Rhodes, the he yielded the floor.

"Dale?" asked the Commander-in-Chief.

"SETI, a.k.a. Search for Extraterrestrial Intelligence, is defunct, Mr. President," replied the Head of Department D. "Lack of funds, lack of support, lack of results. Many of SETI's high profile members have since found other interests. After all, why spend time and energy searching for the truth when fiction is so much more interesting?

Opening the file on Project Blue Book after SETI was terminated was the smartest thing we ever did.

"The fanatics have waded through all the reams of alien abduction accounts, UFO sightings, and crop circle hoaxes. They have actually been of some help in correlating incidents that our personnel never connected. Of course, the Department has been monitoring the Internet for key words relating to alien encounters. In effect, we have 'volunteer experts' unwittingly working for us around the clock. Only twenty people outside of this room know that Department D has picked up where Blue Book left off."

Department D was a small, but extremely well funded, independent subdivision of the CIA. The reasoning behind it was that independence and power would give the U.S. an edge if an extraterrestrial dimension were ever to develop. The rest of the intelligence community would be thrown into a state of chaos. Adaptability and foresight would be the characteristics of the new leaders in espionage. Department D was designed to establish that lead.

"The man I have immediately supervising the project, Colonel Doyle, has been doing a great job. If anything significant happens, day or night, I hear about it within the hour."

"And?" asked the President.

"Nothing yet, Mr. President. Doyle and I have a standing meeting three times a week. This morning's report was remarkably underwhelming. I thought he'd find something for sure after the incident at Graham. Ken interrogated every man on the base. The aliens were either routed or destroyed without a trace. We combed the base from ceiling to floor. Nothing."

"Where's Doyle now?"

"With General Chey's permission, Mr. President, we've assumed command of a small army base in New Mexico as temporary field Head Quarters. There was a major in command. I don't recall his name. Hennessy Barracks boasts a compliment of some 500 men and staff."

"What's that, about three companies, General?" asked Chatham.

"Yes, sir."

With a wave of his hand, the President let it be known that he was not impressed by the Secretary of State's rudimentary knowledge of military organization, and wanted no further interruptions. He was very interested in what Schmidt had to say.

Schmidt continued. "Hennessy is well equipped and the staff is excellent, gentlemen. Most of them are assigned to test fiber optic communications systems and train field support techs for special operations. The equipment is state-of-the-art. Some even experimental."

"So, it's a training base for spies," The President concluded.

"That's why it's not on any map," said General Chey with subdued pride.

"Gentlemen, I don't relish the chore of signing my name to letters for families of dead soldiers," said Rhodes. "And I don't like having to tell them that their sons, husbands and fathers died as victims of 'friendly fire' in a training exercise. It's a lie and it makes the U.S. Army look incompetent. Hell! It makes ME look incompetent. I don't like that. Not one bit.

"I want these monsters. I don't care what you have to do, but I want them. I want them for the lives they cost us, and for the resources they've forced us to waste so far.

"Their ship has been completely destroyed. Nothing could have survived the blast from fifteen nuclear warheads. Challenger confirms no remnants of the intruder. I want to feel equally confident that any aliens that have been deposited on the ground have also been neutralized. The nest of them in Sudan was destroyed at the cost of two hundred fifty American soldiers. Exterminating their murderers will be small enough consolation for those boys, but I intend to at least give them that.

"Now, unless there is something else ..." The President waited a moment for questions then said, "That will be all, gentlemen. Thank you for your help."

*   *   *   *   *

"There can be no consolation for the comrades we've lost. This entire world doesn't have enough collective soul to repay the losses," Tur said with an intense passion that was rare for a So Wari.

Then, almost as if he had become self-conscious about the emotional content of his words, his demeanor became cold. "No matter. As we've all grown tired of hiding in the shadows, a more aggressive posture is clearly indicated. The weapons Devit has fashioned are more than equal to any arsenal these vermin can muster.

"Still, there's no need to waste resources. This culture is sufficiently fragmented to make subjugation a matter of applying strategic pressure to weaknesses."

Tur met the eye of each of his meren. "You see," he said, "in the end, it comes down to a battle of wits."

Chapter 23
LA COSA NOSTRA

"Are we getting all of this?" Colonel Doyle asked his assistant as he watched the monitor screen intensely.

Dixon's answer was a little rushed. "Yes, sir. Every interview has been recorded from three angles. Editing will be done at your discretion."

"Good, good ..." Doyle said absently, transfixed by the series of questions the various interviewers asked of Vit Na. He made notes on a pad as he listened.

"... So you didn't just build a giant space ship and take off to some distant world," Professor Morgan said.

"Of course not, Claude. We made a number of colonies on the way to our present home," Vit Na answered.

"What I still don't understand is how your people could have done that. There are certain limitations that even your people would have been forced to observe. For example, there are only a few earth-sized planets in this solar system. We have investigated Mars, Venus, and several moons of the outer planets. We haven't found a trace of life, much less intelligence anywhere."

"I suspect you're looking in the wrong places, Claude. You see—"

"Underground! You built settlements under the icy surfaces of the moons. That's why we haven't seen any of your ancient colonies."

"No. Not exactly. Again I don't have all the details, but my ancestors colonized the gas giants."

Morgan had already asked the obvious question. Vit Na continued, with a vague answer. "A physicist would be better suited to discuss the particulars, but as I understand it, retexturing the gas worlds had to do with establishing a platform at a distance from the gaseous body sufficient to reduce the effective gravity field to match that of Earth. Large platforms were woven of polymers derived from waste material. They floated on the surface of the gaseous atmospheres. There's more to it than that, but that's the gist of it."

"To say that I'm intrigued would be an understatement. You must tell me more about. ..."

Morgan droned on about the technicalities of space colonization, but Vit Na was no longer listening. *Come on little chief. I know you're watching me. Come get me! I have what you want. The power you crave.* She tracked the monitoring cameras as they followed her every gesture around the gymnasium. He was up there, this Doyle. She could feel it — not with her personal field, but something else. Something more ... basic. It was as if she had another sense she hadn't previously known about, but the knowledge seemed perfectly natural.

She instinctively fed Morgan coils of uninformative answers. She spoke in riddles, with never-ending "I don't know's" and "That's not my forte's." She made it plainly obvious that she would not let the new chief get anything cheaply. What he wanted, he would have to come after himself. *How deep is your patience little chief? Do you even know you're being tested?* she wondered. Somehow she knew he did.

"The little bitch is being evasive," Doyle said aloud. Major Dixon inquired. "Sir?"

"Huh. Oh, I was just thinking out loud, Dixon. That lizard is feeding this guy crap by the shovel. She knows much more than she's telling him. Any idiot could see it. Mendez and these assholes he's hired have been treating her with kid gloves. No wonder they haven't learned shit."

Dixon didn't answer. The new "Old Man" was now on his feet and pacing. He didn't want to debate interrogation tactics and Dixon knew it. He was deciding how much info he could get out of the alien before he had to kill her. Dixon had seen this look before on the faces of other men — men of power with a hunger for more power. Ernie Dixon had seen this same look in the mirror of late.

This look could kill.

* * * * *

Major Dixon had been up all night. He was now, de facto, Colonel Ken Doyle's right hand. He felt like Doyle had plunged that hand to the bottom of a cesspool and asked him to pull the stopper. Dixon was in over his head. "Sir, we have everything we need on order. We can have it with in the week."

The colonel shot him a cross glance. "Within THIS week soldier. It's Friday already."

"But sir, the cost. We've already spent more money than we had in our budget, plus that chest of cash you brought with you."

Doyle spoke without turning. "In this matter Uncle Sam has given us carte blanche. Understood?" He didn't wait for a reply. "Now, run down the inventory I ordered."

"Inner Vision's next generation MR scanner. The Sensidyne 6000 biochem analyzer. The Bull's Eye laser probe. The Hermes One containment isolation system, and the Crick's Step Ladder nucleotide sequencer. That's the bulk of it, sir. Then there's the $1.2 million in conventional equipment and civilian support staff you asked for. Most of this stuff I've never even heard of before and my dad worked for GE."

Doyle looked at the young major dubiously. "Of course you haven't. They're mostly prototypes. We don't even know if they'll work. We're sort of ... testing them for these folks." Major Dixon still looked uncomfortable. "We do it all the time." Doyle finished.

Dixon knew he was treading across thin ice. He decided to drop the subject and get to a safer topic. "We can get the inventory delivered, but the question is: where to put it all? Hennessy Barracks can't even accommodate all that equipment much less utilize it."

"It's not coming to Hennessy Barracks, Major, It's going to San Francisco."

Major Dixon was dumfounded. "Sir?" he said.

"We're going to need more operating funds. Are you up to it, Major?"

*   *   *   *   *

So. He wants to meet me on his own terms. Vit Na now found herself in a cell that was even smaller than the original one ... and more heavily fortified. *So now I know something else about this Colonel Doyle. Not only is he bold and ambitious, but he's cautious as well,* she mused. Her feet and hands were bound firmly by steel bands to the arms of a make-shift forechair. Even her tail was restrained. *I really find myself looking forward to this interrogation,* she thought.

Colonel Kenneth Doyle entered the cell without reservation. He spun a chair around and sat in it backwards, resting his arms on top of the back of the chair. When he tipped the chair forward as he sat, it resembled a forechair. *Interesting!*

Doyle was flanked by two personal guards. One was that same Sergeant Jerry McCray. He stood silently behind Doyle and made that threatening gesture with his fingers again. Vit Na wasn't sure if Doyle knew it or not.

"So, Vit Na. How's tricks? Are you enjoying the hospitality?" Doyle said, with a smile. She noticed that it was a different kind of smile, this one had. It conveyed no comfort, no warmth. Just a hunger. It brought to mind that broken tailed rat. Reminiscence of its fate brought a smile to Vit Na's face. The smile was almost a reflection of Doyle's.

"I've been very comfortable. Thank you for asking. Your sergeant there has made me feel so safe in the confines of my quarters. Now, how can I help you?" she said smoothly. *Lets see how he handles that,* she thought.

Oddly, his smile broadened yet seemed to fade at the same time.

"I'm glad you asked. I've been listening to your conversations with the other—"

"Oh, Colonel? I was under the impression that eavesdropping was considered impolite, even in this culture," Vit Na interrupted. Again she smiled, a pretty, disarming smile.

Doyle's smile faded further.

"Yes. Well, survival sometimes supersedes etiquette, my dear. As I was saying, I've been watching you very closely. I think you know that. I also think you know more about your friends and their technology than you will admit." He waited for a response. He only receive another smile accompanied by an intense glare.

"You may not realize this, but we did get one of your compadres." The shock value of that statement was obviously effective. "Oh, didn't anyone tell you? I guess not. Oh, don't get excited. And don't get your hopes up for rescue either. It's dead." The calm quickly returned to her face, but Vit Na had to wonder, *Who did I lose?*

"Whatever it was, it put up a hell of a fight. It was no match for our weaponry, though. Maybe you're not all so high and mighty after all."

Vit Na answered him smoothly, "Then why am I here, Colonel?" Tilting her head back, she still managed to look downward at him even though she was in restraints.

"I'm glad you asked," Doyle replied. He snapped his finger for the third man in the room to hand him a tablet. "Just how did they make you invisible?" Vit Na tensed imperceptibly. *I thought I had put them off of that topic,* she thought.

"As I told Dr. Mendez, I don't understand the technology used to do that," she said.

"I know. You're just an archeologist," Doyle said. He leaned forward in the chair again. "But I'm not Mendez. So tell me again. This time with feeling." The other guard had handed him some kind of mechanical device that Doyle now switched on to life. Instantly, electric current lanced through Vit Na's body.

Fortunately, it was a surprise which she was able to control easily. She noted the reaction her initial response drew from the men before her and decided to duplicated it each time the current flowed. Meanwhile, she increased the impedance of her skin to the point that a hundred fold increase in current would cause no significant discomfort. *If they believe they are doing me harm, manipulating the situation may become all the easier.*

"Please don't make me hurt you again, Vit Na. That's really not my goal. Just answer my questions as truthfully as possible and let's all just get along. Okay?" That deviant smile returned with as much sparkle as ever. "Now one more time. Why were you at Graham AFB?"

She hesitated just long enough to effect the resignation the circumstance called for, then answered just before Doyle hit the buzzer again. "We were a reconnaissance team. Our leader wanted to know just what we were up against. I was sent to guard the team leader's back. I guess I didn't do such a good job of it though."

Doyle didn't swallow that as readily as she had hoped. "How were you selected for the mission in the first place?" he asked suspiciously.

"I was not a volunteer, that's for sure. As nearly as I can guess — and that's all I can really do — it was on the basis of my size."

Doyle leveled his chair with all four legs on the floor and said, "Explain."

"Many of my people are too large to stealthily negotiate your corridors and stairways," she said. Vit Na recognized their hesitation as the colonel and his men decided to believe the lie or not. She added, "I was the wrong size, at the wrong time in the wrong place. So I got picked for a suicide mission. After all, who needs an archeologist when you're at war?" She waited for the response.

"That's a good question. Why did your mission require an archeologist, Vit Na? I assume you weren't picked at random," Doyle asked.

Damn! He's better at this than I thought he'd be. His thinking really embodies military training. I must watch what I say. "This started out as a scientific expedition," she said aloud.

"And what was the nature of this mission?" he asked.

She thought through possible interpretations and misinterpretations of her most likely answers, before replying. "We were searching for fossilized microbes. They were a missing piece of an important puzzle on my world."

"And your job, specifically?" Doyle prompted.

She smiled to herself. *Fascinating. I had wondered how this culture was driven without the pressures exerted by predators. This Doyle is the missing link. They breed predators from within! Doyle is as focused as any hunter I've seen. He has already devoured Mendez and has probably undercut his superiors in the Jing Pen military machine. This may prove an interesting contest. Modern intellect against primitive pack mentality.*

Doyle cleared his throat to remind her of the electrical stimulator. Ignoring the threat, Vit Na smiled pleasantly. "I'm sorry. I was distracted for a moment."

Doyle affected offense. "Sorry if we're boring you. We'll try to be a little more entertaining." He fingered the controls of his torture device menacingly.

She spoke. "My job was to locate sites of major city ruins in the remains of the continents we left behind."

Doyle's interest was piqued. "Ruined cities? What ruined cities?" He then raised a hand and rephrased. "A better question would be, where are these ruins?"

"The ruins were a myth. Any remnant of our civilization is mired deep in fossilized excrement — what you call oil reservoirs. There's no way to get to it, even with your greatest technology. Sorry." She sounded convincingly sincere.

"What about those treasures you mentioned? Dragon treasures?" Doyle looked down at his note pad to remind himself of the details. "You told Mendez that the dragons used some kind of crystal device to store data. Where would be the most likely place to find such gems?"

She looked trapped for only a moment before starting to answer, but she was cut off.

"And don't give me any of that 'I don't know crap.' As you have pointed out, you're 'just an archaeologist.' No one could know where to find 65 million year old equipment better than you!"

He had her there. There could be no other reason for bring an archeologist countless light years into outer space unless she were assigned to locate valuable artifacts, and she knew it. *And so evidently does he.*

"You mentioned that there was another one of us captured ... and killed. May I see him?" Vit Na asked, now staring the colonel down.

"Why? What good will it do you?" He seemed to consider the request for a moment, then consented. He nodded to the corporal to his left. "Tingley? Bring in the 'specimen.'" The corporal took off to fetch the item.

Doyle pressed on.

Efficiency, Vit Na noted.

"So, tell us about your military strength here. Your friends may have been able to hide from those boobs in Washington, but I know we didn't get you all. In fact, I know we didn't get anybody who isn't expendable to him."

Vit Na cocked an eyebrow. "Who is HIM?" she asked.

"Why your leader, of course," Doyle answered. "I know he must be out there somewhere, reconnoitering, biding his time."

She regarded him carefully for a long moment. He just smiled back at her. Waiting.

"You have a remarkable sense of military strategy, Colonel. However do you come by it?" she asked, almost angrily. His smile broadened. "Easily." *This is a true predator,* she decided, *and at least for right now, he has the sharpest teeth.*

"That was an interesting conversation you had with Ms. Washington yesterday. How does your society view mixing of the races?" The question probably was not as facetious as it sounded, Vit Na decided. She sensed that this Jing Pen did not waste words often. "Do you root for the underdog, or is it survival of the fittest?"

Vit Na almost laughed as she answered, "A little of both, actually."

Corporal Tingley returned, nervously carrying the "specimen" draped in a small, white sheet. "Ah. Here's your friend now." He reached up, took the package from his subordinate and held it in his lap. "Now, I hope you two weren't very close." He ripped the sheet off of a charred, dismembered forearm and hand.

Vit Na couldn't help but recoil at the site of the So Wari limb. She didn't even hear herself gasp in horror, "Tur!"

"Who is Tur?" Doyle asked intensely. Vit Na hesitated for just a heartbeat. Then answered, with resignation. "Tur is the one you seek. He is the Leader."

"Too bad he went head first into the fray. Looks like he's one dino who is permanently extinct," Doyle clucked. Vit Na strained against her restraints in anguish.

"Vit Na. Just who was this Tur to you anyway. Your boyfriend?" Doyle was cruel, almost taunting now.

She countered with restored calm and an unexpected weapon: candor. "No, he wasn't my BOYfriend. He was my BEST friend. I understand your tactics and your intentions as well. You want to know if you can cross breed me or the nucleic material from this bone tissue with an animal you can control." Doyle was momentarily taken aback by her keen insight. She sighed, "I'm never going to see him again!"

Doyle's levity resumed. "Sure you will. You'll both live happily ever after in dino heaven."

Vit Na shook her head. Her eyes closed tightly. "You vicious little beast. You think your little band of ruffians can stand against So Wari power? You'll see the shadow of death before he does."

Doyle, still laughing, said. "That'll be some trick considering his condition and all." He shook the seared hand in mockery.

"So Wari power doesn't look that tough to me." McCray added.

"You asked about our military strength. A war is first won in the heart, then in the mind, then in reality. That was an example of a warrior's heart. To fight against all odds so that others may triumph. Sacrifice is too weak a word for this phenomenon." Vit Na said. Then nodding to the severed limb, she stated. "The one who made this sacrifice wasn't Tur. The remains are too small."

"So, we're supposed to get scared because you've got a bigger T-Rex up your sleeve? We'll burn the next one down just as easily. You see, now we're ready for you." Doyle said with confidence.

Time to shake him up a bit. "The meg you so proudly mock was severely wounded. Notice the irregularities of the finger bones? They've all been broken. This warrior survived that first explosion in space. Healing took place within hours. Not only did he survive your worst, he stood head-to-head with your combined armed forces. More over, he did it unarmed. He single-handedly decimated your pitiful armada. This one," she added with reverence. "Stihl was his name."

The humans were silent for a moment. Doyle handled the 'specimen' with newfound respect. The other two showed more fear than anything else.

Trying to rally courage in his men, Doyle taunted her again. "You make these So Wari sound like Jedi knights or something!"

Vit Na responded solemnly, "Or something."

"So, what are we going to have to fight now, the champion or what?" His demeanor was more serious now.

Vit Na's tone had become grave. "Now you will face Tur. HE is like nothing you've ever imagined. The So Wari, as a people, have not lost a war in the seventy million years of their history. They represent the vanguard of the most successful coalition of species this galaxy has ever known.

"No intelligent race in the stars would ever consider challenging a So Wari head to head. They are the ultimate martial artists, on EVERY level. You should take pride in the death of this one." Again she gestured toward the arm in Doyle's lap. "You've seen nothing. Tur has been working around you as one would to avoid getting the pulp of crushed insects on one's foot ... Until now," she spat.

"Earlier, you mentioned war. Are we at war with him now, Vit Na?"

"You've made the mistake of placing yourselves in harm's way. Well, you have Tur's undivided attention. Now there's no place for you to hide — not even in this military underworld you've created, Doyle." She left off mention of his rank for the first time in the interrogation. He didn't notice.

"You know nothing of WAR. You play games of dominance with your kin and call it war. You don't even have your Si Tyen benefactors to guide you. You've slain all the dragons," she added.

Doyle searched her eyes for hints of a bluff. "He can't be all that. He'd have made his move already," he said.

Vit Na sounded sympathetic now. "By the time you see him, it will be far too late."

Ken Doyle faltered. "You make this Tur sound like some kind of super God-fucking-zilla ..."

Vit Na smiled thinly. "No. More like your Satan."

A hush fell over the men. Even Doyle could find no words.

Vit Na's voice cut through the silence like a razor. "You started this game, Doyle. Now you're alone on the field with Him, and you don't even know the rules."

Chapter 24
THE ART OF WAR

The morning was cool. Jonathan Rhodes stood on the verandah overlooking a calm meadow. The secret service man sitting by the door was his personal body guard, Mike Palmer. The six-foot-four, 260 pounds of muscle sipped on a hot cup of coffee. The President was half finished with his own cup. He was grateful for the solitude Camp David afforded him. The other secret servicemen were stationed at various check points. Inconspicuous, but ever vigilant.

The First Lady and children were visiting family this weekend. He had the cottage all to himself ... and twenty-five guards. The President nodded to the agent on the porch and retired to the library. There, he looked for a pair of glasses he had left on the bookcase. Upon finding it, he shut the door behind him. Settling in at his desk he proceeded to catch up on some work he had brought with him.

"There appears to have been a misunderstanding, Jonathan Rhodes. One that should be cleared up forthwith," intoned an unexpected visitor. The President looked up to see Tur addressing him from the center of the room.

Telescien technology allowed Tur any conceivable metamorphosis. His current height of two meters was limited by the dimensions of the room. Assuming such a diminutive size made him uneasy so, Tur stood with an unusually formal posture. This telescien projection was not as elaborate as the one he used in the Tomet encounter, but it would serve his purposes today.

The President was startled by the intrusion. He looked past Tur to check if the door was open. It was not. He did not recall seeing or hearing it open since he himself had entered the library.

"Who are you and what are you supposed to be dressed up as? Furthermore, how did you get in here?" Rhodes asked indignantly. He touched a secret alarm under his desk as he spoke.

"I am Tur, High Commander of the Efilu Realm. I have been monitoring you people since our hostilities began. You seem to have a number of misconceptions about us," he replied.

Just then, the door knob turned. Before the door could begin to open, Tur thrust his tail against it, holding it shut. "This is a private conversation," he said. "I don't like to repeat myself and you can't afford to miss anything I say. So let's dispense with any distractions shall we?"

Tur waited a moment for President Rhodes to absorb the meaning of his words. Seeing that had failed, Tur clarified, "Dismiss your guards. They can't protect you from me anyway. If I wanted to harm you, the deed already would have been done."

Rhodes looked his guest in the eye as he pondered his options. With no more than a nod to Tur, he crossed the room and opened the door. Tur made no move to stop him. "Mike, I have an unexpected guest. I accidentally touched off the alarm. Settle the men down for me. There's no need for alarm. There's no danger. Do you understand?" he said.

The monologue was well rehearsed and Mike Palmer did understand perfectly. The President was in no immediate danger, but the small force of secret service men were to surround the library from every conceivable exit. Palmer could not see the second party, and made no effort to try. Someone else WAS in there. No one but the President was to get out without being apprehended or killed.

Rhodes closed the door and returned to his desk. Tur watched him carefully as he sat. He made a mental note of the human Commander-in-Chief's clumsy attempt at trapping him, before continuing his own remarks.

"You have been acting on the assumption that we are alien invaders, coming to this Earth, as you now call it, to subjugate your people."

Rhodes folded his hands on the desk in front of him and said, "And you're not aliens?"

"No."

"Then what are you?"

Tur was becoming impatient, but he knew some basic information was necessary if these animals were to keep out of his way. After all, they had never encountered superior beings before. They didn't know how to act.

"Our races left this world long ago. About sixty-five million years ago, actually. An accident threatened to render this world uninhabitable. Our ancestors chose to migrate to safer worlds where we had more opportunity to expand.

We took representative specimens of every species with us to keep our new worlds viable and similar to Fitu, which you call Earth. Some of our people stayed behind in an effort to resurrect this dying planet — animal rights and such. Obviously, they were successful in getting the process started before dying out from the toxins our previous salvage efforts had failed to eliminate."

Jonathan Rhodes nodded as he considered the story. "So in other words, this world was once yours."

"No. I mean this world is still ours. By Efilu law, any soil that has given birth to Efilu life is the charge of the Greater Society, to manage as it sees fit. There is no statute of limitations on this law. The fact that you yourselves have a similar law should make the situation simple enough for you to understand."

Rhodes raised an eyebrow before responding. "Are you referring to the law of Eminent Domain?"

"It would seem most applicable," Tur said, with approval at the President's grasp of the situation.

"Just how many of you are there on Earth now, Commander?"

Tur was puzzled by the question. *What possible difference could that make to him?* "Twenty, all told," he answered.

"... And your ship?" Rhodes asked. It became clear to Tur that this vermin was preparing to bargain with him. Tur decided to watch as the Jing Pen chieftain played out his options.

"We presume it was destroyed in your second assault, along with the majority of our equipment."

"I take it your people have certain ... special needs?"

"Of course," Tur conceded. The President nodded again as he did when making important decisions and casually swung his chair around to look out the window behind his desk. Tur was amused by this odd behavior.

"I can't promise you anything on the spot. Our government doesn't work that way," said Rhodes. Tur interrupted him. "Your title is Commander-in-Chief, is it not?"

"Yes, but I answer to other parties empowered to place certain checks on my authority. May I suggest that we set aside a reservation suited to your special needs ... in exchange for the benefit of some of your extensive knowledge?"

Tur sat on his haunches now and folded his arms. "And you expect to bargain with us for advanced technology?"

Rhodes shrugged. "You can't expect us to put ourselves out on a limb simply out of the goodness of our hearts, can you?"

Tur didn't smile, although he was even more amused by this attempt at extortion.

The President continued. "You, personally, don't have very many choices. You're not leaving. Oh, and you can attack me, but they'll kill you." The President gestured towards the men on the other side of the door.

"I'll be replaced by the Vice President, and your people will still have the same problem, but now they'll be down by one. With a total number of twenty — I'm sorry, nineteen — and no way home, that's not a choice you can afford to make." President Rhodes did sincerity well. He waited for Tur's response.

Tur stood and walked past the outer doorway. "You don't know what I can or cannot do," he stated.

"Where are the rest of your people hiding?" Rhodes figured he had nothing to lose by asking.

Tur thought about it. He had nothing to lose by answering. "We took over one of your bases. The one in the Aleutian Islands. You call it Thompson Air Force Base. It serves us well," he said.

Rhodes was taken completely by surprise. "You can't be serious. That's impossible. We've been getting regular and accurate reports from that base for weeks. That facility is among the most heavily guarded in the country."

Tur answered slowly and deliberately. "Yes. We've virtually mastered your language — and your routines."

Then with astonishing speed, Tur turned, flung a closet door open and dashed through it. The President heard the door latch behind Tur. He immediately went for the library door. He opened it and beckoned in the guards, directing them into the closet.

There was a jagged hole torn through the floor. The wood looked as if it had disintegrated from rot. Rhodes watched a heavily armed man drop down through the hole while another shown a flashlight down on him. The man in the hole looked around at ground level then up at the President and Mike Palmer. He shook his head.

Jonathan Rhodes slammed his fist against the closet door frame.

"Damn!"

*　*　*　*　*

"So why did you tear the hole in the floor?" Bo Tep asked. Tur recounted his meeting with President Rhodes in good-natured fashion.

"They have no concept of telescien technology," he answered. "Given this one's ambition, I'd like to keep it that way." Suddenly, the humor left his voice. "Something unexpected ... I think that this fur mite is actually going to challenge us. I told him about our utilization of that base we just abandoned."

The new Efilu headquarters was nestled under undisturbed corn fields in Iowa. One benefit of mini-wave travel was that they had made it there completely undetected. "If I'm right, they'll attack that base with everything they have," Tur said, then hesitated.

"But there's something else?" Jeen prompted.

"This 'government.' It's not a true republic as we were led to believe. It's more of an administrative bureaucracy. We need to know who this Commander-in-Chief answers to, and what unseen influences control his administration. I have another meeting with him in the morning." Tur stood and indicated for Bo Tep, Jeen and Ikara to follow him into the monitor room of the newly fabricated Efilu headquarters. "We have a lot of work to do," he said.

* * * * *

The next morning, President Rhodes was up early again. This time he was in the Oval Office reviewing security measures for the White House. The secret service contingent had tripled, supplemented by marine special forces. All were armed to the teeth. He would NOT have a repeat of the Camp David fiasco today. If this Tur had the balls to return ... some how Rhodes knew he did ... feared he did.

The President's special committee had hardly seated themselves when Rhodes entered the cabinet conference room. He started chewing out General Schmidt and the Chairman of Joint Chiefs for their incompetence, even before taking a seat himself.

"Dale, what the hell am I paying you for anyway? You tell me about this glory boy, what's his name?" Then pointing to Chey, he said, "And you assure me that everything possible is being done to find these aliens —correction, dinosaurs — and one shows up at Camp David of all places?" He pounded the table for emphasis. "You call that security?"

Rhodes stopped to take a cleansing breath, then continued. "Check the security of the phone lines, and not just for tapping. I have reason to believe someone may be fooling around with our data systems.

"I've brought in someone who has some interesting ideas you gentlemen should think about," he said, pointing to a visitor seated at the table. "I'd like to introduce Dr. Derrick Barnhill from the University of Toronto. America's top paleontologist, Will Parker, is nowhere to be found. It's as if he and his colleagues just dropped off the face of the Earth. None of our other top paleontologist have Dr. Barnhill's credentials ... or discretion.

"Dr. Barnhill was kind enough to join us at a moment's notice. Maybe we can combine resources to get some leverage against these monsters. They must have some weakness or else why would they have left when things got rough on Earth millions of years ago?"

Dr. Barnhill added, "Or more importantly, why have they returned?"

"Another potential weakness. Good point, Professor. I want to know exactly what we're dealing with. I want you and your—" The room went silent.

Tur stood at the opposite end of the table as if he had been there all along.

"You have some nerve coming here!" Rhodes exclaimed. Tur paced casually around the table in silence taking note of the oddities displayed there. Rhodes went on. "You break off negotiations begun in good faith, including a generous off—"

Tur abruptly cut him off. "We were not in the midst of negotiation. I was explaining the facts of life to you to save time and energy." Tur circled back to the opposite end of the table and met the President's glare. "Obviously, it was an exercise in futility. Now we are going to have to do this the hard way."

Jonathan Rhodes stepped on the hidden alarm button in the floor before responding. "So, I guess you're going to disintegrate us with a death ray from your ship. Oh, I forgot, your ship has been destroyed. Pity. Then I guess you'll have to send your vast armies to punish us. Oops. That's right, there are only twenty of you, aren't there? Well, what are you going to do now, beat us up one at a time?" He expected to see Mike Palmer come charging in with a SWAT team at any moment. It didn't happen.

"No interruptions today, Rhodes. I need your full attention. Your subordinates may stay if you wish," Tur said.

The President quickly calmed himself and addressed his staff. "Gentlemen, I'd like to introduce High Commander Tur of the Efilu Empire."

Tur said nothing, but continued to stare into the President's eyes. "Commander, I'd like my staff to stay. They can learn a lot from this encounter."

"With such limited powers of retention I can't see where they'll be of much help to you," Tur said blandly.

Rhodes ignored the jibe. "Now, I presume you're here because you have a counter proposal?"

"There's no need for proposals," Tur said. He sat on his haunches and made himself comfortable. "You took hostile action against a facility you thought we occupied. That was a premature act."

Rhodes blurted out, "You could never have escaped that attack — if you were there at all. You were lying, weren't you?."

"First lesson: I have no reason to lie to you. It's a waste of thought. Second lesson: I like brevity. Your future responses are to be to the point. There's no need to embellish. My decisions do not waver with details or excuses. Third: since you were aware of our presence there, that attack represented a declaration of hostilities on the Efilu Realm. Claims of ignorance can no longer apply." The committee members turned to the President for the counterpoint ... and to see if he would blink.

"Tur, no matter how powerful you may be, you have no resources here. Even if you have lasers or blasters or whatever, they some day will run out. You don't know the terrain, you have only a handful of men and you are trapped here. You'll have to deal with us eventually. This is our world, now. You HAVE to negotiate — if not with me, then with my successor. We are not going to just go away," Rhodes said.

Then he added, with more confidence than he really felt, "He who knows when to fight and when not to fight will be victorious. You're kind has had its time in the sun. Make way for the new."

Tur pursed his lips with disappointment. "I expected you to be briefed earlier. It seems your species has limited organizational powers as well. You should know why I'm here today."

"And why is that exactly?" The President asked. Tur responded coolly. "Damage control." A hush fell over the room.

"Your tribal by laws proclaim these United States as a democracy headed by an elected Commander-in-Chief. However, we spent the better part of yesterday afternoon learning otherwise," Tur said pointedly. The air in the room became heavy for Jonathan Rhodes. The other men seemed tense as well.

"This republic was run by a few economic factions. Major decisions simply represented compromises between them. We had to change our entire approach," Tur said.

Genuinely curious, Rhodes asked, "Your approach to what?"

"Management of course. We have identified each faction and come to terms with them. Nelson Dithers was the last hold-out. He took a little coaxing to come around, but eventually, he did. The others fell into line with much less persuasion."

Seeing the confusion in their faces, Tur felt his own aggravation returning. "We have simply brought them all to the same side of the table," he added.

Chatham broke the silence of the other senior staffers. "And what side of the table is that?"

An expression that was nearly a smile crossed Tur's face. "My side."

"What makes you think WE will keep quiet? Tur, we have access to a telecommunications network that can broadcast information to virtually every corner or the globe. What do you think will be the response to an alien invasion? The armies of the world will pursue you relentlessly until you are cornered and finally destroyed," said the Secretary of State.

Tur inhaled and exhaled slowly in exasperation. "I'm rarely guilty of being too subtle. I see now that subtlety is a relative concept, so I'll speak plainly. You have no armies, no media, no following. I do. Try to expose me and I'll have your own friends remove you. Permanently."

Rhodes seethed for a moment, then said, "Americans have much more integrity than you credit them with. This isn't over yet."

The So Wari was losing patience. "You're a little dense. The point is, this conflict is over. It was finished while you slept. Your entire power base has been co-opted in a bloodless coup. I now control the economics, politics, communications and trade in the nation you call your United States. To control the military effectively, I need this office as well."

Rhodes wasted no time in responding to the offer. "You'll never have my cooperation in selling out the American people. I'll fight you tooth and nail."

Tur eyed him calmly. "Be careful. There are those in my camp who feel that the entire human species should be eradicated. That would be a potentially time-consuming course of action, but it's feasible if it comes to that."

Body language was clearly universal. Tur realized the rest of the humans in the room were all distancing themselves from President Rhodes. The President was scared now. He didn't know how or why, but he believed that Tur could and would kill every human being on the planet.

"The very fact that you mention an option so drastic suggests that you can't. I'm sure there is some law — some limitation — that prevents you from committing genocide, even if you are capable of doing it." He swallowed hard.

Tur just stared at him with a cold, deep stare.

"In fact, if you could do it, you would have done so by now and dispensed with the theatrics." President Rhodes felt that he had regained some ground with that statement, until the phone on the table rang.

Tur gestured for the man to answer it. The President did. He switched on the speakerphone.

"Rhodes? This is Dithers," the assemblage heard. The board chairman of the world's largest telecommunication company never made direct calls to the President. The President picked up the receiver.

Nelson Dithers sounded scared. "Jonathan, I don't know what's going on here, but I got a visit last night from someone who asked to remain nameless. No one saw him but me. I've told this story once before, and everyone thought I was crazy. He said you would know what was going on.

"He touched my nine-year-old grandson, Jason. Just touched him! Now Jason's been admitted to Georgetown Hospital in intensive care. He's in unbearable pain, and the cause is unknown. The doctors have tried everything they know to break it. Nothing is working! They can't even break it with general anesthesia. The child has been placed on a ventilator. The doctors say his EEG shows no change in the brain wave activity. He's still awake ... and writhing with that excruciating pain. This creature said that if he gets any more resistance he'll touch the rest of my family. I have 32 grandchildren!

"I'm an old man, Jonathan, but if this happens to another one of my children, you never will be. Give him what he wants or I'll destroy you myself!" The voice was replaced by a dial tone.

Rhodes stared at the receiver blankly, then replaced it. He sat to recover from what he had just heard, when the phone rang again. Hesitantly, he opened the line.

"Mr. President?" It was a familiar voice. "Mr. President, why are we on yellow alert, sir?" It was Admiral Healy.

"What are you talking about, Healy?" The President asked.

"I've spoken to every nuclear sub commander in the Pacific, Sir. Every ship is on yellow alert. Only your password can do that and only when used with that of the Secretary of Defense and the Chairman of the Joint Chiefs of Staff. We thought it was a malfunction, but it won't respond to any override command on our end, Mr. President. Please tell me if we're about to go to war, and with whom."

The President looked at Secretary Mason for support. He found none. "Rest assured, we are not at war and we're not going to war with anyone. Stand down all weapons immediately. That's a direct executive order, Admiral. Do what ever it takes to follow it. Rhodes out."

He avoided Tur's gaze for a moment. Then looking up after what had seemed to him like an eternity, said, "What are you trying to prove with these threats?" Rhodes trembled. One could almost feel the table shake as he did so.

Some said that Jonathan Rhodes had nearly supernatural intuition when it came to reading an opponent. His instincts told him that he didn't want to read this one any further, and that no mortal man should. Now it was too late.

"If you need my help, you had better negotiate a little more amicably, Tur," said Rhodes, still posturing.

"I did not say I needed you, Rhodes. I just need this office. The Vice President will do nicely if I am forced to remove you. I have no interest in compromising."

"There must be some middle ground," The President said, almost begging now.

Tur spoke with little emotion. "You will cooperate because you're a politician. You have no real loyalties. This is all an endless game to your kind. It's more important to you than eating, breathing or procreation. You'll do anything necessary to remain 'in the game,' no matter who suffers for it. Now that you realize 'the game' is not over, you'll play by the new rules. Or not at all."

They all realize that if they resist the path through the new maze I've set, life will go on without them, Tur observed. *A Jing Pen can always be replaced by another who is more willing. As long as they play along, they'll cling to the remote, albeit futile hope, that they can change the rules along the way. Recognizing this weakness was simple, at least for me. Too bad Ikara had so much trouble recognizing this option. it has always been obvious.*

Every man in the room realized that the United States of America had, as Tur described, been the victim of a bloodless coup. Now they were just fighting for personal survival. The eternal unsaid law of politics is: Only fight to the death when there is no tomorrow.

Otherwise, go with the flow.

"This is the essence of War," Tur said. "I don't need your mythical 'death rays' to subjugate this world. What I am capable of doing is beyond your ken." Tur raised a heavy eyebrow at the small audience.

"You have translated winning as ruling, losing as vanquished. The truth is, winning means surviving and losing means not. To challenge me means losing." Tur looked around the table to confirm comprehension by the attendees.

The President found his voice. It came out as a hoarse rasp. "You can't just come in hear and treat us like pawns in some chess match. We are men!"

Tur looked at him as if he spoke an unintelligible language. "What's the difference?" He waited honestly for an answer to his question, before clarifying their respective positions. "Your species has always played its little games. I am merely changing the rules a little."

"So, now we play your game, is that it?" Rhodes asked in frustration.

"So Wari don't "play." You have no choice except that between cooperation and destruction. I can go through your entire line of succession and your public would never know the difference. Plausible reasons for the changes can always be manufactured. Every one of you knows that or you wouldn't be here," Tur explained. "I will leave the details to the survivors."

He stood and walked away from the table. His image began to glow a little as he prepared to dematerialize. Before he faded, he turned to the President. As he spoke, he had no way of knowing that the mixture of light and shadows made his stiff, long ears look vaguely like horns. His deep-set eyes shone crimson. His spiked tail wrapped around his feet, completing the sinister image.

"You need to understand this: There will be order on this planet. My order. I only need a few of you to restore it. It doesn't matter to me which of you I use.

"Overall, nothing need change. You will still answer to the powers that be. From now on though, THEY will all answer to me."

Chapter 25
ESCAPE FROM ALCATRAZ

"EYES ONLY" was stenciled in red across the document. Colonel Ken Doyle scanned down to the middle of the first paragraph in search of a single word.

"T.U.R."

He said the name aloud. A cold sweat broke out along his spine. Doyle read the rest of the communiqué. It was an acronym: Transcontinental Unrest Resolution. The content was chilling, in light of Vit Na's warning.

FROM: THE OFFICE OF THE CHAIRMAN OF THE JOINT CHIEFS OF STAFF.

TO: ALL FIELD COMMANDERS

SUBJECT: OPERATION T.U.R.

TRANSCONTINENTAL
UNREST
RESOLUTION

1. ANY SUSPECTED ALIEN ACTIVITY WILL BE IGNORED. SUCH ACTIVITY WILL NOT BE INVESTIGATED ON ANY LEVEL. ANY SEARCH OPERATIONS OR INVESTIGATIONS THAT ARE CURRENTLY BEING CONDUCTED WILL BE TERMINATED IMMEDIATELY.

2. ALL LINES OF COMMUNICATION WITH JCS WILL REMAIN OPEN. ANY AND ALL FILES ON SUSPECTED ALIEN ACTIVITY WILL BE SENT TO JCS OFFICE AT THE PENTAGON.

3. THE RISING PUBLIC HYSTERIA RESULTING FROM THE 'APOCALYPSE SYNDROME' HAS INCREASED THE ALREADY ALERT CONCERNS OF THE ADVISORY COUNCIL. THIS RESULTS IN THE INVOCATION OF A PRESIDENTIAL EXECUTIVE ORDER MANDATING MARTIAL LAW.

4. MAJOR GENERAL DALE SCHMIDT HAS BEEN ASSIGNED AS TASK FORCE COMMANDER. HIS ORDERS WILL SUPERSEDE ALL LOCAL AUTHORITY. ANY RESISTANCE CONSTITUTES A BREACH OF EXECUTIVE ORDER, THE PUNISHMENT OF WHICH IS DETENTION AND SPECIAL COURT MARSHALL.

5. ALL MEDIA OUTLETS HAVE AGREED TO SYSTEMATICALLY REDUCE THE AMOUNT OF "ALIEN"-RELATED INFORMATION THEY DISSEMINATE, IN SUPPORT OF MARTIAL LAW. VIOLATORS OF THIS PLAN WILL BE IN NON-COMPLIANCE WITH THE EXECUTIVE ORDER OPERATION T.U.R. AND WILL BE HANDLED ACCORDINGLY.

6. THIS MEMO SUPERSEDES ALL PREVIOUS ORDERS. ALL FOLLOW-ON ORDERS WILL BE ISSUED BY THE PRESIDENT AND JCS.

The document was signed by General Michael Chey and countersigned by the President himself. All signatures were accompanied by the appropriate seals.

"Even the President?" Doyle said aloud. This meant a major shake-up in the government. No, not just a shake up. Not just a conspiracy. This had all the earmarks of a coup. By whom? Wishful thinking hoped for a left-wing faction take over.

The local television news was on mute as he mulled over the memo. He clicked past CNN, CNBC and C-SPAN. All the familiar faces were on the air. There was not a hint of trouble. He switched over to the Armed Forces Network. Again, not a hint — not even a break in the scheduled programming. Then at the end, there was a clue — almost as a footnote. Reassignments.

Major General Dale Schmidt had been assigned as the assistant to the Joint Chiefs, and stationed at Pentagon City. It was ostensibly a promotion under any other circumstances, but why now? And who would be replacing him?

Major Dixon walked in while Doyle was pondering his new position.

"Sir?"

"Huh? Oh, it's you. Come in. What's our status?"

"Fort Alcatraz was completely operational as of 21:00 hours. I just stopped by to make sure your office was satisfactory and to see if you needed anything. Anything wrong, sir? You look upset?"

Doyle hadn't realized that it was so obvious. "I'm just a little tired. What's the status of Hennessy Barracks?"

Dixon was caught off-guard by the question. "Lieutenant Colonel Lyle Hampton officially relieved me at 15:00 hours today, Sir." There was a subtle "who the hell cares" tone in his voice. He went on with what ended up more like a formal debriefing than a casual answer. "Our guests were escorted over at 13:00, including Matthews and Olsen. 'The Captive' was transported at 14:00. All traces of its presence have been eliminated. As of 21:00 hours, Alcatraz Island was completely secured."

Alcatraz had been a tourist attraction in the San Francisco Bay area for years. A colorful history surrounded it. The Native American protest of the early seventies bore late fruit. The federal government finally capitulated and agreed to renovate the facility as a joint Native American administrative headquarters.

The renovation was to be completed by the Army Corps of Engineers over a ten-year span at a cost of one hundred million dollars. It was dirt cheap, all things considered. Then Senator Henry Mason chaired the oversight committee. The trade-off was that the Armed Forces would have access to the facility while it was under construction, or until the renovation costs were paid in full.

The Colonel pulled a few favors out of his hat and rattled a few skeletons in some tightly shut closets in order to gain the run of the Island. Now he was worried that his shenanigans would backfire on him.

Doyle also realized that Dixon was too sharp a soldier for him to keep a development like Operation T.U.R. from him.

"Ernie, we've got a little problem here," Doyle hadn't even noticed when the Major came to full attention. "What do you make of that?"

Doyle said, as he handed Dixon the memo.

Dixon's brow furrowed as he read. "It sounds like we should have taken Vit Na's warning a little more seriously, Sir."

Doyle ripped the memo out of the other man's hand. "No shit, Sherlock!" He sat down before saying another word and hoped his shaking was less apparent from the seated position. "He's trying to send her a fucking message. The question is, how much time do we have to accomplish our goal?"

"Well, Sir, all the hardware is in place and running. Reassigning personnel is going to be a problem from now on." Dixon tapped the document laying on the desk. "There are about half of the technical staff we're going to need. Even taking into account the talents of Mendez and his people, we're still short about eight essential men for what needs to be done."

Doyle drummed his fingers impatiently on the desk. "We'll use civilians."

"Sir?"

"Civilians, damn it! I have files on five ex-naval officers who serve on the faculty at the UCSF hospital and zoology department. Then there's you and me, Ernie. We'll have to make do with that."

Ernie Dixon inhaled, ready to voice a metaphor about the difficulties of steering a ship and rowing too, but caught himself. He knew Doyle was aware of it. The colonel was just in too deep.

They were in too deep. It was either sink or swim.

*　　*　　*　　*　　*

Vit Na wasn't fully awake yet. She felt different somehow. It wasn't just the overwhelming effect of the ether. There was something else. She lay on the cold metal table with a feeling a human might have described as déja vu. This table was smaller and colder than the previous ones, although by objective measurement, it was almost identical to the one she awoke on weeks ago in Hennessy Barracks. It was a moment later before she realized she was strapped to it. She tried to scan the area with her personal field and almost choked on her own saliva as she gasped.

Gone! She double checked. *Nothing. Loss of consciousness should not affect a personal sphere of influence. Have I been found out?* All hope of escape was gone. Without the energy she had sequestered in her personal field, she had no chance of bypassing the security networks. Vit Na had not cried tears of despair in over fifty years. She shut her eyelids tightly now against the indignity, only to force the soft, gentle droplets out of the corners like a cascade of pearls.

A hand appeared from nowhere to brush the tears away. *Who?* She looked up. The face was familiar even through the tears. There was a moment of relief. She thought it was Clyde Olsen come to rescue her. *Must be a hallucin ...* Her flesh went cold. It was Sergeant McCray.

"This is your new home, Vit. I know. I know. No need to thank me. Those tears of joy are enough." He stopped laughing and said, "Better get used to it. No one ever gets out of here. This is the Rock." He turned to go, then faced her.

"You know I never noticed how pretty you were until I saw those tears." He touched her face, then gave her a surprisingly gentle caress. "I never felt anything so soft. Tingley, come feel." He beckoned to Corporal Tingley. The man came closer, but did not touch her coat.

"Tingley, you're such a wuss!" He rubbed her head. "She can't hurt you. Look." Before either companion or captive could respond, he bent over and kissed Vit Na deeply in the mouth. He smiled as she spat his saliva out of her mouth with disgust.

"See? No harm done? The eggheads say this thing's biologically compatible with us or something. It's like letting a dog lick you face. It's perfectly safe! Loosen up ... and take over. I'm off duty as of 22:00. I have a poker game with the army boys tonight and do I feel lucky!" He rubbed his hands together, looked at Vit Na and laughed.

"Don't worry about Tingley kissin' on you, Vit. He doesn't like girls much. Oh, that's right, you're not really a girl, are ya?" He affected a terrified look and went out of the door, with the echoes of his laughter fading slowly down the hall.

"He's a real jack-ass," Tingley said after the laughing died down. "Are you all right M-Miss?"

Vit Na barely heard him. She was sobbing softly. Tearlessly.

How dare he? How dare he?

Corporal Tingley shook her again. "DON'T TOUCH ME! Don't you ever touch me," She snapped. Vit Na regained her composure. She endured one final shudder, then looked coldly at Tingley as he spoke.

"He had no business taking liberties with you that way. He has no right to belittle everyone the way he does." He paused thoughtfully for a moment.

"Do you have ... people who like their own kind ... where you come from, Miss?"

Vit Na didn't blink when she responded. "Again, Corporal?"

"Homosexuals. Gays! That's what he meant. When he said I don't like girls." The corporal looked agitated. "They say we screw thousands of men a year, but I only had one friend ... and he's gone now."

Vit Na allowed the distraction. "What are you talking about?"

"My sexual preference is men. Males," he said reassuringly. "Even if you were a man, I would never make such an assumption. To touch some one without invitation is taboo. What about your people? They're an advanced race. How do you live with those among your people who have alternative tastes?"

Vit Na looked puzzled for a moment, then thought to herself, *Ah.*

"We don't tolerate them," she replied. She watched his reaction.

"You can't mean that you're as backward as these Neanderthals," Tingley retorted in dismay.

Vit Na said in her most soothing voice. "You don't understand. We don't tolerate homosexuality because it's a waste, not out of moral judgment. The only way your kind knows to express intimacy is through sexual intercourse. We do have intimate relationships, but they are non-sexual. There is a difference between intimacy and sexuality. We mate only for a short time each year. Those encounters are for the advancement of the species, not for whimsical and frivolous reasons."

Tingley looked at her skeptically. "Come on, are you telling me you don't enjoy sex?"

"Of course not. I love it! We all do. That's not the point. It has its time, it has its place and it really is not so important what your mate looks like. We have our mates and we have our friends. With very few differences, one male's organ feels pretty much like any other's when its inside you. From what I'm told, the reverse is also true. We just enjoy the moment to its fullest, and cherish the memories."

Tingley looked disappointed. "And then?"

Vit Na said lightly, "And then we look forward to the next one! Homosexuality only serves a purpose during times of overpopulation, or pestilence, when the urge is uncontrollable, but fecundity is undesirable. Even then, there are more constructive ways of using that energy than wasting precious seed."

The corporal thought about it and nodded. "Interesting philosophy."

Vit Na took advantage of his receptive mental state to probe his knowledge. "What happened while I was unconscious, Corporal?"

Tingley was caught off-guard. "Oh, they etherized you. I've never seen that done intravenously before. I always thought that IV ether was lethal."

Vit Na prompted him. "I have a strong constitution."

Tingley caught the hint. "Yes, well ... they did an MRI on you. You know, that magnetic resonance thing. They had some problems with it, I hear."

So that's what happened to my personal field! It was stripped by the magnetic scan. It must have distorted the image beyond recognition. I'll just have to convince them to run me through it again so I can get it back. Its probably my only way out of here.

"I think I can help you with that. The ether is very toxic." *But it won't be next time!* "My body went into a kind of generalized seizure activity that scrambled your image. A clearer picture can be obtained while I'm awake."

Tingley squinted one eye at her and asked, "Why are you being so helpful with our study of you?"

Vit Na thought to herself, The *plausible lie.* "The alternative to getting non-invasive data from me is not appealing."

Again, Tingley nodded in understanding. "I'll let 'em know." He draped the sheet back over her restrained body and left the cell. Vit Na breathed a quiet sigh of relief.

* * * * *

Javier Mendez sat in one of two chairs in front of Doyle's desk. He was rubbing his fingers together absently. Hoyt Matthews was seated in the other chair. They had been granted a reluctant extension on their progress report. The cumulative data led to more questions than answers.

"No wonder these people ruled the Earth," Mendez muttered. Dr. Matthews came a dazed reverie, and said, "What?" He looked at his watch. "I know, Doyle's late."

"No. Not that. Look at the resources we've poured into this project so far and what have we come up with that Vit Na hasn't already told us? Nothing."

Dr. Matthews commented, "Kind of nice to work with such fancy equipment though."

Mendez conceded his point grudgingly. "Doyle's a real patron of the sciences." The scanning electron microscope Doyle had "acquired" for use on this project was but one of the technical marvels that filled the cubicles and halls that formerly comprised Alcatraz Penitentiary. The cells made very pleasant, if monotonous office space. The mess halls, rec. rooms and laundries had been converted into labs, conference rooms, computer centers and auditoriums. The "Good Colonel" planned to get the most out of his prize captive. He had spared no expense.

"What kind of man is this Doyle character any how?" Matthews asked.

Mendez hesitated for a moment as he considered the question. "The worst kind."

Matthews pushed the issue. "What business did you have with him that you got to know him so well?"

Mendez looked up in thought, blinded by the halo that surrounded the fluorescent ceiling light. The answer that Matthews had so lightly asked for had eluded Javier Mendez a thousand times. "I wouldn't know where to begin. Much of our activities were sanctioned by the government. Many more weren't. He has a way of getting you're mouth to make promises you conscience can't live with. Most of our work is still classified ... but you wouldn't believe some of the—"

The door opened behind Mendez. Matthews recognized the new arrival.

"Speak of the Devil."

"And he'll make you a deal, doctor," Colonel Doyle sneered as he entered the room.

"Why are we here?" Mendez asked coldly.

"Your progress report. You and Andy Griffith here are overdue for one."

"When we have something to report we'll tell you. So far we have nothing but new questions. What did the MRI show anyway?"

Doyle looked peeved for a moment, then honestly said; "Nothing."

Mendez looked at him quizzically, then briefly at Hoyt to see if he had any insight into the response. The other man just shrugged.

Mendez asked, "You mean there was nothing unexpected?"

"No, I mean we saw nothing that made sense. Just a jumble of static and noise. No image. We tried to reconfigure the data four times. Nothing. The man guarding her on the last watch says she had some kind of seizure from the ether, but I'm not sure that I buy that either. At any rate, she says we may have better luck if we repeat the procedure while she's awake. That's fair. She knows the next step is dissection and she wants to delay that as long as possible. So do I.

"I had an idea about an electromagnetic aura surrounding her. It would explain some of the MRI readings," Doyle conjectured. "We took some Kerlian photographs of her."

Mendez was at the edge of his seat. "And?"

"Stone cold normal. We compared them with some control photos we took of the staff. No difference." He crossed to the comfortable chair behind the desk, then sat. "We went ahead with the scan. It was technically adequate. The radiologists are reading it now."

Mendez scrutinized Doyle as he sat there with furrowed brow. "There's something else eating you, Ken. What is it?"

Doyle squeezed the bridge of his nose between his thumb and forefinger. "I had to release two members of your team today. Robyn Washington and Clyde Olsen." Before being asked, he expounded more freely than Mendez had ever known him to speak before.

"The big brass wanted to know why Project X is still intact after that memo from the Pentagon. I don't so much mind turning Washington loose. She's harmless. Olsen worries me, though. I just know that son-of-a-bitch is going to pull some bullshit stunt."

The Colonel stopped talking for a moment as he watched Mendez's new idiosyncrasy, then asked, "Why do you keep rubbing your fingers together like that?" Mendez stopped, self-conscious.

"Oil from Vit Na's skin. Very smooth. Very light. It feels good! I guess I've been doing this for hours." He noticed Doyle's concerned look. "Is there a problem I should know about?"

"One of my men was found dead in the john tonight. He had been playing cards with some of the other non coms. There was some drinking and maybe a little light drug use. I don't know. All I do know is that a perfectly healthy thirty-five-year-old soldier just keeled over and died."

"Why, Ken, I didn't think you cared."

"I don't. What bothers me is that he was the second to the last man to have contact with Vit Na!" Mendez's jaw dropped. "Yeah, not so funny any more, is it?" Doyle said sarcastically.

"Does this other man remember anything out of the ordinary going on between your dead man and Vit Na?"

"Nothing at all. He says she was completely restrained the whole time. Funny thing though, he was surprised but not too broken up about this McCray's demise."

Dr. Matthews speculated out loud. "Still, no one else has suffered any ill effects from contact with Vit Na. It could be just a coincidence." The Colonel added his usual skepticism to the dialogue. "There's an old saying in the intelligence game, Doctor: 'Coincidence is a conclusion of exclusion.'"

Mendez placed a hand on Matthews' arm to silence any further discussion. "We'll check all the specimens from this McCray and Vit Na for any matching traces of toxins."

The colonel nodded. "Go to it. In the meantime, I can't risk any more men. Bruce Stahl and Hollingsworth have a little surprise in store for our guest."

* * * * *

I've got to get out of here while I can. It's only a matter of time before they figure out what I'm doing. That stupid sergeant didn't make things any easier with that disgusting saliva drinking ritual. They'll never find the traces of venom in him or in my normal secretions, but they'll suspect ... and I just can't afford that!

She was in what at one time was a solitary confinement cell. The overhead light was very bright; the space, small. The fortified steel door was electronically controlled from the outside only. A small square opening was enclosed by steel bars.

The new guards were like living nightmares — monstrously huge, and grotesque. They rivaled Tralkyz in size, but their build was bulkier. There was something else unnatural about them, too. Vit Na had no time to think about it though. She had to concentrate.

One of the beasts jammed its snout in between the bars in the small opening in the door and bared its teeth. The portal was obvious designed for communication with prisoners. At the same time, it prevented effectual harassment of visitors from the occupant. Today, Vit Na was glad it worked both ways.

She wove her fortified personal field in and out of the maze of computer circuitry that made the new Alcatraz facility manageable. She smiled as she over came one system after another. She needed no modems or accessories to conquer cyberspace. She just needed to get past those infernal security measures. She had been at it for hours now.

Music played gently in the background. Max Hollingsworth intended for it to soothe the strange animals left to guard her. *Bears!* she realized. *I knew I had seen references to such creatures. That size can't be natural. Growth enhancers of some kind must have been employed. ... And all that metal hardware they're wearing doesn't look very friendly.*

Just then, a number of familiar faces entered the outer room: Hollingsworth, Stahl, Mendez and Matthews, led by a grinning Colonel Doyle.

"It looks like your assessment of your friend's talents were accurate. He has taken over the central government and imposed a loose version of martial law. We underestimated him."

"YOU underestimated him. You were the only independent human who knew anything about him." Vit Na said gyrating rhythmically to the music. "I assume you are plotting some kind of counter measures." *I won't underestimate this man again!* she promised herself.

"Nothing you can do anything about. I don't know what happened to my man McCray and I don't care. What I do care about is that you remain safe and secure in my custody. Some of your friend's orders are actually working to my benefit. I've been able to justify the restoration of Alcatraz Island under the guise of preparation of short-term high security detention facility. Everyone knows that California is known for its radical dissidents. It also gave me a free hand to have air force personnel and equipment reassigned to me for security purposes. It works out nice.

"Even these little pets were easy acquisitions under the T.U.R. Mandate. I like them," he said pointing to the bears. "They follow orders without question and I never have to worry about security breaches."

There were four of them. Kodiac bears were naturally the largest land carnivores on the planet. Stahl, Mendez, and Hollingsworth had developed them for use in battle. A judicious use of growth hormone increased their size by over thirty percent. They were trained to use an array of surveillance and telemetry equipment in conjunction with an impressive arsenal of heavy weapons no three humans could hope to carry and operate. No elite soldier in the world stood a chance against one in hand-to-hand or even knife-to-hand combat.

A similar process had produced Akita dogs the size of small horses. The two species worked as a team very effectively. They were the ultimate combination of speed, strength, ferocity and endurance coupled, with expandability. Doyle could always breed more.

Stahl was working some kind of control device that directed the bears' behavior. *Hmm. If I can get into that control program,* she conjectured, *I could make this exit short and simple — and cripple their command chain in the process.* She continued her interface with the security system, expanding her efforts to include the control mechanism for the Kodiacs.

"We've learned a lot from you, Vit Na. I intend to learn much more," Doyle said. He grinned that horrible grin he often used before doing the unthinkable. "You like music I see," Doyle said with a trace of suspicion.

"I like to dance, I told you that before," Vit Na replied, smiling prettily. "I'm glad you're happy. You're going to be my trump card. If worse comes to worse I can use you as a bargaining chip with Tur."

"No you can't. Even if he discovers I'm alive, he'd never negotiate my release. As far as he is concerned, I am a casualty of war. My final duty to him is to do as much damage to the enemy as possible with what remains of my life." *Almost there ... Got it! I now have control of the whole system ... but ... hmm. Why can't I activate the weapons system? There's an activation override switch. It operates manually. This will be tricky, but I think ...*

"Vit Na, tell me something, I know why I'm smiling. Everything's going my way. What I have a little trouble with is the reason you're smiling."

She stopped dancing. "I'm smiling because I know something you don't know," she purred.

Go ahead. Jump, Doyle. The colonel motioned for the bears to come closer to the cell door. Their guard was up. He hesitated at ordering the weapons to be activated.

Why is he so damned cautious? she wondered. *Well, looks like he needs a another little push.* The lock to the cell door clanked open and the door suddenly swung open with the desired effect. The bears growled a warning then fell silent.

Instinctively, Bruce Stahl flipped on the weapons system activation switch. Vit Na smiled broadly. She turned a bear toward the shaking Bruce Stahl via the remote communicator in the beast's middle ear. The machine guns blazed to life, cutting his own short. The pellets destroyed the control box. Humans scattered.

Vit Na activated another bear. The two heavy machine guns crisscrossed the small room with three hundred rounds. She saw Doyle remove his side arm from its holster and tip the heavy steel table over for cover. Hollingsworth, and Mendez made it. A wounded Hoyt Matthews was dragged to safety while bleeding profusely. Stahl looked like ground beef by now.

Vit Na was still separated from the exit by an armed Colonel Doyle, who fired futilely at the bears. She aimed the ursine machine guns at the lights and fired. When they stopped sparkling, the windowless room was pitch black.

Now or never! she resolved. Perfectly at ease in utter darkness, Vit Na smoothly negotiated the fallen bodies and debris in the room, and leapt silently over the table. She evading Doyle's blind aim with no effort at all. Vit Na commanded the bears to face one another before making them fire their the weapons again.

She opened the outer door and slipped out before the humans had a chance to turn around, adjust to the bright light from the hall, and recognize that the movement wasn't reinforcements coming in, but Vit Na going out. The door slammed shut behind her and locked electronically.

Good! ... but I'm not free and clear yet. I can minimize use of blending by creating holographic illusions in the surveillance network. Once out, I'll crash the whole system. By the time they sort everything out I'll be miles away from here.

She made her way through the complex, evading confused soldiers and staff. She used blending sparingly when she was in direct sight of armed men. Near the main exit was the security center. She counted eight guards. Then it occurred to her: The *alarm. All this commotion and they're still here? They're confused because there's no alarm. Well, we'll just remedy that situation.*

At Vit Na's command, the klaxon sounded. The guards ran to the weapons cabinet, broke out the automatic weapons and grenades, then filed out of the room along their preassigned routes. One individual remained: woman, still monitoring the cameras that showed only static. Vit Na slipped in behind her, hooked her tail around the woman's lean neck and slammed her head against the nearest wall. Her skull cracked. She was dead before her limp body slid to the floor.

Vit Na's eyes found the exit from the building. It was less than ten feet away. Just then the door to the lavatory swung open. "Hey, Susan, what's going on out h—" The big sergeant stopped short, seeing the dead body on the floor. Vit Na was caught by surprise, so focused was she on the freedom nearly within arm's reach.

The man was dark-skinned, with straight hair. The name tag on his khaki jacket said "Juarez." Vit Na locked gazes with the new adversary and measured the threat, motionless. Both pair of eyes darted to the sidearm laying on the table between them. Vit Na flipped it and the table out of reach of the man with her tail. The man turned back to the intruder and smiled as he reached into his combat boot.

"I don't know what you are, but you're fucking with the wrong guy today," he warned. He flipped the blade into readiness with the dexterity of one who had done great harm before with pleasure. He assumed a combat stance, within arm's reach of Vit Na. The weapon was non-government issue, she observed. She knew how these soldiers normally were armed. *This one looks like he knows what he's doing,* she surmised. He feinted several passes to the chest and throat then smiled more broadly at the unarmed Melkyz.

With a frightened, desperate look she half extended her hand claws. His attention went to them and he backed off a foot or so. A distinct clicking sound crisply broke the silence in the room. Juarez looked down at the source. He only caught a glimpse of the sickle shape claw on her toe before it blurred into motion. He looked up to see Vit Na backing away before he realized his throat was cut.

His last act in life was to try to choke back the bleeding with his hands. The switch blade dropping to the floor with a clink between quivering knees. He never fully appreciated the elegance of her cut. She had reached all the way back to the vertebra in one stroke.

Vit Na watched him until he stopped moving. *Odd. He was a trained soldier. Why would he deliberately draw attention to his most deadly weapon instead of away from it?* There were no further complications in the effect of her escape.

The February air smelled cool and sweet in here nostrils. She looked back at the Island, still visible from the woods in the moonlight and breathed aloud, "Free!"

Chapter 26
BATTLE LINES

Devit reported in after inspecting the new core of Pentagon city. It was secure from the world of man. Colonels from three of the armed service branches stood at each door which interfaced with the old structure. No human with less than the rank of colonel or navy captain was permitted entry. The officers had the glazed look of Volition Override that Devit had developed to make the most of the available Jing Pen personnel.

Dropping an electromagnetic static field into the frontal lobe and limbic system to cut away and replace the intrinsic neural activity was quick and easy. Jeen wasted no time in encoding telecommand receptor engrams into the fields. The system operated as did any gel con, and was responsive to focused Efilu thoughts. It solved the problem of human resistance to telepathic command.

"We are secure, Commander," reported Devit. "Exterior to this gel core, the building called the Pentagon shows no trace of disturbance. The top-ranking officers are all inside. Out there," he gestured with his head, "we control everyone down to the rank of lieutenant. The rest will follow our orders through them."

Tur nodded absently as he read through the most recent reports from the U.S. military network. The data was getting thick and monotonous, but it was no deterrent to So Wari diligence.

Jeen watched him for a while before asking, "Why are you spending so much time on those routine reports? I've all ready read them all. There's nothing of consequence there."

Tur didn't respond. Jeen tried a different approach. "Maybe I can help," she said, reaching an open hand toward the sheaves of paper.

"You wouldn't see it," he answered directly and firmly, with little more than a glance to meet her inquiring eyes.

"Wouldn't see what?" she pressed.

"The clue," he answered. Jeen had been doing well since Ikara's outburst. They all had felt relief at the return of Tur's aggressive style, but now he seemed distracted again. She felt her frustration rising. "What clue?"

Tur realized that it was a fair question and lowered the tiny pages from his face. "These Jing Pen know more than they're telling. Not all of them, but enough of them to be dangerous. This intelligence community is so fragmented, and they each have their own agenda. One group doesn't know what the other is doing.

"You can add to that the fact that they receive more electronic data from their satellite facilities than they can correlate under normal circumstances. Now that every one of them is transmitting everything, these idiots are completely inundated.

"Your point, Commander?" Jeen asked patiently.

"There are records of a project called Blue Book that was responsible for collecting data on extraterrestrial sightings, abductions, invasions ..." Tur returned to his reading.

Jeen shrugged, dissatisfied with the response. "Any validity to the reports?"

"None. It's mostly trash. Hoaxes, rare natural phenomena, occasional Solar Fletts that get temporarily trapped in the atmosphere and feed on random magnetic fountains until they can break loose of the planet."

Intrigued by the last mention, Jeen pursued it. "Solar Fletts?"

"Sorry, Stellar Fletts," he corrected. "They're harmless to us."

"So?"

"So, the Jing Pen have spent millions of dollars on monitoring these vague events ... and hidden it well from the public. How do you think such a paranoid mind-set would react to an actual attack?"

Jeen's eyes widened. "Then you think Stihl and Vit Na are alive?"

"No. Not really. I saw Dirm's report. Stihl couldn't have survived, but they may try to exploit his remains. They're heavily into cloning research. Vit Na, on the other hand, may still be alive. If so, I feel personally obliged to retrieve her ... or her remains."

Jeen asked calmly. "How will you know?"

"There will be ... an inconsistency in the status reports. Something very small, down-played." As he said that, he noticed something unusual in the command roster. "Hennessy Barracks," Tur read aloud. "it has changed command three times in the last two weeks. Dixon, Major, Army. Doyle, Colonel, Air Force. Hampton, Lt. Colonel, Army."

He laid the stack of papers down on a ledge of the three-story chamber. "Jeen, pull up the tactical map of US bases," he instructed.

She activated the gel console and complied silently. Her eyes darted rapidly back and forth over the field. "It's not on the map," she finally said.

"Bring up everything we have on Hennessy Barracks. I want Chey in here immediately."

* * * * *

"Search completed, sir. She's not on the Island." Major Dixon reported upon entering the lab.

Colonel Doyle was sitting on a lab stool, deep in thought. "Okay, we go to Plan B."

"What's Plan B, Colonel?" Hollingsworth asked. Both Doyle and Dixon looked at him with contempt.

Doyle said shortly, "Find the subject, Hollingsworth. Wherever she is."

Hollingsworth pressed, "Is this to be a 'search and destroy' mission, sir? She still has the fail-safe device in her chest." His words were heavy with venom.

Doyle remembered the plastic explosive wired to a radio transponder that had been placed in Vit Na's chest wound during her recovery. He answered him with more sympathy than he thought possible. "No, I want her retrieved alive if possible. The detonation receiver has a range of about four hundred yards. She's beyond that for sure. The plastique won't leave very much behind if used. I want at least some tissue recovered intact."

"She didn't leave much of Stahl intact," Hollingsworth said. Doyle had already chosen to ignore that subject when Mendez and Matthews burst in.

"I got something you need to see, Ken." Mendez dashed his report on the table and flipped several pages. "Here!" He stabbed at the center of the page with his finger.

Doyle looked at the graph, puzzled. "What the hell does this mean?" Mendez had almost caught his breath by now. "This a spectroscopic analysis of the oil I was rubbing between my finger yesterday. After you implied that it might be lethal, I scraped as much of it together as I could for analysis. Its innocuous to us, but its index of refraction is identical with that of air."

Dixon was completely in the dark. "What does that mean exactly, Doctor?"

Doyle answered the question for him. "It means that she can become invisible at will! Damn it, why didn't you know about this sooner?"

"To find something, you must first know what you're looking for." Hoyt Matthews interjected. "This discovery was pure serendipity."

Doyle was now on his feet and pacing the floor. "Luck or not, she now has four advantages: the power of invisibility, superior strength, superior intelligence and the freedom to use them all."

"You left one out, Ken." Mendez had long since stopped acknowledging rank when addressing Doyle. "She has the ability to control animals. We may not be able to depend on trackers to find her."

"Not necessarily," Dixon interrupted. "She went directly for Stahl in the confinement area. Why?" There was a collective pause as everyone tried to catch up with Dixon's train of thought. "He controlled the bears! She achieved some kind of override, but to do it, she had to knock out the primary control box." It made sense to them. No one else was so specifically targeted.

"So, we may have limited use of conventional police dogs, which she could rip to pieces if they caught her," Doyle said in frustration.

"I can fix it." Everyone in the room turned to look at Hollingsworth. "Bruce and I worked on this years ago. I know the system better than anyone ... alive. Give me some technical support and I'll set up a random radio signal receiver in the head gear. She'll never be able to get a fix on the frequency in order to override our control."

Doyle clapped his hands once with genuine enthusiasm. "You have carte blanche, Mr. Hollingsworth. Let's go people!"

*   *   *   *   *

The northern California woods were cold. A light snow covered the frozen ground. Wherever there was a broad patch of virgin snow, Vit Na circumvented it; or took to trees, leaping trunk to trunk. In the distance, a pack of dogs barked ... nearing. *They have systematically cut me off from accessing any computers or telephone lines,* she raged inwardly. *I should have gone towards the city instead of running for the forest. STUPID! I have to find some way to signal Tur and the others.*

I sense more of those bears and dogs, but no men. I wonder why?

She worked her way up the heavily wooded hill and saw the answer. A hundred yards away, a handful of men lay in ambush. Equipped with night vision goggles, listening devices and automatic weapons with silencers, they awaited their quarry. *They're going out of their way to keep this little chase quiet. Why not just squeeze me between the beasts and soldiers?* Vit Na vacillated for a moment, while deciding which force to confront. She had tried to order the dogs and bears in another direction, to no avail. Something had changed. They didn't respond to her signals anymore. She didn't look forward to having to face those savages on even terms. The men were easier targets.

A red light flickered to life on an adjacent tree. *Infrared motion detectors,* she noted. Muted shots zipped through the cold night air, ending in an inhuman death cry. A deer — a ten point buck — had triggered the device. Vit Na looked up. There was a similar device on the tree behind which she hid, but it hadn't been activated yet. She turned her ears forward to focus in anticipation of their next move.

A light slit the darkness, stopping at the fallen animal. "It's just a deer. Stein and Johnson, go get it and drag it out of the line of fire. We don't want it distracting the bears and dogs, or warning the subject."

Two men ran furtively through the woods to the cooling corpse. Obviously, the detection chain had to be deactivated. Vit Na took advantage of the opening in the perimeter, following so closely she could feel the warmth of their breath. Blended, she could hide her footprints in the drag path of the deer. The carcass was disposed of and the threesome trekked back to the fortified position. Vit Na evaded the movements within the little camp, all the while listening to the plans unfold.

"The Major says that we lay low after the detection grid is done. The nerve gas ready?"

"Yeah, sarge. I can start launching the grenades at the first signal." Vit Na looked at the crate behind her. "Toxic" was stenciled across the face of it. *They want to flush me into that section ahead and gas me and those beasts all at once. I guess they really are expendable. I'll listen a bit longer, to learn their strength and position before moving out of the area. Maybe I'll do a little inconspicuous damage before I go.*

The gas masks were piled on a rack in front of her. "These have all checked out sergeant. I put the rejects in the can to avoid confusion. They say that this stuff causes permanent brain damage," said the lower ranking soldier.

"Nice work, Smitty. Let's take no chances," his superior said. Seizing the opportunity, Vit Na used her little finger claw to make tiny triangular tears in the masks, at the seams. Against positive pressure, they would appear intact. The negative pressure resulting from inhalation within the mask would suck outside air into the mask, like a one-way valve.

The gas was stored in canisters that were stacked on their sides. *Hmm. Metal.* Laying her hands on the crate, she managed to build up a low-grade magnetic force field. She used total mass of the containers for leverage, and made small punctures in several of the bottom canisters. The gas concentration wouldn't build up to toxic levels for hours, but when the top canisters were removed, the rate of gas flow would increase exponentially within the camouflaged tent. *Six less animals to contend with,* she thought with satisfaction.

She learned what she needed to know, identified the scent of the odorless gas for future reference, then disappeared into the darkness.

*   *   *   *   *

Doh couldn't be happier. He had the opportunity to not only observe the Jing Pen in their natural habit, he could actually discuss their behavior with them. "What do you know about the theory of analogy, General?" he asked.

Doh imagined his own distant ancestors at the same stage of evolution as this Jing Pen scientist. *Fascinating!*

"Biologically?" asked General Schallek, Ph.D. He was the chief investigator in the Army's biological defense division. "The principle of Convergent Evolution holds that two given organisms of different phylogenetic origin and stages of development can arrive at similar solutions to the same problem. The best known example is flight.

Birds, insects and bats all fly with the benefit of wings."

The doctor was seated at his desk facing Doh, who had perched himself against the fourth floor railing over looking the central atrium. Weepf was standing on the floor of the atrium. Her head came up to the middle of the third floor. She glanced up at the mention of wings. Choosing to ignored them, she continued to monitor satellite communications on the console in front of her.

"Of course, the respective structures have different origins," Dr. Schallek pontificated. "The bird has feathers that fan out from its upper limb to assume aerodynamic perfection, whereas the common fly takes advantage of outgrowths of its exoskeleton. The less efficient bat uses modified hands to fly."

Doh was thoroughly entertained.

"Man, by contrast, has taken lessons from mother nature and combines the greatest features of all three to create flying machines that are superior to any nature has devised so far," Schallek continued.

Weepf was out of his line of sight. He didn't notice her following his shadow absently with her eyes, as he spoke.

"Our technology more than makes up for what we humans lack in physical prowess." A look of consternation crossed his face. "I still can't understand how your people survived the climatic upheavals of 65 million years ago. Granted you have made some miraculous accomplishments, but we would have surpassed you had we started on a level track. The fact is, the complex mammalian brain is capable of more functions, and is faster than any other in nature.

"First, we dream, then we comprehend, then we create," Schallek bragged with impunity now. "For example, a mere forty years ago, the microwave oven, cellular phone and space shuttle were science fiction. Now they are reality. If your people had this kind of capacity, you would never have been cast out."

Doh was confused for a moment, then actually offended. "What do you mean 'cast out'?" he asked.

"In biblical terms, the serpent — i.e. you people — were cast out of Eden. The Genesis story was never taken literally until now. This attempt to take over our world is doomed to failur—"

Doh interrupted him. "You have either heard or told too many of your fire side stories. You're beginning to believe in your own myths. If anything, man was made in OUR image. Mankind has been the interim custodian of this world, and look what you've done. Pollution, mayhem, disorder everywhere!" Doh spoke with brutal candor.

Schallek was startled by the intensity of Doh's response. He recovered his composure and countered, "We will learn your strengths, weakness and finally your technology. We will win in the end. Oh, not me personally, but mankind. The Laws of Nature favors us, even with all of our flaws."

"Your species has delusions of grandeur," said Doh. "You are expecting some version of War of the Worlds that you'll win by discovering some miracle weakness that we've overlooked. Man's worst fears are only born of the familiar. The most hideous nightmares — only combination of your actual experiences. Such dramatic assaults are too crude. Subliminal weapons are so much more effective. It's no wonder you have anticipated our influence over your species erroneously.

"Natural forces are always terrifying when they're beyond your control. Yet a virus need not be as lethal as HIV or Ebola to incapacitate billions. To be effective, it simply has to leave them chronically dysfunctional. Then the survivors become still a drain on the target society.

"Unrelenting winters? Decades of drought and fires? Civil war? Just think about it. You vermin barely hold your own against the forces of chaos. What chance could you have against us?"

"Divine Law: The will of God," was the General's nearly desperate retort.

Weepf had never seen Doh angry before. It was refreshing. She now joined the discussion, which was developing into a debate. "You speak of law, fur mite. Two things make a law work. The first is its acceptance. The second, more importantly, is its enforceability. The most natural of laws dictates who will win and who will lose: SURVIVAL. On this world, in this time, WE are the ultimate force. Therefore, WE are the Law.

"Your ancestors competed with mine in an environment where proto-mammals had all the advantages. You still lost! We were small and weaker, but smarter. Here we are again in conflict 220 million years later, and it looks as if the outcome will be the same.

"Sun Tzu's wisdom indeed! You quote ancient So Beni battle philosophy as if were your own!" Weepf's eyes narrowed at the little man. She had risen on her toes in order to catch him with a downward gaze. "You must have learned something about war. Do you think you have learned enough to compete with me?" she said with a smile.

Weepf opened her hand as if to allow some invisible object to alight on it. "We have crushed opponents that could reduce this planet to cinders." She clenched that hand into a fist.

After a pensive pause, Weepf looked almost sympathetic. "In all candor we should never have come into conflict. We are on ... different orders of existence. You don't even realize that you never had a chance." A radio was playing music softly in the background. Vanessa William's "Colors of the Wind" was in full swing when Weepf speared her elongated fifth finger through the machine.

"You may have us now, but when the combined armed force of the USA realizes this alien conspiracy—" Gen. Schallek boasted.

"They'll what? Show us some real destructive power? We already have your top officers and executives. What good do you think a few lackeys who were effectively trained never to question authority will do for you?" She settled down flat-footed

The doctor looked frustrated beyond control.

"Well, what about phasers?"

Weepf glanced upward over the railing without moving her head to give a terse, verbal response. "Don't MAKE me hurt you."

*　　　*　　　*　　　*　　　*

"Do you have one of my people in custody? Yes or no, General?" Tur was like an avalanche momentarily poised at the brink of a cliff.

Sweat beaded on General Chey's forehead. Tur demanded evenly, "What's going on at Hennessy Barracks? I won't ask again!"

Chey swallowed hard in anticipation. Jeen and Ikara discovered that there was an entire level of consciousness that they could not directly access through their machinations. Pain was deemed an unreliable incentive to truth telling. Tur had devised a more direct form of persuasion.

Tur hesitated for the briefest moment before clenching the force field he had woven round the human's nervous system. The eviscerated pulp of General Russo's brains smacked the wall between Gen. Chey and Gen. Schmidt, and dribbled down to the floor.

General Russo was responsible for the entire southwestern sector for the Army. He didn't have the necessary answers. The inquisitor's eyes turned to the next in rank.

Angry and frustrated, Tur gripped Dale Schmidt by the torso, with his thumb pressed firmly against the fragile sternum. "Schmidt, you are the immediate superior for this Colonel Doyle. Are you going to tell me what I want to know or is this going to be a short year for senior officers?"

Schmidt, unlike Russo, did have the answers; he was just too slow in giving them up. The mangled mess was more than the Chairman's stomach could stand. General Chey's lunch made a sharp contrast on floor next to Dale Schmidt's viscera. While on his knees, scrambling to maintain balance in his own excrement, Michael Chey could not stop telling the Efilu Commander about Hennessy Barracks.

* * * * *

The quiet little cafe was typical of San Francisco night clubs: subdued, smoky, and intimate. Carla Shedrick was hot tonight and the room loved her. Robyn Washington cast a furtive eye through the crowd, looking first for Doyle's men, who she was sure she had eluded, and secondly for her contact.

He was sitting at a table in the front row. It was not the best choice of seating if one wanted a clandestine exchange of information. Adrian Dunbar started the standing ovation that ensued. Even after the crowd joined him, he still stood six or seven inches above the rest.

Washington took a deep reminiscent breath, then crossed through the throng. She could see his handsome smile from the door. It became more disarming as she moved closer to him.

Some things could never go back to the way they were. She was no longer a naïve seventeen-year-old college sophomore, and he was no longer a suave, senior communications major about to start an internship at the local news station. Now he was a hot, up-and-coming investigative reporter gone associate producer. Every network head-hunter was after him ten months before, but it was TransWorld News that got him, thanks to their international exposure and a high six figure salary.

There he stood, head and shoulders above the rest: the producer of the highest rated news program on TWN ... and the one that had got away fifteen years before.

"Robyn!" he shouted, as he saw her cutting through the crowd. He pulled out a chair and seated her gallantly. He kissed her lightly on the cheek before he sat down. "How are you?"

Washington was self-conscious. "I don't know yet. Hey, can we sit somewhere less conspicuous?"

"Where?"

She searched the dim corners of the room, and spotted a booth that had just been abandoned by jubilant fans. "There," she pointed.

Dunbar began to lead her across the club to a couple of empty stools at the bar. "No, not here. That booth there." She took him by the hand an led him around the bar impatiently. The pair slid into the booth, and faced each other across the table.

"What's with all this cloak and dagger bit, Robyn?"

"Look, A.D., you know I don't go in for theatrics, so just believe me when I tell you this is some serious business we're into here. Both of our lives are in danger if I've been followed."

"Okay, so stop wasting time and spill it."

She paused for a moment, not sure where to begin. "First of all, I have no evidence to support what I say, but you know me well enough to know that I'm telling you the God's honest truth."

He said nothing, but returned an intensely receptive stare.

"... Aliens and dinosaurs rolled into one?" A.D. said, after a several moments of careful listening. "So how did you get out alive? That's the kind of info that people disappear for having."

"It's complicated, but I think they control part of the government somehow." His mouth dropped opened skeptically. "Dinosaurs. In the White House," he said. He thought for a second, then added humorously, "Now, wait a minute. Maybe that's not so farfetched."

"I'm serious now. Someone made Doyle release the whole team. Of course, he's had us followed as discretely as possible. I hope I lost them. They can't be that good."

A.D. laughed softly. "Look at this attitude! So THEY'RE not smart enough to keep up with you either?"

She caught his meaning. "That's not what I meant. I just mean they aren't FBI or CIA. They're not trained in espionage techniques."

"Well, ... we'll hope not," he said. Their coffee arrived. It was the best she had smelled in weeks.

A.D. sipped from his cup, and pondered his next move. "Any chance we can get an interview out of someone who can confirm—"

Robyn shook her head. "No way. No one involved in the military is going to cross Doyle. Now, in that, they are well-trained."

"You mean in loyalty?"

"No, I mean in obedience."

She looked deeply into her black coffee. "Do you think you can get it on the air?"

"I don't know," he said. A.D. was always very honest with her. "Maybe if you actually came on the air ..."

She drew a deep breath. She had known in her heart it would come to this. She absently drummed her fingers on the mug as she estimated how long she'd live in freedom after revealing the capture of an alien visitor ... or how long she'd live, period.

"What's she like?"

Robyn snapped out of her reverie. "Huh?"

A.D. repeated his question. "I said, what is she like, this ... alien."

Robyn scrambled to catch up with his line of thought. "Vit Na? I guess she's remarkably like many women I know. Stronger, more confident, though. She seems like she's accustomed to having her way in many matters, but is very adaptable to strange circumstances. Mostly, she seems alone."

She thought about her choice of words for a moment, appreciating the irony of a linguist unsure of words in her native tongue. Then she affirmed, "Yeah. Alone, but not lonely. There is someone just for her that she keeps in her heart. Someone named Tur."

As she pondered Vit Na's fate, she felt embarrassed about how trivial her own danger was by comparison. Robyn followed the familiar lyrics the songstress was elegantly weaving through the air by tapping out the rhythm on her own coffee cup. The finale in that rich contralto that was Ms. Shedrick's hallmark. *"... Just get here if you can."*

The piano tinkled in the background through the applause as Robyn thought aloud. "I was just thinking about how powerful this song is. You know, Adrian?"

The last time she called A.D. by his full name, he ended up making breakfast for her.

* * * * *

"I want a mini-wave fully armed and six meren ready to go, Devit," Tur instructed. "You know who you are," Tur said to the remaining Efilu contingent, as he prepared for the assault ahead.

Bo Tep, his two aids, Dirm, Devit and Los stepped forward. "We'll transport the mini-wave across the continent in Air Force One," he added.

Bo Tep offered, "The mini-wave would be faster moving under its own power."

Tur didn't even look up as he answered. "We are talking about a patch-work mini-wave imitation. We can't push it. The plane will attract the least attention and no one will question the squadron of fighter jets escorting it. We need to conserve our energies any way we can."

Tur directed his attention immediately back to the Weapons Master, his plans solidifying. "Devit, you will arm the jets — standard issue, nothing fancy. You might as well utilize them to the fullest. WE will be fully armed and ready upon arrival. I will lead the recovery maneuver. You all will maintain maximal dispersal of any counter-offensive efforts."

The main body of the Efilu was to be left under Weepf's command.

"Weepf, you will carry out the mission in case of any ... delays," he said. "The sooner the algae gets home, the better off the Realm will be. There is still enough gelcore to assure complete invulnerability. Any questions?" Tur looked around briefly, not really expecting any.

"Then I—"

"What provisions have you made for air cover after the Jing Pen escort is exhausted?" Weepf asked smoothly.

"None. We can handle anything they throw at us from the ground."

"Like Stihl?"

She knew that the issue was like a raw nerve to both Tur and Dirm.

"Stihl was unarmed and unsupported. There is no similarity between the two situations."

"Still, the loss of any of you seven could seriously jeopardize the completion of MY mission."

"You will be the only senior staff member with any military experience left here. Without you, the mission will be over. You stay here. End of discussion."

When a So Wari felt it necessary to actually say it, it really was the end of all peaceful discussion. Weepf said no more.

Chapter 27
ARMAGEDDON

"He must be responsible. No one else would have the know-how. The question is, why?"

"You've got to calm down, Colonel," Hollingsworth implored.

"That's all we need now, a human traitor!"

Mendez objected. "You don't know that Clyde sabotaged the system. This Vit Na has shown inhuman brilliance and ingenuity ..."

"Bull shit, Javier. All of the alien's tricks were software-related. She had no access to the mainframe downstairs. That room remained secure throughout the entire escape. Someone else had to do it. Hell! Even my men aren't savvy enough to wreck the system this badly — present company included. I want Olsen arrested. Dixon!"

"I'm on it, sir," Ernie Dixon had been furiously working one of the few PC's not connected to the house mainframe. "Here it is. Olsen, Clyde. Born Rochester Minnesota, April 4, 1968. Graduated MIT, twenty-third in his Class of 1990. Never held a regular job for more than nine months. Political organizations: none. Social organizations: Greenpeace, SETI, Society for the Preservation of Sacred Native American Burial grounds. Save the Whales campaign '87. Participated in a number of animal rights demonstrations ..."

"That proves nothing." Hoyt Matthews found his voice in the fray.

"The boy has no history of subversive behavior?" Dixon snapped his fingers for attention.

"Here, here! Thrown out of ROTC for unauthorized experiments with explosives. He also qualified with automatic weapons."

"That's it! I want Olsen picked up if possible, but I want him taken out of this equation," Doyle spat. "There are enough variables in it already."

A sergeant entered, handed Major Dixon a print-out and left.

"Sir? The inventory reports," said Dixon. "An M60 with grenade launcher, 600 rounds of ammo, and a .45 automatic with three magazines are missing. The depot door was forced."

"Ernie, I want that renegade dead!" Doyle looked around the room for any opposition to the decree. There was none.

* * * * *

They aren't taking any chances. Troop formation in five layers. The little chief didn't expect me to strike first. Now he'll be even more cautious ... more ruthless. Vit Na heard barking in the distance. The spotlights shining through the darkness meant more bears. Lots of them. There was no way to avoid a confrontation.

Clumsy humans had made easy targets. Bloody bodies lay strewn about the dark forest floor, victims of her nocturnal prowl. A small alcove in the face of the mountain had served as a temporary refuge from both chase and cold. She knew she dared not utilize any of the small caves, for fear of booby traps. She watched as the assault bears climbed the hill towards her position. If they didn't already sense she was there, they were sure to stumble over her on their way through. She steeled herself.

The angle of the hill allowed her to clear more distance with the leap downward than she could have on level ground. Her trajectory landed her in the midst of the ursine squadron. Immediately, she cripple the lead bear and proceeded to take the others out in the same brutal fashion. A tail to the throat, a toe claw to the eye or midriff, and a straight punch to the spine took out the majority of the party before they knew what hit them.

The surviving bears that could still defend themselves circled Vit Na. They numbered only three. Vit Na also circled, executing each crippled bear in passing where they lay. The odds were not in her favor. Success so far had been the result of surprise and bluff ... at her feet, she spotted an equalizer. She hefted the heavy weapon from a fallen bear, aimed at the com link and fired. She hit two before the remote human controller began returning fire.

Line-of-sight parabolic trajectory. Those laser targeting beams may work in my favor. If I can just stay one step ahead of their movements, she thought. Her reflexes were so much faster than the primitive mammals, that she evaded nearly all attacks.

Then she was caught full in the face by a paw. The claws barely broke her skin. It was quite effective in breaking her rhythm, however. Vit Na saw the laser beam as it crossed her torso. She nearly cleared the beam before two rounds tore through her flesh.

She rolled, barreling between the legs of one of the disarmed bears, which still standing. It took the remaining fire in the spine. Rage overwhelmed the beast with the machine gun and it charged Vit Na. Its movements effectively made aiming the automatic weaponry it bore impossible.

Ignoring the pain in her hip, she rolled backward, allowing the bear's momentum to carry him up and over. Its claws dug deeply into her flesh before she manage the tight tail grip necessary to snap its neck. She spun the limp body to one side and rose shakily to her feet.

By now the dogs had doubled back and were waiting for an opening to attack. Vit Na emptied three hundred rounds from two salvaged weapons. The entire pack was wiped out before the overheated weapons jammed.

At that point, Vit Na's unsteadiness marched into bone wrenching convulsions. She dropped the guns and sat amongst the dead. She took a cleansing breath, made a brief assessment of her injuries and then staggered off over the hill. The echo of more dogs grew in the distance.

*　　*　　*　　*　　*

"What is the closest threat to Alcatraz Island?"

Devit checked the map before responding to Tur's query. "The naval base at Alameda. Six battleships and one air craft carrier are stationed there."

Tur paused for the briefest moment, then commanded, "Take it out. Jets only. When they run out of ammunition, order them to crash into any military hardware that remains intact." He pointed. "Set us down in San Francisco Bay. There, we'll split the mini-wave into three sections, as planned."

Tur drummed his fingers on his knee in the cramped Air Force One jet. "Let's do this quietly. If Vit Na is alive in there, I don't want them alerted until the last possible minute."

Bo Tep rubbed his chin. "'Quiet' takes time. Just how long do you plan to spend on this operation?"

Tur raised his head slowly. "As long as it takes."

"Casualties are proportional to the duration of a strike, but I'm sure you realize that. There are only seven of us. How many of us can you afford to lose?" he asked. Tur didn't respond.

"Do you have any ideas on minimizing this trip?" Devit asked, addressing his question to no one in particular.

Bo Tep looked at him. "Not yet, but I'm sure I'll think of something."

Devit smiled, an expression most unusual for him. "I already have a plan."

* * * * *

The watchtower was still manned. Guards criss-crossed each other's paths, never letting themselves out of each other's sight. Alcatraz Island was tranquil, but not the abandoned facility U.S. federal records indicated. In Bo Tep's estimation, it looked like a military installation expecting company. Devit's plan was ludicrous. Just ludicrous enough to work.

"Just watch. If the profile of the human patrolman holds, curiosity will do the job for us. If not, well, we can still do it your way," Devit said.

He nodded to Bo Tep. Devit then plucked a feather from his coat and dropped it from the segment of the mini-wave the three meren now piloted. It wafted toward the guard tower and landed gently in the north corner station. The Efiluan trio waited.

The first guard looked at the plume from a distance. He tipped his head quizzically. His eyes lifted towards the night sky searching for the great bird that lost the feather. The mini-wave was hidden in the darkness. The soldier took two steps closer, then paused. He looked around suspiciously, then crossed the cat walk to the resting quill.

"Wow!" he mouthed. Devit smiled in the darkness. The man stroked the long, white plume. It was luxuriously soft and delicate. "Hey, guys!" the guard whispered as loud as he could. "Come here!"

They all converged on the north tower. Devit nudged Tur gently in the ribs and said, "Time to go to work."

With that, he slinked across the blackness by way of the mini-wave bridge, then caught hold of the tower, below the position of unsuspecting humans. He climbed into position and silently counted.

"Check it out. Have you ever seen a feather this big?"

"Nah, man! I'd hate to see the buzzard this came off of. Hey Weiss, you know a little about birds, don't you?"

"Yeah. A little. I was in the Audubon society in high school. Let me see that." After an intense, but brief examination, the soldier said, "I've never seen a feather like this. Even ostriches don't grow feathers this big ... more than just big, the pattern is weird." He drew his finger along the length of the plume. *Soft!* He repeated the action several times. "It just flows." Weiss marveled.

As Devit knew he would, the Jing Pen called Weiss drew his fingers down the quill against the acute angle of fibers, expecting them to give way with the same yielding softness. Before his hand had reached the stem, Corporal Weiss lost two finger tips and a thumb. The other men watched in mute horror as the digits dropped to the ground.

Devit took the opening to silence all three before they could draw another breath. Two well-thrown rigid quills to the throats of each flanking guard sent them gurgling and sputtering blood as they fell to their knees. An opened palm to chin thrust the neck of a third man beyond the breaking point, in yet another silent death.

Only the fingerless one was left. Alone, in shock, Weiss' life ended with a chest full of penetrating spines from Devit's back, when their struggle forced him against a handrail.

"Well," Devit was saying as Tur and Bo Tep joined him on the parapet. "That's that. Nice, quick, and quiet."

Tur was not impressed. "Quit showing off. You could have taken them out just as easily without the theatrics. Let's go."

Bo Tep caught up with Devit and whispered a comforting thought. "It was great ... and more fun than anything else we've done so far. Good work." Cautious to avoid the sharp angles of Devit's quills, Bo Tep patted him on the shoulder.

Tur was kneeling at a communication cable. "Devit!" He called. "Can you access this system from here?" The Ironde stepped up to the cable, the fiber optic strands skillfully exposed already by a surprisingly nimble Tur.

"I don't know," Devit answered. He reached deep into the gel core of the mini-wave and pulled out a handful of goop that swiftly configured into a gel console. He attached it to the mass of glass threads.

"I can access some of the main system from here, but it looks like somebody is expecting trouble. The thing is loaded with safeguards."

Tur turned a wry smile. "Jing Pen safeguards? You're kidding me!"

"Don't laugh, sir. Within the parameters of their technology, they can be very resourceful. The lock-out is configured to keep out a rogue program of their own design. I can by-pass some of the programmed barriers, but most of them are physical. We'll have to take them out in that fashion."

Tur slammed his fist into his own thigh. "I'm tired of this tip-toeing around. I'm not built for this kind of turtle-spit. Disable as much as you can, then we go in and kill anything non-Efilu we meet." That was a general order and everyone heard it.

The High Commander took the lead. However, he had to crouch and crawl through many of the corridors leading to the main hall. Devit made better time through the narrow passages and found the main engineering section.

His assimilation of the data was nearly instantaneous. The most efficient method of securing the Island was to use the mini-wave. It was discharged forthwith, like a force of nature rushing ahead of the infiltrators, softly neutralizing every Jing Pen it washed over. Along the way, its secondary directive was to widen the necessary passages to allow the larger Efilu to follow.

Dirm was the first to report in.

"She was here, sir." Tur felt himself rocked emotionally. He hid the reaction by pretending to catch an overhanging pipe for balance. "Any ... remains?" Dirm was nothing if not discrete with his superiors.

"I should have been more clear, High Commander. She was here, but she left. There are signs of a violent escape and a desperate pursuit. Which explains the scant troops and lack of resistance."

Tur was all steel. "How long?" he asked. "Two hours, maybe a bit more." Dirm answered without hesitation.

Tur was already moving toward an exit as he called over his shoulder.

"Track them."

He waved his hand indicating the building in general. "Burn it down."

*   *   *   *   *

Vit Na felt cold, that deathly cold one feels following acute blood loss. Her spleen did auto-transfuse enough blood to keep her conscious and mobile, but efficient combat was out of the question. Her mind was exhausted and unfocused. She would have to rely on instinct alone to get passed her malefactors.

Remember, I am the hunter! she drilled herself. *I will pick them off one at a time.* In a moment of clarity, she thought, *The ship. I have to signal the Repam. I'll need a power source ... and just hope I don't burn myself up in the process.*

Vit Na heard those stupid canines again. She clutched the oak tree she rested against with her claws. Normally, she could have pulled an object four times her own weight into the highest branches, but she now struggled to scale every inch. She hung upside down from a branch twenty-seven feet off the ground.

The inverted position set gravity to work in her favor. Her head began to clear. Vit Na blended into the snow-covered branches. Dogs whisked by below her, the slower bears following their lead. One of the bears hesitated beneath her. The action caught the attention of one of its companions. They both raised their noses to sniff the wind for the faint scent.

Now! Vit Na told herself, as she grabbed one beast by the head and wrenched it 180 degrees with all her might. The other was watching its partner fall for no apparent reason, when an invisible claw raked out both its eyes in one swoop.

The bear too, had instincts. It lashed out with its own great might, now completely blind and in pain. It struck solidly. Vit Na was too weak and tired to effectively dodge. The dangling Melkyz was knocked to the snow-blanketed ground by the blow.

The bear howled in agony then wandered blindly into the night. The sound of the dogs could be heard to grow louder. *Highest Mother!*

They're coming back! She had no strength and she left blood-stained footprints with every agonizing step.

Vit Na felt like a cornered animal. In truth she was little more. She heard automatic gun fire in the distance, the dogs barking and howling in pursuit. Now survival demanded the unthinkable.

I've been burning calories with impunity. My nutrient reserves are exhausted. She remembered how back in the cage, she had known that at some time, somehow, this decision would have to be made. She would have to eat the fallen bear.

Her stomach was too empty to vomit at the thought of eating raw mammal flesh again. Survival ruled all etiquette. She tore into the flesh. No aristocratic niceties, just savage, urgent hunger. She finished the liver, heart and most of the fat underlying the skin. Then she braced herself for the fight of her life. Dead leaves crackled.

The dogs still could be heard barking in the distance. The clumsy footfalls slipping and sliding nearby on the ice belonged to a Jing Pen, a man! She sprung at the lone human, pinning him to the ground. An involuntarily wave of nausea repulsed her.

"Vit Na, wait! It's me. Don't you know me? It's Clyde. Clyde Olsen! I've come to help." In her frenzy, Vit Na could neither recognize nor hear the man. She also could not bring herself to take another bite of mammalian flesh.

Out of desperation, she began ripping at his mind with all of her own. He screamed a long, silent scream that only she could hear and enjoy. Vit Na devoured his memories, his beliefs, even the very pillars of his soul. She left the psychic carcass laying, bereft of volition, in the void of his life's essence. His body, fully intact, rested motionlessly on the frosted ground. She took his weapon, her head clearing again.

Her mind took advantage of Olsen's most recent memories as the rush of calories from the bear's flesh revitalized her own brain. *Power condenser, just over that ridge. I've got to get to it!*

*　*　*　*　*

San Francisco Bay was ablaze with naval fuel. Under Efilu command, the F-16 escort jets had completed their final sortie against their own navy. Tur's contingent had caught unawares the rear guard of ground troops on Vit Na's trail. In all, the seven Efilu took out three of the eight human companies on the search and destroy mission for their fugitive companion. The soldiers never knew what had hit them.

Even Tur didn't expect to see what lay over the hill. Twenty Kodiac bears, all an average height of eighteen feet tall, and ready to kill.

It didn't take Tur long to respond, even to the unbelievable. He skewered the first bear to charge his way with his spiked tail and slung the flailing body back at the rest of them. Bo Tep, flanked by his two bodyguards, went after the crazed bears that broke ranks. He cleared a path for the smaller meren to spear through the crowded hill unmolested.

Dirm, having experienced human combat technique firsthand, was prepared for artillery use. His body armor was solid and fortified with a contact force field. He disabled the artillery and allowed Los and Devit to mop up the scattering humans and Akitas. Los slashed the animals left and right with his forearm blades, running past them at speeds they couldn't hope to match or evade. Devit simply threw his natural projectiles with lethal accuracy.

Tur too was forced to engage the Jing with mostly hand-to-hand combat. The mini-wave was operating at it peak capacity, configured to repulse air to ground weapons at Dirm's suggestion.

Tur could see flashes of light moving away from the battle, led by gun and artillery fire. "Vit Na!" he gasped.

Tur collapsed the mini-wave, engulfed his assault party in it and carried them over the hill. The suspension field charged to disrupt metabolic hydrogen ion transfer. As the mini-wave passed over, its field of influence worked as effectively on the Jing Pen as cyanide gas. They dropped one by one.

* * * * *

Vit Na was trapped. She had successfully made her way to the transformer and used her personal sphere of influence to set up a force field. She had intended to focus an intense multiphasic laser pulse as a beacon to the Repam. The arrival of more fire power than she had seen so far interrupted her plan. It was all she could do to deflect the bullets and light artillery shells reverberating against her shield.

They'll be sending reinforcements soon. I can't stay in here forever! Got to take a chance. With any luck at all, they'll be momentarily stunned by the light, and cease fire for a moment. A few seconds ... That's all I'll need!

The helicopter gunship had spotted her. It came into range just as she made her decision. She readied herself, planted her feet firmly on the ground, raised her hands straight up over her head and focused the blinding purple-white beacon pulse. It lanced through the night time sky.

The helicopter was caught in the beam. The explosion did make a distracting display.

Chapter 28
SALVATION AND RUIN

The brief daylight faded in seconds. Confusion ruled as the color of night returned. Men groped and stumbled with the pain inflicted by the blinding flash through their night vision goggles. Major Dixon's back was to the window of the mobile command center.

A split second after the burst, Colonel Doyle was on his feet. "Who authorized nukes?" he shouted, bracing for the after-shock that never came. The gun ship explosion registered as a vanishing blip on a tactical display screen. "What the hell was that?" he asked. Doyle's attention was now drawn to the random small arms fire on the hillside.

"How did she get a hold of incendiary grenades? Ernie, confirm that blast came from our quarry, and that there are no other high yield weapons missing from the armory that you didn't catch. In the meantime, have those men fall back."

Doyle pulled at his stubbled chin. "Where are those bears any way?"

* * * * *

"They're firing from the Bay!" Devit exclaimed, as he watched the incoming missiles streaking hundreds of yards over head. It was true. The plan to cripple the San Francisco-based naval fleet with a sneak attack had backfired. Reinforcements came in from the Pacific, ten warships strong. They concentrated fire on the skirmish in Muir Woods.

"She's unprotected up there." Tur's thoughts were almost a murmur. Then more firmly, he projected, "Shields up. I want the entire hillside blocked off."

Bo Tep stepped up to Tur, with uncharacteristic discretion. "This 'make shift' mini-wave can't handle the demands you're putting on it. If it collapses, we'll be out here all alone and unprotected ... like Stihl was."

Tur turned full face to him. "She's out there all alone, Bo. I know I'm placing all of us at risk, but I can't help it. I brought her to this Alom- forsaken planet. I can't just leave her in the hands of these savages."

Pleading eyes in a So Wari face were even more incongruous than Tralkyz discretion, or compassion.

"Alright Tur, I'll drop it." Bo Tep said, with a nod. "Let's clean up this mob though. I don't like to have all of these stray animals running wild."

* * * * *

Jeen was running now. She couldn't believe that the operation could have gone as wrong as her reports indicated. Weepf had to see them *NOW!* She came into the central atrium where Weepf was in her usual place, brooding over the fact that she had been left out of the action. The activity in the southwest region was escalating.

Doh was at her side explaining something, when Jeen interrupted.

"We've got problems, Weepf."

"No kidding." The new mission commander emphasized understatement in her own style of sarcasm.

"Have you seen this yet?" Jeen asked, handing Weepf the satellite photos and local California news broadcasts.

Weepf checked the photos twice. Her Vansar eyes enhanced the images. "These photographs have a diffracted quality about them. Normally, I would attribute the phenomenon to poor lens quality, but ... as I recall ... we saw the same type of pattern when the animals attacked the first headquarters."

She beckoned the other Efilu to come closer. "Notice here and here," she instructed, pointing as she spoke. "Warships. The heaviest armament in the U.S. arsenal ... And they are firing weapons."

Frustration painted her features dark. Then suddenly a wry expression. "Tur mentioned cloning, did he not?" she queried. Ikara nodded slowly. "And the mini-wave shielding shows signs of failing? We cannot allow Efilu genes or technology to fall in to Jing Pen hands."

"Of, course not," Doh added "But what can we do? Tur gave specific orders that safety of the algae was to take top priority ..."

Weepf waited patiently for the paleontologist to make his beleaguered point, then said, "Precisely. We can't leave this ball of mud for several months; yet, we cannot afford a compromise of our tactical edge."

"But—"

"This is now an issue of security," she stated. Doh was the only one present who still looked uncomfortable with her position.

One of the generals who stopped his assigned task to try to discern what the commotion was about caught Gober Dil's eye. "What about them?" Dil asked.

Weepf looked at the little general with a smile that chilled his bones.

"Nothing. But the others we burn, the ones that Jeen fixed."

Ikara protested "You can't just leav—"

Weepf put a hand on her shoulder to silence her objection. "It's alright. We will command them to hold the others here indefinitely, but set the cortical field intensity on maximum. The overload will burn out every synapse serving higher functions in their fat little heads within two days. It will look like meningoencephalitis. Their diagnostics will turn up nothing familiar and they'll conclude the cause was a biological weapon gone wrong. The others will be quarantined, especially after telling the story of the Pentagon being taken over by 'alien dinosaurs.'"

Weepf smiled again. "It doesn't matter anyway. This society is already dead. These people just don't know it yet."

Ikara's puzzled look found an answer from the Vansar mer. "Good government is a matter of empathic rapport, just as good security is a matter of habit. You can't compromise on fundamental principles and hope your mistakes get forgotten or compensated for by the system.

"This entire economy in running out of resources. It is concentrating the wealth in the top one percent. They are reducing the work force to save funds, at the same time pushing the remaining workers beyond reasonable limits. They still have to support the growing ranks of the poor and unemployed, with health care, food, shelter ...

"The minions, empowered by desperation, are calling leaders to task and bringing down one staple institution after another: the health care profession, education, law enforcers, finance, entertainers, the legal system, even the politicians themselves. The leaders have become complacent in the belief that the trends simply represent a cycle that will run a limited course and return to an acceptable status quo. I see chaos destroying them in no more than twenty years.

"Remember, we've seen these signs before. WE don't need to do another thing here. Let's go."

* * * * *

Devit's coat was visibly thinning from throwing quills at attacking dogs and men. Los had reached the crest of the hill. "Over here!" he shouted, "They got—" An explosion rocked the top of the hill. Los was no where to be seen.

Tur ignored the loss, and didn't even look for the body when he reached the high point.

At the foot of the hill he saw the mobile command center, guarded by two bears. When the others caught up to him, Tur just pointed as he lead them toward it. Bo Tep silently ordered his left-hand meg to work his way around the battlefield.

One of the sentries growled in confusion at the charging Efilu force. Colonel Doyle came to the window. Instinct recognized the antagonist before intellect did. "Tur ..." he breathed almost inaudibly. "Lieutenant! Turn the turret 150 degrees," he shouted. Noting the confusion on the young man's face, he barked "Now!" The officer complied.

Doyle nearly tripped getting to the gunnery controls, then began firing at will. To his horror, Tur took the brunt of the anti-tank weaponry in stride. "Ernie, raise Bravo Company," he commanded. "Tell them to forget Vit Na. Redeploy them here. If those monsters get us, we're all done."

Major Dixon carried out the order, but imagined he felt the icy grip of death closing around his soul.

The major had no sooner completed his instructions when the rear wall of the vehicle began to peel open. Rig Ejen, Bo Tep's right-hand meg, barreled through the view port as the gash in the back wall revealed his left-hand meg, Di Otz. Man knew not what every Efilu cub knows: Tralkyz always attack in pairs!

The command center rocked for a while, quivering with inhuman screams that issued from the mouths of human victims. Then there was ... silence. The Tralkyz pair came out, not even winded and looking for fresh adversaries. They stepped on the remains of the guard bears Rig Ejen had disposed of on the way in.

A rain of shrapnel signaled the failing of the mini-wave shield.

*   *   *   *   *

"We're on our own now," Devit murmured under his breath. Tur was too far away to hear. He was engaging the tank brigade that had responded to the distress call.

Two tanks vaporized before he could move toward them.

Weepf hovered above the battle site in full glory. Gel-enhanced field compression made her virtually invulnerable. The Translation Horizon she generated allowed her to maneuver far beyond the physical limits of a body with her mass.

"It looked like you needed a little help," she called to Tur defiantly.

An unexpected smile greeted her. "I'm glad you're here. Get that missile fire off of us. We'll handle the rest."

The compliment of smaller Efilu sported mini-wave mass drivers that were designed to spew high-energy free radicals. Configured for supersonic flight, the piloted gel-mecha prepared to rain aerial destruction on mammalian targets. She signaled all "Deathwings" to deploy against the tanks and warships in the harbor. Her orders: "Spare no one."

"Wait!" Tur called to her before she got into the thick of it. "Drop a bit of gel down here. Vit Na is hurt. I don't know how bad yet."

Weepf could see Vit Na laying still on the ground near the smoldering transformer. Tur was too far away to make out the Vansar's grave expression as Weepf complied with his request.

He met little resistance as he made his way up the hillside.

The only light in the early morning sky came from naval jets burning as they fell victim to Weepf's fully-armed fury. Devit came up beside Tur, who was silently bent over Vit Na, obscuring the Ironde's view of her. As he came around to face the High Commander, he saw the grievous site: So Wari tears washing over a broken figure.

Vit Na was breathing agonally. Her eyes were glazed. There was water vapor rising from her body in the chilled night air. Devit felt helpless. His medical training was so limited ... He couldn't do anything.

No one could DO anything.

* * * * *

Weepf had come around after finishing off the bulk of the human air assault force and was closing rapidly on the retreating survivors. She slowed just enough to build up a lethal charge in the rarefied air in front of her. She then plotted the optimal course to spread the energy through the formation of planes, and zoomed through it. The explosions were deafening. Blinding.

Somehow, to her the effect lasted too long. Then Weepf realized the light was coming from above her. Pulsating silently. The sky shone as midday. The source was a familiar, odd shape.

The Repam's stasis field allowed for no vibration, draping the countryside in an eerie unnatural stillness. Weepf looked at the human confusion with glee. Men screamed futile instructions to each other at the top of their lungs. Distraught dogs howled at the light for mercy, to no avail.

The Efilu, communicating telepathically, were unaffected. Most by now had gathered around Vit Na's still form. None of them noticed as the mammals running wildly about the hillside below them simply began winking silently out of existence. When it was over, wisps of ash were the only Jing legacy of the conflict.

A silver thread dropped from the Repam's underside and pooled on the ground a few yards from the group. Car Hom stepped out of it, and approached his companions somberly, knowing already by ship's sensors what most of them were just learning: Vit Na was dead.

Chapter 29
PHOENIX

"We must prepare," Tur said stoically. He displayed no emotion, but there was an overwhelming intensity in the thought projection.

"Of course," Car Hom responded in an appropriately solemn tone.

After a moment, Tur added, "Surprised to see you again alive, old friend." Car Hom didn't know how to take that comment under the circumstances. Yet he noted a touch of warmth in the statement.

"Friend? Since when did you count me among your friends?" Car Hom said, half jokingly.

Tur smiled grimly. "I suppose friends are like fingers: lose one and you begin to keep count of the rest."

The High Commander turned to face his first officer. "I've always considered you a friend," he said. After a pause, he added, "I just never said so."

Sensing discomfort, Car Hom mercifully changed the subject. "I had the hardest time finding you all. When I saw the devastation at the Aleutian base, I surmised that you must have gotten into some trouble. Normally, I wouldn't have been so pessimistic, but knowing that you were all under the influence, I couldn't be sure. Naturally we monitored the air waves for distress calls, but—"

"Wait. Hold on. Under the influence of what?" Tur demanded confusedly.

"Oh. I'm sorry, I should have told you immediately. I must have been distracted. The Inhibition Field. We discovered that not only do the Jing Pen have inhibitory centers in THEIR brains, they actually generate a field of psychic inhibition. It's amazing that you could communicate intimately at all in that static. We discovered that it also interfered with the radial thinking process. Basically it reduced you almost to their level. I'm glad to see you were up to the challenge."

Tur looked momentarily distressed. "If we are at risk for psychic interference—"

Car Hom interrupted him with a gently raised hand. "It's no longer a problem. The stasis field the ship is generating nullifies the inhibitory effect. The mute quality was just a flourish."

Tur gave him an approving shake of the head. "You Super Hunters and your flourishes. Nice work, Car."

"Don't get carried away with praising staff, now," Car Hom said. "I'll have to become the disciplinarian, and I'm getting too old to play the 'bad commander.'"

Car Hom looked over Tur's shoulder. Brajay was there now. Los had been found and it looked as if he might survive, but it didn't look as if he would ever be able to run again. A long, slow death was all the once Acting Commander of the Repam had to look forward to.

They were ready. A congregation of comrades and friends now encircled Vit Na's motionless form. Tur joined them, followed by Car Hom. Someone handed Tur a sharp pair of ritual wrist shears. He accepted them absently, ignoring their significance for as long as he could.

Thoughts reached deep into the stillness that was Vit Na's mind. In unison, they breathed life into that void and slowly, she rose from the cold darkness of the beyond. The specter briefly looked down at her own remains with some remorse at the realization of death. She focused the group, aiding them in funneling some of their life force through the corpse, extracting every iota of memory, feeling and intention ... in essence, her very soul.

The configuration process was private, but lasted only moments. When it was done, the Animem materialized, almost reached for the corporeal form, but suddenly turned away. She reached out for Tur instead. A warm hug was enjoyed by both without shame.

Vit Na Iku, as she had now become, ordered a gel console and proceeded to catalogue information gained while she was held captive. Doh's findings needed correlation with the archives from archeology department. The Animem was helpful in organizing data, but was limited in its ability to analyze the new data brought in by Doh. Preliminary debriefing would take place once on board the Repam, then Vit Na Iku would rest.

"The Repam is fully armed and at 70% of full power. How much of this world would you like to eradicate, Commander?" Car Hom asked. The old Alkyz was absolutely formal in his request. The decision was Tur's alone.

"How did you recover anyway?" Bo Tep asked, approaching from the first officer's left side.

"Remember when we came into this star system and we bypassed the binary planet?" asked Car Hom. "Ages ago, it was the sentry station at the edge of the solar system. It was equipped with supplies and armaments, although no algae. It was of no use to us when we approached, of course, but we were able to dock and repair the ship adequately.

"We did a tight perihelion to recharge the core and here we are. Of course, there is no way of achieving full power from a yellow star without a singularity for energy compression."

"When you were last in contact, the Repam's orbit was rapidly deteriorating. How did you even get out of the atmosphere?" Tur asked.

"That was the embarrassing thing. Once I escape the Inhibition Field, and my head cleared, it was obvious. The damn thing works a lot like the Poison. The only reason the Repam sustained any damage at all was because that pompous idiot brought the nuclear device INTO the ship! The majority of the hull was intact. We were in danger of crashing to the surface of Fitu, even suffering more damage and casualties, but that was all. The ship would not have suffered irreparable damage."

Bo Tep and Tur then finished the explanation for him in unison. "So, you used the force of the second blast to propel you out of orbit."

Car Hom glibly bowed in affirmation. "Simple." Then becoming more serious, he asked, "So, Tur, about your orders? Do we wipe them out or don't we?"

The So Wari High Commander shook his head. "What's the point? It won't undo anything and they really don't represent a significant threat anymore." Without another word, he walked deliberately to the hill.

He returned to where Vit Na's corpse still lay. Tur took the shears he still held in his hand and neatly snipped Vit Na's hands off at the wrists. Custom demanded that the final act be done by the departed's next of kin.

The next part of the ceremony fell to the mission commander. Tur had the misfortune of being both on this voyage.

He gestured into the air with his right hand. It began to glow red. He manipulate one hand around another, never touching one with the other, in a careful complex ritual. The red glow became an intense white, radiant sphere encompassing both hands. He extended his hands together toward Vit Na, but hesitated.

Tur swore he would not humiliate himself again with tears. He squeezed his eyes shut, jerked his head away from the group, snorted once and unleashed a searing white beam. The heat was hardly felt by Tur, but it did dry the lone tear that escaped his eye before it could fall.

He returned to the Lift point where now only Car Hom waited. As the So Wari stood, it looked as if his arms had become too heavy to carry on his shoulders. "Just take us home, Car." Tur's head hung low, he tried to lift a hand to Car Hom's shoulder, but couldn't complete the effort somehow. "I'm so tired." He caressed the limp, dismembered Melkyz hands in his own. "I just want to go home."

*   *   *   *   *

Clyde Olsen still lay writhing on the cold forest floor, as he had all night. Visions of small furry creatures with big pointed ears and twisting tails crawling all over his body haunted him. He remembered seeing alien hieroglyphs and somehow understood their meaning. He had an overwhelming compulsion: *I must get to Tur! He needs me. Needs to know I'm safe.* He stood, and felt off balance. He fell forward more than once. It seemed that something was missing.

When he tried to envision home, his thoughts focused on two drastically different images simultaneously. His mind was reeling. Too many voices were speaking at once, and there was no way to answer.

"Stop that noise! Let me out. Don't tie my tail that way! Quit touching me! Leave me alone."

Leaves blew wildly. To his horror, he saw and recognized the Repam lifting off in the distance. He screamed in distress "Don't leave me!" Then he sat back down on the damp leaves sobbing uncontrollably.

Olsen spoke out loud to himself. "How can anyone hope to live like this?" The sunrise brought little warmth, but more light than he could bear revealed a form most alien to him. He looked at his hands in disgust. He saw pale skin which was sparsely covered with hair, a clumsy physique. His first coherent thought: *Damned to a living hell in my own body.*

Then, his sobbing ceased as if a switch had been thrown. A single desperate thought came to him.

"The Keepers."

EPILOGUE

Tur rested casually in the ancient forechair reserved for the Sentry-at-Arms. His rank of High Commander was now official upon completion of the Retrieval, as the mission was currently being called. He sat quietly during the remaining debriefing session. *Why does everything have to have a grand name in our culture? The Exodus. The Return, The Keepers. I'm getting sick of all of this "Uniqueness."*

The Council was in session. There would probably be jubilation when the public could be informed of the gravity of the situation that they had been told so little about, now that its resolution was at hand.

The former crew of the Repam had given their reports by department. Somehow, Acquisitions was slated for last on the agenda.

A break in the proceedings had been announced. The Round Table chamber had been opened up to the large anteroom, which usually was subdivided into offices, in order to accommodate the recess.

"Very compelling testimony." Some one projected a thought to Tur without identifying himself. It was Thea, resting on his haunches in a dim corner ... listening.

"You realize that 'intelligent mammal' is a contradiction in terms, don't you? What is this Doh trying to prove? No one will believe this story."

Thea was quietly debating with one So Wari who wasn't the least interested in debate.

"Now, mind you, I don't suggest that you are fabricating the story, but we all know the Kini Tod are prone to ... shall we say, exaggeration?"

Tur simply looked at him coldly. “You weren’t there,” he stated. Wary of offending a So Wari, Thea stood and took a step towards the light.

“We will see,” Thea said, still looking back over his shoulder as he walked away from the High Commander. The open section of the room was filled with murmuring meren who also had opinions on what had been learned of the adventure so far.

The Council had reconvened and each delegate had resumed his seat at the Table. The Repam’s senior staff was accounted for, save one: Bo Tep was nowhere to be seen.

“Engage the Melkyz Animem sequence,” Yaw Doar said, looking to Meeth for approval. “With your leave of course,” he added.

Meeth nodded curtly. Vit Na Iku began her humble salutations before recounting for the assembled dignitaries the details of the trek back to Fitu. Tur watched without emotion. He had stilled his mind such that his feelings could not be heard. Memories of his tears flooded back as she referred to the private sequence. He wasn’t sure he wanted to review it.

The Council experienced Vit Na’s four-month ordeal during what was left of the evening. The doubts that initially had permeated the chamber melted away as the extraordinary trek became a part of each of them. There was a long silence before any thoughts were shared.

“What a noble sacrifice. The Melkyz community should feel honored,” said Slijay, an elegant orator. “She has done us all honor.”

“Yes, but be that as it may, we still do not know from whence this plague has come to us. As Vit Na Iku has shown us, this Inhibition Field that the Jing Pen generate is strikingly similar to the Poison itself. This is too strange to be coincident. We may still have a deadly enemy amongst us,” Meeth said.

“Meeth, we’ve been through this. The Quatal made a bold move against us, gambling everything on one clutch. They missed the mark. We all feel terrible about this ugly affair, but it’s over. Give it a rest.”

Car Hom stepped up to Slijay deliberately. The move, although disconcerting reminded Slijay that his last statement could easily be interpreted as a challenge to the Head of the Council. He apologized profusely. Meeth never formally accepted. Instead, he continued his statement as if he never had been interrupted.

“We have taken the liberty of purging the entire algae population.” A general wave of surprised thought projections rippled through the chamber. This Meeth had expected, but he also knew someone would be outraged. It was just a matter of who.

Thea spoke up, boldly. "Don't you think that that's a bit excessive? I mean the threat is gone, why waste the resources? The healthy algae will just supplant the bad." *He shows annoyance, but no more. Someone must feel more.*

"Meeth, I'm sorry, but I, for one, agree with Thea. You had no right to commit those resources to such a large-scale and useless project. We have been watching you. My information on you suggests a string of irrational decisions on your part. This mission for example: what an incredible discovery, but the logic for launching it was flawed. There was never a need to send so much expensive hardware into the unknown. We could have solved our problems from this end."

Meeth allowed Slijay to ramble on uninterrupted. He began to circle the room as the smaller meg spoke. The Sulenz loved attention, and they so seldom got such an opportunity. This one now, unknowingly, held Meeth's attention most closely.

"It's a wonderful find ... The legacy of the Keepers at last comes back to the fold. Let us speak plainly here today. We have been drifting apart for ages. Each of us seeking our own destiny. Subtle friction between our societies is tolerable, but in recent years indifference has become the norm.

"Whatever happened to the days when we cared about each other? When we shared our brother's glory as well as our brother's woes? We have become selfish and cold. These Jing Pen represent a rekindling of the fires that forged our Realm."

Yaw Doar eyed Meeth pacing restlessly as the Sulenz spoke. "What do you mean a 'rekindling,' Slijay?" The Alkyz asked suspiciously.

"An opportunity, brother. When was the last time someone outside of your clan called you brother? I'd guess a lifetime. We have an opportunity to welcome a new society to the fold.

"Alone, scared, confused in a hostile world, the Jing Pen survive and grow, but at a snail's pace. They live, brothers, in our cold shadow, with no one to protect them. They exist at the mercy of those who envy us and our Realm.

"The Quatal tried to get at us through a thing as simple as the algae our livestock consume. What if some desperate foe — or as Meeth has suggested, some deranged faction of our own society — were to exploit the Jing Pen? Those who would might seek to, and conceivably could destroy us through them."

"The fledgling Jing need guidance. Our guidance," Slijay intoned. He momentarily stopped pacing and paused for dramatic effect. "I refer you all to the Pact we swore to up hold so many eons ago: 'No child of Fitu that has achieved sentience shall be denied audience to petition admittance to the Greater Society.'"

Hushed murmurs followed as the ramifications of Slijay's observation sank in. "By definition, whether they have been engineered so or not, they do meet the minimal criteria for claiming Efilu heritage. The Enlightened children of Fitu shall be welcomed!"

The Melkyz delegate Yhm Vel spoke mockingly. "There is a great gap between simple sentience and Enlightenment. They seem more like stepchildren than children by my reckoning."

Slijay responded almost too smoothly. "The Efilu are traditionally a matrilineal society, my dear. It doesn't matter how they were fathered." The argument was all too neat. Consternation and distaste dominated most of the participants in the room— all, save two.

Chybon, the High Tyen, sat at his station, ostensibly devoid of any opinions at all. The other was Meeth, who thought, *I still don't know for sure who is responsible for all of this subterfuge. This Slijay seems to voice a lone opinion. He is eloquent and knowledgeable, but no one is buying what he is selling. ... So far. Still if what this Melkyz Animem says is true, entry of the Jing Pen could prove disastrous. There must be some way to silence this Sulenz.*

"Many of us are testy. The strain of tolerating the substitute food source for months has made us all irritable. Let's table this discussion for now and resume at a later date," Tur motioned. He had been observing the dynamics in the room. Slijay had grown bold ... or desperate.

"That Animem has some Jing Pen psychic components. The chance to learn from them could prove invaluable. They do make references to our images as 'Gods.' It would be quite beneficial to them if we could reverse this Inhibition Factor they are burdened with. On behalf of the Sulenz people, I volunteer our resources to voyage back to Fitu to begin the transfer."

"I forbid it!" Meeth decreed.

"We do not recognize your authority to forbid the return to Fitu," Slijay said. The Sulenz watched Meeth sigh in resignation and droned on. "It is with in our rights ..."

The haunting words of his father Corp echoed in Meeth's mind ... *The Spirit of the Law ... Action!*

Slijay didn't see the deadly So Wari tail whipping at him with at lightening speed. "I can point out—"

The last thing he saw was the horrified looks of his peers as his body was cleft in two by the lethal spikes. Meeth deftly followed through with the wheeling movement, with obvious satisfaction. His expression was exactly as if he had inadvertently crushed an unseen Jing into expensive floor cover. Then he feigned just the right amount of remorse when he looked at Slijay's hewn body at both ends of his station.

"I forgave his transgression once. Twice, I am loathe to grant. I say now that the Jing Pen race is a potential Threat to Life. I don't know what could happen if they were brought here to the Realm, but we all have experience with results of Sulenz biologic experimentation.

"Until we can all clear the neurotoxins built up from utilizing the substitute food source, I don't want any complications from Jing Pen psychic contamination. I hereby move that we seal off the Fitu star system until we can sort this thing out." Meeth sat down and noted that many of those assembled were still staring at Slijay's remains. Tur had come forth to contain the volatile situation.

Meeth spoke for all to hear. "Clearly my irritability may have led to impulsive action here today. Until I have recovered enough to carry out my responsibilities, I will step down as Head of the Council."

Tur took him by the arm, only to be relieved of his charge by two Tyen security meren. *Since when did the Tyen concern themselves with security?* Tur thought to himself.

* * * * *

Martial law had been rescinded less than a month ago. Business as usual had not quite returned to San Francisco. A lone figure stood behind the counter of the little shop at Post and Taylor. "'The Dragon's Lair.' What an interesting name for a store," the old man said. The tall Black woman simply said, "Thank you."

Robyn Washington was working on a translation of a Druid text. The man had the look of a retired college professor. He was bald with a white beard and spectacles. He wore a tweed sports coat with oversized pockets and suede elbow patches. Also, he carried an umbrella as it was quite overcast. Washington smiled at him.

"Do you also fix the computers?" he asked pointing to the sign with his umbrella: "Computer Repairs. Payment Only For Reparable Damage. Free Diagnostics."

She smiled more broadly. "No. My fiancé does that," she answered. The man wrinkled his brow "He must be very good to make such a bold offer."

"You have to leave it over night for the diagnostic," Clyde Olsen said, parting the curtains that separated the back room from the main store area. The older man didn't even raise an eyebrow at the sight of the white man.

"Well," he said. "I have been having some trouble with my desktop computer. It's a little old, but then, so is anything over six months old these days!" he said and laughed at his own joke.

Olsen smiled.

"What's your name son?" the man asked.

"I am called Ol Sen."

The man nodded. "Nordic heritage. Good stock."

"I'll bring my CPU in tomorrow. I had come in from the street expecting the usually comic books, sci-fi and fantasy magazines and paperbacks. This occult collection of books maps and curios could be the envy of any shop in New England or the UK. I'll bring some very old books you may find interesting young lady ... and maybe a dragon or two!" he said with another laugh.

"We'd be very happy to see them." Olsen said cheerfully. The man left.

"Did you find anything new, Robyn?"

"Not much Vit — I mean Clyde. Most of this is the same as the others, containing vague references to dragon hordes, but there is a section in here that actually contains a map."

Olsen stroked his hair backward and frowned. "If it looks promising, we'll check it out."

Washington looked at him with a little concern. "How are our finances?"

Olsen smiled. "Don't worry. We have about thirty-eight thousand dollars after expenses. Your stock market has been very good to us this month."

* * * * *

"Ol Ygar died two months ago, Bo," the Tralkyz emissary had told Bo Tep. "You have been named his successor." The young meg looked as if he had more to say, but was tentative about saying it. Two Si Tyen security meren had sequestered Bo Tep for a private, "preliminary" debriefing. They stood guard at the door to the small conference chamber.

"The Council supports a change in leadership. The Tralkyz haven't led the council in three thousand years. The populace thinks we're due a tour of duty," Bo Tep explained.

"You don't look surprised," the younger Tralkyz observed. Bo Tep smiled. "When you've been through what I've been through in the past four months, there aren't many surprises left."

"Well, here's one for you: You got the go ahead from the Si Tyen quarter."

Bo Tep was more than surprised. He was shocked. "The Tyen? Are you sure?" Bo Tep asked, looking at the two guards at the door.

"Positively. They swayed the lower societies to vote in our favor ... In YOUR favor, my liege."

Bo Tep raised an eye brow at the note of sarcasm. The meg was also a pack leader and nearly eye to eye with Bo Tep. "Watch that, Tee Spuun. I'm not bound by Round Table etiquette yet. I can still take you out and wipe you down," he warned. A smile took the edge off of the threat.

"Anyway, we can finally get a few things changed around here, you think?" Tee Spuun was very diffident for a Tralkyz. *He wouldn't last long in the trials of leadership,* Bo Tep thought to himself.

"I don't know," Bo Tep answered slowly in whispered tones, more to himself than to his dull informant. "Why would the Si Tyen, of all people, manipulate US into a position of power? ME, of all people? I just led the most recent assault against that Tyen in the Forest of Feelings. It doesn't make sense." He tugged at his chin.

"They are very righteous by nature," Tee Spuun offered.

"Yeah, maybe ... maybe," Bo Tep hesitated. *I don't think anyone's that righteous,* he thought to himself. "Anyway it won't matter for years. Meeth is old, but I'm sure he'll be around for a good long time."

In fact, Bo Tep's installation as Heir Apparent to the head of the Council was a very simple affair, down-played by the Tralkyz. For now, he would only be the High Chief of the Tralkyz Lesser Society.

Curiously, he had entered the Round Table chamber just in time to see Meeth being lead out. It was something about the set of the Tyen guard's shoulders that told him something was going very wrong.

Bo Tep found the timing to be very suspicious. The Sulenz were expected to whine a bit but they wouldn't dare charge Meeth, under the circumstances. No one, then, had expected the Si Tyen to press for a ethics investigation. As the acting head of Council Security, Timon had Meeth arrested.

Enter Bo Tep.

The Council's welcome was formal and cool ... all except for the High Tyen's smile. It was warm, almost friendly. Then Bo Tep realized: *He's the one! ... from the forest. I'd recognize that smug look anywhere.* It all made sense now. *The Tyen have been playing us from the beginning. Me, Tur, Meeth, the Council ... even Vit Na ... And it looks to everyone like I'm in on this whole thing!*

He had reached his seat at the traditional head of the Table. The inauguration was casual in its simplicity. Timon, the Si Tyen delegate stood obviously ready to assume the official position as Chief of Security. *It's too pat,* Bo Tep decided. *I have to break this up somehow. They've installed me here for their own reasons. I don't know what they've got on me, but if one of them also gets the top security position too ...*

The new Tralkyz High Chief thought fast. He knew the people he could absolutely trust and rely on were few. More important now than basic competence, was loyalty. "Timon, as of now you are relieved of all duties as head of Council Security. I name Tur to that position effective immediately," he said.

The Si Tyen were visibly shaken. Bo Tep suppressed a wry smile. "I've come to know this meg better than I know my brother on our little outing, and I can't think of anyone the Council could trust more than him.

"As for the Jing Pen and the remainder of Fitu, from this moment on the planet will be off-limits. Completely quarantined. No one goes there, no one communicates with them and no one sends any little 'care packages' to them." He eyed the Sulenz, Ironde and Si Tyen with that statement.

"We can re-examine Doh's records at our leisure. See to it that the information is made available to all interested parties." He nodded to Jeen.

"Weepf, as you are now unemployed, you will head the official study of the Jing Pen and their right to claim Efilu heritage. This session of the Council is here by adjourned."

Short and to the point, Tur thought to himself. *I think I'm going to like this new Council.*

*   *   *   *   *

"Do you want to tell me what this is all about, Sedon? You're not regular security," Meeth said casually.

"And you're not crazy either, Meeth. You deliberately killed Slijay because he threatened to bring the Jing Pen into the bosom of Greater Society." He tightened his grip on Meeth's arm. "We may have lost our voice in Council Intelligence for now, but he'll be replaced.

"You don't win a war by fighting every battle tooth and claw. What does matter is that to survive, any Lesser Society must take responsibility for its members or the Greater Society will do it instead. When our peoples truly understand the difference between simple sentience and enlightenment the remaining answers will become obvious. We've already primed Bo Tep to lead the Council.

Sedon and his companion were leading Meeth deeper into the winding corridors that led to the catacombs beneath the Round Table. Meeth noted a pair of Melkyz hands dangling at Sedon's side.

"You're hoping to get at data on the fate of the Keepers. That's why you supported the Sulenz motion to admit the Jing Pen to the Greater Society," Meeth said, trying not to struggle. *Don't alert them to your next move.*

"You still don't understand. We aren't looking for the Keepers, WE are the Keepers."

Meeth looked at him with both disbelief and horror. "That's right. We discovered millions of years ago how to travel, via astral displacement, to distant worlds. Unfortunately, it requires a combined group effort. We can only send one or two at a time. The drain on our life force leaves many of us sterile. We discovered that too late. Needless to say, our reproduction has dropped off.

"We have had a very weak presence on Fitu for the last five hundred thousand years — since the Great Revolt there. There were complications you know. A few Animem Tyen were left to guide the surviving Jing." The meg shrugged. "It was the best we could do. We have been completely out of contact for four hundred years. We needed you to expose the existence of the human race, to see what the Jing have done in our absence. They belong to Fitu and therefore to us."

The Tyen now took on a more persuasive tone. "We have become stagnant. The Efilu have not admitted a species to the Greater Society in nearly seventy million years. We have to broaden our definition of intelligence to include new species of Fituine origin, even if they are quasi-artificial. The Greater Society is becoming sterile.

"Both the human tribes and the Efilu Realm will collapse if we don't get some new blood into our communities. The Jing will probably end up killing themselves if we don't guide them. They need our help. We need each other, whether you realize it or not.

"The So Wari, at least, are doing just fine on our own. We don't need some fur mites coming in here and getting into everything ... And we certainly don't need mystical guidance in making our decisions. We are not impressed with Level Four psychic tricks," Meeth said resentfully.

The right-hand guard said, a little haughtily, "Actually, Level Six." Meeth's mind raced through the possibilities of what a Level Six psychic could do. He had never heard of such a thing. The revelation came to him like the shock of ice water suddenly coursing through his veins.

"Tyen! YOU were the architects of the Poison."

The Tyen mer had remained anonymous, but now spoke. "Yes, but we can never admit it. For hundreds of thousands of years we have tried to teach these Jing Pen how to Dance Life. They're slow learners. We only wanted to show all Efilu what it is like to—"

With that, Meeth suddenly broke free of the grips that he had been subtly loosening from his arms since they started down the hall. He was able to trap one of his captors against the wall and crush her spine. The other dealt Meeth a crippling blow to the chest. Meeth couldn't tell if he was seeing double or if another Tyen had joined the ruckus.

Meeth knew he was dying with the second blow to his head. With his last iota of concentration, he projected, "Help. Someone! Don't let them into the inner circle of the Council. The Tyen are mad, all of them! They ruin everything they touch! They ARE the Poison! They'll destroy us all! Fight, Bo. Fight ... *Them ...*"

END SEQUENCE

JING PEN TRANSLATOR

ALKZ- The largest and strongest of the Super Hunters. The name evolved into Alkyz after the Exodus. They are well known for their administrative and diplomatic skills.

ALOM (also ALUM)-The inescapable current or river of fate. It both leads and follows one everywhere. The Efilu personalize their particular branch of the stream of time and space.

ANIMEM- Animated memory used for interactive storage of an individual's life experiences, mind, soul and body image. Animem may take tangible form, but are limited to deductive reasoning. An animem cannot internalize new knowledge.

BIM- Measure of energy equal to the radiant energy that strikes a plane the area of a square dyme in one one thousandth of a day at a distance of 50,000 dymes. Modern humans would measure bims in terms of kilojoules.

BOLOK- Livestock used much as cattle are used to day. These were the Triceratops of the Cretaceous period.

DAEBIM- One tenth of a bim. See BIM.

DAEDYME- One tenth of a dyme, or about 1800 miles.See DYME.

DYME- One tenth the distance traveled by sound in a twenty-four hour day. About 18,000 miles.

EFILU- Enlightened children of Fitu. Intelligent peoples who had their origins on Fitu. All are telepathic to some degree. All are descended from what we have come to know as dinosaurs. See EFILU: THE PEOPLES OF THE REALM.

FITU- The Efilu name for Earth.

FORECHAIR- Because of the presence of the tail, most Efilu are not comfortable sitting in a chair with a back. The forechair has a vertical supporting structure in the front for the chest, and a horizontal extension in the rear for the tail. Side arms are usually absent altogether, or are located on the front of the chair, over which clasped arms may rest.

FUR MITE- Efilu slang term for a small mammal.

GEL APPARATUS- A variety of crystal integration machines used for managing, storing and transmitting data. They are coupled with a solution of electromagnetically active particles that act as microscopic construction devices or building block to form a macroscopic tool or structure. (e.g. Gelconsole, gelcore, gelcraft, geldecor, gelfactory). Also, See WAVE.

IRFONDE- Omnivorous people that had a nomadic, loose society, and became well known for their adaptive skill using very little raw material. They became power producers and suppliers for many of the lower societies. The name has changed slightly since the migration, to Ironde.

JING- A broad term referring to mammals. The Efilu make no distinction between Jing with reference to size or species. Also a term of derision.

KAS PEN- Snakes. Genetically engineered reptiles designed to control mammalian (Jing) population. The absence of limbs was an unnatural adaptation to pursuing smaller quarry into burrows against which the primitive mammals had no defense.

KORIBIM- One hundredth of a bim. See BIM.

KORIDYME- One hundredth of a dyme, or about 180 miles. See DYME.

MEG- A male Efilu.

MER- A female Efilu.

MEREN- More than one Efilu.

MINI-WAVE- A gel apparatus that is one thousandth the mass of a wave. See WAVE.

NELKY- Small saurian people of the class of Super Hunters descended from an ancestor similar to the velociraptor. They have the ability to blend into the background of there surroundings. Over the 65 million years since the migration known as the Exodus, the name has evolved to adhere to the nomenclature of Super Hunters (-lkyz suffix) by changing to Melkyz. They are among the most brilliant strategists.

PEN- The modifier used to denote genetic engineering of the natural organism to suit Efilu needs. The name of the natural base organism always precedes the word Pen.

PERSONAL SPHERE OF INFLUENCE- The natural electromagnetic aura that is generated by all living things. The Efilu generate a more intense field than most lower life forms, owing to their high metabolism and tissue density. Furthermore, by means of extra-sensory perception, the field is partially visible to them. To one degree or another, the Efilu have been able to fold and convolute the field into more complex and versatile psychic appendages (e.g. astral sensory probes, electromagnetic emitters, telekinetic pseudopods).

PHOTODYME- The distance traveled by light in ten years.

QUATAL- A defeated enemy race. They were shape shifters who challenged the Efilu in battle ... unsuccessfully.

ROOGS- Large marine people who raise fresh produce and biological power sources as well as design most large space craft. On land they travel in large water filled corpuscles or that are sacks shaped like gigantic red blood cells and float on force fields.

THE ROUND TABLE- A medium sized city, by our standards, that holds the seat of Efilu power. The city is carved from a single hardwood tree trunk. Still living, the tree is fed and powered by saprophytic plants rooted to its circulatory system. Its power source is supplemented by artificially produced energy. The center piece of this structure is the Round Table itself: an elaborate council chamber with an advanced data processing system built into it. The whole structure is the handiwork of the So Beni engineers and has remained intact for over seventy million years. It was salvaged from Fitu fifty years after being left behind during the Exodus.

SENORI- Known to us as the Allosaurus. A wild animal which hunted in packs. It was similar to the Tyrannosaurus, but slightly smaller, with longer, stronger arms.

SENORI PEN- Genetically engineered therapods derived from the natural animal we call the Allosaurus. They were bred by the Sulenz to act as guardians against marauding therapods. They all but drove their natural counterparts to extinction in the wild. Eventually they became like mad dogs, prone to intimidate and loot defenseless peoples. The arms were genetically shortened to limit their ability to fend independently in the wild. They were virtually unstoppable without the use of advanced weapons. We know them by their skeletal remains, as the Tyrannosaurus Rex.

SO BENI- Large saurian people; among the most influential and physically powerful. Their ancestors were herbivores similar to the Stegosaurus. They and their successors were known for their military and engineering skills. They were eventually supplanted by the So Wari. See EFILU: THE PEOPLES OF THE REALM.

SULENZ- Small, almost tailess people who primarily live on insects they raised on ranches or farms in order to exploit their meat and honey. Sulenz adapted the "z" at the end of their name to associate themselves with the Super Hunters. They were never accepted as such. They are among the most gifted of telepaths, but not very popular.

SYNESPRIT- A romantic or philosophical description indicating "as one of the spirit." The terms describes lovers and great thinkers who concur with one another.

TELESCIEN- A pure energy machine with no mass. One of a variety of External Field Appendages (EFA) used by the Efilu for remote manipulation. The compound force field unit is controlled through a telepathy-sensitive interface with its Efilu counterpart, instantaneously, even at great distances. Effectively it's a temporary, god-like automaton with artificial intelligence beyond that of any computer known to man.

TOMET- A peaceful alien race that made the mistake of settling in a star system once inhabited by the Efilu.

TRALKYZ- Second largest of the Super Hunter races. They are unpredictable in every respect, except for their viciousness, and the fact that they always attack in pairs. Pound for pound they are the fiercest of the Super Hunter class.

TYEN- Technically, Si Tyen. They are distant relatives of the So species. These people have developed a pair of oversized dorsal plates that function as wings. A few stayed behind to try to salvage the Earth from the catastrophe the caused by the Sulenz. We know them from our distant memories, as Dragons.

VANSAR- Among the largest avian species in the Efilu Realm. They rival the So Wari and Tyen in size.

WAVE- Large gel apparatus used for extensive planetary or orbital tasks, (engineering or military). Very versatile, it can assume many configurations, but not the nearly infinite number capable by the telescien. It has a potentially greater energy output than a telescien since it has mass. It also is more durable than a telescien.

WILKYZ- Slightly smaller than the Tralkyz, these Super Hunters usually travel alone or in small groups. They possess the ability to merge divergent time-lines temporarily. The effect produces the illusion of greater numbers, for the purpose of confusing an enemy briefly, with overwhelming force.

EFILU
(THE PEOPLES OF THE REALM)

THE SUPER HUNTERS

Alkyz- The largest of the class. Golden brown with ruby red highlights. The fur-like pile is mostly short except at the back of the head, neck, forearms and calves. The ears are relatively small and inconspicuous. Rounded rather than pointed. Size: 25 to 30 feet. 4000 to 5000 lbs.

Melkyz- Jet black to black and white marbled coat. The fur-like down has the consistency of mink or ermine, only softer, with a delicate light oily sheen. They have large, pointed ears and long lean tails. The overall appearance is much like a cross between a kangaroo and a human being. Size: 6 feet, 7 inches to 8 feet from head to toe when standing, 5 to 6 feet when sitting on haunches. 500 to 600 lbs.

Tralkyz- Charcoal gray coats with dull, fur-like plumage. Blue-gray highlights. They are heavily muscled with thick powerful tails. Ears are proportionally smaller than those of Melkyz and have tuft of feathers that fan out from behind them that glow red as a warning or when prepared to attack. Size: Fifteen to 18 feet tall, 2000 to 2500 lbs. *Chiefs are bigger, at 22 to 25 feet tall and 3500 to 4500 lbs.

Wilkyz- Tan, auburn, brown and burnt orange striped coats. Structurally similar to the Melkyz, but a little bulkier in the chest and shoulders. Long and lean with more substantial tails, they stand 12 to 15 feet from head to toe, and weigh 1000 to 1400 lbs.

Vansar- Avian people. Tall and slender, with wings that are powerfully muscled. Super joints allow for conversion from wings to effective arms and hands, almost instantaneously. Brilliantly colored, the plumage is a neat mixture of wide bands of golden yellow, orange and iridescent purple. The bones are hollow and light weight. The Vansar are disproportionately strong for their mass. Size: 800 to 1200 lbs. 25 to 32 feet tall.

PACHYDERM PEOPLES

So Wari- Brown suede-like hides of various shades. The dorsal plates are hunter green. The pointed ears are long and stand nearly straight out from the head; they subtly change orientation to focus on the source of sound without revealing alert status. So Wari are bulky, nearly muscle-bound in appearance, but incredibly fast and agile. They are among the biggest of the land-dwelling Efilu. Size: 25 to 30 feet tall. 5000 to 6000 lbs.

So Beni- Similar to the So Wari. Tan, with yellow and green dorsal plates. Size: Twenty five to 30 feet tall. Forty-five to 5500 lbs. Now extinct.

Si Tyen- (The Dragons) Physique typical of the European winged dragon physique. They had short, gun metal gray mixed pile, with long silvery gray plumage. The build is intermediate, between that of the Alkyz and the So Wari. They stand 28 to 33 feet tall and weigh 5000 to 5500 lbs.

Roog- Marine dwellers. Deep blue green matted pile with moss green patches. Large powerful jaws are set in a humanoid face that sits atop a long neck. They have oversized five-fingered hands connected to very short powerful arms. Their legs are similar: very short and powerful, with fin-like webbed feet. Size: 40 feet long.12,000 to 18,000 lbs.

MISCELLANEOUS SPECIES

Denar- Medium sized fishers, they eat small game and occasionally supplement their diets with fruits and nuts. The coast are an unassuming brown, with reddish patches around the eyes. They are 12 to 14 feet tall and weigh from 1000 to 1200 lbs.

Gen Rost- A cross between an owl and a penguin in appearance, Gen Rost are awkward when walking, and have limited flight capabilities. They have loose, short brown feathers with a few green accents. They live in humid, swampy climates.Size: 6 to 7 feet tall. 200 to 300 lbs.

Ironde- Nomadic by nature, the Ironde are also omnivorous. Large, nearly rotund, they have short thick tails and are covered from head to toe with long, luxurious snow white plumes deadly when stiffened. The face is a deep teal green. Size: 12 to 14 feet tall. 1200 to 1500 lbs.

Kini Tod- Turtle-like appearance. Red-orange armor with green borders and bellies. Short, thick club-like tail. Size: 5 to 6 feet tall. 400 to 500 lbs.

Mit Kiam- Graceful and muscular, the Mit Kiam wear long, fur-like feathers. The coat is a blend of golden tan, brown and red-brown hues. The plumage about the head is particularly spectacular with contrasting highlights and dark tips. They stand 14 to 16 feet tall and weigh 1200 to 1600 lbs.

Notex- This species shows another example of super joint development. Lean, with disproportionately long legs, Notex have hyperspeed capabilities. They can achieve and sustain speeds as fast as two hundred miles an hour, almost instantaneously. Darkly-colored indigo blue, with hints of violet obliquely striped throughout the body. The tail is rigid and moves as a counter balance. They are 8 to 10 feet tall and weigh 800 to 1100 lbs.

Sulenz- Omnivores, feeding primarily on insects and mollusks. With their tiny tails, they are reminiscent of large prairie dogs. They have short, dense plumage which is striped yellow and yellow-green. Size: 700 to 900 lbs. 10 to 12 feet tall.

Tal Genj- Herbivorous people. The coat is rich brown, sporting short plumage with black accents. They have a frill or facial ridge to which an array of flexible antlers are anchored. The effect is that of a neat, complex display of gleaming curls or dreadlocks. They are slender-to-medium in build and graceful. Size: 12 to 14 feet tall. 1400 1700 lbs.

Tan Barr- Fluffy gray down with stripes and patches of purple-to-mauve plumage. They are medium-sized, stocky Efilu. Size: 10 to 12 feet. About 1000 lbs.